"What the hell were you doing out there?" Rhys asked through clenched teeth.

The way he stared at me—angry and knowing and possessive—made me uncomfortable. I fought the urge to fidget by getting pissy right back. "So are you going to tell me why you were looking for me or what?"

His eyes narrowed, and something shifted in the car. He didn't move an inch, but suddenly he crowded me. I felt my power flare, panic following close behind. Oh God—if something happened to Rhys, I'd never forgive myself. I desperately tried to pull it together, but the more I struggled to keep it in my grip, the more it slipped away.

Rhys's fingers lifted my chin, and I opened my eyes just as his mouth touched mine. I gasped at the slow warmth that filled me, head to toe.

"Gabrielle," he whispered. I felt his hot breath intimately, and he gazed into my eyes as he brushed his lips against mine for one more delicate kiss.

More. His sweet kisses didn't satisfy my need. In fact, they only whet my appetite. . . .

"A sexy world of kick-ass action! You'll want to immerse yourself in MARKED BY PASSION, the first in a thrilling new series, complete with a smoldering hero and the toughest, sassiest heroine around."

—Veronica Wolff, author of *Sword of the Highlands*

MARKED BY PASSION

KATE PERRY

FOREVER

NEW YORK   BOSTON

Copyright © 2009 by Kathia Zolfaghari
Excerpt from *Chosen by Desire* copyright © 2009 by Kathia Zolfaghari. All rights reserved. Except as permitted under the U.S. Copyright Act of 1976, no part of this publication may be reproduced, distributed, or transmitted in any form or by any means, or stored in a database or retrieval system, without the prior written permission of the publisher.

Typography by David Gatti
Cover illustration by Franco Accornio

Forever
Hachette Book Group
237 Park Avenue
New York, NY 10017
Visit our Web site at www.HachetteBookGroup.com

Forever is an imprint of Grand Central Publishing. The Forever name and logo is a trademark of Hachette Book Group, Inc.

Printed in the United States of America

First Printing: February 2009

10 9 8 7 6 5 4 3 2 1

For Parisa.
P.S.

And for Nate,
though that goes
without saying.

Acknowledgments

Much gratitude to . . .

Holly Root. She says she's an agent, but she's really a superhero. I'm positive she's got a cape and mask stashed in her desk.

Latoya Smith. She brought this story to life. All authors should be so lucky as to have an editor like her.

The kung fu gang. They unknowingly helped me choreograph the fight scenes. Special thanks to Andre Salvage (who teaches me to fight despite it all) and Jon Chintanaroad (who spent one long car ride brainstorming Gabe's powers with me).

Julie Linker. She loved this story even when it was a germ of an idea. Although I don't know how she'll feel when she finds out I didn't give Gabe a motorcycle.

Veronica Wolff. The gods were smiling on me the day I met her. She always has a shoulder and a glass of wine waiting when I need them. I'd be a blathering heap if it weren't for her unwavering support and awesome critiques.

Katie Salvage. A good friend understands when you

need to disappear for weeks because of a deadline. A great friend will join you while you work, even if you can't socialize, just to spend time with you. Katie is a great friend.

Parisa Zolfagari. She answered the phone every time I called, even though she knew the conversation was going to start with "What if Gabe . . ." She's a smart woman who always knows when to suggest a cupcake pick-me-up. Words can't convey what she means to me.

Nate Perry-Thistle. Nate is love. I'm blessed he's mine.

Also, thanks to Loren Cheung for help with the Chinese lingo (mistakes are my own).

And a special shout-out to the crews at Café Reverie and Coffee Bar, who so cheerfully fed and watered me while I was hammering this story out. If you're ever in San Francisco, stop by and visit them.

MARKED BY PASSION

Chapter One

"Gabrielle Sansouci Chin?"

I froze. In the twelve years I'd been bartending at the Pour House, no one had ever called me anything but Gabe, much less pronounced Sansouci correctly—*sahn-soo-si*—with a French accent, to boot. But what startled me most was the use of Chin, the last name I'd dropped fifteen years ago.

Eyes narrowed, I stopped stocking the refrigerator behind the bar and turned around. A tall hulk of a man stood on the other side of the counter with a package in his hand.

It had to be the contract—I wasn't expecting any other deliveries. My stomach lurched as I stared at the thin box. Probably nerves.

I looked at the guy again. He was more well groomed than your typical deliveryman. Custom suit and manicured nails. More like Lloyd's of London than FedEx. Weird for a courier. Gallery 415 must employ a higher-quality service than most.

His brow furrowed. "Are you Gabrielle Sansouci Chin?"

"Yeah, I'm Gabrielle." How did the gallery know my real last name? I only went by Sansouci, my mother's maiden name. Whatever. As long as they sold my paintings, they could call me whatever they liked—even Chin.

He nodded. "Sign here, please."

"No 'I've got a big package for you' or anything?" He gazed at me flatly. I couldn't resist a glance at his crotch. "You don't think your package is that big?"

His eyebrows arched, but he remained impressively silent.

Some people just didn't appreciate humor. I waved my hand. "Give it to me."

He held out his clipboard, and I scrawled my name on the line he indicated. As I reached for the slim box, he pulled it back. "Sign here, too."

I shrugged and did as he commanded. The gallery really took pains with security. Nice—it made me feel like I was in good hands.

"And initial here. And here."

"A little overkill for just a contract, don't you think?" I glanced up at him as I scribbled "GS," but he just stared back implacably. He waited until the last flourish of the pen before handing over the box.

A shiver ran up my spine the moment I touched the box—so strong I almost dropped it.

He chuckled mockingly. "Good luck," he said, then he strode out the front door.

Weird. I hadn't been so nervous about this showing before. Not that I didn't have cause for the nerves—it wasn't often the premier art gallery on the West Coast offered a one-woman show to a virtually unknown artist. Only the artist that had been booked fell through, and Chloe Evans, the gallery's director, had been desperate to fill the empty spot on her calendar. She'd seen some of my older work, but it was the first two paintings in my *Enter the Light* series that convinced her to take the risk.

Now I just had to produce the last three paintings in the series, and I had seven weeks to do it. I suppose there was a possibility of failing, like if the paintings sucked or I choked.

A very distant possibility. No way was I going to fuck this up. This was what I'd been working toward for the past fifteen years. This was how I was going to make my mark on the world.

Yeah, confidence wasn't an issue for me—not once I set my mind to something. Which made the sudden flare-up of nerves all the more strange. I frowned at the box.

The broadsword-shaped mark on the inside of my right hipbone prickled.

"Hey, Gabe," Jerry called from the end of the bar. "Who was the stiff?"

I held up the box. "Courier."

"Is that what I think it is?" Milo, who sat a couple seats away from Jerry, asked.

My grin was wide and triumphant. "Hell, yeah, it's my contract."

They cheered, clapping and whistling shrilly. My heart warmed. I'd known them from the beginning of my stint here. They'd seen me struggle to make it as an artist—they knew what this show meant to me.

I didn't want to think what it said about me that the closest I came to family were two construction workers who frequented the bar I worked in. Or that my biological family wouldn't have been half as proud of me. Except for Mom, but she was dead.

I blinked away the uncharacteristic moisture that gathered in my eyes as I thought of her. Fifteen years didn't make me miss her any less. It didn't erase any of the guilt over her death, either.

The front door swung open, and a shaft of light broke the bar's afternoon dimness and my dark thoughts. Clearing the emotion from my throat, I turned to greet the newcomer. But then I saw him, and the casual hello I'd been about to say stalled on my tongue.

He walked in tall and broad, his medium-length brown hair fluttering from the wind outside. He moved like a warrior bent on conquering—I half expected to see him clutching a sword. His focused stare made my breath catch in my chest. His vivid eyes were the same blue as my favorite glass sculpture at the de Young Museum—bright and clear but with amazing depth.

The first thing that struck me was this feeling of connection—like I knew him. Absolutely ridiculous—I'd never seen him before in my life. Trust me, I would have remembered.

My second realization: he wasn't what he appeared to be. He wore a fabulous suit. A businessman? No way. Businessmen didn't ooze danger, and he wore power as casually as the custom-made clothes.

And all that power was headed straight for me.

For some reason, the damned birthmark on my hip tingled again. Rubbing it absently, I met him down the bar, away from Jerry and Milo. For privacy.

Being private with him would be fun. A lot of fun. I would have liked to indulge, but with all the work I had to do it'd be foolish to get distracted by a man.

Too bad, though.

"Get you something to drink?" I asked.

He studied me for a long, silent moment before he said, "A finger of scotch, please."

Oh, God—he had a British accent, too. Like James Bond, the ultimate bad boy, come to life.

Did I mention my weakness for bad boys? The flutter of interest I had before flared into all-out lust. I tried not to imagine him rolling around in silky sheets, whispering naughty words to me in that delicious voice of his. Unfortunately, being an artist, my imagination is pretty active.

Focus, Gabe. I resisted the urge to ask him if he had any impressive toys he'd like to share with me and got out a bottle of fifteen-year Laphroaig—the best scotch we stocked.

I poured some into a crystal tumbler Johnny, my boss, kept for himself, covertly studying him under my lashes. He had a scar I hadn't noticed on first inspection—a thin, raised line that bisected the left corner of his mouth. How did a businessman get a scar like that? Trip and fall against his desk?

Intriguing.

As I handed him the drink, our fingers brushed and a wave of heat rolled through me, languid and steamy and seductive. Like it was feeling me out. Or feeling me up. I gasped and jerked my hand away.

His gaze sharpened, its intensity searing. I expected him to say something, some comment about the weirdness that just occurred. He just dropped a bill on the counter and walked away to a table in a dark corner.

I watched him settle in the shadows. I couldn't see more than his outline, but I knew without a doubt he still watched me.

Bizarre. Maybe it was just me. Maybe I was subconsciously stressed because of the gallery show and was looking for an outlet. Had to be it.

"Hey, Gabe." Jerry held out his pint glass. "Before you go all hoity-toity on us, can you get me a refill?"

"Sure thing." I nodded at Milo's glass. "Another pale ale? On the house. We're celebrating."

Milo knocked back what was left of his beer and pushed his glass toward me. I drew their beers and poured a Coke for myself. "For the record, I'm not going hoity-toity. I still plan on working here." It wasn't like this one show was going to make me set for life. But it was the solid start I needed.

"So what does this contract entail? And have you had a lawyer look at it?" Milo's face took on an angelically calculated look. "Because my nephew Murphy is a lawyer."

Jerry whacked his arm. "She knows that, moron."

"I'm just saying I could get Murphy to look at it. We don't want Gabe to get cheated." He shrugged a little too nonchalantly. "And if when they meet and they like each other . . ."

Smiling, I shook my head. He'd been trying to set me up with Murphy for years. I might have been tempted if he weren't a lawyer. I wrinkled my nose. Stuffy guys weren't my thing.

I grooved on guys like Jesse. Everything about Jesse screamed naughty, from his Colin Farrell looks to his job as a mechanic. Not that being a mechanic made you a bad boy, but I'd stopped by his shop once and accidentally overheard enough to know some of the cars they were "fixing" were "relieved" from their original owners.

Of course, Jesse and I didn't date anymore. We used to get together for no-strings sex, but then things changed.

He'd started to hint that he wanted more. I hadn't been sure I had more to give him, so I broke up with him.

I glanced at the table by the door. In appearance, the British guy was the complete opposite of Jesse. Why did I feel like he'd be so much more exciting?

"You know"—Jerry leaned across the counter—"there's a new guy at work who I think you'd like."

Returning my attention to the conversation at hand, I tipped my head and asked, "What's he look like?"

Frowning, he scratched his head. "He's tall. I think."

"Are you talking about the Meyer kid? Hampton?" Milo snorted. "He's no taller than me."

"That's what I meant. He's tall."

"I'm only tall compared to you. He's not tall enough for Gabe. What if she wants to wear high heels?" Milo shook his head. "She'd tower over him."

I thought of pointing out that five nine was hardly Amazonian proportions, but I decided to stay out of this one. They'd get distracted soon enough.

"That's why Murphy is perfect for her. He's six feet. Almost."

Height didn't matter as much as, um, size, but I didn't tell the guys this. I didn't put it past Milo to make Murphy whip it out for a quick measurement—he was *that* intent on hooking me up with his nephew.

"I told Murphy about you." Milo winked at me. "He thinks you sound beautiful. I told him the real deal was even better."

"She's not only beautiful, she's exotic. Like those Eurasian models on your calendar, only her blue eyes aren't fake." Jerry turned to me. "You didn't tell us the terms of your deal. When's the show?"

"In a couple months. I still have some canvases to finish for it."

"We're so proud of you, honey," Milo said. "You're going to knock 'em dead."

"She's going to be the next Matisse," Jerry declared proudly.

Maybe not quite Matisse, but one of the greats of this century.

Wu, my father, once told me I'd never make it as an artist. I smiled in grim satisfaction at the box. I almost wished I were still speaking to him so I could rub this deal in his face. He'd never believed I was good enough at anything. Not a good enough artist. Not a good enough daughter. And certainly not a good enough Guardian.

A lump formed in my throat when I remembered his harsh words the last time I'd seen him, at Mom's funeral. That even my brother Paul would have made a better Guardian, and maybe he should have been marked instead of me.

Yeah, well, that would have been okay with me. Because maybe then Mom would still be alive.

My nose tingled with the onslaught of tears, and I ruthlessly suppressed them. Mom would want me to celebrate my win today. She wanted it for me as much as I did—maybe more. So I raised my glass. "To me. And to the two best guys in the city."

As we toasted, I caught movement out of the corner of my eye and turned in time to see the mysterious Brit slip out of the Pour House. I frowned, which was silly—what did I have to be disappointed about? That he didn't ask me out? Like I had time to date with the paintings to finish for the show.

"Hey, Gabe." Milo's eyes narrowed shrewdly. "You know the paintings you gave us a couple years ago?"

"Yeah." They were bar scenes with dark shadowy figures and red swirly depths. I'd still been struggling to define my style at that time, but they'd been my breakthrough paintings. Only someone who knew them would recognize the two figures at the end of the bar in each painting as Milo and Jerry. It was in the way they slouched over the counter.

"You think they'll be worth some serious cash in a couple years?" He blushed. "Not that I'd sell mine."

I grinned. "Wouldn't that be cool?"

Jerry perked up. "You mean like we could auction them off and then buy a Greek island or something? I always wanted a Greek island."

Milo smacked his arm, but I just laughed. "If the paintings become that valuable, hell, sell them and I'll paint you new ones. But I get to visit your island."

"Deal." He stuck his hand out and we shook. I counted my blessings that he didn't spit first.

My cell phone rang. Johnny didn't care if we took personal calls during non-peak hours. Not that he was around much to care. The past year he'd been traveling more and more with his young stud of a partner, Steve.

I looked at the screen. It was Madame La Rochelle, my surrogate everything. Fate had smiled on me the day I went to the Shakespeare Garden at Golden Gate Park and sat next to her on one of the benches. Aside from offering me friendship and being a replacement for the mother figure I'd lost, she became my mentor.

This one-woman show was all due to her. Well, her and my talent, but my talent wouldn't have been noticed without her connections. Madame La Rochelle was known as the "master maker." She'd brought dozens of great artists into the public's eye. Including Yves Klein, who was famous for having women roll around in paint and throw themselves at canvases.

I flipped open my phone and said in the French my mom had taught me, "*Bonjour, Madame.*"

"*Gabrielle, j'ai parlé à la directrice de la galerie,*" she said without preamble. She was like that—to the point. She always said that she was too old to tiptoe around things. I wasn't sure what "too old" was in actuality, but I figured it had to be close to eighty. "*Elle va t'envoyer le contracte.*"

"I know. I have the contract here." Too excited to maintain French, I picked up the box and waved it as if she could see. "I just got it like half an hour ago."

"What do you mean you got it this afternoon?" Madame said in her heavily accented English. "*La directrice* said she was sending it *demain.*"

Tomorrow? I frowned at the package. "Are you sure?"

"*Mais oui, Gabrielle.* You think I lie?"

"No, Madame, of course not," I said quickly. To incur her wrath was to take your life into your hands. I'd heard she'd once made Picasso crawl on his hands and knees to apologize for forgetting a rendezvous with her.

"*Alors, le contracte* will arrive tomorrow. Bring it and I will have my lawyer look at it, *d'accord?*"

"*Oui, Madame.*" I stared at the box on the counter.

"*Je te verra demain à deux heures. Ne sois pas en retard. À tout à l'heure, mon chou.*"

"Tomorrow at two. Got it. *À demain, Madame.*" I hung up and picked up the package. My stomach roiled with that nervous feeling I'd had earlier. If this wasn't the contract, what was it?

"One way to find out," I muttered. I ripped off the easy-open tab and upended the package. The contents of the box tumbled out onto the counter as if in slow motion.

A scroll.

My heart stopped, and my breath caught in my chest. It couldn't be. Forcing myself to breathe, I closed my eyes for a long moment and then reopened them, fully expecting to see something different before me. But it was still there: one tattered, ancient scroll tied with a strap of leather. Wu's obsession and the bane of my existence. The reason my mom died.

And then it hit me—there was only one reason the scroll would be delivered to me.

It meant my father was dead, too.

Chapter Two

Wu was dead.

An unexpected wave of sadness and regret swept over me. My father was dead. I'd never feel him brush my hair out of my face or see him give that brief nod of approval on the rare occasion he thought I did something right.

But those moments had been few and far between, especially once I'd become a teenager. And the problems between us had culminated in that last exchange when he said point-blank that Mom died because I was careless and out of control.

The bitch of it: he was right. And as much as I rationalized that it had just been a tragic mistake, I didn't blame him. I didn't think I'd ever forgive myself, either.

I looked down at the scroll and felt the old resentment rise inside me, coupled with a new fear that I might screw up again and get someone else killed. I'd told him I wanted nothing to do with this. Mom's death should have proved I wasn't suited to be the next Guardian. I scooped the parchment to put it back into the box before anyone saw it.

As I touched it, electricity shot up through my feet. Strange. I'd never felt a static shock like that. Plus, I shouldn't have felt anything through my boots. I looked down right as the earth started shaking.

Earthquakes were commonplace in San Francisco. Most of them went undetected, but every now and then one hit that made you stand up and take notice.

Like this one.

The liquor bottles behind me rattled, the glasses on the bar danced in place, and the earth rolled under my feet. I grabbed the bar with my free hand and prayed the ground wouldn't open up and swallow me. Because it felt like it might.

"Whoa." Jerry grabbed his pint glass before it jiggled off the counter.

"This is a big one," Milo said as his seat wobbled. "What do you think? Six-point-oh on the Richter?"

"Nah. Feels closer to the Loma Prieta quake in '89, and that was a six-point-nine."

I started to suggest we go stand in a doorway (lesson number one in earthquake safety that every Californian learned in school), only as I opened my mouth, more electricity coursed through me. It reverberated through every inch of my body and jetted out my fingertips and the top of my head.

My hair crackled with static, and I could feel waves from the earth undulate up into me, filling me until I felt like I couldn't breathe. I struggled to move—

I couldn't budge.

Wu's voice rose from my memory. *Gabrielle, remember*

the first rule. The Guardian who protects the scroll pos-
sesses its power.

Aw, hell. This wasn't an earthquake. This was *tŭ ch'i.*

The waves turned into what felt like scalding molten lava oozing up my body. It built in me until I thought I was going to erupt. I felt excruciatingly full, every single cell in my body on fire and expanding.

I wanted to scream from the pain, but all I could do was gasp for air. Drowning and spinning wildly—just like I'd felt right before I lost control and killed my mom. Gritting my teeth, I fought against panic. I wouldn't let it get loose and hurt someone again.

And then it receded, a persistent throb of energy deep inside me.

Heart still thundering, I stared down at the scroll clenched in my hand. *Shit.* I stuffed it back in the box, warring between wanting to get rid of it and needing to hold it close and never let it go.

I shook my head. Next I'd be calling it "my precious" and slinking through dark caverns.

"Gabe. *Gabe.*"

Milo's voice broke through the fog, and I looked to up find them gawking at me with concern.

Jerry's brow wrinkled. "Is this your first big one, Gabe? You look shaken."

"A little. It's been a long time since I felt, um, that." I ducked out from behind the bar, knowing that the earthquake hadn't originated on a fault line, but from me. "I need to go to the back for a sec. Shout out if anyone needs anything."

Milo frowned at me. "You okay, Gabe?"

"Peachy." I tried to smile but knew I failed miserably.

"I'm just going to make sure the stock back there is okay and put my, um, contract away."

"You sure you're okay?" Jerry asked with a frown. "You're walking funny."

Because I had to will my feet to move. My legs felt like they were encased in dirt up to my thighs. "Just off balance. Be right back."

I hurried away as fast as I could. Hugging the box to my chest, I closed the door to the closet Johnny called his office and slumped against it to collect myself.

What the hell had just happened?

Even as I asked myself, I knew. Wu was dead, I had the scroll, and now I possessed its curse. *Tǔ ch'i.* My knowledge of it was limited—I thought of it like the Force in *Star Wars,* only less ethereal and more tied to natural elements—but I recognized it nonetheless from the brief taste I'd had once before.

My birthmark zapped me. I thought I felt the scroll shift inside the box, too, but that had to be a figment of my imagination.

What wasn't my imagination: the current that still reverberated inside my body. As if on cue, it swelled, and that feeling of drowning overwhelmed me again. Closing my eyes, I wrestled to control it before it broke free and caused another earthquake.

Once I managed to will it down, I opened my eyes and found myself crouched on the floor, clutching the package.

I needed to hide it—a temporary safe place until I could figure out a longer-term solution. I searched the office, not happy about leaving it here unattended. I could practically hear my father's outrage at the mere thought. *The second rule, Gabrielle,* he used to say with a grave expression, *is that the Guardian must keep the scroll hidden at all costs.*

"Yeah, yeah," I muttered under my breath as I scanned the room. I understood that it was imperative to keep the scroll secret—not only from the population at large, since it contained knowledge humans weren't ready for, but also from uniting with the other four scrolls floating around the globe. Except I figured the chances anyone would come to a dive bar in San Francisco to look for one—tonight—were slim.

And hiding it in the office was better than keeping it behind the bar with me. I wouldn't be able to keep an eye on it and serve drinks all night, and I cringed at the idea of it being accessible to so many people. In the wrong hands . . .

Well, actually I had no idea what it could do in the wrong hands. Not really. My knowledge regarding the scroll was sorely lacking. Beyond the myth, I only knew normal people couldn't resist the seductive pull of *tŭ ch'i.* Too much power unless one was trained to handle it. Wu used to say without strong moral fortitude, a person could be lured into doing bad things with the powers.

So when I was younger, my training consisted simply of combat—specialized fighting like hand-to-hand, grappling, and weapons—but nothing else. Every time I asked Wu about the scroll and *tŭ ch'i,* he'd blow me off by saying I wasn't ready. That handling *tŭ ch'i* was a great responsibility not to be taken lightly and I'd yet to exhibit that kind of accountability. I guessed my moral fortitude was in question.

I'd been almost eighteen before he relented. Actually, I nagged him into showing me. That was the day my mom died.

I did, however, know rule number three: to unite all five scrolls was bad on a cataclysmic, world-destruction level. Though Wu had never been able to tell me exactly what that meant, just that no one person could handle that much power without being corrupted by it.

There was a cranny of space behind Johnny's Christmas decorations big enough to hide the package. Fighting the urge to continue to clutch the box, I dropped it back there and piled extra stuff on top to camouflage it.

I cursed Wu the whole time. My older brother Paul was the one who wanted the scroll so badly—he should have gotten it. Paul probably knew more about the scroll than I did. He'd certainly been more aggressive about gathering knowledge, to the point of eavesdropping on Wu. Not that Wu noticed—he was too focused on me. Wu never noticed anything about Paul, which sucked, because a boy shouldn't be ignored by his father.

But I figured Wu would turn to Paul once I was gone. I never thought I'd receive the scroll—not when I ran from Los Angeles to San Francisco after Mom's funeral. So what if I was the one born with the mark? It was just a freaking birthmark. You'd think Wu would realize this.

"Stubborn fool," I said with more anger than I'd felt in a long time—to combat the sadness I didn't want to feel at his death. Which pissed me off even more. He'd pretty much disowned me. Why should I have feelings for someone who didn't want me?

The other, less savory part of me was glad he was dead. I hoped it hurt, however he'd died. He deserved no less for letting Mom get killed. Yeah, technically I killed her, but he could have prevented it. He'd been right there. The one in charge. Instead he'd let her die and then railed at me for it.

How messed up was that? I shoved a box on top of the scroll and punched it.

I remembered my mom's lilting French accent, the way she used to stroke down the long length of my hair, and the feeling of total unconditional love that I hadn't felt since. All lost because of one stupid scroll. I didn't care how powerful or valuable it was, I would have traded it for more time with my mom. I would have traded my art career in a heartbeat for ten more minutes with her.

"Damn you, Wu," I muttered, dropping my head in my hands.

"Already done," someone said from behind me.

I whirled around, automatically lowering my weight for attack the way I'd been taught so many years ago. But then I straightened in disbelief. "Wu?"

My father rubbed his chin thoughtfully. "Not entirely true, though, is it? More like I'm in purgatory than actually damned."

If I'd been hitting the tequila bottle, I could have justified this as a drunken delusion. But I didn't drink, and I knew what I was seeing.

He was thin—thinner than he'd been fifteen years ago—but still wiry with muscle. His hair was more gray now than black, but it was still thick. He wore his white gi, pristine because he always ironed it (totally anal if you asked me), with a simple gold satin sash wrapped around his waist.

For a moment, I felt relief that he wasn't dead. But then I got pissed. Really pissed. Anger rose in a dark tide inside me, and I clenched my hands to keep from hitting something. "What the hell is this about? A ploy to manipulate me? I told you a long time ago that I wasn't playing your games anymore."

"And I told you that I wasn't playing any games," he said, his voice terribly hushed.

When I was a kid, it used to freak me out when he spoke like that. It was a sure sign that shit was about to hit the fan. Now it just made me want to flip him off. "What do you call this, then? I told you I didn't want to have anything to do with the scroll or you. So you pretend to be dead and send me the scroll anyway?"

"If I had a choice I wouldn't have sent it to you," he said icily. "But you're marked. Therefore it's yours on my passing."

"Excellent," I said with bite, to cover up that his words stung. I shoved aside the stuff I'd used to hide the scroll and grabbed the box. "And since you haven't died yet, you can take this back."

I threw it at him, hoping it hurt him as much as I hurt on the inside. Only the box sailed right through him.

Right through him.

Blinking, I looked more closely at him, noticing for the first time how he was somewhat translucent and surrounded by a glow.

"Shit," I said succinctly.

He nodded. "For once you're right about something. Only you've yet to comprehend how deeply in shit we are."

Chapter Three

I didn't believe in ghosts. Not that I disbelieved in them, but I never had cause to give them a thought one way or the other.

Only now this glowy thing that resembled a Chinese Obi-Wan stood before me, and I'd thrown an inanimate object through its body. What other explanation was there?

Well, I supposed I could be having a really bad flash-back, but I didn't do drugs. Maybe it was a shock-induced delusion. I closed my eyes, counted to ten, and reopened them.

He was still there, scowling at me.

I shook my head. "You can't be here. I just don't believe in ghosts."

"Yet you believe in a scroll that can lend you the ability to channel the earth's power?"

He had a point. "I've seen that for myself."

"And now you've seen a ghost." He crossed his arms and looked at me like he was defying me to deny it.

I couldn't. "I—"

"Enough," he said abruptly. "We don't have time to debate this. We have a lot of work to do, and we need to start right away."

"We?" I shook my head. "No way. You cannot implicate me in any of your troubles. I walked out, remember?"

"You can't walk out on destiny, Gabrielle."

Sigh. "Not this destiny bullshit again."

"You know our family was specially picked to guard this scroll." His chest puffed out, he raised his arm and orated in his grand story voice. "*One monk, Wei Lin, saw within the overlord's heart and recognized he coveted the sacred scrolls, for the scrolls unlocked the mysteries of nature and man. One scroll for each element. Earth, fire, wood, metal, water—*"

"I know the story." I rolled my eyes. "You repeated it a million times when I was a kid."

"You obviously don't remember it."

Right. I bet I could recite it verbatim. *Centuries ago, a group of monks in a secluded monastery in southeast China, battered by neighboring gangs, developed an art of war. As there were five elements in Chinese cosmology, there were five correlating fighting principles in the art, documented in five scrolls.*

Over time, the monks became so adept at harnessing the elements that they developed other abilities. Each element had its own set of powers, and each secret was recorded in the scrolls for future generations to learn.

Tales of the extraordinary leaked through the provinces, until they reached the ears of one particularly ruthless overlord . . . "Trust me, I remember it."

Wu wagged a finger at me, clearly not convinced. "For decades Wei Lin searched until he found five men worthy to guard them—one man for each scroll. He marked them and then decreed that the mark would be passed down, generation to generation, to the next worthy one. The Scroll of the Earth was entrusted to the Chins, and the next Guardian is you. It's an honor to bear the mark, Gabrielle."

"An honor?" I snorted. A curse was more like it.

The little broadsword-shaped birthmark on my hip prickled.

I rubbed it. If only I could rub it away. "It's a mistake."

He hesitated. Then he said, "It can't be a mistake. The mark doesn't lie."

"Gee—what a vote of confidence." I shouldn't have cared, but it stung nevertheless.

"Hey, Gabe." Jerry knocked on the office door. "You okay in there?"

I had to clear my throat a couple times before I could reply. "Yeah. Be right out."

"Okay, but you've got a customer."

"Right. Thank you." I quickly strode to the box that held the scroll and busied myself hiding it again.

"What are you doing?" Wu asked over my shoulder.

"Putting it away for now. I have to get back to work." I had a customer waiting, and the after-work crowd would be trickling in soon. Ignoring the compulsion to pick up the scroll and take it with me, I stood up and brushed my hands on my jeans.

"You can't go back to work," he said indignantly.

"Just watch me." There was only one way to leave the office, and Wu was blocking it. As much as a ghost could.

I steeled myself and walked through him. It was like

walking through thick, chilled air. Closing the door, I shivered. Talk about freaky. I pushed my hair back and told myself to get a grip.

"Closed doors don't make any difference on this side of life," he said from right behind me.

Caught off guard, I spun around. Without warning, the curse bubbled up inside me, choking me with its intensity. I fought to keep from dropping to my knees. At least if I lost control of the power, I wouldn't hurt Wu—he was already dead. Small comfort.

Hands clenched, I fought to get a grip. Once I caught my breath, I hissed at him. "Leave me alone."

"I can't. We must discuss your new duties—"

"The only duties I need to take care of are waiting for me there." I waved behind me at the bar.

"Right now *tǔ ch'i* is coursing unrestrained through your body. You must learn to harness it, as well as recognize when to use it and how much to draw upon it. There are dire consequences to its misuse."

"No kidding." Not a day passed when I didn't replay Mom staring at me in horror as she gasped her last breath. My nose burned with the sudden threat of tears.

Wu's eyes, on the other hand, were filled with cold purpose. "I'm the only hope you have, Gabrielle. Without my help, you'll destroy not only yourself but everything around you."

"Right, Obi-Wan. Like how you helped when Mom lay on the ground dying?" Anger evaporated my urge to cry. "Thanks, but I think I'll take my chances and deal with the Force by myself."

"It's *tǔ ch'i,* not the Force," he said tightly. "And stop calling me Obi-Wan."

I shrugged. "I figured it was better than Yoda."

"Hey, Gabe," Jerry called. "Who you talking to?"

Oh, great. They couldn't see Wu—I should have realized. He was a ghost. I turned around with a tight smile. "Just talking to myself."

Milo and Jerry exchanged worried looks before facing me with concern written all over their faces. "We know the excitement's been a lot lately—"

"What excitement?" Wu asked, hovering next to me.

"—so if you want us to watch the bar while you take some time off, we could," Milo finished. "I got that guy who was waiting for his beer and rang him up and everything. And I make a mean gin and tonic."

"What excitement?" Wu asked again, closer this time. It seemed ghosts had no sense of personal space.

"I'll make it through the night. And Vivian's arriving at seven. But thanks for offering." I turned so my back was to the guys and faced Wu. "You need to leave."

His mouth firmed. "I can't leave. I told you, I have to teach you what you need to know about your new abilities."

"It's pointless, because I'm never going to use them." I whirled around and marched behind the bar. I could feel Jerry and Milo gawking at me, but I ignored them and pretended to be busy stacking glasses. It gave me the perfect opportunity to fume. I grabbed another couple pint glasses and turned to stack them behind me.

Wu stood between me and the shelves. "You can't turn your back on destiny."

"*Holy shit*." I yelped and dropped both of them. Fortunately they just bounced on the rubber mat behind the bar.

"Gabe!" Milo and Jerry yelled at the same time. "Are you okay?"

"Sorry." I waved off their concern. "I just lost my grip."

"Gabrielle, you were chosen to protect the scroll. The mark proves it." Wu pointed to my hip.

I hated that blemish. I should have had it covered with a tattoo like I'd wanted to when I first left home. The idea of being voluntarily poked with needles didn't appeal to me, though.

Three regulars entered the Pour House and came up to the bar. "Hey, Gabe," they called out.

Wu frowned. "Gabe?"

Giving him a look that said he needed to stop harassing me or face the consequences, I turned to my customers. "The usual, guys?"

I bent down to pull three Budweisers out of the refrigerator and felt something clammy and cold brush my skin. With a small yelp, I dropped a bottle. It shattered and sprayed my boots.

Damn, damn, damn.

Milo leaned over the edge of the counter and peered down at me. "Are you sure you're okay, Gabe?"

"Peachy," I said through gritted teeth.

"Gabrielle, fetching beer is beneath you."

I set two bottles on the counter and got a replacement for the one I dropped. "Nine bucks, guys."

Wu hovered in front of me, his torso sticking out of the bar. "Gabrielle, you can't ignore me."

"Wanna bet?" I muttered as I pulled change from the register.

The liquor bottles behind me began to rattle.

"Whoa," Jerry exclaimed. "Is that another quake?"

"Feels smaller." Milo pursed his lips. "Probably an aftershock."

I had the sneaking suspicion the seismic activity was just a ghost having a hissy fit, mostly because it felt different. More of a superficial shaking than something that started in the bowels of the earth. So I ignored it and helped the couple who walked in. By the time I served their drinks, the shaking stopped. And Wu was gone. Thank God.

Jerry whistled. "I don't think I've ever felt an earthquake last that long."

"Me either." Milo shook his head. "The big one's coming."

They clanked bottles to that. Then Jerry said, "But my stool didn't shake. Kinda strange."

Chapter Four

$\mathcal{M}$y relief at Wu's disappearance was short-lived. All evening he kept popping up when I least expected. I dropped more beer bottles than I had since I first started working at the bar. The harder I tried to pull it together, the more out of control I spun.

And if the haunting wasn't enough, the scroll obsessed me, as well. I felt compelled to check on it every few minutes to make sure it was still safe and hidden away. Not that I could—it was an especially busy evening. As I poured a shot of tequila, I had the fleeting thought that this was what the rest of my life would be like.

Depressing, to say the least.

By the time the other bartender, Vivian, arrived, I was frazzled. Not a good thing, because dealing with Vivian was trying at best.

In my defense, I'd tried to befriend her, but she'd never been open to it. I didn't know why she disliked me from the moment she set eyes on me. All I knew was that she took pleasure in making my life hell but was a total angel whenever a man was around.

She sauntered in half an hour late—typical for her—dragging Jesse behind her, clinging to him like a leech. Flipping her fake long blond hair behind her shoulder, she rubbed her boobs on his arm and shot me a mean grin.

My eyes narrowed. Jesse and I were only friends now, but that didn't mean I wanted to see my archenemy hanging on him.

The trembling began again, a churning deep in the ground that I instinctively knew started with me and resonated down into the earth—not the other way around. Fear shot through me. Closing my eyes to calm myself, I fought back the welling energy with all my willpower. I didn't like Vivian, but that didn't mean I wanted to kill her, either.

The quaking subsided as quickly as it stirred. I rubbed my temple, drained. Maybe a priest would be able to exorcise *tŭ ch'i*. It was like a demonic possession. Kind of. I wondered if it mattered that I wasn't Catholic.

As soon as Jesse's gaze fell on me, he pried himself off Vivian's arm and headed straight to my section of the bar. To her dismay, I'm sure.

"Hey, babe." He slid onto a stool and frowned. "What's wrong?"

"Just a headache," I said with a weak smile. Without asking, I grabbed a glass to fix him his usual: mineral water with lime, made to look like a gin and tonic. The whole time, his puzzled gaze followed me.

But I knew he wouldn't pry even though he could tell I wasn't myself. We respected each other's privacy. There were trade-offs, of course—like I couldn't ask him why he didn't drink alcohol. But at times like this, respecting his past seemed a small price to pay. I certainly didn't want to talk about mine.

"Thanks." He flashed me a half grin and set a bill on the bar. I don't know how many times I'd told him he didn't have to pay, but he always did. Way more than he needed to. I'd tell him to stop, but it aggravated Vivian, so I let it pass.

I never said I was perfect.

Vivian huffed and stormed off to the office, probably to deposit her things. I had a brief flare of panic, worrying about her finding the scroll, but Vivian would never sift through the crap in Johnny's domain. It might mess up her manicure.

"Sorry about that." Jesse shook his head. "I met up with her outside the door and she attached herself to me."

"You don't owe me any explanations." I was used to seeing women, and occasionally men (this *was* San Francisco, after all), go crazy over him. It was his bad-boy look: the tattoos on his arms, leather jacket, worn jeans. More than that, I didn't mind seeing him with other women. It was just Vivian I objected to.

Sometimes his casual possessiveness got on my nerves. I hadn't dated anyone in the year since I broke up with him, but I bet if I brought a guy around, Jesse would flip out. Especially if the guy were a dark warrior disguised in a suit.

I glanced at the table where the British guy had sat and was struck by a fresh wave of disappointment that he was no longer around.

Just as well. He seemed like he'd be high maintenance. High maintenance was the last thing I needed.

"Are you sure you're okay?"

I blinked at Jesse. I'd forgotten he was there. "Just peachy."

"You only use 'peachy' when you're anything but."

Something that felt an awful lot like chaos rose in my chest—something that had nothing to do with *tǔ ch'i* but was just as uncomfortable. Swallowing the panic in its wake, I picked up a rag and wiped the counter.

"I struck too close to home, huh?"

Best to change the subject. I tossed the rag aside and tried to smile. "I wasn't expecting you tonight."

His lips quirked at my obvious segue, but his eyes looked sad. He played along, though. "I heard the news through the grapevine and I came to celebrate."

I froze as his words registered. He heard about the scroll? How? Did he see Wu? A shot of alarm coursed through me. I did a quick survey of the bar—it'd been a long time since Wu had made his presence known. Was he wreaking havoc behind my back?

"Hey."

I frowned at Jesse. "What?"

"Sure you don't want to talk about it?" He traced the turned-down corner of my mouth. "You don't seem yourself. I thought you'd be more elated about the gallery show."

The gallery show. Right. "Today's been a little overwhelming, to tell you the truth. How did you hear? I haven't told many people."

He cocked one eyebrow.

Right. How silly of me. He had connections.

"Want to know what I had in mind?" His low, rough voice made me frown. I knew he used it on purpose—to bring us back to familiar, sex-without-strings territory.

But it just sounded wrong. It was missing something. Like a British accent.

Leaning on the counter behind me, I hid my discomfort behind a friendly smile. "Celebrate, huh? What were you thinking?"

He reached out and took my hand, his gaze on my mouth. "I thought we could go back to your place."

I could tell he was imagining kissing me. Sometimes when he didn't think I was looking, he'd get that look in his eyes, like he longed to get me naked again, but never as blatantly as right now.

And it annoyed me. What part of *I don't think we should see each other anymore* was ambiguous? I was about to tell him he needed to back off when *tŭ ch'i* started to bubble up inside me, hot and molten.

An image of Jesse lying on the ground, his dead gaze sightlessly accusing, popped into my mind. I recoiled with a gasp, tugging my hand out of his.

He caught hold of my apron strings and pulled me forward before I could scramble away. "Tell me what's going on, Gabe."

There was something in his eyes that I'd never seen before—something too serious. If I wanted to be honest, I'd admit that he'd been looking at me like that a lot lately.

Honesty was overrated.

The curse still rippled, but I didn't feel like it was about to erupt. Still, I wasn't going to risk touching him. I gently pulled my apron from his grip. "I've got to get back to work."

Disappointment darkened his gaze, but he flashed his crooked bad-boy grin. "Maybe I'll stick around and walk you home. In case you change your mind."

I sighed. "Jesse, I'm not going to change my mind."

"I have a lot to offer, babe." The words were spoken casually, but I heard the loaded meaning behind them.

Ironically, I was saved from answering by Vivian. Feeling her death stare boring into my back, I turned around right as she ducked behind the bar. Out of the corner of my eye, I saw her bony elbow swing wide, aiming for my midsection, and deflected it. She was so predictable.

"Hello Viv," I said sweetly.

She glared at me, and I knew without a doubt that she'd witnessed my whole exchange with Jesse. She'd been trying to get him into her bed forever. Seeing him with me really got to her. I tried to be a better person and not feel good about that, but I couldn't help gloating. Just a little.

Usually I would have taunted her more, but tonight I just wanted out of there. I closed up my register and cleaned up the broken glass and spilled alcohol in record time. I supposed I could have let Vivian clean up—she was supposed to close, after all—but if I left things a mess for her, she'd retaliate tenfold. Besides, Jesse's eyes were on me the whole time, and that infuriated her.

"Done?" he asked when he saw me toss the rag into the bin.

"Done. But, listen, tonight's not good. I have a few things I need to take care of." Going around the counter, I pressed a quick kiss to his cheek and walked away before he could say or do anything.

I hurried to the office, put on my jacket, and unburied the box. *Tŭ ch'i* tugged at me when my hand touched the box. I tensed, waiting for it to explode to life, but it died down with a weak ripple. Thank God. Relieved, I turned around and found Jesse in the doorway.

"What's the package?" He nodded at the box.

"Just some papers I got today."

"For your show?"

I studied him with narrowed eyes. What was with all the questions? And why did he show up suddenly tonight? Why was he so insistent on going home with me? Could he know about the scroll?

Tŭ ch'i swelled, echoing my suspicion. I fought it back, but I couldn't help but be distrustful of Jesse's interest. Only how much of my doubt was justified and how much was real?

Oh, God—Wu's crazy delusions had transferred to me along with the scroll. This was *Jesse*. I shook my head to dislodge the suspicions. Soon I'd believe I was being followed by black helicopters.

Jesse frowned. "What's wrong?"

"Nothing." I clutched the box tighter. "I'm just tired. It's been a long day."

He took a step closer. "I can help you with the tension."

"Jesse—"

"Come on, babe." He snaked his arms around my waist. "Take me home with you. I miss you."

His embrace was warm and familiar. I waited for the zing of sexual awareness I'd always felt with him. Nothing.

Instead, I remembered the way my body had gone up in flames at the one glancing touch of the British guy's hand. Just thinking about it now made my nipples tighten, and I felt a rush of longing.

But not for Jesse. And I didn't want to give him the impression that he was the one turning me on, so I shrugged out of his hold and clutched the box to my abdomen as if it was a shield. "I'm too tired for this."

He stared at me; God knows what thoughts were running through his head. Then he tucked a strand of my hair behind my ear and said, "I'll walk you home."

"I—"

"Just to make sure you're safe," he cut into my protest.

Normally, I would have scoffed at such an offer—I'd spent my entire childhood learning the finer points of kung fu, after all. But I felt shaky with the scroll on my person, and having a brawny guy with me was that much more comforting. So I nodded. "Okay."

The whole six blocks to my apartment, I was torn between keeping Jesse at arm's length, worrying about whether Wu was going to suddenly pop out of nowhere, and being hypervigilant about having the scroll out in the open. Call me paranoid, but I had a weird feeling I was being watched. And not in the Brit's hot, expectant, sexually charged kind of way. More menacing.

At the rate I was going, I'd be a basket case by the end of the week.

"You're in a hurry tonight. You that tired?"

No—that freaked out. I was roaming the streets with the equivalent of an atom bomb in my hands. I walked even faster. "A lot happened today."

"I wish—" He shook his head, shoving his hands in his jeans pockets. Instead of continuing his thought, he sped up to keep pace with me. "Let's get you home."

My apartment was on the fringes, as I called it. Ten years ago, the part of the Mission where I lived was definitely dangerous; now it was only somewhat questionable.

Apartment is kind of an exaggeration, though. It was minuscule, even by San Francisco standards. The front room fit my futon, and I could fry an egg and take a shower at the same time, which made it convenient that I didn't cook.

But the reason I took it, except for the cheap rent, was the back room: my solarium slash painting studio. It'd been a porch at one time but was enclosed at some point with glass. It was incredible—not huge, but the natural light that filtered in during the day was amazing. It made the frigid cold from the lack of insulation worth it.

We arrived at my front door without incident. I unlocked it, but before I could thank him for the company and send him on his way, he slipped inside past me.

"What the hell?" I muttered. I followed him, closing the door behind me. Then I locked it for good measure. No sense in taking chances when the scroll wasn't secure yet.

My birthmark tingled as if agreeing.

Jesse poked his head into the bathroom and then casually checked out the kitchen before disappearing into my studio.

It seemed like he was scoping things out. Was he checking for another guy? The Brit came to mind, and I snorted as I pictured his elegance in my meager shack.

I'd get down to the bottom of Jesse's weird behavior—after I stowed the scroll away. Walking briskly, I went into the little kitchenette and put it in the safest place I could think of: the refrigerator. No one would look for it there.

As I closed the refrigerator door, I paused. Maybe I should check it first. I hadn't looked at it since I hid it in the office, after all. I'd just make sure everything was in order, maybe open it and take a look—

"Gabe? What are you doing?"

Jesse's voice reverberated in my head. Blinking, I realized I had the fridge door handle in a death grip.

He leaned in the doorway between the kitchen and my studio, concern furrowing his brow. "Gabe?"

Strange. I forced myself to step away from the fridge and faced him. "What were you doing?"

"What do you mean?"

I frowned at the caution in his tone. "It was like you were casing the joint."

"Just checking out your work. I didn't think you'd mind. You used to show me your paintings." He brushed the back of his hand across my cheek. "Did I tell you how proud I am of you?"

That shut me up. Not even Madame La Rochelle had told me she was proud of me, though it was implied. But of all the people I wanted to hear that from, Jesse was the last. I pulled back, a little, but it was enough that he noticed.

The corner of his lips lifted. "I seem to be hitting all your buttons tonight."

I opened my mouth, but I didn't know what to say so I just closed it again.

"Funny how fearless you are except when it comes to emotions." Sadness tinged his smile. He reached out to chuck my chin, and then he moved past me. "See you around, babe."

Dumbfounded, I stood in the kitchen, staring after him. I heard the door open and click shut.

What was up with him? I knew that he was still hung up on me, but he never pressed the way he did tonight. It reeked of desperation.

Why would he, of all people, be desperate?

Shaking my head, I went to deadbolt the door. Except as I stepped into the living room, I found one irritated-looking ghost hovering next to my futon.

"Who was that man?" he demanded, arms crossed.

"None of your business," was my automatic answer. Then I said, "What the hell are you doing here, anyway?"

"I told you I'm here to prepare you for the Guardianship."

"And I told you I don't want to be Guardian. End of story."

"The choice isn't yours to make."

The hell it wasn't. But I knew better than to argue the point with him. Shrugging out of my jacket, I dropped it on the floor and climbed onto my futon. I kicked off my shoes and pulled the covers over myself, clothes and all.

"Gabrielle, stop hiding. You need to face this. It's time to stop running."

Ignore the ghost, I told myself, huddling deeper. *He'll go away.* Eventually. Hopefully.

"Is this how you want to spend your life?"

Hard, though, when he wouldn't shut up.

"Living like this?" he continued. "Looking like a punk?"

I stiffened. He must mean the blue layers in my hair. I'd started dyeing my hair to downplay our resemblance—I didn't want to be reminded of him. I'd continued coloring it because I liked the expression. Blue was my favorite. It matched my eyes. It was tastefully done and minimal. I did not look like a punk.

"Frittering it away working in a bar and sleeping with men you care nothing for?"

I shoved the covers aside, pissed. It'd been over a year since I'd slept with anyone, and that was Jesse. Of all the things to accuse me of, being a slut was the least true. "You don't know what you're talking about."

Wu glared back at me. "Your mother would be so disappointed in you."

Direct hit. Hissing, I hopped off the bed and stabbed a finger at him. "I will not let you or a scrap of decaying paper control my life. I make my own choices, and Mom would be happy about that. She hated the scroll."

"That may be true, but—"

"*May be true?*" I snorted. "She gave up everything for you. She was going to be one of the top photographers of our time, and she stopped showing because you didn't want that kind attention on the family. And how did you show your love? By caring more for the scroll than you did her."

He glowed brighter, almost indignantly. But he didn't say anything. He couldn't say anything. How could he dispute the truth?

A bubble of energy drew up through the ground and filled my body. Fists clenched, I took a step toward him. "So don't you dare tell me how she'd feel—"

Before I could say anything more, he vanished.

"Damn you!" I swung my fist at the spot where he'd been standing.

Some *tŭ ch'i* shot out before I could stop it. Once I yanked it back, I looked around, expecting to see carnage but relieved to notice nothing had happened.

Shaking, I slumped on my futon. At least tomorrow couldn't get any worse.

Chapter Five

*H*alf the night I tossed and turned. The other half I dreamed that my father lived in my refrigerator and that a giant roll of paper chased me down the street whenever I left my house.

Okay, I also had dreams about my mom, although I don't know if you could call them dreams, since nothing happened. They were more like one snapshot that flashed over and over: only Mom's eyes, the vivid blue she'd passed on to me, full of shock and recrimination the moment before she died.

Needless to say, I didn't feel rested when I got out of bed. My head throbbed like I had a hangover, which made me wish I'd at least had something to drink. I considered going back to sleep, but I couldn't face more nightmares.

And I had a lifetime of this to look forward to. Yay, me. At least it felt manageable this morning. I could feel it inside me, but it was dormant, not threatening to engulf me. Plus I hadn't had any ghostly visitors. Yet.

I was making myself a stiff pot of coffee when

someone knocked on my front door. Taking my cup, I went to see who it was.

A courier—the typical kind, in battered, holey clothes, bicycle shoes, and a bag slung across his chest. He bowed over his clipboard, and all I could see of his head was his dirty dreaded hair. "I have a package for Gabrielle San-saucy."

I stared at the package suspiciously, but since I didn't believe I was heir to any other magical ancient texts, I nodded. Plus, he pronounced my last name incorrectly, which was actually reassuring. "I'm Gabrielle."

"Cool. Sign here." He held out the clipboard, lifting his head and looking at me for the first time. His eyes widened. "Whoa."

Ignoring his drool, I signed beside the X. I didn't underestimate the effect I had on the opposite sex, but come on. I was wearing an old sweatshirt and yoga pants.

"Thanks, man." He gave me one last all-over look, as if to memorize me for future wanking material, and grinned as he handed me the package. "Have a great day."

Right. I nodded and closed the door. I didn't waste a second opening the package this time—I ripped open the tab as soon as the deadbolt slipped home.

This time it really was the contract from the gallery. I stared at it for I don't know how long, trying to figure out how I felt. Sad, pissed, stressed, guilty—everything except ecstatic, which should have been at the top of the list.

Another thing that should have been at the top of my list: working on my next canvas. I had seven weeks to finish the three remaining paintings in the *Enter the Light* series. Normally it wouldn't have been a problem, but I had a time bomb in my fridge. How could I concentrate on my art with that looming over my head?

And it was nonnegotiable: Chloe agreed to show my other twelve canvases only because of this new series. Without the next three paintings, I might as well kiss the art show good-bye.

"What is that?"

I spilled my coffee over my hand and the package. "Damn."

Arms crossed, Wu frowned at me. "Fighters set their weight when they get scared. They don't jump like a bunny."

"Well, I'm not a fighter." Even as the words came out of my mouth I knew they were a lie.

"What's that, then?" He pointed to the corner of the room.

Grabbing yesterday's T-shirt to clean up the mess, I didn't have to look to know he meant the foam mat I'd rolled up and duct taped—I used it as a sparring dummy when I worked out. Wince. "I stretch my back on it," I lied.

He raised his eyebrows, his disbelief clear.

Okay—I liked fighting. A lot. I still practiced my forms and shadowboxed with my makeshift, duct-taped partner. But no way was I admitting that. It felt like a betrayal to Mom, who didn't want me to become like Wu.

I may not admit I still worked out, but I had the feeling Wu could see straight through me, much like I could see through him. Not that working out changed anything. "I am *not* going to be the next Guardian."

"You can't fight destiny."

"*This*"—I shook the package in front of his ethereal face—"is my destiny."

"What is that?"

"The contract from the art gallery that wants to feature my work." I smiled with bitter triumph. "You were wrong."

"What do you mean?"

"You said it was all a pipe dream and that I'd never make it as an artist. But I'm doing it. The best gallery on the West Coast offered me a showing."

"That hardly matters." He waved his hand dismissively. "The most important thing right now is getting your power under control."

"That's it?" I gaped. "I just told you I accomplished the incredible and all you can focus on is how I can't keep it together?"

"You caused a tidal wave last night."

I paused, frowning. "Excuse me?"

"You caused a tidal wave. Well, a small one," he conceded reluctantly. "Nevertheless, you let the scroll's gift overwhelm you. Again."

My heart stalled, and I went cold with fear. Was anyone hurt? I started to ask him, but I saw the look on his face and realized he was manipulating me.

Well, I'd had enough. I pointed away from me. "Out."

His aura intensified. "Stop acting childish and accept the fact that you have a duty to fulfill. You can't run wild anymore. You have responsibilities."

"The only responsibilities I have are to myself."

"We didn't raise you to be so selfish."

That barb hit a soft spot, but I stiffened my spine. I refused to let him play me. "It's not selfish to work your ass off for what you want. And you know what? I'm not letting you ruin this for me." I headed to the bathroom.

"Running away again, Gabrielle?"

I whirled around and pointed a finger at him. "Which is it? Running wild or running away?"

"With you, they aren't mutually exclusive," he said coolly.

I don't know why that hurt as much as it did. I knew he had a low opinion of me—I shouldn't have been surprised by his words. What did I expect? That he was going to see I was talented and accomplished in myself? That I was good as I was? That I wasn't a failure?

Right. I shook my head. I was such an idealistic idiot.

And there was one thing he was correct about—my running away. I slipped my arms out of my sweatshirt and pulled it over my head.

"What are you doing?"

"You were right. I'm done running." I dropped the sweatshirt on the futon. "Especially in my own home. If I want to get undressed, I'm getting undressed."

"Undressed?" His voice practically squeaked.

"Yep." I reached behind me for the snaps of my bra. I hadn't popped even one before he was gone.

"Good." I speared a hand through my hair and went to get dressed. Madame La Rochelle expected me, and that wasn't something I could flake on.

I was out the door and about to close it when I heard Wu say, "Where are you going, Gabrielle?"

Looking in, I expected him to come rushing after me, but he just stood in the living room. "What? You aren't going to follow me to work?"

A frustrated look pinched his face. "I can't."

"What do you mean you can't?"

"I'm tied to the scroll," he mumbled. "I can't go beyond a certain distance from it."

Good to know. "Then I guess I'll see you later." I closed

the door before he could get another word in, knowing I'd have to deal with his anger when I returned home.

What else was new?

The feeling of being watched hit me a couple blocks after I left my apartment. I paused to look around. A busy late morning in the Mission like usual—nothing stood out.

"Now you're just being a freak," I muttered to myself. Maybe the scroll had infected me with paranoia as well as its mad powers.

Shaking my head, I stopped at the corner store to buy the *Chronicle* before hopping on the bus. The unusually long earthquake and resulting high waves overnight were mentioned on the front page, but the article was brief. No one was injured. Thank God.

Madame La Rochelle lived on the other side of town, both literally and figuratively. Her neighborhood, Pacific Heights, and mine were at complete opposite ends of the spectrum. Crackheads hung out on my street; the only things on her street were her neighbors' Mercedes and BMWs.

Hopping off the 22, I walked the few blocks to her home, a three-story Edwardian. I rang the bell at the gate and waited until she buzzed me in.

Unwrapping my scarf, I dropped it and my coat on a chair in the foyer, which, incidentally, was as big as my entire apartment.

Madame had original artwork from all kinds of modern masters hanging in her house—it was like walking through a museum. Minus the security. I didn't know how many times I'd chided her about her laissez-faire attitude regarding protection. She always replied that if the paintings were stolen it'd only add to her infamy.

I couldn't count how many times I'd visited over the years, but the house still awed me. The building aside, the furniture was all antique. Each time she served me something to eat or drink, I worried I was going to spill it and ruin some priceless thing.

"Madame?" I called out. My voice echoed from the high ceilings.

"*Je suis dans la cuisine.*"

Gripping the packet that held the contract, I headed for the kitchen, which was at the back of the house. It was my favorite room, mostly because it was less formal than the rest of the house. It also had one wall of floor-to-ceiling windows that overlooked the entire bay.

"*Bonjour, mon chou,*" she said when I entered. She turned to put a kettle on the stove. "*Tu as reçu le contracte?*"

Trust her to get down to business. I bent to kiss her papery cheeks. "Yes, the contract arrived this morning."

"Give." She made a give-me gesture with her fingers.

Her English wasn't great, even though she'd lived in the States for over twenty-five years, so I wasn't sure she'd understand much of the legalese, but I handed it over anyway.

She hobbled to the kitchen table and seated herself. Without a word to me, she pulled it out of the sleeve and began scanning the contents.

I frowned at her. "Are your joints okay? You're moving stiffly."

She waved a hand to dismiss my concern, never lifting her head. I rolled my eyes and finished making coffee for the two of us. By the time I'd poured two cups, she was on the last page of the contract.

I carried over the two delicate china cups. "How does it look?"

"*Tu l'as lu?*" she asked, accepting her coffee.

"*Pas vraiment.* I just flipped through it."

"*Bien.*" She waved a hand to the cupboards. "*Il y a des biscuits dans le placard.*"

Because I'm not one to turn down sweets of any kind, I went to fetch the tin of cookies from the cabinet. So Madame couldn't complain that I was a barbarian, I put a bunch on a china dish before I set them on the table. Then I took two. "So will I be signing my life away?"

She shrugged in her expressive Gallic way and set the contract aside. "*Je ne sais pas.* The language is confusing, *non?* I will give it to my lawyer and he will tell us."

I nodded and lifted my cup to my face to breathe in the aroma. I could feel Madame's eagle eyes studying me, and I wondered how long it would be before she pounced.

Exactly eleven seconds. "You do not seem content. Are you not happy about *le contracte?*"

It wasn't the contract I was down about. I just shrugged. Shrugs went a long way with the French.

Not this time, though. Her fine eyebrows furrowed and her lips pursed. "*Mais pourquoi tu n'es pas contente?* This is all you want all these years, *non?*"

"Yes." I sighed. It was. It was what Mom wanted for me, what she'd wanted for herself and would have accomplished if I hadn't messed up and killed her. I should have been overjoyed.

Hard to feel overjoyed when you had the crushing weight of a curse on your shoulders. It'd be one thing if I could expect *tŭ ch'i* to unleash predictably (like with every full moon or something), but it was completely random, as far as I could tell. I did a small internal nudge to test it and it barely flared.

"*Ah, je comprends.* You are in shock, and maybe a little scared, *hein?*" She patted my hand knowingly. "You will be *merveilleuse.* You will see. Madame La Rochelle is never wrong."

I smiled at her modesty. "Of course you're not."

"How is work on the next painting coming?" she commanded as she reached for a cookie. "You have started it this week, *non?*"

I pretended to be engrossed in my coffee.

"Gabrielle." She set her cup down with a sharp clatter that made me wince. "You have very few weeks left. The contract is for the series as well as the twelve other canvases. There is no series if you do not finish the last three paintings, and you cannot finish the paintings if you do not start them."

"I know. I'll finish them." I frowned at a cookie before I bit it.

"Sitting here eating is not finishing them," she pointed out.

I imagined trying to paint with Wu's ghost standing over my shoulder and criticizing every brush stroke while he chastised me for not living up to my obligations. Yeah, that was going to be real successful. "I just have a few things on my mind. Some personal business."

She sat up straight like a tenacious little dog catching a scent—a scent of something distasteful. "Personal business? What is this personal business?"

"The thing about personal business is that it's usually personal," I said with a smile. I set another cookie on Madame's saucer as I took another for myself, hoping it might distract her.

She made a sound only native French people could pull off—something between a snort and a harrumph. "There is no personal business between us. You tell me everything."

Not quite. And especially not this time. I clamped my mouth shut and lifted an eyebrow.

Her eyes narrowed. "*Je le decouvrai, ton secret.*"

Hell, no, she wouldn't discover my secret. But a statement like that would only have made her more determined, so I smiled enigmatically and poured the two of us more coffee.

She was silent all of thirty seconds before she started in on me again. "I worry, *mon chou*. This is—how does one say?—a lifetime chance."

"A chance of a lifetime," I corrected.

"You must work hard now. Harder than ever." She frowned. "Unless you change your mind and do not want this."

"I want it." Every fiber of my being went behind the words.

"*Donc,* you must be serious, because there will not be another chance. If you lose this opportunity, it is lost. *Tu comprends?*"

"*Oui, je comprends.*" Basically she was saying if I blew it I could give up any hope I had for ever becoming a known artist.

My heart felt sick at that thought. I rubbed my chest and tried not to think negative thoughts, but Madame had augmented the frisson of doubt I'd been feeling all day.

No—Madame had done nothing. It was Wu that screwed with my confidence. Wu, the scroll, and *tŭ ch'i*. Since they came back into my life I'd been spiraling chaotically. I could deal with chaos as long as I felt like I was in control.

I didn't, though.

Madame clutched my hand, bringing my attention back to her. "I worry, *mon chou,* that your mind is not where it should be. *Pour réussir, il faut être complètement dédiée.* You must be completely dedicated."

"I am." Even to me it sounded like a half-assed reassurance.

"You must clean your mind from distractions and paint." She pointed a wizened finger at me. "That is most important."

"I know." Except I had the mother of all distractions tucked away in my refrigerator—and a ghost to prove it.

Chapter Six

*B*y the time I'd gotten to work the next evening, I'd decided Madame was right—I couldn't afford to be distracted now. I had to focus on the goal and push everything else aside.

So wouldn't you know it that the biggest distraction I could imagine walked back into the Pour House that night.

Carrie (the other bartender on duty with me) was the one who noticed him first, given that I was bent under the bar stacking clean glasses. She nudged me with her foot. "Gabe, get up here and check this guy out."

"You, too?" I asked with a grin. "I'd expect Vivian to go crazy over a guy, but I thought you were immune."

"My studies may not give me time to date, but I'm not immune." She sighed. "You'd have to be dead not to drool over this guy."

I chuckled.

"And if I were Vivian, I wouldn't have offered to share him with you," she stated. "In fact, I would have knocked you out with a bottle of bourbon to take out any possibility of competition."

Carrie *was* night and day from Vivian, and I loved working with her. A history doctoral student by day, she worked part time to supplement her financial aid. She had great stories about her professors, she didn't insult Manuel the busboy, and the customers loved her. Best of all: she didn't pry. She respected boundaries enough not to push them.

She hinted a few times at getting together outside of work, and I'd actually been tempted. I hadn't had a female confidante since—well, since my mom. Madame was great, but not quite the same thing.

"Come on." Carrie prodded me again. "He's headed this way. You don't want to miss out on this. And on your way up, can you pull out a Sierra Nevada from the fridge?"

Shaking my head with amusement, I stretched to grab a bottle.

"Hurry." She kicked me this time.

"No man is worth this harassment," I muttered as I stood up. I rolled my eyes at the dazed look on her face. As I turned my head to see what the big deal was about, my gaze collided with dark crystalline blue eyes.

Him.

"I told you," Carrie murmured under her breath. She grabbed the beer and left me alone with the British guy.

Just like the last time, I had the sense that I knew him—more than just from having seen him before. My body came to attention, but at the same time it relaxed. The vague headache that had plagued me since I received the scroll eased. Even *tŭ ch'i* seemed to recognize him, calming to a gentle ripple from the seething burbling of the past few days.

Weird.

His gaze trained on me, he sat down at the same table as before, in the darkest corner of the bar. I had the impression he expected me to drop everything and go to him, and the impulse to do just that pissed me off. I wasn't any man's beck-and-call girl. I bent to no one's will—not anymore.

So I took an order of froufrou drinks from a gaggle of young women. I'd decide when I was going to go over there. I was in control.

Not that he was going to appreciate that. I covertly glanced at him. He looked like he was used to being in control, too. I bet it'd be quite an experience butting heads with him.

A shiver that felt an awful lot like anticipation crawled up my spine. I was going to get that opportunity—I just knew it.

Aware that his gaze remained focused on me, I took my time whipping up the drink order. Then I helped the next patron and the next, until everyone waiting for my attention had been served.

Except for him.

Wiping the counter, I shot him another surreptitious peek. Then I slipped out from behind the bar and went to him.

He watched me approach, thoughtfully stroking his scar with a long finger. "Games like that won't work with me, love," he said.

I tipped my head to the side and insulted him. "If you thought it was a game, you aren't as observant as I thought."

He casually lifted one eyebrow, but his gaze sharpened with renewed consideration. "I don't believe anyone has ever called my powers of observation into question."

"Consider yourself no longer a virgin. If you want a drink, you need to order it at the bar." I sauntered back to the bar like my heart wasn't pounding in my chest. I felt like I was baiting a tiger. The trick was not getting mauled in the process.

As I ducked under the counter, I hoped I hadn't irritated him into leaving. Something that felt very much like panic flared at the thought. I didn't want him gone—I just wanted him to know I wouldn't bow down to him.

But it worked. He slid into the barstool directly across from me as I pulled two beers for another customer. I glanced at him, careful not to show my sense of triumph. Not even I was that stupid.

After I delivered the beers and rang up the transaction, I turned to him. "Scotch?"

"Please."

"Coming right up." Turning around, I stretched to get the bottle off the top shelf. I could feel his eyes roving my body, so I wiggled my butt a little extra. I poured a fat finger of scotch into a crystal tumbler and set it in front of him.

He raised the glass. "Thanks for the show."

I shrugged. "Figured a suit like you could use the thrill."

"Know many suits?"

"Fortunately, no." I smiled sweetly.

"You don't know what you're missing, love." Taking a sip, he watched me over the rim of the glass.

"Somehow I don't believe you're like most suits. If you'll excuse me." Before he could reply, I went to help the guys farther down the bar. They flirted with me as I drew their beers. While I'm friendly, I never flirt back. Causes too much trouble.

I glanced back at him. To flirt with him would be like flirting with a wolf—dangerous and plain foolish.

Because he stared at me, I wandered back over to him.

Once again, he beat me to the punch. "Working here you must get a lot of men asking you out."

The edge to his statement surprised me. I thought I misinterpreted his tone—wishful thinking on my part—but I leaned into the bar and really looked at him. It was right there in his eyes. He tried to mask it, but I could see tinges of it in his blue eyes. A hint of reluctant jealousy and something darker.

Against my better judgment, I pulled a Vivian (minus the abundant cleavage and the bitchiness) and leaned over the counter so my top gaped. I was playing with fire and knew I should back off, but I couldn't. In a caressing whisper, I said, "It must really burn you up knowing I won't be leaving with you."

Okay—maybe with the bitchiness.

A hint of amusement replaced the jealousy. "I don't recall asking you to."

"You didn't have to."

"Be careful, love. I might take that as a challenge."

Then he leaned in so close I could feel the heat of him and smell his sexy maleness mingled with scotch. His finger whispered into my cleavage—a chaste brush against the skin at the draped vee of my top.

A delicious shiver ran down my body, and I felt my cheeks flush. God, I hoped he didn't notice how my nipples just woke up and said *Bonjour!*

I took hold of his finger and leveraged it backward to peel it off me. Not because I didn't want him to touch me—quite the contrary—but he needed to know that I wasn't going to let him do whatever the hell he wanted. "I'm not that kind of girl. I don't even know your name."

He was silent a moment, as if he were wondering what kind of girl I was. Then he stretched his hand across the counter. "Rhys Llewellyn."

"Gabe Sansouci." To my credit, I didn't hesitate in shaking it. Nor did I gasp at the sparks that shot from the contact—though I would have been justified. I'd never felt anything like it. It was like *tǔ ch'i* flowed from me to him and back. No boundaries, no beginning or end. A limitless connection.

More importantly, for the first time since I received the scroll, I felt like *tǔ ch'i* was under control. His touch somehow siphoned some of the excess from me—at least that's what it seemed like to me.

Staring at him, I waited for him to keel over, but his face betrayed nothing. How could he not feel *anything?* It felt like thick molten lava blanketed us. I wanted to fan myself with my free hand, but I didn't want him to think he was the one affecting me so badly. Not when *he* looked so unaffected.

"Gabe." He held my hand in his in such a way that I knew he was intimating I wouldn't be released until he wished to do so. "Is that short for Gabrielle?"

Chills raced up my arms at the way he drawled my name, like a sinful dessert to be savored. "Everyone calls me Gabe."

"I make it a point never to follow the masses." He let go of my hand.

Ignoring the piercing sense of loss at the sudden

withdrawal of his touch, I tensed as I waited for *tŭ ch'i* to come crashing back. But nothing happened. The light feeling of being unburdened persisted. Weird.

As it was, I hid my wrist behind my back. "You obviously don't follow the masses. You ended up at the Pour House."

The corner of his mouth lifted.

I suppressed the urge to trace his scar with my tongue by busying myself wiping the counter. "I doubt it's your usual type of haunt."

His gaze flickered down my body for a brief instant before returning to my eyes. "It has its charms."

"Enough to appeal to a man like you?" Raising my eyebrows, I looked him up and down too.

"What kind of man am I?"

The kind that's trouble. Tossing the rag aside, I said, "The kind who knows what he wants."

He swirled the scotch, studying me. "Astute."

"I'd be able to figure out what that is if I were astute." Because he wanted something. From me. An egotistical thought, yes—but I knew in my gut he was here for me and me alone.

The way he looked at me—warm and intrigued and possessive—confirmed it. "It shouldn't be difficult to ascertain," he said.

"Maybe not." Except with everything that had happened lately, I had a hard time believing this was simply masculine pursuit. "Maybe the real question isn't what you want but why you want it."

"Perhaps." He watched me over the rim of his glass, like a predator waiting for his prey to make a wrong move so he could pounce. "Although the more interesting question is what I'll do when I get it."

His husky, accented reply conjured images of sin. I could just see what he'd do, and it involved a gigantic bed with billowy silk sheets. Hot, wet kisses. Maybe even dark chocolate licked off smooth skin, but that might have been wishful thinking on my part.

Resisting the urge to fan myself, I said, "Excuse me," and headed to a group of people waiting to be served.

Coward? Maybe. But I needed a moment to regroup. I was already in over my head with everything in my life— I didn't need another complication. Rhys definitely fit in the complications category.

I glanced at him from under my lashes as I reached for a lime wedge. I needed to stay away. Though somehow I didn't think he'd stay away from me. At least not until he got what he wanted.

Call me paranoid, but this had the scroll written all over it. I couldn't discount the fact that he'd shown up almost exactly when I received it. Coincidence? My gut said there was no such thing.

"Hey." Carrie sidled up to my left. "It's tapering off a bit. It's cool if you want to leave early." She nudged her chin in Rhys's direction.

I smiled. "I'd like to leave early, but not because of that."

Her grin dimmed. "A major hottie and you're going home alone? Are you feeling okay?"

Chuckling, I untied my apron and tossed it in the bin under the counter. "Just a little tired. Are you sure you can handle it till closing?"

"Manuel and I have it covered."

I ducked out from behind the bar, keeping my eyes forward so I wouldn't catch anyone's eye—namely Rhys's. I'd slip out before he knew I was gone. With any luck, he'd think I was taking a break. All I needed was a few minutes' head start.

Bundling up, I sneaked out the back door and pulled it closed. I turned to make my getaway when I felt someone watching me from the right. I whirled around to find Rhys waiting for me.

Not sure whether I should be angry or wary, I tipped my head and blinked at him benignly. "You'll get your suit dirty leaning on the wall like that."

"I'll buy another."

I wrapped my scarf around my neck, taking my time because I was rattled. Had he been the one spying on me all along? Intuition said no. The feeling of being watched was different this time. Not menacing—just hot. "It's a nice suit. Custom-made, isn't it?"

"Of course." He straightened and walked toward me.

"You know, lurking in alleyways is a good way to get yourself mugged." I steeled myself, ready to attack.

But he only took my arm and began to walk with me. "Are you telling me you're dangerous?"

If only he knew. I waited till we were on Mission in view of all of humanity before I disengaged my arm. "Thanks for the escort. I can make it on my own from here."

"My car is over there." He pointed to something sleek and black and so expensive-looking I was amazed its wheels hadn't been stolen. "Let me give you a lift."

I shook my head. "I pride myself on being a little bit smarter than that."

"Now it sounds like you're saying *I'm* dangerous."

Laughing, I edged away. "That's an understatement, I think. Good night."

He grabbed my hand before I could hightail it out of there. "Meet me tomorrow."

Caught off guard by his abrupt command, I sputtered for a second before I said, "No."

"Why not?" He gazed at me calmly, obviously waiting for my arguments so he could coolly dispel them.

There were hundreds of reasons I shouldn't ever see him again, starting with the paintings I had due and ending with the scroll. But what came out of my mouth was "I don't know you."

"I'm offering the opportunity to get to know me." He drew me closer. "And I'd like to get to know you."

I shook my head. "I can't imagine I'd be all that interesting compared to the type of women you usually meet."

"The fact that you're resisting is reason enough for me to be interested." His thumb whispered over my pulse, as if to point out that I wasn't unaffected.

The fact that I *was* affected was the issue here. And tempted. I tugged my hand. "Thanks, but I have to pass."

Surprisingly, he let me go. Slipping his hands in his pockets, he studied me. Then he said, "If you change your mind, I'll be at Ocean Beach. One o'clock."

Before I could respond, he walked to his car. I gaped after him, admiring his boldness (and the rear view). He glanced at me over the roof of his car before he got in. I stood in the cold night air and watched him drive off.

Because I was somewhat paranoid, I headed in the wrong direction and doubled back—twice—before I headed home. Just in case.

He didn't follow me home. Call me crazy, but it disappointed me. As I let myself inside, I vowed I wouldn't meet him tomorrow afternoon. That'd just be stupid.

Chapter Seven

I can't believe I'm this stupid," I muttered to myself as I got off the 5 Fulton at Ocean Beach. I glanced at the time on my cell phone: 1:20. Maybe he'd have given up hope that I'd arrive. Maybe he'd be gone.

I refused to analyze the pang of disappointment that thought brought on.

Wrapping my scarf tighter around my neck, I walked down the sand. It was good that I came, even if he was gone. The rhythmic crash of the waves soothed *tŭ ch'i* to a lull, and the tang of the air pacified me. What we San Franciscans called a beach didn't even qualify compared to Southern California, but I always found comfort in the familiarity of the sound and smell. Who cared that it was frigid and overcast most of the year?

Certainly not Rhys. I looked left and saw a lone figure sitting on a dune farther down. The fluttering in my stomach told me it was him, so I took a deep breath and went to face the music.

He knew I approached—I was sure of it—but he stared

at the waves, one leg out straight and the other bent with an arm resting loosely on his knee. Even wearing a thick sweater, dark jeans, and a casual jacket he looked expensive. And mouthwatering.

Rhys looked up, a hint of a grin lifting his lips, as if he could read my thoughts. "Gabrielle," he said when I reached him.

Tŭ ch'i surged, as if excited by Rhys's presence, but then quietly receded again. Odd. Frowning, I plopped down close but not too close. "I shouldn't be here. I should be working on my next painting."

"Then why are you here?"

Good question. But no way was I ready to answer it. "Why are *you* here?"

"Perhaps for similar reasons."

"I doubt that," I muttered. All night I'd thought about it. A man like Rhys didn't come after a woman like me unless she had something of value, and the only valuable thing I had at the moment was the scroll. Paranoid? Yeah. Wu raised me that way.

Rhys picked up my hand and studied it. "Will you tell me about your painting?"

I tried to suppress a shiver as he traced my lifeline with a long finger. "I thought I was here to get to know *you*."

"I did say that, didn't I?" He smiled and turned his body to face me instead of the water. "What would you like to know?"

Why he was here. Why he found me so fascinating. What he looked like without any clothes on. How his hands would feel on my . . . Clearing my throat, I jerked my chin toward him. "How did you get that scar?"

He automatically touched it. "It's not such an interesting story, love," he said lightly. "It was long ago. I was conducting a business transaction that didn't go as smoothly as I would have liked."

The part of me that had a thing for bad boys jumped in excitement. The saner part of me said *run*. "Business sounds hazardous."

"It can be cutthroat at times."

"I bet." I stared at his scar, wanting to run a finger over its raised surface.

Before I could ask any of the hundred other questions in my head, he said, "Tell me about your art."

"There's not much to tell." Especially at the moment, since I hadn't painted anything in days. I winced. "I have my first gallery showing in a couple months."

"That's quite an accomplishment. Perhaps you'll invite me to attend."

My stomach twisted at the thought of Rhys looking at my work. Normally I wasn't fazed by other people's opinions (except Madame's, of course), and it unnerved me that his opinion could matter.

Needing some distance, I pulled my hand from his. A chill stole over me and I huddled in my coat, hugging my knees. "Most people would call coming to the beach in the middle of winter insane."

"It reminds me a bit of where I grew up." Taking off his jacket, he draped it across my shoulders and pulled it closed under my chin.

Burrowing into it, I furtively inhaled. It smelled like him—mysterious, warm, and forbidden. "Where did you grow up?"

"Wales. In the countryside. Not on the ocean, but close enough to feel its pull."

"You're a country boy?" I pointedly stared at the casual clothes that cost more than my entire wardrobe put together.

"I grew up in the country," he clarified. "I haven't lived in the country since I was seventeen."

"But you miss it?"

"Not at all. The only thing that made living there tolerable was the distant thunder of the waves," he said in a way that I knew that topic was closed for discussion.

That didn't mean I wouldn't pry. "You don't miss it, but you come here because it reminds you of it?"

"Sometimes it's good to be reminded of the past." He brushed back the wind-loosened strands of hair from my eyes. "To remember how much is at stake in the present."

Caught in his quietly intense stare, I could barely swallow. My words were a whisper. "How much is at stake?"

"More than I'd care to admit." He massaged my furrowed forehead until I relaxed. "I have a treat for you."

I blinked at the segue. "A treat?"

Eyes on mine, he slipped his hand into the opening of his coat at my neck. It hovered over my pulse, a teasing caress that set my heart pounding. Slowly, he slid the back of his hand down over my scarf, over my collar, not stopping until it rested over my chest.

Despite the layers I had on, I could feel the heat radiating from his hand. My nipples hardened into tight, needy peaks, and I had to fight the impulse to rub myself against his knuckles. I held my breath to avoid the slightest contact, not releasing it until he reached into his coat's inner pocket and drew out a small white bag.

He held it out to me.

"Do I want it?" I wasn't sure if I meant the little bag or the passion he offered.

"I think you do," he said in his low, sexy accent.

Afraid he was right on both counts, I took the bag. It had a small sticker seal—Teuscher. Teuscher chocolate was like manna from the gods. I glanced up at him before I broke into it. "What if I didn't like chocolate?"

"It's dark and sinful. It went without saying that you'd like it."

Picking a piece, I ignored his burning gaze and bit into it. I sighed at the smooth, rich taste. I popped the rest, savoring each chew. M&M's were everyday food, like a hamburger, but Teuscher was like splurging on filet mignon.

Rhys turned my chin so I faced him. "You have some on your lips."

Before I could do anything, he leaned forward and I felt his breath caress my skin.

My heart thundered in my chest. I wanted to get up and run far away from him. I wanted to close the distance and take him into me, physically and emotionally.

And it scared me. I'd seen what loving Wu had done to my mom. I hadn't wanted anyone like that—ever. Hands on his chest, I pushed him back. "I need to go."

He studied me, entirely too knowingly, before he dropped his hand and sat back. "Sometimes, Gabrielle, one needs to accept one's fate."

If I didn't know better, I'd think he was talking about more than what was going on right here. But now wasn't the time to get into that. I shrugged out of his coat and handed it back to him as I stood.

"I'll take you home," he said, standing.

"I'll take the bus." The last thing I needed was to be enclosed in a small space with him. Because I knew I sounded ungrateful, I softened my voice and said, "Thanks. This was"—Exciting? Illicit? Foolhardy?—"interesting."

The corner of his mouth hitched in amusement.

"Well. Um. See you." I waved and started to walk away as quickly as the sand let me.

"Gabrielle."

Freezing, I turned around.

"You forgot this." He strode to me, holding out the Teuscher bag.

I looked at the chocolate, just as tempted to leave it as I was to take it with me, because I knew with every bite I'd think of him. Which is what he wanted. I narrowed my eyes. "You're evil."

"I've been called worse," he said with a smile. Lifting my hand, he flipped it to kiss the inside of my wrist before setting the bag in my palm.

Speechless from the sparks shooting through my body, I took a step back, and then another. Turning, I headed back to the bus stop. I could feel him watching me go, and I was overcome by the strongest urge to go back to him.

Clutching the bag of chocolates, I forced myself to walk faster away.

Chapter Eight

*M*y brief reprieve from *tŭ ch'i* came at a cost. It was back in full force the next day, and fighting to hold it in exhausted me. I'd planned on getting some painting done before work but the compulsion to pull out the scroll was so strong that I couldn't make myself walk beyond the refrigerator.

Finally I just gave up. I sat on my futon with Rhys's little bag of chocolate, hoping it'd distract me from my headache. No luck. Not even my shower as I got ready for work perked me up.

I'd walked a couple blocks before I registered the prickle up my spine. Someone was spying on me again.

My imagination? Possible. I was either losing it or someone was actually tailing me, and I was leaning toward the latter. The only thing I knew for sure: it wasn't Rhys this time.

I glanced in a storefront window, hoping to catch whoever it was. But I was on Mission Street with half of humanity, and my shadow was too clever at staying hidden. So I did what could be a brilliant move or utterly stupid—I turned onto a less-traveled side street.

The feeling persisted. I picked up the pace, my heart pounding. There could be only one reason I was being followed. If this guy knew I had the scroll, how safe was it hidden in my fridge?

My mark stung as if punctuating my fear.

Then I got pissed. For having the scroll foisted on me. For getting sidetracked from my art. For letting a cowardly punk who couldn't even face me scare me.

"No more," I said through gritted teeth. Using a group of guys ambling toward me as cover, I ducked into a recessed doorway. I waited a couple seconds and then peeked.

There he was. Narrowing my eyes, I tried to get a better look at him, but the dim lighting of the street coupled with winter's early sunset impaired my vision. All I could see was a man, dark, about six feet tall and kind of bulky. But I knew for sure it was my tail—he looked left and right as if he'd lost someone.

Something about the way he moved was familiar. Frowning, I retreated into the alcove again. I was just about to take another peek when someone grabbed my arm and tugged me out of my hiding place.

Gasping in surprise, I automatically palmed up toward his face.

"Hey!" He blocked my strike, so instead of hitting his nose it redirected to his cheek. He grunted at the impact but caught my wrists and held me tight.

I was about to ram my knee into his groin when he said, "It's me, Gabe."

"Jesse?" I stopped my knee just in time and quit struggling.

"Who did you think I was? Jack the Ripper?" He let go of one wrist to rub the side of his face. "You pack a punch, babe."

"That's all you have to say?" I jerked out of his hold and whacked his chest with a fist. "You scared me to frickin' death! What the hell were you doing following me?"

He frowned. "Trying to catch up to you. I saw you and figured you were going to work. Wanted to walk with you."

"Why the hell were you lurking, then?"

"I wasn't." He stepped back as if repelled by my anger. "I just thought we could spend a few minutes together."

"Oh." I blinked. I was about to tell him how sorry I was for jumping down his throat—damn the scroll and its infusing paranoia—but he was already walking away. "Hey. What happened to walking me to work?"

He looked over his shoulder but kept going. "I can tell when I'm not wanted. Sorry I frightened you."

"I do—" *want you*, I finished mentally as he turned the corner and disappeared. Except I didn't—not the way he wanted me to want him—and I liked Jesse too much to lead him on that way. I thought to go after him to make sure he was okay and that our friendship still stood, but somehow I doubted he'd be receptive.

God, I sucked at relationships.

To cap off my already not-so-stellar evening, Vivian was on shift with me. But I managed to stay clear of her by doing the menial, downtime chores she hated doing. Mostly. She did her best to harass me anyway.

I was quartering limes when I heard her whistle.

"Hel-lo, handsome," Vivian drawled softly.

I rolled my eyes, not bothering to look up to see who she was talking about. She tended to go for men who didn't want her, and sometimes it was too painful to watch her get slapped down.

Though sometimes I really enjoyed it.

"Wow." She whistled softly. "His suit must have cost as much as I make in a month."

Suit? Rhys? My gut did a strange flop and my body tingled, a strange combination of excitement and *tǔ ch'i*. I looked up expecting to see Rhys bearing down on me.

Instead it was a wiry guy with short hair. Damn. Pouting, I cut a lime into wedges and grabbed another as I said, "A guy who spends a lot of money on clothes won't let a salivating woman near him."

"You aren't fooling anyone. I know what you're up to." She shoved me aside. "I'm serving him."

"Jeez." I glared at her. "Watch it, will you? You almost made me slice off my finger."

But she wasn't paying attention to me. Her imitation of a come-hither smile stretched her thin lips, and she leaned across the counter in a patented move to show off her ample boobs. "What can I get you?" she asked huskily.

Poor unsuspecting guy. I shook my head. Though if he was stupid enough to take her up on her silent offer, he deserved whatever he might contract.

"You can get me a Bombay Sapphire and tonic while I speak to Gabby."

I stopped midcut and looked up. No one had called me Gabby since—

The man in the expensive suit stared straight at me. He looked like a grown-up, edgy version of—

I blinked. "*Paul?*"

My brother smiled. "Hello, Gabby. Long time."

Searching his eyes, I waited for the recrimination to surface. I remembered what he'd said to me after Mom's funeral—that I was to blame for Mom dying and how I wasn't worthy of the Guardianship—and my heart broke all over again. Even though he was four years older, he'd been my confidant and playmate growing up. If anyone could have understood that it'd all been an accident, it should have been him. But he'd still held me responsible.

Only I didn't see anything in his gaze but cautious greeting. Why was he here after all these years? My gut said the scroll. What else could it be?

Longing pierced my heart. Seeing him brought home just how much I'd missed him.

His smile deepened with amusement. "Don't recognize me, Gabby?"

"It's Gabe now," I replied inanely. "No one calls me Gabby anymore."

"Gabe. That suits you. Simple and to the point." He unbuttoned his suit coat as he perched on a stool. "But you'll always be Gabby to me."

"Here you go." Vivian slid the gin and tonic in front of Paul and batted her eyes at him. "My name is Vivian."

"Thank you." It was polite, but the casual dismissal was loud and clear nonetheless. He took the drink and gave me his full attention. "I'd like to talk to you. Alone."

Vivian's lips puckered into a sulky moue.

As unevolved as it was, I couldn't help smirking. In the old days, I would have given Paul a high five. "Sure. I'll take a break."

Wiping my hands on a towel, I started to slip out from the bar when Vivian's claw grabbed my arm and jerked me back. "You have to be selfish and hog everything, don't you? It'll all come back at you, and you won't be laughing then."

With a snarl, she turned on her heels and marched to the other end of the bar.

"She's delightful," Paul said dryly as he led me to a free table in the back corner. "You've got a real friend in her."

A light feeling I hadn't felt even when the gallery offered me the showing filled my chest, and I grinned. "We've been BFFs from way back."

He chuckled.

"So." I sat down. "This is a surprise."

"A good one, I hope," he said with a tinge of anticipation as he settled across from me.

"I hope so, too," I replied softly, drinking him in.

He studied me just as intently. I wondered what he saw. Was it as weird for him to see me grown up as it was for me to see him? Because he wasn't what I expected.

Yes, he looked familiar—almost eerily like looking in the mirror and seeing a masculine version of myself. We were both an equal mix of French and Chinese, sharing Wu's thick, straight black hair and Mom's lean height. We both had high, sharp cheekbones. Paul had Wu's dark eyes, though. I had Mom's.

But he looked polished, almost hardened now. The rounded edges he had as a youth were gone.

He reeked of money, too. I mean, we'd been better off than most, but we weren't rich. Now he had that ultra-rich look that I'd seen in people who went to the gallery openings Madame took me to. His black hair was perfectly cut and styled, his nails manicured. And Viv was right—his suit was expensive. I wondered what he did to earn clothing like that.

"It's amazing," he said, shaking his head. "You look so

familiar but so foreign at the same time. You've grown up nicely. I like what you've done to your hair."

"My layered streaks are a far cry from your *GQ* look."

He shrugged. "You always had your own style. Remember your gypsy phase?"

"Oh, God." I laughed. "I must have held the Guinness World Record for most scarves worn at once."

He grinned. "You even used tablecloths. Which was okay until you cut down that heirloom tablecloth Mom's grandmother gave her."

At the mention of our mother, we both sobered. Frowning, I played with the frayed edge of my apron. Finally, I just couldn't hold back any further. "Not to sound ungrateful or anything, but why are you here, Paul?"

Sorrow flooded his eyes. "Dad is dead."

I blinked, startled but not sure why, since I already knew Wu was dead. I cleared my throat and asked what I hadn't been able to ask Wu. "How?"

"They say it was an accident." He took a large sip of his G and T.

"*They* say?" I frowned. "Who says?"

"The coroner and the police."

"The coroner was called?" I asked incredulously. Shouldn't Wu have mentioned that? "How did he die?"

"I understand it's standard procedure for the coroner to respond." Paul took another sip of his drink, his knuckles white from clutching the glass. "He fell down in the bathtub and broke his neck last week."

The irony of him dying in a freak bathroom accident when he skirted danger with the scroll was almost humorous. But then what Paul said registered. "When did he die?"

"Last week. I didn't find out until four days ago, and it took me that long to track you down."

How was that possible? Yeah, I used my mom's maiden name and my official address was listed as the bar's, but he had money, and money bought results. It would have taken someone with research skills an hour to find me—tops.

I shook my head. It probably didn't mean anything. He'd most likely not been thinking clearly after Wu's death. He'd idolized our father, after all. He used to follow Wu around like a puppy dog. Wu never gave him the time of day—I was the focus of his mania. I'd envied Paul's anonymity, but I knew he viewed Wu's treatment as rejection. I hoped they'd patched that up after I was out of the picture. "How did you find me?"

"My private detective."

"Your private detective." I nodded like everyone had a PI at their beck and call. "What was it you said you do now?"

"I'm in business. Import–export."

"Right." It was on the tip of my tongue to ask him how many kilos of coke he moved each year, but he spoke first.

"I didn't come here specifically to tell you about Dad." He frowned at his glass, revolving it in careful clockwise circles.

He seemed like he needed prompting, so I obliged. "Why did you come, then?"

"I feel bad about Mom's funeral."

He shocked me so badly I almost fell off my chair. "Excuse me?"

Paul nodded. "I shouldn't have said those things to

you. It was cruel and uncalled-for. You were suffering as much as the rest of us. Probably more."

I didn't know how to feel about this sudden confession. For the longest time I'd waited for him to call and apologize for that day when he turned on me, but after a couple years I gave up. I watched him play with his glass and wished I'd thought to bring myself a glass of water to fiddle with, too.

"I have no excuse. I should have come sooner, but I was building my business, and the years got away from me . . ." He shook his head. "And then Dad died and I realized I couldn't put it off any longer. You're the only family I have left, Gabby."

The lump in my throat made it impossible to say anything.

He leaned forward, his eyes blazing. "I want to be what we used to be. Despite everything, we were best friends growing up. Do you miss me as much as I miss you?"

"I missed you." And I really did—for a long time. But I'd written him off. At the time, I'd felt justified. Now I felt like I'd betrayed him, too.

"Do you think you can forgive me for what I said?" He reached for my hand and clasped it in his. "Can we be friends again? I don't expect to walk back into your life and have everything be okay. I know I've let too many years go by. I'm just asking you to give me a chance to be your brother again."

My heart ached with longing. God, I wanted that *so badly*. I'd give anything to have a big brother again. I'd give anything to be able to talk to someone about the Guardianship—someone who knew the history and understood. Emotion clogged my throat, so I just nodded.

"Good." He blinked a few times and cleared his throat. "We'll have dinner. There's so much to talk about."

"I like food," I said inanely.

He grinned, and I caught a glimpse of the boy I used to have stick fights with. "You always did. Especially candy, just like Mom. I remember how you two used to sit on the porch and share M&M's."

Our special time, Mom called it. She used to tell me there were many secrets to being a woman and she wanted me to know all of them.

"I used to be so jealous of those moments, even though Mom always made sure she and I had our own special time together. I miss her, Gabby." He frowned at the ice melting in his glass. "Do you ever think about the day Mom died?"

My shoulders tensed, and I hunched down just a little in the chair. I hadn't expected him to mention that. I wasn't ready for it.

"She laughed when I told her she shouldn't go outside because you and Dad were practicing. But she wanted to take more pictures of the roses, so she went anyway. One minute she was smiling and happy, and the next . . ." He shook his head and took another swig of his drink.

The guilt in Paul's gaze shocked me. It never occurred to me that anyone else would feel responsible. It made me feel that much guiltier myself.

"I wonder how things would have turned out if I'd insisted she should stay inside." He squeezed my hand. "It was bad of me to blame you. I think it was to lessen how responsible I felt myself. And you couldn't help that you couldn't control *tŭ ch'i*. You were only eighteen. It was too much of Dad to ask of you. Especially when you were so focused on your art."

The energy that had been pulsating under the surface surged, probably responding to my emotions. For a moment, I thought it was going to break loose, but I managed to shove it back with sheer will.

Oblivious of my struggle, Paul let go of my hand and sat back in his chair. "I'm sorry. I hadn't meant to bring all that up, not the first time I saw you again."

"It's okay." It had to be said if we were going to be friends again. Besides, who'd understand better than me?

"I have all of Mom's photos." His lighter tone told me we were done with the heavy talk. "I had them shipped up from LA to my suite here in the city. You should come by and pick out the ones you want."

"I'd love that," I said with my whole being.

He smiled. "Good. They're yours as much as mine. And then there's the matter of Dad's estate."

I wrinkled my nose. "Since when did Wu have an estate? He was just an accountant."

"I specifically meant the scroll."

"What about the scroll?"

"I know you never wanted to deal with the responsibility of the scroll. It's not what you were meant to do. So I came to offer to take up the role of Guardian for you."

Tŭ ch'i flared for a second, but I clamped down and stifled it. For some reason, I parroted Wu's words. "You aren't marked."

"It's the only thing I didn't inherit." He swirled his drink so the ice clinked rhythmically. "You've got to admit I got Wu's focus and discipline, not to mention his sense of responsibility."

The five-year-old in me pouted. "If you say you deserve the scroll because you're four years older, stronger, and more competent, I'm gonna pop you one."

Paul laughed and shook his head. "You're still so defensive, Gabby. I didn't mean to step on your toes. You know you're a good fighter. It's just I know you've always wanted to be an artist. The scroll will only get in the way of your plans. The plans Mom had for you."

Didn't I know it.

"If I took over the Guardianship, then you could concentrate on your art and whatever else you want to do. You'd be free."

So tempting. And so easy. "You'd make that sacrifice for me?"

"It's no sacrifice. I know you see it that way, but I've always felt honored by that part of our family history."

The mark on my hip ached, and I rubbed it with the heel of my hand as I studied him.

"I'm not pushing you, Gabby." He swirled the ice in his glass. "This is your decision. Because the scroll is in your possession now, isn't it?"

I had the impulse to lie and say *no*. Silly, considering this was my brother. Wu was the one with the conspiracy-theory mentality, and not even he would think to mistrust Paul. "I have it."

"Where are you keeping it?"

"Someplace safe," I answered vaguely, looking around to see if anyone was eavesdropping on us.

"I know you'll keep it secure until I pick it up. I'll have my lawyers draw up the necessary papers for you to sign. To relinquish your ownership, of course."

I shook my head. "It's not your responsibility, Paul. I can't pawn it off on you."

He paused, his frown bringing out an eerie resemblance to Wu. "Why not? I have the means to keep it safe. You wouldn't have to worry about it, and you can concentrate on your art. It's a win–win."

"I know, but—" I shook my head. I should have just handed it over to him. He'd offered me the perfect out. I could let him deal with the burden and all the crap that went hand in hand with the Guardianship. I could be free to live my life the way I'd planned. The way Mom had wanted it.

And he was right—he'd be the ideal Guardian. He was everything I wasn't. Most importantly, he wanted it.

But something held me back. And my birthmark stung, which normally wouldn't have fazed me, but the sharp, pinlike pain struck me as a warning. What it was warning me about I couldn't guess. "I need to think about it."

"What are your doubts?" he asked reasonably.

"I can't put my finger on them."

He leaned forward and lowered his voice. "It's just that I'm worried about you. I don't want you to be burdened with hurting another innocent person."

His statement hit me like a wall of ice water. In my mind, I saw Mom lie before me, her eyes blank in death but somehow still wide with shock. I felt a faint rumbling of power inside me, and I wrapped my arms around my middle, as if that'd help contain it.

"Damn it, I didn't mean it like that. I'm sorry. Are you okay?" He frowned with concern. "It's been so long since I've been a big brother that I'm muddling it. I just want you to be safe and happy. Do what's right for you, Gabby. I'm here to support you. If you need help, you know where to come."

"Thanks." My shoulders relaxed, and the tension in my gut eased. "I appreciate it, Paul."

"It's what I'm here for. Speaking of helping out . . ."

He reached into his interior suit pocket and pulled out a business card. "My personal contact info is on the back. For you, I'm available twenty-four/seven. Don't hesitate to call."

"Okay." I took the card. *Chin Enterprises, Paul Chin, CEO*. I shouldn't have been surprised. Paul was always an overachiever, but it was hard reconciling the boy who used to take every opportunity to yank my hair with the head of a corporation.

"Call me and we'll set up dinner." He leaned back in his chair and downed the rest of his drink. "I want to hear more about this art show you've got coming up."

I blinked. "You know about that?"

"Of course." He smiled indulgently. "It was in the report from my PI."

"Oh." Right.

"You know, my company often gives grants to artists. I could pull some strings." He held his hands up. "I'm just throwing it out there. You should be painting full-time. You don't need to work here."

"I like it here." I tried to moderate the defensiveness in my voice as I slipped his card into my pocket. "But thanks. I'll think about it."

"Great. I'd love to help." He stood up and buttoned his coat. Then he held his arms out to me.

I hesitated only a moment before I slipped into his embrace. It felt foreign—man arms instead of the spindly boyish limbs I remembered. His chest was hard with muscle, and even his scent was different. Expensive. Luxurious. I burrowed closer, trying to find something familiar. But that was irrational—a person changed in fifteen years. Especially the fifteen years between adolescence and adulthood.

"I'm sorry I waited so long to find you, Gabby." He stroked his hand down my ponytail and pressed a kiss on my forehead. "Call me, okay? Soon."

"Okay." I smiled. As I watched him leave, it struck me how out of place he was here. I picked up the empty glass off the table and ducked back behind the bar.

Vivian was waiting for me. "Ran him off, huh?"

"Actually, Paul gave me his number." I flashed the business card just to piss her off.

"He did," she said flatly, a sour look in her eyes.

"Yeah. He invited me to dinner." I grabbed a Bud from the mini refrigerator, opened the bottle, and plunked it in front of one of the regulars, who leaned patiently across the counter, an empty bottle dangling from his fingertips.

"Thanks, Gabe." The guy dropped a bill on the counter.

I nodded at him before I gave Vivian a brilliant smile. "Paul wants to get to know me."

"Maybe he's desperate." Her tone reeked with spite.

"Or maybe he's just discerning," I replied sweetly.

"Humph." She flipped her hair behind her shoulder and flounced off.

I heard her slam a bottle onto the counter and stifled a grin. Without a doubt, I was going to hell for harassing her like that. At the moment, the joy of rediscovering my brother eclipsed any guilt. I turned to help the next customer, feeling more positive about things than I had since I'd received the scroll.

Chapter Nine

*S*o, Gabby"—Vivian chuckled—"you never said what type of work your *brother* does."

Gritting my teeth, I continued to pour tequila shots for my customer. Vivian had been grilling me about Paul ever since that night he came in—she overheard me tell a customer he was my brother. I was *this* close to strangling her. Not because of the questions but because she was agitating me, and that was making it difficult to keep *tŭ ch'i* reined in. I almost lost it when she casually commented that if she married him we'd be sisters.

And it was only Tuesday. I had to look forward to a week of this.

She leaned her wide hips against the counter next to me. "He must be like a lawyer or something. Only lawyers wear suits that expensive."

I would have taken great pleasure in telling her she was wrong, but not giving her info would piss her off more. So I paid special attention to mixing a Jack and Coke and kept quiet.

"Or maybe he's in movies. Is he a producer? He's too well dressed to be a director. Kinda strange that in all these years you never mentioned having a brother." She studied her manicured talons. "Especially since he's obviously rich. Shouldn't you be mooching off him while you do your little drawings?"

I faked a smile for my customer and slid the drinks across the counter. Then I wadded up my apron and tossed it into the dirty rag bin. "I'm outta here."

She frowned at the clock. "You still have an hour on your shift."

"I know." I left her sputtering, probably because she wasn't done trying to pry details about Paul out of me, and went to get my coat from the office.

Frankly, I didn't know what to say about Paul. I'd been so happy at the thought of him back in my life. I'd almost called him that night to set up our dinner, but I'd been dealing with the Guardianship's effects. Namely the constant dull throb of my head and the uncontrollable urges to shift mountains.

"Damn *tǔ ch'i*." I could feel it pulsing just under the surface, waiting for me to show weakness so it could be free. At least that's what it felt like.

I leaned my forehead against the door. For the past four days, all I could think about was his offer. I should just give the scroll to Paul and wash my hands of it. He gave me the perfect out: it'd be with someone who revered it—wanted it—and it'd still be in the family. I'd get my brother back, and I'd be free of *tǔ ch'i*. Rule number four said the Guardian possessed mad powers while the scroll was in his possession. It stood to reason that if the Guardian passed the scroll on, the powers would go, too.

But Paul wasn't marked.

I scowled at the thought. Who cared? I certainly didn't.

Even as I thought it, I knew it was a lie. There was a reason Paul wasn't marked. I didn't know what it was. At this point, I'd be inclined to believe it was simply a cosmic joke—on me.

What I needed was an impartial party—someone I could talk to who would offer me nonjudgmental advice.

Carrie. Not only did I genuinely like her, but she was smart and levelheaded. She'd make a good voice of reason, and she'd been hinting that she wanted to hang out together for a while now . . .

On impulse, I pulled out my cell phone and dialed her number, but it went directly to voice mail. Damn. Probably in a dusty library somewhere.

"Well, Paul's not exactly impartial." I tapped the phone to my lips. The only person left was Jesse.

I banged my head against the door, which made me wince again. I wasn't sure Jesse was still speaking to me after the other day.

One way to find out.

He answered on the third ring. "Gabe."

No sense in drawing things out. "Are you busy now?"

The pause was lengthy, and I could feel him weighing my words. Finally he said, "Nothing I can't change. Meet you at the bar?"

I shook my head. "I'm clocking out early."

"Then I'll see you at It's Tops. Half an hour okay?"

"Yeah." I'd get there early, but I could wait. It's Tops had great fries.

As I walked up 20th, I felt that prickling sense of being followed again. This time, instead of overreacting,

I ducked my head and walked briskly. It wasn't like I was leading anyone to the scroll.

Except the feeling not only persisted, it intensified. By the time I turned on Valencia I had to make a conscious effort not to run away.

And then a sleek black car with subtly tinted windows pulled over, rolling at a crawl alongside me.

Fear strangled my breath. In my head I heard Wu instructing me from long ago. *If someone attacks you, finish the fight then and there. Never allow him to take you to a second crime scene. Your chances of escaping alive diminish drastically on their turf.*

So I stopped and faced the car, my hands curling into ready fists. I was ending this now.

The car stopped and the passenger window glided down, confusing me. Were they going to drag me inside through the window?

And then I saw the driver and my back stiffened. "What are you doing here?" I asked, more than a little peeved.

"Saving your ungrateful arse," Rhys Llewellyn answered, sounding just as irked. "There's someone following you. Get in."

I studied him through narrowed eyes. "How do I know this isn't a ploy? You could have set this up. Maybe you're the one following me, hoping to trick me into trusting you."

"Love, I wouldn't have to resort to such drastic measures, and we both know it." His features hard, he pushed open the passenger door. "Now get in the bloody car before something happens."

Because I could feel the person behind me ramp up to make a move, I dove in and slammed the door shut. I heard the lock engage, and the car roared away from the curb and down the street.

Inside, it was warm and smelled secure, like leather and powerful man. I felt myself relax and wondered if that was wise. After all, I'd just willingly stepped into the lion's den. How safe was I really?

"What the hell were you doing out there?" he asked through clenched teeth.

"Walking," I replied as flippantly as I could.

His hands tightened on the steering wheel. "On a deserted street, late at night? I gave you credit for more intelligence than that."

My hackles rose, but instead of rising to his bait, I cast bait of my own. "What exactly are *you* doing here? I find it hard to believe that you happened to conveniently turn up when I needed you."

"You know just as I do that there's no such thing as coincidence. I was headed for the bar and happened to see you."

"So you followed me."

He glanced at me. "Don't get your dander up. I didn't follow so much as tried to catch up to you."

"Right."

"We both know you wouldn't have gotten into my car if you didn't feel safe with me, love."

True. I hunkered in the seat and pouted. He had me there.

We drove in silence for another couple blocks before I realized how close to It's Tops we were. I pointed to the right. "Pull over there. I'll get off at the corner."

Rhys pulled over and, letting the car idle, turned to face me. Somehow his expression was shrouded, as if he were in shadows. Even so, I could clearly see the vibrant blue of his eyes.

The way he stared at me—angry and knowing and possessive—made me uncomfortable. I fought the urge to fidget by getting pissy right back. "So are you going to tell me why you were looking for me or what? I'm late meeting someone."

He was instantly alert, as if he sniffed another male in the picture. "Who?"

"A friend."

His eyes narrowed, and something shifted in the car. He didn't move an inch, but suddenly he crowded me. "What sort of friend?"

I recognized the danger in his voice. A smart woman would deescalate the situation, but no one's ever accused me of being smart. "Just a friend," I said in a way that suggested the opposite.

He grabbed my knee so quickly I barely saw him move. "A man?"

Smiling sweetly, I patted his hand. "Jealous?"

"Insanely," he said through gritted teeth.

His growl startled me—the passion behind the one word plus the fact that he'd admit it. Hell—that he'd feel it, considering we barely knew each other. When I spoke, my words sounded confused and questioning even to myself. "You don't have the right."

"No, I don't." He took my arms and shifted me to face him completely. I could feel his urge to shake me, but his hold, while firm, was tender. "But I find myself wanting the right, despite myself."

"Gee, thanks for making me feel wanted." Scowling, I tried to shrug off his hands.

"Do you want me to want you, Gabrielle?"

I lifted my chin and met his turbulent gaze head-on. "Not at all."

He stared, searching, for several heartbeats. Then the fire in his eyes banked, and the corner of his mouth curled in satisfaction. His hands gentled, his grip becoming a caress. "For someone who's supposed to embody harmony, you are the least harmonious person I've ever met."

I opened my mouth to ask him what that meant when *tǔ ch'i* flared.

Oh, God—if something happened to Rhys I'd never forgive myself. Closing my eyes, I desperately tried to pull it together, but the more I struggled to keep it in, the more it slipped away.

His fingers caressed my face, and I opened my eyes just as his mouth met with mine. I flinched at the shock his lips caused, and then I gasped at the slow warmth that filled me, head to toe.

"Gabrielle," he whispered, nuzzling my nose with his. I felt his warm breath intimately, and he gazed into my eyes as he brushed his lips against mine for one more delicate kiss.

More. The sweet kisses didn't satisfy my need. In fact, they only whetted my appetite. So I parted my lips, ready for the real thing.

And Rhys let me go.

Dazed, I blinked as he sat back in his seat, taking all his heat with him. The desire to touch him was so strong, I shoved my hands in my coat pockets.

As if he couldn't resist, either, he reached out and ran a finger along my lower lip. "Love?"

"Hmm?" I couldn't help it—I flicked it with my tongue. I felt his body tense, and my body tightened in response.

When he spoke, his voice was thick and gravelly. "You didn't want to be late."

"Late?" *Jesse.* I completely forgot about him. "Right. I have to go."

Rhys unlocked the door, but he grabbed my hand and stopped me before I could step out. Eyes on mine, he kissed the inside of my wrist. Then he nipped it with his teeth.

Goosebumps broke out up and down my body, and my nipples tightened with the need for the same kind of attention.

He rubbed his thumb over my pulse and smiled darkly. "Remember that when you're talking with your *friend*."

The way my nipples ached, I was unlikely to forget it anytime soon. But I wasn't telling him that. Frowning, I started to scoot out.

He didn't let go of my hand. "Take a cab home. I don't want you walking the streets alone. Please," he added when I started to protest.

It was the *please* that got me. By the way it stumbled from his lips, I could tell he wasn't accustomed to using the word. I didn't know what to think, so I just nodded. "Okay."

He released me, and I climbed out. Closing the door, I headed straight to the diner, conscious of him watching the whole time. He didn't drive off until I was safely inside. Which was when I realized how utterly still *tǔ ch'i* had become. I couldn't even feel it twitching.

Strange. I couldn't help but think I should know what happened and why. The fact that I didn't made me feel all that much more incompetent.

God, I hoped Jesse would convince me to give the

scroll to Paul. My brother would be better equipped for this.

I sat in a booth at the rear of the restaurant, my back to the wall and facing the entrance. I chose to think of it as caution rather than paranoia.

The waitress shoved a glass of water in front of me without any acknowledgment and went back to the kitchen to bark at the cook. I took a sip, wishing the scroll came with Jedi mind powers. I could will her to bring me fries and a Coke.

Jesse arrived on time. I tried to smile at him as he slid into the booth, but my mouth felt tight with tension.

He nodded at me and lifted his hand to signal the waitress, who arrived posthaste. Of course. He ordered a Coke and fries for me and coffee for himself. Gross. I wouldn't get coffee in a place like this, but working in a garage made you impervious to bad java, I guess.

Jesse waited until the waitress scurried away before he spoke. "So what's wrong?"

"Everything."

He raised his eyebrows.

"Okay." I leaned in and lowered my voice. "Let's say you inherited something you didn't want."

"What did I inherit, and why don't I want it?"

"If I told you, I'd have to kill you."

His lips quirked. What he didn't know was that I wasn't really joking. "Seems like a dangerous inheritance."

I rolled my eyes. "You don't even know."

The waitress came back to deliver our drinks, taking extra-special care to make eyes at Jesse before she left. At least she wasn't flashing her boobs like Vivian would have.

He lifted his coffee cup to his lips. "So are you going

to tell me, or are we going to play guessing games all night?"

Here went nothing. "I inherited this, um, artifact, and my brother offered to take it off my hands."

"What kind of artifact?"

"An old one." I leveled him a *don't ask* look.

"I see." He paused, toying with the rim of his cup. Then he said, "I didn't know you had a brother. I thought you were on your own."

"We haven't been in touch. We'd had a falling-out." Understatement of the year.

"But he wants this thing you inherited."

"He's willing to take it off my hands," I corrected.

"And you want to keep it now."

"Um, no. I'd love nothing more to get rid of it."

Jesse stared at me. I had no idea what he was looking for, but it made me uncomfortable. He'd been trying to see deep inside me like this more and more lately. I wasn't a dummy—I knew I had walls around myself and that he was trying to find the chink that'd make them crumble. He just wasn't the one I wanted to pick at the stone.

Rhys popped into my mind, with his intense eyes and soft, soft lips. He was welcome to try to scale my walls any day. I was suffused with heat all over again, remembering how his mouth had brushed against mine. I wondered what he'd say about all this.

I shook my head. I barely knew him.

Out of the blue Jesse asked, "Did you just inherit this artifact?"

"Yeah." I frowned. "Why?"

He shrugged. "Just wondering why you've been acting so strangely. You could have told me."

That I now possessed some weird curse and had a ghost chilling at home? I didn't think so. "Sorry."

"Here are your fries." The waitress smiled coyly as she set the plate and a bottle of ketchup in front of Jesse. His smile was reserved, and when he pushed the fries toward me I felt a childish sense of retribution. I refrained from sticking my tongue out at her, though.

He waited until we were alone to ask, "So what are you asking me?"

Propping my elbow on the table, I leaned my chin on my fist. "What would you do if you were me?"

He shook his head. "I'm not—"

"No," I interrupted. "I'm asking you because you're my friend and I trust you. I know you'll give me an honest opinion."

My emphasis on *friend* wasn't lost on him. I tried to read his eyes as he studied me, but they were dark and inscrutable. Finally he said, "Let me get this straight. You inherited an artifact you don't want, but your brother wants it."

"Yes."

"So where's the problem?"

I pursed my lips. "I was the one who inherited it. If it were meant to be his, wouldn't it have gone to him?"

"Who gave it to you?"

"My father."

He frowned. "I thought your father was dead."

"Um, I may have exaggerated that a bit." I hurried on. "But he's dead now." And I had the ghost to prove it.

"You didn't like your father, so why would you care if he wanted you to have this artifact or not?"

I scrunched my nose. "It's hard to explain."

"Try."

"Well—" My birthmark itched, but I tried to ignore it. I wasn't giving in to it. "This artifact is passed down to one person in every generation, and I'm it. It's tradition. If I give it to Paul, I'm bucking tradition."

"You're an artist. Aren't you supposed to buck tradition?"

"I'm asking you what *you* think."

He grew serious. "I'd give the artifact to your brother."

I frowned. "Really?"

"Yeah." He picked one of my fries and bit it. "You don't want this thing, and your brother does. It's still in your family, and then you're free. Isn't being free your thing?" he asked with a tinge of bitterness.

My frown deepened. "But—"

"There's no but, Gabe. What's the big deal? Just give him the artifact if you don't want it."

I recoiled at the anger in his voice. "Why are you pissy?"

"Because you ask me what I'd do and then argue about it." He pushed his cup aside, dropped a couple bills on the counter, and started to slide out of the booth. "Are we done?"

"*No.*" I grabbed his arm to keep him in place. "I came intending to get your advice, but now I feel like this is about us and not the sc—um, artifact."

His hand clamped down on mine where I held him, and he leaned in. "Gabe, what do you want from me?"

I frowned. "I told you I wanted your—"

"Forget this artifact bullshit." His grip tightened, and his eyes narrowed with emotion. Passion? Fury? Toss-up. "What do you really want from me?"

Frustration bit at me, and the ground shifted. I forced

myself to relax before I spoke again. "Why are you bring-ing this up now? All this time—"

"All this time I've been waiting until you felt comfort-able enough with me to let me in. To realize that we're more than *friends*. But you keep pushing me away." He shook his head. "What does that say about me that I keep trying despite it all?"

I may not have wanted him the way he wanted me, but I didn't want to lose him or the familiarity of our relation-ship, either, and it felt like that's where this was going. "I have let you in. I trust you more than I've trusted anyone in years."

"You didn't call me to tell me about your showing," he pointed out flatly. "And this bullshit about an artifact—"

"Is totally true," I said defiantly, even though I knew I hadn't been completely honest with him. Still, my lies were of omission, and I lifted my chin, daring him to say otherwise.

He smiled sadly and stood to go. "If you say so, Gabe."

If I let him go, I had the feeling that he'd be lost to me forever, and that spurred me to panic. Grabbing his hand, I swallowed a huge lump and said, "I'm not good at this."

"I know you aren't, but I don't think honesty is too much to ask for."

"Um." I bit my lip. "How honest are we talking?"

He shook his head, bent down, and dropped a kiss on my cheek. "I'm outta here."

"Wait," I called as he turned to leave.

Pausing, he looked over his shoulder.

"Are we okay?" I asked in a timid voice I didn't recog-nize as my own.

Jesse stared at me so long, for a second I thought time had stopped. Then he said, "I'll call you" as he left the diner.

It didn't escape my notice that he hadn't answered my question.

Chapter Ten

Someone was following me. Yeah—frickin' again. The itching feeling started as soon as I stepped out of It's Tops, and I knew it wasn't Jesse—I saw the punk reflected in a window and there was no hot Brit to step in this time.

I'd meant to honor my promise to Rhys and catch a cab, but no way was I going to stand around and be a target for some stalker. So I started walking.

Briefly, I considered letting whoever followed me to catch up so I could question him with my fists. *Tŭ ch'i* swelled eagerly, goading me into action. Fortunately, the exercise of walking restored my common sense, not to mention my control. Stifling the rush of energy, I decided to deal with him more cleverly.

I'd ditch him.

And I knew just the place. I just had to get there before I got mugged (because who knew what this guy would do).

Picking up the pace, I headed for Archie's, a martini bar on Valencia. It'd be crowded (safety in numbers), and because of a particularly disastrous date a few years ago, I knew that the women's restroom window opened to a small alley.

When I saw the gleaming blue neon of the bar, I relaxed. Swearing to myself that if I got out of this all right I'd do a little practice sparring on my makeshift dummy, I walked inside and headed to the bar.

It'd look suspicious if I didn't order a drink, so I slid onto a barstool at the far end and ordered a martini. Half my attention was on the front door to make sure my tail didn't surprise me. The other half watched the bartender drown my gin with vermouth.

The guy on the stool next to me lurched into my space and elbowed my arm. "Thish ish a great place."

I nodded politely as I dropped a bill on the counter for my drink and tip.

"You're pretty." He grinned sloppily. "I am, too."

Rolling my eyes, I pretended to take a sip of my drink.

"Wanna kish?" he asked, leaning over and puckering his lips.

"Maybe when I get back from the restroom. Save my seat?" Smiling, I touched his shoulder suggestively. Guilt stabbed me, and I knew I'd be karmically punished for this, but he was the perfect cover. I stood up and hurried to the ladies' room.

I had a foot on the windowsill when a woman stepped out of one of the stalls. She came to an abrupt stop and gaped at me.

"Date from hell," I said with a grimace, hoisting myself up.

"Oh." She nodded sympathetically and washed her hands. "Smart move."

The ground was too far away to jump safely, so I hung on to the frame and dangled myself lower before dropping the last couple feet. Not wanting to linger, I took off at a run. To be safe, I wound my way up and down random streets before I finally headed home.

I opened the front door to find Wu hovering next to the futon. I felt a pull from the kitchen—a relief, because I recognized it as meaning the scroll was still there. I forced myself to ignore it and shrugged out of my jacket.

He frowned. "You're huffing. Have you been running?"

"A little." I dropped my coat on the floor.

"You're embarrassingly out of shape."

"This coming from the man who died from falling in the bathtub," I shot back as I pulled out an athletic bra, sweatshirt, and lycra yoga pants.

The glow around him diminished, and his face went blank. "Yes, I was taking a shower."

Something about the way he said it made me pause. "And you slipped."

His forehead wrinkled. "I don't remember."

If I looked in the mirror, I'd probably have identical lines creasing on my brow. "How could you not remember how you died?"

"I was taking a shower," he repeated, his gaze distant. "Something made me turn around, but I don't remember anything after."

I didn't like the sound of this. "What made you turn around?"

"I don't remember."

"Were you followed much when you were Guardian?" I didn't remember stuff like this happening, but I'd been a kid.

"What?" He snapped out of the daze, his focus sharp on me. "Why do you ask about being followed?"

"Well, maybe you heard someone coming after the scroll."

He scowled. "Don't be ridiculous. Rule number two states that the Guardian must keep it hidden at all costs. No Chin has *ever* betrayed the Guardianship in all the generations we've secreted the scroll."

Then how come I was being followed? Because I sure hadn't spilled the secret.

"Why did you ask?" he asked again.

"Just curious." Like hell I'd tell him what was going on. He'd totally blame me.

He drifted toward me. "You can't just ask such a question and then dismiss it."

Yeah, but I also wasn't sure about telling him I was being followed. He was already a pain in the neck—if he suspected the scroll was in danger, he'd be even more annoying. It was bad enough working out while he was in the same room. If only he'd leave.

An idea hit me. I dropped my clothes on the floor and started to pull my shirt over my head.

"What are you doing?" he asked, his voice an octave higher.

"Getting undressed for bed."

He squeaked and then disappeared without a trace.

Grinning, I put on my workout clothes and pulled out my duct-taped sparring buddy.

I'd never admit to Wu that he was right, but he was. I hadn't practiced in a while, and with recent events it seemed a good idea to brush up on some moves. I knew my instincts would kick in if I were attacked, but better to be prepared. A rolled-up foam mat wasn't the same as practicing with a live body, but in a pinch it'd do.

I beat it up steadily for over an hour, starting slowly with simple punches and kicks. Once I had the flow, I practiced a few throws and pictured leverages (hard to actually perform leverages on something that doesn't have joints).

I'd just executed a rather brilliant jab–eye poke–sweep combination when I heard, "You lost your balance."

"*Shit.*" I whirled around with a small yelp to find Wu hovering cross-legged over my bed.

"You aren't setting your weight properly." He frowned. "It's causing you to lose your balance."

I didn't give a damn about my balance at the moment. "Stop sneaking up on me."

"This is troubling," he said as if I'd never spoken. "Balance is essential, especially for the Guardian of the Book of Earth."

Whatever. I put the foam dummy back in the corner.

"What are the five elements?"

He fired off his question so suddenly it was like a strike. I stammered. "Excuse me?"

"Each scroll is based on one of the five elements in Chinese cosmology. What are they?"

If I didn't answer, he'd hound me all night. Sigh. "Earth. Fire, water . . . And, um—" It wasn't wind—that was a Western element. Shit. I knew them, but the more I struggled to say the last two, the more blank my mind got.

"Wood and metal."

"Right." I snapped my fingers. "I was about to say that."

Exasperation lined his otherworldly face. Then he

continued like I hadn't said a word. "For each element there is a correlating fighting principle. The properties of wood include flexibility. The fighting principle that goes hand in hand with it is leverages.

"Fire is strength and persistence, which translates to punches and kicks.

"Metal is best described as unyielding and determination—power moves.

"Water, which represents wisdom and intelligence, teaches the psychology of fighting.

"Earth encompasses all. It represents patience and hard work. Stability and balance. Obviously, its fighting principles are yielding and the use of balance points."

"Obviously." I knew I sounded snotty, but I couldn't help myself.

Wu didn't even pay attention. "Stability and balance are key for manipulating *tǔ ch'i*, the energy endowed by the scroll. Without stability and balance, earthquakes and tsunamis happen."

His accusatory tone irritated me. What I hated most was that I couldn't argue with his point. "There were no tsunamis, just big waves."

He pointed a finger at me. "You must learn to control *tǔ ch'i*, or you'll be susceptible to the impulses of the scroll."

Oh, please. "And once you start down the dark path, forever will it dominate your destiny."

"This is not a joking matter, Gabrielle," he snapped. "The scroll is powerfully seductive. Its call can entice you into doing things you don't mean to. It enhances the natural inclination of the person who holds it."

My birthmark prickled.

"You must practice control before you're lured to read

the scroll." His eyes narrowed. "You haven't looked at it yet, have you?"

"No." Tempting now, though.

"We'll begin practice in the morning."

"What do you—"

He vanished again.

"Hey! Come back. I wasn't done with you yet."

Nothing.

"Sure, decide to go poof when it's convenient for you," I muttered.

As if hearing Wu's warning, the scroll tugged at me. *Tŭ ch'i* flared, as if answering the pull. I took a couple steps toward the kitchen before I realized what I was doing.

I paused. Not that I believed Wu, necessarily—he was something of an alarmist. It was, after all, just an old scrap of paper.

What would it hurt to spend some time looking at it, anyway? Just a few minutes. I might learn some important things. I bet it'd feel cool to the touch. Soothing.

Maybe just a little reading.

Tŭ ch'i pulsed under my skin as I walked to the refrigerator. I got the impression it was eager, too. I mentally made myself calm down before taking the scroll out.

A rumbling echoed deep under my feet the moment my hand closed on the parchment. I freaked as I felt *tŭ ch'i* flare. It threatened to spike right before I stifled it. I waited another ten seconds to make sure everything was still before I took the scroll into the living room.

Settling onto the futon, I entertained the idea of reading it in some hidden place so Wu wouldn't stumble upon me. A silly thought, since of course he'd home in on it. I shook my head and unfurled the bane of my existence.

I don't know what I expected, but it wasn't the endless

pristine Chinese calligraphy, untouched by time. Crisp, not like it'd been handled by countless people over God knew how many centuries.

"Weird," I said under my breath as I traced the bold characters.

Here begins the Book of Earth, wherein . . .

Gasping, I turned to see who spoke, but then I realized the words echoed in my head. I touched the lettering again.

Here begins the Book of Earth, wherein lies the truth about man and energy. For energy is but a tool, good or bad determined by he who wields it . . .

"Holy shit," I mouthed. You could read it if you just touched it? Who knew?

I pulled back my finger. The Book of Earth. Maybe the scrolls were called books back in the day. Or maybe there was a glitch in my instant translator.

Wu used to tell me about the scrolls, but just the story about how the monk Wei Lin recognized that a neighboring overlord coveted them, and how Wei Lin stole them from the monastery and sought out five men to keep the scrolls safe. Five scrolls for five families.

He never went into any detail, though—except for the four rules. The intricacies of the scroll and *tŭ ch'i* were a mystery to me. All this was new.

"Wonder if he'd even tried reading it," I mumbled, running my fingers over the first words again. I let them sink in before I continued.

Fifteen minutes later I was battling to keep my eyes open. With each word I traced, I found myself snuggled more deeply into the comforter.

I yawned, tried not to think about how tired I was, and read another line. Then I read that line over again—twice.

Not because it was so interesting, but because I didn't understand what the hell it said. What did *the shallowest stream is the same as the deepest river* mean?

It took me another fifteen minutes to come to some conclusions.

One: the scroll could solve the worst case of insomnia ever encountered. Fighting was exciting. This scroll—not so much.

Two: it was beyond confusing. I admit I was never great in reading comprehension, but I wasn't stupid. I could read a paragraph and summarize it. But I had a feeling that if someone asked me what I'd just read, I wouldn't be able to say anything. Except that it had to do with trees and birds and stuff.

Three: the trees and birds and stuff. I got that it was the earth scroll, but the author could have used fewer nature analogies. No need to go overboard.

Four: there were no instructions on how to handle *tŭ ch'i*. At least not in the beginning of the scroll. It figured that the author would make you read to the end before revealing any useful secrets.

And having the scroll in my hands didn't abate the strength of *tŭ ch'i*. If anything, it felt like it'd had a boost of vitamin C. I had to concentrate to keep it from manifesting.

"I'm done." I tossed the scroll on the floor and snuggled into the covers. Closing my eyes, I tried to relax enough to fall asleep, but each time my tension faded, *tŭ ch'i* surged.

It was going to be a long night.

Chapter Eleven

After another fitful night of sleep, I woke up late, groggy and feeling hungover. *Tǔ ch'i* roiled in me like rancid fast food, making me want to puke to get rid of it. I felt bloated with it this morning.

Needless to say, Paul's offer looked *really* attractive.

I considered going back to the beach. I'd felt peaceful there. I just wondered if the peace stemmed from the waves, Rhys, or a combination of the two.

But I remembered the way *tǔ ch'i* flared last night when Rhys had touched me, and I shook my head. Not him. Except it'd calmed down after he showered me with those almost nonexistent kisses.

Do *not* think about those kisses right now.

With a groan, I rolled out of bed. I needed to get some work done today. My shift didn't start until six, but it was January, so I only had a few good hours of light to paint by.

I took a moment to pull on an old sweatshirt and leggings on my way to the fridge. Grabbing the scroll off the floor, I stood there, clutching it in my hand, for only a few seconds before returning it to its hiding spot. Then I hesitated only a few more before going out to my studio.

Frigid out. People had the misconception that California was all sun, palm trees, and blond people in swimsuits, but that was so wrong. Especially in San Francisco, where the winters could be cold and wet. And fog was the norm all year round.

Shivering, I sat on the stool and propped my bare feet on the rung to keep them off the cold floor. I studied the painting until my mind was clear and I was in my creative space. I dabbed some azure, white, and ochre on the palette, picked a brush, and leaned forward.

Right before my brush touched the canvas, something shifted and *tŭ ch'i* swelled. Before I could stop it, the earth opened to me, and it and I connected. That was only way to describe it: connecting. As if I extended down into the earth and it flowed into me, no beginning or end.

The same feeling I'd had the first time I'd touched Rhys.

For a split second, I felt free, like anything was possible. But then it morphed. Instead of an equal give and take, *tŭ ch'i* overpowered me, forcing me to bend to its whim. I tried to reel it in, but it shoved back with staggering intensity.

I didn't like it. Struggling against it, I mentally pushed away to keep from being mired. When I was finally free, I found myself sprawled on the floor, gasping for breath.

"What the hell was that?" I mumbled, shaking my head to clear it. I almost expected Wu to pop out and answer. He didn't, and I didn't know whether that was a relief or not.

It took a couple tries before I could stand. Woozy, I

teetered on my heels, holding on to the stool so I wouldn't topple over.

"Food." Eating something would make me feel better. I stumbled into the kitchen and grabbed a bag of M&M's—my breakfast of choice—and returned to the studio. Opening the bag, I popped them one by one, setting the blue ones on the easel's tray. I hated blue M&M's. Totally unnatural.

After a third of the bag, I decided to get back on the horse. So to speak. I reached down to pick up my discarded brush and emptied my mind to get into the zone, but as soon as I mentally crossed into that space, *tŭ ch'i* began to rise again. I blinked to snap out of it right as I got that drowning-in-dirt sensation.

Because I'm stubborn, I tried two more times. It accomplished nothing except giving me the mother of all headaches and making me feel supremely pissy.

I picked up the bag of M&M's and chewed angrily. Being overwhelmed by the curse every time I tried to paint was bad. Very bad.

"That's not a healthy breakfast."

I turned around to face Wu and made a show of sticking another in my mouth.

His lips firmed with disapproval. "You won't train well without real food."

"Then it's a good thing I'm painting and not training this morning." God, I sounded bitchy. Maybe I was hanging out around Vivian too much.

"You're wasting your time with this painting." He glided over and waved dismissively at the canvas. "It's nothing more than dabs of color. Your true worth lies in being a Guardian."

Whatever. Turning back to my painting, I tried to picture what needed to happen next, but I couldn't see anything beyond the chaos of *tǔ ch'i* churning. Like it was waiting to pounce.

"Speaking of being a Guardian," he continued like this was a normal conversation, "you *must* begin to eat better. You can't train well if your brain is addled by sugar."

I slowly popped a red M&M.

His exasperation vibrated at me. If I'd turned around to look at him, he probably would have been glowing. "Gabrielle, we need to begin training right away. I explained it last night. You have a decent foundation in fighting, but an essential part of protecting the scroll is to understand the power it imparts to you." His voice hardened. "You have to be able to wield the power accurately and without consequence."

Another accusation. My spine stiffened. Wu and Paul's faith in me was staggering. "Why don't you just say what you're thinking?"

"You don't know what's in my mind."

"It doesn't take a telepath. You think I'm a failure. You always have." My glare dared him to deny it.

He folded his arms and gave me his flat, omniscient gaze. "Do you think I see you as a failure, or is that how you see yourself?"

I blinked. What a sneaky attack. And I couldn't defend against it. So I jammed the last of my M&M's in my mouth and stood up. "I'm going to take a shower, and then I need to get some work done before going to the bar."

He shook his head slowly. "One day, everything you've been running from will catch up to you." Before I could tell him what he could do with his Jedi wisdom, he vanished.

"Seems to me like you're the one always leaving and

unavailable," I yelled, swiping the spot where he'd been standing with my arm.

Fuming, I marched through the kitchen. As I passed the fridge, I ignored the impulse to check the scroll and hurried along to the bathroom. I slammed the door shut, turned the water on hot, and stripped.

I hadn't lied about needing to work—I absolutely needed to get cracking on my paintings. I just wasn't sure it was going to be possible. Especially here. I stepped under the spray and immersed myself.

If I went somewhere else, would *tŭ ch'i* be as much of a distraction? Maybe, maybe not. At least Wu wouldn't be hovering over my shoulder pestering me every five seconds. That was enough motivation for me, even if it was going to be a struggle carting my supplies elsewhere.

Unless I gave the scroll to Paul. Then he'd have to deal with Wu and his insanity. I was only hesitating because of a stupid broadsword-shaped blotch.

The birthmark stung, like someone poked a pin into me. I rubbed it with my loofah hard enough that my skin turned red.

By the time I finished my shower, shook my hair out, and applied some eyeliner and lip gloss—the extent of my cosmetic talents—I'd come to the conclusion that until I was ready to hand the scroll over to Paul, I needed to find an alternative place to work.

I pulled out my cell phone and called the only logical choice.

"Âllo?"

"Madame, c'est moi, Gabrielle."

"C'est l'après-midi. Tu ne travailles pas maintenant?" She sounded concerned. *"Il faut finir les peintures. Tu n'as que quatre semaines."*

"*Oui, je sais.*" She didn't have to remind me of the deadline. "That's why I'm calling. I thought maybe I could do some work at your house."

Silence. Then she said, "*Qu'est-ce qui s'est passé?*"

"Nothing's happened," I lied. "I just need a change of scenery. And this way you can crack the whip and make sure I stay on schedule."

"Why do I feel you are not truthful with me?" Before I could say anything, she said, "*Bien,* come paint here. I make room in the kitchen."

"*Je le ferai, Madame.* I'll do it when I get there." I grimaced at the thought of her moving furniture. She was spry, but she wasn't as robust as she once was. "Okay? I'll be over there in the hour."

"Okay, Gabrielle." She chuckled. "You are worse than a mother, *non? À tout à l'heure.*"

"See you soon." I hung up, packed up some supplies and a couple canvases, and schlepped everything to the bus stop.

Madame La Rochelle met me at her front door. "Something is wrong, Gabrielle. I feel it here." She patted her chest.

"Nothing's wrong, Madame," I reassured her as I carted all my stuff into the kitchen. "I just needed a change of venue. For inspiration."

"Then I hope my kitchen is good inspiration, because you must finish the series, *n'est-ce pas?*"

Tell me something I didn't know. I gritted my teeth. "I will, Madame."

"*Bien.*" She watched me arrange my easel and set out my painting supplies discreetly in the corner. When she was satisfied that I'd properly settled in, she clapped her hands together. "Now I make some coffee?"

"I'll do it. You sit."

"You spoil me, Gabrielle," she protested, but she sat nonetheless. I'd just poured the hot water into the press pot when she said, "All these years you say you can only paint at your home, in your little *atelier*. Why do you change now, Gabrielle?"

"I was having trouble focusing at home." I set the pot on the table, along with two china cups. Not a bad answer, really. Truthful without being *too* truthful. "I thought I'd try something new."

She didn't reply, but I could hear her thinking that my focus had better get better really soon. As I poured coffee into the two cups, she waved toward her refrigerator as she took a sip. "*Il y a un peu de gâteau. Chocolat.*"

Chocolate cake was even better than the shortbread she usually offered. I hopped up to get it. "Is it from Delanghe?"

"*Mais oui, bien sûr.*" She huffed. "From where else would it be?"

I grinned. "Silly me."

As I was setting the leftover cake on the table, the gate buzzed. I looked longingly at the cake. Sigh. "I didn't know you were expecting anyone. I'll get out of your way."

"Nonsense," she said crisply as she started to stand. "You belong here more than anyone, and there is plenty of cake and coffee. However, I do not know who it could be."

"*Asseyez-vous,* Madame." I motioned her back to the chair. "I'll get the door."

I buzzed the gate open, wondering who it might be. I knew Madame had a ton of friends, but their visits never corresponded with mine.

The weirdness of that struck me, but I shrugged. She was orderly—she probably liked to keep the parts of her life compartmentalized.

And, really, I wouldn't have anything in common with her friends anyway. It sounded like they were all jet-setters who hung out with people like the royal family and the Picassos. I hung out with two construction workers who drank Budweiser and a mechanic who stripped stolen cars on the side.

Tightening my ponytail, I swung open the door, but my polite welcoming smile melted into a frown when I saw who it was.

Rhys Llewellyn stood in front of me, looking delicious in designer jeans and cashmere sweater. I might have asked him to turn around so I could check out his butt if I hadn't been so blown away by him showing up on Madame's doorstep.

"Isn't this a surprise?" he said, not sounding shocked in the least.

Chapter Twelve

I gaped at him like an idiot for several stunned seconds before I recovered. Then I scowled. "What the hell are you doing here?"

"Visiting an old friend."

I narrowed my eyes. "What old friend?"

"Clothilde La Rochelle, of course. Or don't you know whose house you're in?"

Mocking bum.

He cocked his eyebrow like he could hear my thoughts. "Aren't you going to allow me in?"

He was asking for more than entrance into Madame's house—I could tell. And, God, was it tempting. His magnetism pulled me, and I caught myself leaning toward him. I held myself rigid despite the irrational desire to press myself to him and let him heat me up. But I couldn't get away from the spicy tang of him, clean and warm and exotic. Did he smell like that against his skin?

I looked up and his eyes ensnared me. I could paint those eyes. Part arrogance, part erotic knowing, that look could sell a million paintings. The whole package was devastating.

Package.

My eyes drifted down his body to rest on that part of his anatomy.

He stuck his hand in his pocket, drawing his pants tighter against his groin.

My gaze shot back up to his face. His scarred lips had the barest uplifting, but his eyes flashed with amusement.

I shrugged. "Not bad."

"I've never had complaints," he said as he brushed by me.

Suddenly too warm, I stepped back to put some distance between us. The corner of his mouth twitched, but I didn't care. Let him be amused. Self-preservation was more important than dignity, and I didn't trust myself not to combust if he came too close.

Closing the door, I skirted around him. "Madame La Rochelle is in the kitchen."

To my annoyance, he headed down the hall like he'd been there hundreds of times. Why hadn't Madame ever told me about him? And why did he show up not only here but at the Pour House after all these years?

Suspicious, I kept a scowling eye on him as I followed him back.

Madame gasped (happily) when he walked in behind me. "Rhys! *Vous visitez à San Francisco? Pourquoi vous ne m'avez pas téléphoné?*"

"*Parce que vous adorez des surprises,*" he replied as he leaned to kiss her on both cheeks.

Scowling, I slouched onto a chair and tried not to be affected by his delicious accent, which got more delicious when he spoke French.

"Vous êtes aussi belle que toujours, Clothilde."

I rolled my eyes. Bullshit artist. Okay, Madame *was* really beautiful, but he was totally playing her. He must not know her well enough if he thought she wouldn't see through him. I waited for her to slam him, but she just giggled.

Giggled. And was she blushing?

"Rhys"—she held his arm and gestured toward me— *"je vous présente Gabrielle. Gabrielle est peintre."*

"Yes, I know she's an artist." His icy-hot gaze swung back to me. "And we've already had the pleasure of meeting."

"The pleasure was all yours, I'm sure," I said with a sickeningly sweet smile as I pulled the cake closer to me.

"Gabrielle." Madame frowned distinctly at the plate and my coffee.

Sigh. It was one thing to wait on him in the bar—that was my job—but the idea of serving him here chafed. But since Madame expected it, I got up and pulled out a china cup and extra plate for him. To express myself, I dropped them in front of him with a loud clank.

One corner of his mouth lifted.

"So what are you doing here?" I asked as I poured him coffee.

"Gabrielle, why do you act like this?" Madame frowned at me. "Rhys is an old friend."

I looked him up and down. He was *not* old. The friend part I doubted, too.

"Gabrielle is just being protective." He lifted the cup to his lips. "She doesn't trust me."

Madame looked between Rhys and me, her gaze curious and probing. I could see the wheels turning in her head even before the unholy matchmaking light lit her eyes. She knew of Jesse, but she'd never warmed to the idea of him. She'd actually pulled out champagne when I told her I broke up with him. I'd always thought it was because she didn't want me to get distracted from my vocation. Guess I was wrong.

"Rhys, Gabrielle is quite accomplished. She is being featured at Gallery 415."

"Is she?" he said as if I hadn't already told about the show. At least he didn't tell Madame about taking me to the beach—she would have been all over that.

"How long do you visit San Francisco?" Madame asked.

"It depends entirely on my business."

I pretended like I didn't notice the way he stared and I forked a massive chunk of cake into my mouth.

Rhys laughed, a low, rich chuckle that reminded me of the expensive chocolate he'd given me. But his laugh faded as I licked a bit of whipped cream from my lips. I could tell he was remembering licking the chocolate from them. Hell—I was remembering that, too.

"*Très intéressant,*" Madame mumbled.

No, it wasn't. I quashed the sudden arousal, glared at him to let him know what I really thought, and focused on my cake.

"Rhys," Madame said in that strident tone she used when she was scheming. "Perhaps you will be able to attend Gabrielle's exhibition. She is quite talented. You will be enamored, *j'en suis sûre.*"

I rolled my eyes as I shoveled in another bite. Enamored, my ass.

"Your intuition is flawless, Clothilde. I'm sure I'll find her"—he lingered on the word before continuing—"*work* fascinating."

"Gabrielle, Rhys is very knowledgeable about art. His collection far surpasses the little pieces I have."

Translation: he spent big bucks on art and had a house that rivaled a museum. In other words, be nice to him and maybe he'll be your benefactor.

I glanced at him from under my eyelids. By the heated way he gazed at me, I was pretty sure his idea of *benefactor* would involve owning my body in addition to my art.

My suspicions were confirmed when he said, "I collect things."

And he wanted to add me to the list.

The idea of him owning me—you couldn't convince me that he'd go for anything less than total possession—intrigued me even while I balked at it. A small part of me wondered what it'd be like to be under his care. A very small part.

Tipping my head to the side, I feigned ignorance. "What do you collect?"

"Anything that strikes my fancy."

I raised my eyebrows. A declaration, and right in front of Madame.

Not that she minded. In fact, she was eating it up. Beaming, she turned to me. "*Rhys est entrepreneur.* Very successful. He conquered many obstacles to win his place in life. Like you, Gabrielle."

"What obstacles?" I eyed his expensive sweater. No way were we anything alike.

"Let's just say I wasn't born affluent." His smile held an edge that told me very distinctly that this conversation was over.

"Isn't that interesting?" I propped my chin on my fist. I'd assumed when he said he grew up by the ocean in

Wales, it'd been in a large manor home—the kind you saw in British period pieces. "How exactly were you born?"

"In the gutter," he replied in a hard tone.

I blinked. He meant that. I glanced at his scar again. What was he hiding? And why?

Madame patted his arm as if comforting him. "Rhys, Cécile says you bought her *pied-à-terre* in Paris. It is very nice of you to let her continue to stay there when she is in town, *non?*"

Cécile? I frowned at him. Was she a girlfriend? Why else would he let her crash at his place after he bought it from her? I glanced at him to find him watching me, his gaze amused.

Bastard. Not wanting to give him the satisfaction of admitting my curiosity, I tuned out their discussion on what was probably Rhys's millionth home and cut another piece of cake for myself.

I forked a bit into my mouth and wondered again what Rhys really wanted with me. A coincidence that he popped up everywhere in my life, including here?

Right.

So why did he decide to stalk me? He all but stated he wanted something from me. Just sex? The scroll? Frown. It was the only reason anyone wanted me these days. Except Jesse.

Maybe Madame sent him to check me out. I studied her. I wouldn't put it past her. She could be devious (once, she engineered a whole weekend party in Napa just to set up one of her friends with a man). I'd have to ask her when I got her alone—no way was I having that discussion with her in front of Rhys.

"I need to get going."

Madame's cup clattered onto its saucer. "Are you not going to paint?"

"I'm out of time. I have to get to work." I washed my dishes, set them to dry, and wiped off my hands before I kissed her good-bye. "*Je vous appelerai, Madame.*"

Rhys stood up, as well. "Perhaps I can give you a lift."

"No."

Madame blinked. "*Pourquoi pas? Il n'est pas meurtrier.*"

Not a murderer? Yeah, I wasn't entirely convinced of that.

"My car is waiting outside. It's no trouble." He gave a disarming smile, but it didn't reach his eyes.

"I can take the bus." I flashed a fake smile, as well.

"You complain that the bus does not come so well here," Madame pointed out. "Rhys will drive you to work."

Even ten minutes in an enclosed space was too long. Trusting him wasn't the issue here—I didn't trust myself. I seemed to have developed a weakness for expensive-looking men.

Well, one in particular.

Only I knew better than to butt heads with my mentor. I wouldn't argue, but I'd do my own thing. I bent down and kissed her. "Talk to you later, Madame."

"Perhaps Rhys will help you become inspired, *n'est-ce pas?*" The twinkle in her eyes was unholy. "Of beauty, he is *connaisseur.*"

I shook my head. "I don't—"

"I'm happy to help," Rhys interrupted from behind me. Close behind me.

Feeling the heat radiate from his body, I stiffened. It was almost like it was reaching out and wrapping around me like a cocoon.

I didn't like feeling this way—like it was out of my hands and I was at his mercy. I glared at him over my shoulder. "Do you mind?"

"No, actually."

"But I'm sure *Cécile* will," I said with a saccharine smile.

"Perhaps. She did have her sights set on me for her great-granddaughter."

Oh.

He flashed his wicked smile at me before leaning down to kiss Madame on either cheek. "A pleasure as always, Clothilde."

Beaming, she patted his cheek. "*Venez me rendre visite.*" She shot me a sidelong glance before winking at him. "I make sure to have your favorite sweets, *non?*"

He gazed at me. "I find myself more intrigued with the spicy of late rather than the sweet."

Whatever. I turned and strode out of the kitchen.

Rhys caught me at the front door—literally. One moment I was about to walk out, the next his long fingers wrapped around my arm.

"That eager to get to work?" he asked, pulling me to an abrupt halt.

I faced him, feeling *tŭ ch'i* bunch up inside me. I clenched my hands to keep it from spilling out. Not that I'd mind zapping him, but I wouldn't want to bring down Madame's house—she had too many priceless pieces of artwork. "You know, I'm happy to set you up with someone so you have something better to do than pester me. I'm sure Vivian would love to take a drive around the block with you."

"Vivian?"

"A woman I work with." I bared my teeth in a smile

even as my body throbbed. I'm pretty sure it was *tŭ ch'i*'s pulse. At least that's what I was telling myself. "She's super sweet. You two are perfect for each other."

"I don't want perfect, love." He drew me closer to him. His gaze roamed over my face, scorched a path down my neck, over my body, and back up again. It stopped at my lips for a heart-pounding second before locking on my eyes.

An image of the two of us popped into my mind. Naked, we were pressed so close that I couldn't tell where he began and where I ended. Fire wrapped around us, and I burned wherever he touched me. His mouth latched first on to one nipple and then the other, his hands gripping my waist like he needed to be grounded and I was his rock. He licked his way down my belly right to the spot that was dying for his touch. He breathed on me, hot and moist, and it excited me more than I ever would have believed possible.

Then his tongue swiped over me, leisurely and confident. Heat burst inside me, unleashing *tŭ ch'i*. Its molten energy spilled from me to him, bathing him in energy without harming a hair on his head.

"Come," he whispered urgently.

I blinked, suddenly back in Madame's foyer. "What?"

"Come," he said again, leading me out the front door. "My chariot awaits."

My cheeks burned with embarrassment and then anger—at myself for launching into such a vivid daydream. Or nightmare, depending on how you looked at it.

I was so busy beating myself up that I didn't realize he'd taken me all the way to his car until he opened the passenger door.

"Wait." I braced my hands on the roof to keep him from pushing me into the seat. "I never said I'd let you take me to the bar."

He smiled in that bare, minorly amused way of his. "Are you scared of me?"

"I'm not scared of anything." Except perhaps *tŭ ch'i*, but it seemed to be behaving itself at the moment.

"Then what's the harm with me giving you a ride?"

I immediately pictured myself straddling him, rocking on top of him in delicious abandon. My cheeks burned hotter. "Somehow I doubt that's all you're offering me."

He stepped into me so I was pressed between him and the car. "If I offered you more, you wouldn't accept."

The contrary part of my female makeup bristled at his assumption. But of course I wouldn't accept more. Really.

He smiled slowly and bent his head so his hot breath brushed my neck. "Gabrielle?"

I shivered—a combination of his presence and the way he said my name. I'd never liked being called Gabrielle—too formal for me—but coming from him it sounded round and sexy and scarlet. "Yes?"

"Get in the bloody car."

"Fine. But only because I like the leather." And because I had questions to ask him.

He stepped back and held my elbow to help me in.

"I'm perfectly capable of getting in a car on my own," I grumbled. But he'd already closed my door and gone around to the other side. I waited until he pulled away from the curb to say, "I'm surprised you drive."

"How is it surprising?"

Rubbing my temple to ease the constant ache I had of late, I angled myself toward him. "I would have thought most guys who are as obviously well-off as you would have a chauffeur."

"I like to be in control."

"No kidding?" I deadpanned. "I would never have guessed that about you."

He shot me a look that I declined to interrupt. Then he said, "No one speaks to me like this. They don't dare."

I shrugged. "Then I feel sorry for you."

"Do you?" He glanced searchingly at me again and resumed full concentration on the road.

I looked at the way his hands held the steering wheel. Masterful. I bet he'd be masterful in bed, too. I remembered the daydream I had and flushed all over again. I would have fanned myself if I thought I could get away with it without him noticing, but I knew there was no chance of that.

Annoyed at the turn my thoughts had taken, I went on the offensive. "Why were you at Madame's house today?"

He cocked an eyebrow at me. "I didn't realize it was a crime to visit one's friends."

"Oh, please." I crossed my arms and glared at him. "Credit me with some intelligence. You didn't happen to just show up there, just like you didn't happen upon the bar I work at."

"What do you think is going on, Gabrielle?"

That was the problem—I didn't know. I couldn't exactly ask him if he was following me because of the scroll. I tried changing tactics, hoping he'd let a clue slip. "You never said what you do."

"I'm in acquisitions."

"Acquisitions." I pursed my lips. "That's as detailed as saying you collect things."

He said nothing, but he looked annoyingly amused.

I shook a finger at him. "For the record, I'm not some bauble you can buy because you fancy it. So get that look out of your eye."

His lips did that barely amused thing again. "Precisely what look is that?"

"The one where you're thinking of gobbling me up." Put that way . . . Not that I'd be interested. Much. "What do you acquire?"

"Whatever I think I can sell at a profit. Mostly businesses, but occasionally other matters, such as estates or art. If the deal is big enough."

Running my hand along the leather, I said, "You must do pretty well."

"I'm good at what I do." He glanced at me. "Is your headache back?"

I blinked at the sudden change of topic, realizing I'd been absently massaging my temples. I dropped my hand. "I didn't sleep well last night."

"Perhaps you're sleeping in the wrong bed."

I frowned at the edge to his voice. "It's none of your business what bed I sleep in. The Pour House is coming up on the right. Pull over in that bus stop."

Surprisingly, he did as I said. I thought for sure he'd fight me.

"You're assuming you know me," he said.

"Don't tell me mind reading is part of your skill set," I retorted, trying to make light of it. Truthfully, it was freaky. I already felt more linked to Rhys than I wanted to be. I didn't need more evidence of it.

He came to a smooth stop in a bus zone. "You're bloody defensive."

I didn't need to be psychic to know he was pissed—it

was in the tightness of his jaw. Which pissed me off, because he had no right. "Whatever. I'm outta here."

Popping open the door, I hopped out of the car before he could stop me. I slammed the door shut and started to walk away.

The car rolled forward and the window eased down. "Gabrielle."

I looked inside at Rhys, who leaned into the passenger seat. Pointing a finger at him, I said, "Don't even think about—"

"If you don't start to control the energy, you're going to drive yourself mad. Call me when you're ready to learn how." The window rolled up and he sped off, leaving me gaping on the sidewalk.

Chapter Thirteen

*F*irst thing the next day, I went back to Madame's house. Not to paint. I know that should have been my main concern, but this was as a reconnaissance mission.

I needed information. I needed to know how Madame and Rhys were connected—and what that connection meant to me. Factor in his veiled comment about *tŭ ch'i* . . . I had this wretched feeling in my heart that she'd somehow sold me out.

Madame La Rochelle waited for me in the foyer, her gaze serious. Before I could ask her anything, she said, "Gabrielle, *la directrice de la gallerie m'a appelé hier. Elle s'inquiète. Elle voudrait les peintures complètes.*"

I could understand Chloe being nervous about the paintings—she was forced to take a chance on an unknown artist—but demanding to have the completed ones seemed extreme. It probably wouldn't have seemed so extreme if I had something to show her. "What did you tell her?"

Madame shrugged expressively. "What can I say, Gabrielle? I say I will ask."

"Thanks." I rubbed my forehead.

"*Moi, je m'inquiète aussi.*" She turned and waddled down the hall to the kitchen. "Gabrielle, it is not only your future. It is my reputation, as well, that you risk."

Ouch. "I know, Madame. I swear I'm going to finish the series."

She nodded as she set a pot of water on the stove. "*Je sais. Et tu ne travailles pas aujourd'hui, n'est-ce pas? Tu peux peut-être finir la peinture que tu as commencé.*"

"Um. Yeah." She looked so hopeful that I hesitated telling her I didn't come here to paint. "Actually I just wanted to ask how you know Rhys."

"Rhys Llewellyn?" She perked up. "*J'adore Rhys.*"

She looked so enthusiastic, I felt guilty for doubting her. "He showed up at the bar. A few times."

"*Oui, je sais.*"

"You know?" I gaped at her.

"Of course, Gabrielle. I sent him."

"*You?*"

"He collects much art, and he has influence over many people. I am happy he takes an interest in your exhibition."

I groaned. She was looking out for my career. It didn't explain Rhys's mention of *tŭ ch'i*—that still wigged me out—but at least Madame didn't play a nefarious role in this.

"I was much pleased when he called to ask about you," she said as she readied the press pot.

"Wait a second." Frowning, I shook my head as she offered me a coffee cup. "I thought you said you told him about me."

"Yes, Gabrielle. After he asked if I knew you." She shrugged expressively. "He is connected in art, *non?* News of your talent reached his ears."

Given his parting remark, I doubted it was my talent he was interested in. Question was, how had he tracked me? And what did he want? "Do you know how I can reach him?"

"*Mais oui, bien sûr,* I know how to contact Rhys. I write his number for you." I watched her scribble onto the pad she kept close to the phone. She tore the piece of paper with a flourish and held it out to me. "*Voilà.*"

"*Merci,* Madame." I slipped it into my jeans pocket.

"I admit, I am surprised you desire to call him. You were not very nice yesterday, *n'est-ce pas?*"

I recognized the subtle reprimand. "He deserved it."

"He deserves many things, but your anger was not one of them." She studied me. "He's also had a difficult life."

I stiffened. She didn't know anything concrete about my past—I wasn't exactly chatty about my youth—but it still chafed big time that she compared my youth to his. "I've got to get out of here. Thanks for the info."

"Always you run, Gabrielle. One day all will catch you, *non?*"

I had a flashback of Wu saying the exact same thing to me. I wanted to grimace, but I smiled jauntily as I bent to kiss Madame's cheeks. "Then I'll just have to run faster, won't I?"

Shaking her head, she shooed me. "*Vas-y. Appelle Rhys et puis viens finir tes peintures.*"

"*A toute à l'heure,* Madame." I left before she could launch into another full-scale rant about my lackadaisical work ethic.

At the moment, I needed to figure out what to do about

Rhys. I believed Madame when she said she sent him to me because of his art expertise, but that didn't explain how he knew about *tǔ ch'i*.

I pulled out the scrap of paper as I walked to the bus stop. No time like the present. I flipped open my cell phone and called before I could chicken out.

No answer. Wouldn't you know it? I left him a short message asking him to call me and hung up. I was about to put away the phone when it rang.

Paul. Aw, hell. I reopened it. "I haven't called you to arrange dinner yet."

He laughed. "Which is why I'm calling you."

I rubbed my head. "I'm so sorry."

"It's okay, Gabby. I didn't call to chastise you. I was thinking about you and thought I'd see how you were."

"Oh." I blinked. "That's nice, then."

"Are you okay? You sound strained."

"I'm peachy. Just tired."

"Understandable. You're burning the candle at both ends." He paused. "I'm just offering this because I want to help, so don't get defensive and think I don't think you're capable."

I chuckled. "Am I that bad?"

"Always have been," he said cheerfully. "The fact that you haven't changed is actually reassuring. Anyway, the offer for a grant still stands. I can have it expedited. Being sister of the CEO should have some perks."

"I'll think on it, Paul. I appreciate the offer," I added so he wouldn't think I was an ungrateful brat.

"I'm happy to take the scroll off your hands, too. I bet that'd alleviate much of your stress." He continued quickly, probably thinking I was going to jump down his throat. "You don't have to surrender it to me if you want to take on the responsibility. We can just place it in my safe for security."

"Let me get back to you on that. My bus is here." I pulled out my Muni pass. "How about dinner Sunday? Are you free? I'm not working."

"I'll have my assistant free my schedule. Shall we say seven? I can send a car to pick you up."

Scummy bus or chauffeured ride? Tough decision. But I really didn't want him or his driver to see the hovel where I lived. "That's okay. I can meet you."

"Are you sure? It's not an inconvenience in any way."

"I'm positive. Where do I meet you?"

"How about my suite? I'll have them send up dinner. That way you can look over Mom's pictures, too. Sound good?"

I cleared the lump from my throat. "Sounds great."

"I'm staying in the penthouse at the Fairmont. See you at seven."

I hung up. At least my rekindled relationship with Paul was going well. Now if only I figure out Rhys's deal, learn to control *tŭ ch'i, and* finish my paintings in time.

Sigh.

Because going home held no appeal, for obvious reasons, I headed to the bar. I wasn't supposed to work today, but there was always stock work to do. The extra hours wouldn't kill me, and keeping busy would help me figure things out.

It didn't occur to me that Vivian might be there until I reached the Pour House. I paused outside the door, wondering if I should just go somewhere else. But I had no place to go, so I braced myself and walked inside.

When I saw Carrie behind the bar, I felt like I was

being rewarded. I smiled in relief. "Thank God it's you. I thought Vivian would be working."

She laughed as she stacked clean glasses. "No wonder you were so happy to see me. I'd rather face a pop quiz than Vivian."

"Tell me about it." I ducked under the bar and dumped my stuff beneath the register.

"Not that I'm not happy to see you, Gabe, but what are you doing here? Isn't today your day off?"

"I needed to get away from painting." And everything else. "I thought I'd come take care of the stock orders. I noticed we were getting low on tequila last night."

Leaning against the counter, she folded her arms and studied me. "Painting not going well?"

More like it wasn't going at all. I swallowed the burst of panic. "That's one way of putting it."

Carrie nodded, turned around, and poured two cups of coffee. She doctored one up with lots of sugar and left the other black. Pushing them across the counter, she slipped out from behind the bar and waved me to join her on the other side. "Girls' time. Come on."

For a second I was transported back in time. Mom stood in front of me, concern on her face and a bag of M&M's in her hand. *Qu'est-ce qui s'est passé, ma douce?* she'd say as she escorted me to the porch for our special girls' times.

"Gabe? Gabe? Is it that bad?"

Carrie's worried voice brought me back to the present. I blinked away the tears in my eyes and joined her. "I'm fine."

"You didn't look fine." She stared at me in sympathy. "You looked like your heart was broken. Is this about a guy?"

Looking into her guileless eyes, I wondered what she'd say if I told her the truth—that I was plagued by a scrap of paper that gave me the ability to draw energy from the earth, and that it came with a ghost.

If someone told me a story like that, I'd think they were off their meds.

"Did some jerk hurt you? Want me to beat him up?" She pursed her lips. "Come to think of it, you'd probably do a better job of that than I would. But I could sit on him to help you out."

I laughed at the image of perky little Midwestern Carrie helping me take someone on.

She frowned. "It wasn't that funny."

"Oh, it was." I picked up my coffee and sipped some. Enough sweetness to restore me. I sighed happily. "How did you know how I take it?"

"I'm quite observant." She picked up her own mug, making a face as she drank. "So tell me about your guy trouble. Is it the British hottie?"

"Rhys? *No.*" I felt my cheeks begin to burn. "Well, yeah. But not in that way. He's not my guy."

"I don't know if I believe that." Carrie grinned. "But first tell me what he did."

"It's not what he did." I slumped on the stool, warming my hands on the mug. "I just don't know what he wants."

"Sex," she said with the surety of an expert.

I blinked. "Sex?"

She nodded. "And then some."

"What does that mean?"

"He totally wants you. You guys smolder together. But it's more than that, too." She shrugged as she lifted her cup. She took a sip, shuddered, and set the coffee back down. "He looks like an all-or-nothing kind of guy."

"I think he has ulterior motives," I admitted, hoping she wouldn't ask me what.

"Maybe." She shrugged again. "But the fact that he wants you trumps all."

Did it? I wasn't sure. Especially if the scroll was involved.

If. I snorted. There was no *if.* He'd sought me out, finagled his way into my life, and then mentioned *tǔ ch'i.* There was no doubt.

"You need to ask him what he wants," Carrie said, as if reading my thoughts. "Right now."

"Now?"

"Okay, maybe after we finish drinking our coffee." She wrinkled her nose at her mug and took another evidently agonizing sip.

I shook my head. "You obviously don't like it. Why are you drinking it?"

"I love coffee. I just like it sweet. Like yours." She sighed deeply and gazed at my cup like it was her long-lost love. "But I've got to cut down my sugar, or else my butt's not going to fit in my jeans. I should have become a gym teacher instead of a scholar."

Smiling, I pushed my cup toward her. "Live a little."

"Oh, you're evil." She stared at it like it was a gigantic hairy spider. "And here I've been trying to help you by listening to your woes."

"Why is that?" I asked cautiously.

"Because we're friends."

She said it like it was the most obvious thing in the world. Jesse always said I closed off. Maybe it was time to let someone in. I thought about it a moment and then nodded. "You're right."

"Of course I am." She took a quick sip from my cup,

closed her eyes in ecstasy, and then reluctantly gave it back to me. "I've got to get back to work. You call Mr. Hot Stuff and talk to him. It'll be one less thing on your plate, and then you can get back to being productive."

She made it sound so simple. "What if he doesn't answer?" I asked.

"Call him again." Carrie looked at me like I was loony. "You're a warrior. Warriors don't stop until they've taken care of business."

I nodded, not sure I agreed but willing to give her the benefit of the doubt. Pulling out my phone, I hit redial.

It went directly to voice mail.

Three hours later, I'd finished all the stock work, and since Carrie had the steady flow of customers under control I had no excuse to stay. But before I gave up and went home, I decided to call one last time. I turned my back to the bar and waited for his voice mail to kick in again.

"I didn't picture you as the type to wait by the phone," a too-familiar British voice said from behind me.

I stiffened, annoyed that my erogenous zones instantly leapt to attention. Slowly, I turned around and tossed my phone onto my pile of stuff. "Don't flatter yourself."

He smiled. "Never."

"Where have you been all day?" I asked before I could stop myself.

The satisfaction that lit his eyes really pissed me off. "Meetings," he said as he sat down on a stool. "Miss me that much?"

Maybe just a little. Not that I'd admit that to him. "I have some questions. About your offer."

"Of course you do, love."

The bastard. I reached up to pull down the good scotch, poured him a couple fingers, and slid the glass toward

him. I frowned at the amused glint in his eyes, but I didn't
back down. Trying not to get distracted by his roguish
scar, I watched him take a sip.

God, he had a nice neck. I remembered his scent and
wondered how he'd smell right there at the crook. Just
as spicy and hot as I remembered, I bet, plus a hint of
naughty.

"Join me?" He waved to the dark table in the corner.

"Yeah." I ducked under the bar and followed him.

There was already someone sitting there, hidden by
the shadows. Rhys looked at him and arched an eyebrow.
Sputtering nervously, the man collected his drink and
scurried to another seat.

Unbuttoning his expensive suit coat, Rhys held out my
chair and calmly settled next to me as if he hadn't just
intimidated someone out of their seat.

Mentally girding my loins, I leaned closer so he'd hear
my low voice over the din. "Tell me what you meant by
the energy."

"Coy doesn't suit you, love. You know bloody well
what I meant."

How did he know about the scroll? Or that I had it?
I looked for anything in his gaze that would tell me he
was playing me, but it was totally direct. "How did you
know?"

The corner of his mouth hitched, but this time there
wasn't a trace of amusement on his face. "Because I'm a
Guardian, as well."

Chapter Fourteen

*W*ait a sec." I shook my head to clear it. "I think I heard you wrong. I could have sworn you said you're a Guardian."

Rhys arched an eyebrow. "Five scrolls, five families. You have one, which means four others are floating around the world."

"Yeah, but *you* aren't floating around the world. You're here." I frowned. "Where's your mark?"

"Will you show me yours?" His gaze dipped down my body.

My damn birthmark tingled. I put my hand over it, mentally telling it to shut up. "I'm asking for proof."

"Is that what you're asking for?" His eyes on me, he angled his body to block us from the room at large, slipped his tie loose, and began unbuttoning his dress shirt.

My entire body flushed at his slow striptease, but I kept my gaze steady. I refused to show weakness.

God, I wanted to reach out and help him undress.

I swallowed thickly as he pulled one side of the shirt

open to bare his chest. Lightly sprinkled with dark hair and surprisingly defined for a suit. But from manual labor, not the gym—I could tell from the shape and tone of his muscles. Faint scars scored his tanned skin—if this was another era, I would have thought his definition came from swordplay. He certainly had the build of a warrior.

I frowned. That messed with my image of him.

"Satisfied?"

Not until I could run my hands over him. But then I realized he was asking about the mark. I looked closer and saw it—a brown, broadsword-shaped mark right over his heart. Somehow I was positive that it'd be hot to the touch.

Not wanting to give in to temptation, I sat on my hands. "How did you find me? *Why* did you find me?"

"Does it matter?" He leaned forward. "If I can help you control it, do you really care?"

If I could control *tŭ ch'i,* I could paint again. But, yeah, I did care, because how did I know he wasn't a baddie who wanted to take the scroll when my back was turned? He himself said he collected things. I didn't want the scroll, but I didn't want the wrong person to get it, either.

He must have known I was going to protest, because he reached for my hand and put it right over his mark. It scalded my palm, pulsing between us for a split second before the energy surged inside me. I gasped, feeling his power mingle with mine, limitless and bright. Just as suddenly, it receded, leaving me bereft and longing for something I couldn't name.

"Which scroll?" I whispered.

His voice was as husky as mine. "Fire."

Figured. Heat radiated from him. I knew I should pull

away, but I couldn't, instead giving in to the compulsion
to trace it with my fingertips.

He shivered, his eyes burning, and he pressed me
harder against him. "You feel the energy under your skin,
constantly pulsing. Compelling you to use it. The strain
of holding it in makes you feel as though you're going to
alternately explode or go mad. You look over your shoulder, always expecting someone to attack you for what you
hold. All the while, you wonder if today is that day you
slip up and kill someone yet again."

Blink. I couldn't say a word, trapped in the fire of his
eyes. *He knew.*

"I can help you, Gabrielle." He lifted my hand to his
lips. His breath warmed me clear to my toes and back.
"Let me help you."

My body wavered toward him, but I still had the presence of mind to say, "What's in this for you?"

"Nothing."

"Nothing," I repeated flatly. "You used God knows
what kind of resources to find me, and you want to help
me from the kindness of your heart?"

"I do." He flipped my hand over and kissed my wrist.

I felt the gentle flick of his tongue on my sensitive skin
and almost jumped out of my skin. If he felt like this on
my wrist, imagine what he'd feel like if he kissed—

Stop that, I commanded myself. He was doing this on
purpose to distract me into submission. "No good. You'll
have to define the terms better."

"There are no terms."

"That's what worries me. Obviously I have something
you want." I leaned in until our lips almost touched.
"Bad."

His gaze dropped to my lips before returning to my eyes. "And you believe I'll do anything to get it?"

"Yes." Risky, being this close to him. Even his scent was seriously drugging.

He rested his hand and mine over my heart this time, which beat hard and fast. I wanted to tell him my mark was lower, but I wasn't sure having his hand down there was wise, especially in public. "Perhaps you're the one who will agree to anything."

Before I could answer, his lips claimed mine. Hot and searing, I felt the kiss all through my body. My hand gripped his shoulder for balance, and I curled into the heat of it. He flattened his palm over my nipple, and I thought I was going to spontaneously combust.

Rhys growled and somehow turned up the intensity so all I could think and feel was him. His free hand tangled in my hair, as if he was afraid I'd pull away before he could finish branding me. As if he wanted to mark me.

Like the myth had marked me.

Dangerous. I was playing with fire, and I didn't have an extinguisher big enough to douse this. Panting, I pushed him away. "I can't do this, especially at work."

He scanned my face. I thought he was going to protest, but he just asked, "How do you feel?"

"Huh?"

"Tell me how you feel."

Tingly and turned on beyond belief. But I wasn't going to admit that to him. "Good."

"And your head?"

My headache was gone. In fact, *tŭ ch'i* was the least intruding it'd been ever. I scowled at him. "What did you do?"

"Since fire is energy, I'm adept at giving and taking

it." The corner of his mouth kicked up. "One of my many talents."

"Right." If only I had useful talents. The only thing I'd managed to do so far was register on the Richter scale.

He let go of me slowly, like he didn't want to, and re-buttoned his shirt. "Call me when you're ready."

Torn, I watched him walk away before I went back behind the bar.

If I called Rhys, I'd owe him. And when he called in the marker—I had no doubt he would—it wouldn't be something like dog sitting or washing his car. He'd want something big. Bigger than sex—he probably knew he could get me in his bed without having any hold over me.

It'd be good, too.

"Hot." Carrie came to stand next to me, an empty beer bottle in her hand. "I almost went up in flames when he took his shirt off."

"He just unbuttoned it a little," I corrected weakly.

"Thank goodness, because I'm not sure the sprinkler system in here could handle that kind of heat." She grinned knowingly at me. "Better hope you can."

Didn't I know it. I had the sneaking suspicion I was in real danger of getting burned.

Chapter Fifteen

I should have been excited that it was Sunday—I was having dinner with Paul tonight—but instead I woke up in the early afternoon feeling like I'd wrestled a two-hundred-pound python all night.

Any relief I'd felt from whatever Rhys did to stifle the effects of *tǔ ch'i* were long gone. In fact, it'd come back with a vengeance. My entire body ached from the strain of repressing the energy. Worse: I had a terrible hangover from it. My head throbbed with every breath I took.

On top of it all, I felt paranoid. Rhys's blue eyes had followed me in my dreams for the past three nights. My gut told me there was a lot he wasn't telling me.

I was freaked out enough to want to talk to Wu. Yeah, that was saying something.

Not sure how to get him to show up, I took the direct approach: I stood in the middle of my living room and yelled for him. "Wu! Wu, I'm feeling an earthquake coming on."

"*Tŭ ch'i* is nothing to joke about, Gabrielle," he said from behind me.

I whirled around to find him drifting cross-legged over my futon. "Jeez. Stop sneaking up on me like that."

He raised one arrogant eyebrow. "Are you ready to begin your training in earnest?"

"No," I said just to see his expression sour. I really needed to grow up one day soon. "What do you know about the other scrolls?"

The glower on his face cleared. "*One scroll for each element,*" he recited. "*Earth, fire—*"

"That's not what I'm asking." I rolled my eyes. "I'm asking if you know who keeps track of the other scrolls. The other four families."

"Of course not. Have you forgotten rule number three?"

"No." Uniting the scrolls was bad juju. How could I forget any of the rules when they'd been so drummed into my head? "So there's no Guardians' Association? No annual meetings or reunion barbeques?"

Brow furrowed, Wu shook his head. "You're speaking nonsense."

"All I want to know is how you'd track down another Guardian."

"You wouldn't," he said resolutely, crossing his arms. "Wei Lin separated the scrolls for a purpose. They weren't meant to be reunited. To gather the scrolls together would mean—"

"I know. Cosmic destruction." So why was Rhys here? He had to know the rules, right? And I still didn't know how he'd found me. The only thing I did know was that if I wanted answers, I was going to have to pull them out of him.

"This is all immaterial." Wu stood up and hovered over me, as if to intimidate me into submission. "Instead of being concerned about things that have no relevance, you should be focused on learning how to be a proper Guardian."

If I told him how relevant my questions were, he'd accuse me of being the leak. Like I wouldn't know better than to tell people I had the scroll.

I grabbed my jeans from yesterday off the floor and pulled my cell phone out of the pocket.

Wu wavered in my peripheral vision. "Always busy with your social life," he said with scorn.

Hardly, but I let him think what he wanted. I redialed Rhys's number.

Imagine my surprise when he actually answered. "Miss me, love?"

He sounded intimate, as if he were next to me, whispering the words directly into my ear. While we lay in bed. I cleared my throat so I wouldn't sound like I wanted to jump him. "As if."

His husky chuckle hit me deep.

Crossing an arm over my chest, I tried not to notice how my nipples had perked with interest. "I need to see you."

"Is this a proposition?"

The questions provoked all kinds of sinful images. Like ripping his dress shirt off him and licking his mark. My hand tightened on the phone, which creaked in protest. "No proposition. I need more information, and then I'll be ready to deal."

"Deal?" Wu drifted in front of me. "What's this about a deal?"

I turned my back to him again and focused on Rhys. "When can we meet?"

"I'm a busy man, love."

"But you want this, for whatever reason, so I'm sure you'll make time," I responded mildly.

"You're turning me on playing hardball, Gabrielle. Will you deliver, I wonder?"

"Count on it." I hoped he didn't hear how breathy I sounded. "What are you doing tomorrow night?"

"What's wrong with tonight?"

"I have plans."

His voice hardened. "With your friend again?"

"Maybe," I lied.

"Careful, love. I tend to win any games I choose to play."

Not this time. But I didn't want to get him any more riled up, so I sweetly asked, "So tomorrow night?"

"Yes," he said abruptly. "I'll let you know where."

He hung up. One day to wait for answers. I guess I had no choice but to accept that.

But tomorrow I wouldn't take anything less than the whole truth. If only the scroll came with a magic lasso like Wonder Woman had.

Pulling some clothes from the drawer, I headed to the bathroom. I paused in the doorway by the kitchen. Was it my imagination, or did the fridge look really vulnerable? *Tŭ ch'i* burbled inside me, echoing my worry.

Maybe I should take the scroll with me. So no one else got to it. Or to read more if I got a break. It couldn't hurt to know more about the art. I really didn't need to paint right *now*. It could wait a while. And maybe if I read more it'd teach me how to really use *tŭ ch'i*. Maybe I could learn how to zap Vivian . . .

"What the hell." I jerked back. Those weren't my thoughts. I may not like Vivian, but I didn't want to hurt her. Heart pounding, I hurried into the bathroom and slammed the door.

"Where are you going?"

Startling, I turned to find Wu's face coming through the bathroom door. "Damn it, stop doing that. Who'll take care of the scroll if I die of fright?"

He ignored me and looked at my clothing. "Where are you going?"

To Madame's to try to paint before dinner with Paul. What else could I do? Sit around and fret? But it was none of his business, so I simply said, "Out."

"Gabri—"

I started to tug my shirt over my head.

"Eep." He disappeared in an embarrassed poof.

Cleaning up and changing as quickly as I could, I headed out before Wu reappeared. I walked up to 16th Street, caught the 22, and rode it all the way to Pacific Heights. I got off the bus at Clay, intending to walk the rest of the way to Madame's house. But on impulse, I made a detour to Alta Plaza Park first.

Ignoring all the yuppie parents, the kids in trendy Gap clothing, and the large dogs, I found a patch of grass where the sun shined. In January the sun never felt warm, but I needed the light. It felt clean.

As I did a few exercises to calm my thoughts, *tŭ ch'i* came to life. It met the pulse of nature around me, and suddenly I was part of every tree. I was every blade of grass and could feel the energy of every living thing in the soil.

What I couldn't feel was my own body.

Panic rose in my chest. *Tŭ ch'i* crested on it, choking

me. I felt myself drowning with energy, unable to stem its tide.

The ground below me began to tremble.

"*No.*" I clenched my eyes shut, determined to get it under control. The rumbling stopped right away, but *tŭ ch'i* raged inside me, dangerously volatile for much longer.

By the time I opened my eyes, I felt depleted.

That's when I noticed a creepy guy sitting on a bench, watching me.

I wouldn't have thought anything about it, except I had the same menacing sensation I'd had the night Rhys picked me up. He slouched, wore baggy clothes, and had a hat pulled low over his face.

Talk about obvious.

Normally I would have marched over there and confronted him. But normally I wouldn't feel as wiped out as I did now—if he attacked me, I doubted I'd be able to hold my own.

Because I didn't want to lead him to Madame's house, I walked to Fillmore and waited till a free cab careened up the street. Flagging it at the last possible moment, I jumped in and had the cabbie drive me around in circles until I was certain we'd lost the tail. Then I had him drop me off in front of Madame's.

I staggered up the walkway. God, I hoped she had something sweet. I needed something to revive me.

She met me at the front door.

"Do you have cake?" I asked before she said anything. I took off my coat and tossed it on a chair that was probably worth more than I made all year, tips included.

"Of course." She waved to the kitchen.

Fortunately, she waited until we were seated and I'd

scarfed down a huge piece before she started in on me. *"Gabrielle, je m'inquiète."*

"Why are you worried?" Though I could probably make an accurate guess.

"Something is not right. I feel it here." She patted over her heart. "I fear what bothers you will prevent you from success."

A portent? I shuddered. I forced a smile to my lips. "I'm fine. In fact, now that I've had some sustenance I think I can paint."

She didn't look like she believed me.

Leaning over, I kissed both her cheeks. "I swear I'll do this. *Je vous jure, Madame.*"

"Oui, je sais. I go so you can work." She stopped as she reached the kitchen doorway and turned around. *"Et Rhys? Vous avez parlé?"*

"Yes, we've talked." I rolled my eyes. "You're all hot and bothered about me finishing the series. You shouldn't be encouraging me to see him."

"I think he is good for you. Perhaps he will inspire you. *Parce que ta muse, elle est en vacances, non?"*

"No, my muse isn't on vacation." I huffed in exaggeration. "I'll finish the paintings, okay?"

"Okay." She shrugged in her expressive French way that conveyed exactly what she thought and toddled away, waving a hand over her shoulder.

"Like the doubts are helping me," I muttered as I piled my dishes in the sink. After I washed them, I dragged a stool over to the corner where I'd deposited all my stuff. I rolled the wheeled table Madame cleared for my supplies and perched on the stool to examine my work.

Hours later, I hadn't made any progress. Yeah, I'd picked up a brush, I'd dabbled some paint on a palette.

But no progress. Every time I tried to get in the zone, *tŭ ch'i* started to roil. Slowly, like thick, heavy lava—not so I felt as out of control as I did at the park, but enough that I knew I could get to that point in the blink of an eye. What if I caused another earthquake, this time strong enough to bring Madame's house down? I wouldn't be able to forgive myself.

Rhys's offer was tempting. Hell—Rhys was tempting. It'd be so easy to let him help me.

Easy, but not necessarily right. He didn't make the offer out of altruistic impulses. He didn't get to where he was by giving away his expertise. I couldn't underestimate what his price might be. Factor in my attraction for him . . .

Tossing the brush aside, I cleaned up and went to find Madame, who was reading in her living room.

"*Fini?*" she asked, setting her book aside.

Not even close. "For today."

She lifted her cheeks for me to kiss them. "*Donc,* I will see you tomorrow?"

"I'll let you know." I didn't know when Rhys would call or want to meet. "*A bientôt,* Madame."

Instead of lecturing me about how my deadline loomed closer by the hour, she just picked up her book again. "*Au revoir,* Gabrielle."

Strange.

I considered hopping a cab again, but I opted for the 1 California because there was one approaching when I walked down Fillmore. Besides, I didn't have that creepy sensation of being watched.

Not knowing where the penthouse suite was, when I arrived at the Fairmont I went straight to the concierge. Despite my ratty jeans in the posh hotel, he politely escorted me to the elevator and swiped me up. After calling Paul to check.

Paul met me at the elevator with open arms. "I'm happy you're here, Gabby."

Even his casual attire was expensive-looking. As I returned his hug, I tested his shirt. "Silk?"

"So they say." He wound his arm around my waist and pulled me through a doorway. "I just called down for dinner, so it'll be here in half an hour. I thought maybe we could look at Mom's photos while we wait. I have them in the living room."

I had to swallow a couple times before I could reply. "I'd love that."

He tugged my ponytail and guided me to a fancy couch like the ones in Madame's house. "Can I get you something to drink?"

"A Coke would be great." I took off my coat and was about to drop it when I actually noticed my environment. "*Holy shit.*"

Paul glanced up from the wet bar and grinned. "Not bad for a hotel, is it?"

"My entire apartment would fit in just one corner of this room." I turned in a circle, gaping at the crazy opulence. I walked to the French doors that led to the terrace. Beyond, half the city was on display. "Hey, I recognize this place. Isn't it the room where Sean Connery got his haircut in *The Rock*?"

"Yes." My brother walked over and held out my drink. "The bathroom fixtures are all made out of twenty-four-carat gold, and there's a two-story domed library."

"You've come up in the world." I took a sip of the Coke. Even that tasted better than usual. "Is dinner going to be like the spread in *The Rock,* too? Because I could get behind that."

He laughed and gestured me to sit down next to him. "I have Mom's pictures here." Pulling out a bundle from under the coffee table, he methodically arranged them in front of us. "I didn't know how many you'd want, so I brought them all. Pick whichever ones you want."

I set my drink on a side table and leaned forward to pick one up. But I stopped just short, hesitating. Feeling like I wasn't worthy to touch her work.

"Gabby, she loved you." Paul took my hand, infusing me with comfort. "She would have wanted you to have them, despite everything. She loved you best."

Tears sprang to my eyes. It took me a moment before I had them under control enough to reply. "She loved us equally, just in different ways."

"Aren't you going to look?" He nudged my shoulder with his.

"Yeah." I inhaled deeply and let it all go. Then I reached for the first one.

A rose in bloom, probably from her garden. Mom loved gardening. There were more still nature pictures, followed by portraits of random people I didn't know. I set a few aside to take home.

The next picture froze me. It was a black and white of Mom with me as a teenager. We sat on the top step of our porch, laughing, her arm squeezing me tight and a bag of M&M's dangling from her hand. For a second, I swore I could hear her rich laugh and smell her familiar vanilla scent.

"You've got so much of her in you. The shape of your eyes, their color." Paul fingered the photo. "Soften your cheekbones and lighten your hair and you'd be her spitting image."

I shook my head. I had too much of Wu in me for that.

"Yes, it's true. Your fingers, too." He picked up my hand and studied it. "You have Mom's fingers. I bet that's where your creativity comes from."

Touched by the sentiment, I smiled faintly as I traced over her image. "I like that."

"You should have this one, too. To remind you how much of her still lives." He added it to my small pile.

Tears pricked my eyes. Blinking them back, I picked up the next one in the pile.

One of me and Paul.

I had no idea when it was taken—maybe I was around five? Which meant Paul would have been nine. It was taken at the beach, the ocean a hazy blur in the background. My spindly legs looked even skinnier in baggy shorts, and my ponytail was a crooked mess on the side of my head. I had a bucket in one hand, a shovel in the other, and a lopsided pile of sand in front. Paul stood over me, obviously trying to show me how to make a sand castle. He had that exasperated look he used to get when he got fed up with my stubbornness. Still, I beamed up at him with my gap-toothed smile.

He must have been on the same wavelength, because he said, "I probably still get that look when you don't listen to me."

I face him. "You're still trying to help me, though."

Nodding solemnly, he chucked under my chin. "I always will, too."

Chapter Sixteen

The next day, I woke up to the picture of me and Paul, which I'd propped against the broken lamp at my bedside. Seeing it, a sense of belonging I hadn't felt in longer than I could remember blanketed me. I felt such peace that I decided to go to Madame's and paint, after all. I thought I was in a good space—mentally unburdened.

Wrong. I couldn't focus at all. An hour after sitting down, I dropped my brush onto the easel's tray and got up to pour myself some more coffee. Like I needed to get more jacked up.

In my defense, my inattention was partly Madame's fault. When I arrived, she was all over me, questioning me not only about why I was having a hard time painting, but also about what my deal was with Rhys. It took half an hour of fast-talking on my part to reassure her enough that she left me alone to work. For the painting issues, I convinced her I had a major case of nerves. I didn't even bother to explain what I had going on with Rhys.

Actually, I couldn't explain what I had going on with

Rhys. Stirring sugar into my coffee, I frowned. Maybe after I met with him today I'd have a better idea.

If he called.

Resisting the urge to check the clock for the tenth time in the hour, I went back to my workstation. At least I had a place to paint until I figured out what to do about the scroll and Wu. Paul's offer hung heavy over me. In a way, I wanted to give him the scroll because he deserved it so much more than I did.

Which I was also guilty about. Mom always said that life was big enough for only one passion, and art was mine. Still, I couldn't banish the niggling feeling that said I was letting everyone down, including myself, by not fully taking responsibility as a Guardian. I was doing okay with *tǔ ch'i*—as long as I stayed away from my house.

My cell phone rang, startling me out of my thoughts. Setting my cup down, I reached for it and looked at the screen. My heart began to pound when I saw it was Rhys. Flipping it open, I answered it coolly. "Yes?"

Silence greeted me. Then, his voice warm with sympathy, he said, "Having a bad day, love?"

His concern drained the fight right out of me. Sighing, I rubbed my temple. "A little."

"Can I do anything to make it better?"

A million ideas popped into my head, and all of them involved us getting naked. "I don't know how to deal with you when you play the nice guy."

He laughed, a low rumble that I felt deep in my core. "I'm hardly nice."

"No, you wouldn't think that, would you?" But somehow I knew he was. Which was at such odds with his ruthless businessman persona. I sighed again. "So what's the plan for tonight? I work until ten."

"I'll meet you at the bar." He paused. "Gabrielle?"

"Yes?" I asked suspiciously.

"I look forward to it," he said, and he hung up.

I shivered as I closed my phone—in anticipation or portent, it was a toss-up.

One thing was certain: I definitely wasn't going to get any work done. I took my time putting away my materials, said good-bye to Madame, and rushed out of the house before she could quiz me again. I went home to clean up and change, lingering in the shower to avoid running into Wu. No sign of him, but I wasn't going to look a gift horse in the mouth.

Not looking forward to starting the week off with Vivian, I took my time walking to the Pour House. But I had a pleasant surprise when I walked in and saw Carrie.

"Vivian switched tonight for Sunday," she explained as I slipped behind the bar and wrapped an apron around my waist.

I smiled genuinely for the first time all day. "Excellent."

She laughed as she slid a beer across the bar top to a patron. "She's not that bad. As long as you keep your boyfriend out of here. But then, I don't threaten her like you do."

"I don't do anything to threaten her," I said sullenly.

"You don't have to. Your entire being threatens her. You're stunning, smart, talented, and everyone loves you." She shrugged. "Vivian has to try especially hard to be everything you are without trying. She hates that. I'm surprised you don't have a knife sticking out of your back."

"It's not for lack of her trying." I frowned at Carrie. "You're pretty and smart and talented, too."

"I'm pretty in a Midwestern kind of way. She doesn't aspire to look innocently corn-fed, she strives to be exotic and sexy. Like you. Only like I said before, you don't have to try, because you're that way innately." She held a finger up. "And there's one last important thing."

"What's that?"

"The hunks don't fawn all over me like they do you. Like that British guy."

At Rhys's mention, my palm tingled as if feeling his mark all over again. "He wasn't that hunky."

"Liar. I thought my heart was going to explode with excitement when he took his shirt off."

I rolled my eyes. "I told you he just unbuttoned it a little."

"Even I'd make time for him if he asked me out. Except between school and work, I'd have to stop sleeping to fit him in." She grinned. "I bet he'd be worth it."

Against my will, I felt a surge of warmth through my body, almost as if he were next to me. I remembered how I'd reacted to his whisper of a kiss and silently agreed. Hell, he hadn't even really kissed me yet—not in the soul-deep way I wanted. "If you think that, you need to get out more."

Carrie shrugged as she put a bottle of vodka back in the well. "There's the time thing. And I haven't met any guy that's more interesting than the historical heroes I research for my thesis."

"That's just sad."

"Don't knock it. Some of those historical figures were studs. But I'll take those guys just the same." She nodded at the two who walked in, her smile impish. "There's always time to flirt with a cute guy."

I shook my head and turned to serve the four women

waiting at my end of the bar. The first three were easy orders—a glass of wine and a couple gin and tonics. The fourth wanted a Kissin' Candy.

Luckily, I was good at mixing fancy drinks and knew a lot of them by heart, including a Kissin' Candy (which was disgusting, by the way—like a liquefied chocolate-covered cherry). Johnny's tutelage. I couldn't count how many hours he spent teaching me all these obscure drinks no one ever ordered.

When I passed her the glass, she took one sip and grimaced. "This is *terrible*."

Was the cream bad? Possible—we didn't make many drinks with cream. "I'll mix you another."

"Of course you will." She pushed the glass back across the counter and tossed her hair behind her shoulders.

I frowned but took the drink. I sniffed at it—it didn't smell off. I would have tasted it, but she seemed like someone who'd have cooties.

Opening a new carton of cream and making sure it was fresh, I mixed another one. "Here you go."

She grabbed it off the counter and took a tentative sip. This time she gagged. "What *is* this? It's certainly not a Kissin' Candy."

"Yes, it is," I said firmly.

"Trust me, it's not. I had one at the resort in Indiana where it was created, and this is nothing like what they served me there. This has amaretto or something in it."

"Right." I nodded. "Because that's what a Kissin' Candy calls for."

"It does not."

I glanced at her friends. To their credit, they appeared embarrassed. It told me they'd seen her act like this before.

Still, I was here to make her satisfied. "Would you like me to make you something else?"

"No." She smacked the counter with the glass. "I want you to make this right."

"It is right," I said through gritted teeth.

"Are you arguing with me? Because I'm in customer relations, and you *never* argue with a customer. At my company—"

Tŭ ch'i bubbled up as if it felt my blood boiling and wanted to join in on the party. It shot up through me, filling me, empowering me. It drowned all the ambient noise from the bar, and my tension melted.

But then the woman's whiny voice amplified until it was all I could hear. My shoulders scrunched up toward my ears in an effort to block the noise—it didn't help. If anything, her voice grated even more.

My eyes narrowed as I stared at her. *I want her to stop.* I braced my hands on the bar, ready to tell her to get out, when the entire bar started to shake. Violently.

"Earthquake," someone yelled.

The shout pierced my thoughts, like a bright light cutting through a hazy fog. Suddenly I could see— well enough to know it wasn't really an earthquake. It was me.

I reeled it in, but not before the light fixture overhead broke and fell right on the annoying woman.

"*No.*" I gasped, rushing to the other side of the bar.

She lay there, out cold. Her expression was strangely peaceful, at odds with the large, violent gash on her head. I gaped in shock, unable to breathe, watching the blood flow steadily out of her.

One of her friends knelt beside her. "I can feel her pulse. I think. Someone call 911."

Frozen, I couldn't do anything but stare. The only part of me that wasn't paralyzed was my stomach. It twisted sickeningly, only partially due to residual *tǔ ch'i*.

Minutes later, the paramedics arrived. I watched them do their thing. As they carted her off, I couldn't help myself any longer. I grabbed one of their arms. "Is she going to be okay?"

"She'll live." He frowned. "But it's tricky with head injuries, you know? There may be internal damage."

I nodded, stepping back. I stood there, a hand covering my mouth as they took her away.

Carrie stepped in next to me and half hugged my waist. "Pretty crazy, huh? Are you okay?"

"Peachy," I managed to say as I slipped out from her hug. "Excuse me."

Walking woodenly, I went to the office and scrounged my jacket's pockets. My hands trembled so badly it took several tries before I could extract the cell phone from the pocket. Flipping my phone open, I searched until I found the number I needed.

He answered on the third ring. "Gabby?"

Tǔ ch'i rumbled softly, as though protesting my decision.

"Gabby? Are you there?" Concern shadowed his words.

"Yeah, I'm here." Better Paul—the one person I could trust—than Rhys. Yeah, this was best for everyone. "Paul, the scroll is yours."

Chapter Seventeen

*I*magine my surprise when, an hour later, I looked up from wiping the bar to see Paul walk in.

The moment I saw him, *tŭ ch'i* struck, doubling me over with the effort not to bring the building down. Still I felt it slipping from my fingertips, so I pressed my fists into my belly. If I let it loose, at least it'd be aimed at me and not anyone else.

"*Gabe.*" Carrie knelt on the floor next to me, her hand on my back. "Are you in pain? Should I call another ambulance?"

"*No.*" I wanted to shake her hand off me—I would *not* hurt her, too—but I was afraid to move. Maybe if I just concentrated.

But I heard her gasp. I managed to lift my head enough to see her hand several inches away from me, pressing against an invisible barrier.

Her eyes were impossibly wide as she tested it. "What is . . . ?"

I had to suck it up. By the sheer force of my will I

retracted *tǔ ch'i* until it was contained back inside me. Just.

Carrie's hand shot forward, knocking my shoulder.

"Ow." I rubbed it. Damn, she had a heavy hand for being so slight.

"What the heck's going on?" She waved around me, her brow furrowed in confusion. "I swear a second ago you were surrounded by some kind of force field."

"Don't say that too loud. They'll come for you with a straitjacket." Using the counter, I hefted myself to standing.

"Yeah, you're right." She took another swipe at the air. "Maybe I've been studying too hard."

"That's probably it," I said, feeling bad about misleading her.

"Gabby?"

I turned to find Paul standing at the bar, worry lines wrinkling the space between his eyebrows. "I didn't expect to see you tonight," I said.

He studied me, his frown deepening. Stretching across the counter, he felt my face. "Do you have a fever? You're pale and sweaty."

Something inside melted at the apprehension in his voice. "I'm okay. I was just overwhelmed for a second." I reached out to Carrie, but I stopped short of contact, afraid I wasn't safe yet. "Can you keep things under control? I need a quick break."

"Of course." She shooed me with both hands. "Go. I've got it covered."

"Thanks." I untied my apron and stumbled out from behind the bar.

Paul took my arm to steady me. "Did something happen?" he asked in a low voice.

"Um, you could say that."

"Then it's good that I came." He led me to the table in the dark corner, the one Rhys preferred. "I'll take the scroll off your hands and you won't have to worry about it anymore."

"I don't have it on me."

"My car is waiting outside. After you get off work, we'll stop by your place and pick it up."

Shaking my head, I blinked away the sudden tears. "You're so good to me."

"I'm your big brother," he said as if that explained everything.

He was, and he was really good at protecting me. But I was his sister, too, and how well would I be protecting him if I let him have the scroll? Rule number four stated whoever possessed the scroll also possessed its power. I couldn't control it, and I was marked. How would he be able to deal? Even if he just locked it up in a safe, he'd be susceptible to its pull—I was certain of that with every throbbing molecule in my body.

I needed to rethink this. I pressed my hand to my forehead. Hard to think when your head was about to split open.

"Gabby." Paul reached across the table and took my other hand. "I'm really worried about you. Maybe we should go pick it up now."

"*I need to think*." I closed my eyes. "Tomorrow. Let's talk about this tomorrow."

"Tomorrow may be too late." He took hold of my hand in both of his, his eyes warm with serious concern. "This is really taking its toll on you. I can't lose you to this, too, Gabby."

I couldn't lose him, either, and if I surrendered the

scroll and its power to him, I was afraid that was exactly what would happen.

I *wouldn't* lose him. Which meant I'd have to find another solution for the scroll. "No."

"No what?"

"No, I can't give you the scroll."

He frowned. "Are you sure that's a good idea? You look like you're falling apart."

"Yes, I'm positive."

Squeezing my hand, he leaned across the table. "You're exhausted, Gabby. Sleep on this and we'll talk tomorrow. If you still feel strongly about keeping it, fine, but right now you're not in the right space to make such an important decision."

Fair enough. I nodded. "But I'm telling you I doubt I'll change my mind again."

"I only want what's best for you, Gabby." He squeezed my hand and stood up. "Are you up to working tonight? I can give you a ride home."

"No, I'm better now." I got up and hugged him tight. "I—Thank you."

He held me for a long moment and then released me slowly. "Take care of yourself. Call me if you need me, whatever time of day."

"Okay."

A tug of my ponytail was his good-bye. I watched him leave, wishing I'd told him how much I loved him. Those three words just didn't come easily to my tongue.

I dragged my carcass back behind the bar. Carrie looked at me in question, and before she could ask I said, "I'm fine. Really."

She reached around me for a bottle of Grey Goose. "You don't look fine."

"How do I look?"

"Like you were run over by a truck."

I nodded. Accurate analogy.

"You aren't dating the rich guy, are you?" she asked, returning the bottle back to the shelf.

At first I thought she meant Rhys, but then I realized she was talking about Paul. "*No.* Of course not."

"Oh, good. Can you hand me a Bud from the fridge?"

"Why?"

"Because a customer ordered one."

I would have rolled my eyes if I'd had it in me. As it was, bending for the beer was more effort than I was capable of. "No, I mean why is it good I'm not dating Paul?"

She shrugged as she began mixing another drink. "Something about him rubs me wrong."

"He's my brother," I admitted as I slid the beer toward her.

"Oh, crap." She stopped mid-shake, turning red from her chest all the way to her hairline. "I didn't mean—"

"It's okay." I smiled reassuringly at her. "I've noticed he can be overbearing to the help. Normally, he—"

"Normally, he gets what he wants. At least that's how he looks." Carrie frowned as she poured the drink into a glass. She gave me a pointed look as she wiped the counter. "Be careful not to get between him and whatever that is."

It was on my tongue to defend him, but Carrie went to deliver the drinks before I had the chance. It was okay. I could understand how she'd get that impression of him. I just knew him better.

My birthmark pricked in warning, and *tǔ ch'i* surged again—not as strongly as before, but given my depleted state, it was more than I could handle. I mumbled a quick excuse to Carrie as I rushed out of the bar to the alley in back.

I was doubled up against a wall when I heard the back door open. Figuring it was Carrie checking up on me, I waved blindly. "Go away."

Strong hands hauled me up. Muffling a cry, I bit my lip to keep the energy contained inside me.

"Shite." He propped me between the wall and his body, freeing a hand to lift my face. "How long have you been this way?"

Rhys. I whimpered with relief. If anyone could help, it'd be him.

He cursed under his breath and tipped my head back. I was about to protest that his grip was too firm, but he covered my mouth with his before I could utter a syllable.

My hold on *tŭ ch'i* dissolved. I panicked, mentally flailing to keep it together, but then I felt reassuring heat and the cocoon Rhys wove around us.

Safe. I let go a little more, opening to him, drawing his warmth into me. But something widened between us, a chasm that scared me, and I started to step back.

Only he didn't let me. His hold on me tightened, and with a moan he deepened the kiss and pushed us both into the uncharted territory. But he must have sensed how freaked out I was, because just as abruptly he pulled us back to the present.

I lifted my head, panting. My hand rested on his chest, right over his mark, and its heat radiated through his clothes to my palm. I licked my lips—I swore I could taste him on me still.

His fierce gaze scorched me. "What happened tonight?"

I sagged against his chest. I fit so well, it felt so perfect, that I withdrew again. "I don't know what happened. It just got out of control."

"Agree to let me teach you, Gabrielle." He placed a warm hand on my neck, holding me so I couldn't pull away. "You're going to destroy yourself this way."

The emotion in his eyes took my breath away. I blinked as I realized he was more concerned about me than his favor. "Why do you care?" I whispered hoarsely.

His thumb rubbed my jawline. "Why do you think?"

I didn't know what to think. "Why are you here?"

"I told you—"

"No." I took my hand from over his mark and propped myself against the wall so I wasn't supported by him. "Why did you come here to find me? You said there's no such thing as a coincidence. You must have known I was coming into my Guardianship."

"Now isn't the time to discuss this."

"No, but tomorrow's not going to be any different." Crossing my arms, I glared at him. "Tell me."

He was silent for so long I didn't think he was going to say anything. Then he said, "The reason I came to find you doesn't matter any longer."

The pit fell out of my stomach at his reply. I wasn't going to like this—I could tell. But I needed to know. "It matters to me."

"If you don't learn to bend, you're going to break."

"Stop giving me cryptic bullshit." I punched his shoulder. "I just want a straight answer from one person. Is that too much to ask for?"

"No, it's not." He sighed, brushing my hair from my face. "I came for your scroll. I came to take it from you."

Chapter Eighteen

I think I just hallucinated." I shook my head to clear it. "What did you say?"

Rhys frowned. "You bloody well heard what I said."

Hands on my hips, I glared at him. "But I was hoping I heard wrong."

"You didn't." Raking his hair, he turned away. Muttering a curse, he faced me again, his expression resolute. "I came to relieve you of your scroll."

The realization that I'd been manipulated hit me all at once. Instead of being interested in me, it was really the scroll he yearned for. It was more important to him, just like it was more important to Wu.

That hurt.

"You fucking bastard," I hissed.

He reached for my arms. "Gabrielle, don't blow this out of proportion."

"Don't blow this out of proportion?" I barked an incredulous laugh as I jerked away from him. "You just told me that your goal is to take the scroll—"

"Was," he corrected.

"—from me. Which means that the interest, the kisses—*everything*—was a lie." I clenched my hands as anger mixed with the hurt. "I'm not stupid, Rhys. I can see what you were doing. You were playing me."

"I'm not—"

"Stop lying to me," I yelled, banging him with my fists.

He grabbed my wrists. I immediately raised my knee to nail him in the balls, but he anticipated my move and pinned me to the wall, my hands alongside my head and his body flush against mine.

We both breathed heavily. With every breath I took I inhaled his cayenne scent, and the pain twisted my heart just a little more.

"You will listen to me, Gabrielle," he ordered.

Irritation poured from his gaze. And maybe regret, but I told myself I was imagining that. I lifted my chin, mentally throwing daggers at him.

"Yes, I came here intending to relieve you of the scroll. A new Guardian, I knew you'd be too overwhelmed by the duties to be fully aware. I was there once myself, after all." He shook his head. "Quite frankly, I wanted the power. When I ran away from the asylum, I'd vowed—"

"*Asylum?*"

"A boys' home," he clarified. "An orphanage, to you Yanks."

"Oh." Madame said he had a rough childhood, but a rags-to-riches story? Seemed hard to believe.

He must have sensed my disbelief, because his gaze hardened. It was the flatness of his voice that told me he wasn't faking it. "I grew up in an orphanage in Wales. No one knew who my parents were or where I was from. I turned up on the doorstep one night, no note, no identifying features."

Despite myself, I glanced at the spot over his heart.

He glanced at his mark, too. "At the asylum, they didn't know about the scrolls. Neither did I until I was seventeen and my scroll showed up by messenger. By then I'd already started my illustrious career."

"Acquisitions," I said bitterly.

"In the purest sense back then. I had nothing. I had less than nothing. I was determined that I'd never want for anything ever again. I wanted everything and then some." He smiled without humor. "When I received the scroll, a new world opened to me. I had my first taste of real power. The more I learned, the more fascinated I became. If one scroll was powerful, two had to be exponentially so."

"So you decided to take mine?" I asked hoarsely. "Why not one of the three others?"

"Fate," he said simply. "I found you first."

"Lucky me." Feeling sick to my stomach, I tried to pull my wrists out of his hold.

"But then I met you. I *touched* you"— he held me firmly in place and pressed closer, his heat wrapping around me—"and what I wanted changed. I want you infinitely more than I've ever wanted anything. Even more than I want the scroll."

"How nice for you." Space—I needed space. I was afraid I'd cave in to the seductive feel of him, just like I did every time.

"It's not nice," he bit out. "It's damn inconvenient. Especially with the way you fight me at every turn."

A lick of energy stole through me, and I struggled in earnest. "Stop trying to influence me with your powers."

"I'll use whatever I have at my disposal to make you see reason," he said fiercely.

"What is reason, Rhys?" I asked just as intently.

"Reason is that we're meant to be together." Passion blazed from his face, a warrior bent on conquest. "I want you, and I know you want me, too."

I shook my head. "You want my powers. Having me means you also have the scroll. You'll have your cake and be able to eat it, too. You'll have the scroll in your greedy hands and be able to use it whenever you want."

His eyes shifted, tipping me off that there was more. I glared at him suspiciously. "What is it?"

He hesitated, but then he said, "I wouldn't have access to your powers just by having your scroll."

My gut told me this was about to get even worse. "Explain."

"Yes, anyone would be able to learn some of the secrets the monks put into the scroll just by reading it, but there's a ward, if you will, that endows the Guardian with the essence of the scroll. That's where the real power lies."

"Which means if you took my scroll you'd have that power."

"No, Gabrielle." His tone was almost apologetic. "The powers don't get passed on until you die."

The bottom fell out of my heart, and I felt the blood drain from my face as comprehension hit me.

He stepped forward. "Gabrielle, listen—"

"I don't need to hear any more." I sounded shrill to my own ears. "You meant to *kill* me."

He held me firm as I struggled to get free. "I told you I came intending to take the scroll."

"Which means my death," I yelled.

"It did," he said quietly. "But it quickly became evident

I would sooner be able to rip my own heart out than hurt you."

I gaped at him, not sure what to say. What was there to say? He just admitted he'd come here to kill me. No pretty words could change that.

"Gabrielle, listen to me," he insisted, his voice low. "I told you before. I met you and I realized I'd come for the wrong thing. It's you I want, not your scroll. Just you."

A caustic laugh rose up my throat, but something in his eyes stifled it. In them, I saw what he wanted—what could have been—and sadness wilted me. "How can you expect me to believe that after what you've just told me?"

"The truth is in my eyes when I look at you. It's in every touch. You just have to look." His hold on me eased so he cradled me instead of keeping me prisoner. "You have to trust in what you see. In me."

Yeah, that was the problem. I could count on one finger all the people I trusted. And then there was the fact that Rhys had deceived me. How did I know this wasn't part of his grand scheme? "I can't."

"Can't or won't, Gabrielle?" he asked, his voice low and flat.

"What does it matter?" I tried to wiggle away. "Let me go."

Surprisingly, he did. Only even though he stepped away from me, I could still feel the imprint of his body on mine, the heat of him stamped on my skin. I didn't know whether I wanted to hold on to the sensation so I'd always remember it, or go home and shower to wash him out of my life once and for all.

Neither thought comforted me.

"This isn't the end of it, Gabrielle." He stood, hands in

his pants pockets, deceptively casual. Like a snake about to strike. "I'll do whatever it takes to prove myself."

I hugged myself. "You can't honestly believe there's anything you can do to change my mind, do you?"

"Yes, in fact, I do, love." Before I could sputter a response, he wrapped his hand around my neck and tilted my head to kiss me.

"*Stop.*" I put my hand between my mouth and his.

He clasped me tight to his chest, as if he was worried I'd slipped away. "I can feel your heart pounding in rhythm to mine, Gabrielle. You want me, even if you won't admit it. A heart doesn't lie."

"Neither should someone who wants a relationship." I shrugged out of his embrace. "I'm not some object to acquire or steal, Rhys. And, frankly, even if I got over this, I'm not sure I could ever be more important to you than the scroll."

Silence stretched taut between us. He looked like he wanted to say something, but then he flashed a bitter smile and turned to leave, his footsteps echoing down the dark alley.

I slumped there, a fist pressed to my traitorous heart. What the hell was I going to do now?

Chapter Nineteen

I went home early and did what I was born to do: I painted.

Since I'd taken all my best supplies to Madame's house, I had to rummage through a box of old stuff to find a couple adequate brushes and paints that weren't too dry. Setting up a fresh canvas, I stripped out of my clothes into a sweatshirt and sat down at the easel.

Rhys must have somehow siphoned off some of the excess energy inside my body, because *tǔ ch'i* was remarkably dormant. So dormant that when I picked up a size four bright and the palette, I felt like I could actually work.

Staring at the canvas, I knew what the next painting in my *Enter the Light* series was supposed to be—I'd planned out all the canvases in detail months ago. Only I couldn't bring myself to start it. What I'd envisioned felt pale and easy. Without turmoil. No hint of struggle, as if starting a new life was a piece of cake.

Instead, I dabbed the brush in the paint and cut the whiteness with a wild, dark swipe.

An image took shape—a man cloaked in darkness. Strong, powerful features. Shadowed. A hand reaching out—giving or taking, it was uncertain.

Selecting another brush, I painted. No thought. I let my emotions drive my hand. I poured all the fury and pain—the longing—onto the canvas.

By morning light, I was mostly done with it. I dropped my brush and flexed my hands. I glanced at the photo Paul had given me, clipped to the edge of my easel. Holding my fingers out, I compared them to Mom's hand. Maybe Paul was right.

Exhausted, I shuffled out of my studio. As I passed through the kitchen I stopped in front of the fridge, struck by the sudden urge to read more of the scroll.

"No." It was my thought, but at the same time it wasn't. The more I was home, the closer I was in proximity to the scroll, the more it infringed on my consciousness. I couldn't explain it. It wasn't exactly placing thoughts in my head—it felt more like it picked out the thoughts I normally kept buried and magnified them.

Wu's face materialized right out of the refrigerator door. "What are you doing?"

"*Jeez.*" I jumped back, my hands poised to defend. "Stop that."

"If you were more present, you wouldn't startle." He scowled. "And how many times do I have to tell you to set your weight, Gabrielle?"

"Can't deal with this." Shaking my head, I forced one foot in front of the other, over and over until I stood by the futon.

"Since you're awake for once, we should work on a few

things." He drifted until he wavered at my side. "Your fighting skills are woefully rusty."

Stripping out of my clothes required too much energy, so I just dropped and pulled the covers over my head.

"Gabrielle?"

I ignored his muffled voice, closed my eyes, and let consciousness fade.

My cell phone rang incessantly, all morning long, until I finally turned it off.

Unfortunately, my sleep had been so disrupted that when I got out of bed in the afternoon I felt like I hadn't slept at all. The bright side: no sign of Wu. The downside: my headache was back.

A shower didn't perk me up, and neither did eating the few stale M&M's I found in a kitchen drawer. Groggy, I rooted around my bed for the cell phone so I could check my voice mail.

Carrie and Paul had called a few times each, both concerned about how I was. Madame left a message asking me about the paintings. I made a face, deleted it, and played the next one.

"Gabrielle, I—" Rhys's husky voice stalled.

My entire body went on alert.

There was silence. A curse. Then with a frustrated exhale he said, "I can't be sorry for my original motives, not when they led me to you," and he hung up.

I snapped my phone closed and dropped my head in my hands. My chest ached with longing. I wanted to believe him—I wanted that *so badly*. But how could I? I'd known him for days—how could I even be thinking of trusting him? He was a man who'd obviously do anything to get what he wanted.

If only there was no scroll. Then I could paint and have regular relationships without the constant worry of ulterior motives or that I'd hurt someone. Then I'd know for sure whether Rhys wanted me for myself or for an old scrap of paper.

Although I figured I knew the answer to that already.

Needless to say, my mood was less than stellar when I arrived at work. Again. A fact everyone noticed based on the way they skirted around me.

Except Vivian, who was especially annoying with all her gleeful comments about dating my brother. She seemed oblivious that she was flirting with danger. I was tempted to unleash on her—just a little. God knew she deserved it. But I kept to my side of the bar and managed to control the impulse.

Barely.

Because I was so focused inward, I didn't notice who walked into the bar until Vivian elbowed me. "He's so fine. Don't think you can keep him to yourself. I know he didn't come here just to see you."

I froze, martini shaker clenched in my hands. Rhys? I had the urge to dive under the bar until he went away. But I refused to let him make me a coward, so I forced my head up—and just about passed out from relief when I saw Paul.

The spot right in front of me cleared and he stepped in. "Gabby."

Tŭ ch'i surged, catching me unaware. My heart lurched as it strained to get away from me, but I managed to rein it in. Breathing hard, I turned around and finished filling an order for a customer, but really I didn't want him to see me struggle.

God, I needed to figure out how to deal with this. I

couldn't continue like this—I was a menace to society. How long before I lost it again and hurt someone else?

By the time I delivered the drink and collected money, I felt in control enough to deal with him. "Hey, Paul."

"I've been worried all day, Gabby." Brows drawn, he looked seriously pissed. "You didn't return my calls."

Wince. "Sorry. I worked early into the morning and then woke up only in time to get to work."

"I didn't know what was going on. I kept imagining the worst. Like Mom—" Exhaling deeply, he ran a hand over his hair.

"Sorry. Really." I stretched across the counter to squeeze his hand. "I'm not used to being accountable to anyone."

He tried to smile. "Get used to it, because I'm not going anywhere."

Tears sprang to my eyes. I wanted to lay my head on his shoulder and spill everything.

"Hey." He lifted my chin. "Are you okay? You look exhausted."

"I painted late."

His brow furrowed, making him look so much like Wu. "My offer still stands."

My breath caught in my chest, remembering the last time I heard the very same words. Though I was more inclined to entertain this one. "Thanks."

"Both offers."

A slightly tipsy guy shoved his way in next to Paul, jostling him. "Excuse me, can I get a drink?"

Paul shifted to give the guy some space before returning his attention to me. "I want you to let me help you, Gabby, but I'll support you no matter what decision you make."

"You don't know how much I needed to hear that." I didn't think I could love him more than I did right then.

He smiled. "In the meantime, maybe we could have dinner again."

"I'd like that."

"Good." The delight on his face lifted my spirits. His expression became cautious as he said, "And if you change your mind about the scroll . . . Well, I'm here. Even if you just need someone to talk to."

"I'll call you." I awkwardly hugged him across the bar. "Thanks, Paul."

He nodded and tapped his hand on the bar. "You're busy, so I'll get out of your hair."

I watched him leave. My heart rejoiced that he was making such an effort to make up for lost time. My mark twinged uncomfortably.

"*Excuse* me." The drunk guy lurched into the counter. "I need a beer."

He didn't, but I gave him one anyway. Who was I to judge what he needed and what he didn't?

It was an atypical Tuesday night—hopping, so I shouldn't have had a moment to think. But I did.

And all my thoughts centered on the scroll. One thing was sure: I needed to find a safer place for the scroll than my refrigerator. I needed to get rid of it in a way that put it out of everyone's reach. Even my own.

When my shift ended, I told Vivian I was clocking out and left before she could complain. Exhausted after the long day, all I wanted was my bed and a week of sleep. Hell, I'd settle for a whole night. I left the Pour House with plans to go straight home and crash.

I didn't factor in someone tailing me. And this wasn't someone interested in keeping me safe. I wondered if

Rhys had had a change of heart, but as soon as I had that bitter thought I dismissed it. In my gut, I knew the waves of menace emanating toward me could never be from him.

Growling under my breath, I turned off Mission onto 23rd. I frickin' did *not* want to deal with this tonight. Couldn't anyone give me a break?

Anger rose in my chest, so high I almost choked on it. I could feel *tŭ ch'i* tingling on the edges, waiting for the right moment to jump in and spike my system.

I should confront the asshole. I stopped in my tracks, tempted.

Better idea. I began to run—hard and fast—toward Bartlett Street. Red Crush, a popular restaurant and bar, sat on the corner of 23rd and Bartlett. No, I wasn't going to ditch him through the restroom window—I just wanted the noise to cover up any noise he might make when I impressed upon him my displeasure at having my plans screwed up. Plus Bartlett was usually deserted at night.

When I reached the street, I slowed down, looking behind my shoulder to make sure he saw me turn. *Tŭ ch'i* pulsed with anticipation, mixing with my own adrenaline—a heady combination.

I waited, hands clenched and ready. *Tŭ ch'i* radiated through me and gathered into my fists.

The guy barreled around the corner.

"Hey," I called, stepping out from the shadows. I cold-cocked him with a right jab straight to his nose.

He staggered from the impact. I blinked in surprise—I barely felt the impact on my knuckles.

Not wanting to give him the opportunity to retaliate, I shoved the thought aside and followed with a left hook to his jaw.

He spun to the side and fell face forward with a loud *"Oof."*

Dark satisfaction flared in my gut. I jumped on his back and wrapped my arms around his neck in a choke. Lifting a forearm to arch his head back, I hissed in his ear. "Why the hell are you following me?"

When he didn't reply, I applied more pressure on his throat. I waited for the choking sounds, expecting to feel his fingers dig into my arms to break the hold—only nothing happened.

I leaned over and looked into his face. His skin appeared dark, but the lighting was dim. He had nondescript features, but the one thing that stood out was the purple bruise rising on the side of his face. He was out cold.

"Damn it." I let him go and sat on his back. I'd knocked out my best source of information before I extracted any from him.

With a huff of disgust (at myself), I got off him. I felt *tŭ ch'i* urge me to do more—to crush him into the ground. I gasped in horror when I realized I was moving toward him to kick his ribs in.

"Shit." I clawed a hand through my hair and hurried away.

Instead of going directly home, I walked the hood. Briskly—to work *tŭ ch'i* out of my system. I was so engrossed in my thoughts I rounded the corner and walked straight into someone.

We both yelped at the collision. I set my weight, my fist cocked and ready to strike, when I registered that the surprised face in front of me belonged to Carrie.

"Crap, Gabe." She patted a hand over her heart. "You nearly scared me to death."

"You startled me." I lowered my hand and looked at the street signs. What was she doing out here so late?

She gaped at me. "Were you going to punch me?"

"I didn't know it was you." Though I should have had an inkling I wasn't in danger—not a peep out of *tŭ ch'i*. "Why are you out so late so far from your apartment?"

"I was on my way home from the library, and I thought I'd stop in at the bar to see how you were." Her big round eyes widened. "You didn't even hesitate. It was like you were ready to hit. Hard."

"I'm sorry—"

"You've really got to teach me how to do that."

I blinked. "Excuse me?"

"Seriously. I'm always out late, either at the library or work. I'd like to know how to take care of myself. Like you." She smiled and held a hand up. "I know you're busy getting ready for your show, but maybe when things have settled down. Just think about it."

"Okay," I said, simply because I couldn't think of anything else to say.

"Are you still feeling sick from last night?" She frowned. "You're shaking, and you look shell-shocked or something."

I hid my hands in my pockets. "I'm peachy."

"Um, okay." She shrugged off her frown. "I should get going. I've got a rendezvous with a dense historical tome."

Still dazed from my last encounter, I just nodded.

Her brow furrowed, and she put a hand on my arm. "Are you sure you're okay, Gabe?"

"Yeah," I managed to say. "Just tired."

"Okay." She nodded, but she didn't look like she

believed me. She removed her hand and stepped back. "I'll see you at work, then."

"Right. Be careful getting home."

"Always." She waved over her shoulder.

I started down the block.

"Hey," she called a moment later.

Stopping, I turned around.

"We should hang out sometime. Outside work," she added as if I might not understand. "Just us girls."

Girl time.

As a kid, I was so different from the other girls that even if Wu hadn't monopolized my time with combat training, I doubted I would have clicked with them. Then for the past fifteen years I'd been so focused on my goal I hadn't taken the time. Not that I had the inclination, either. Calling me a loner was understating it.

But that day at the bar when Carrie had made me coffee and we talked about Rhys was nice. Really nice. More girl time was oddly appealing. So I nodded, somewhat shyly. "I'd like that."

"Great. We'll talk, then." Carrie's smile lit up the dark city block. "See you later."

Buoyed, I headed home, taking a circuitous route, of course. My cautious delight over the possibility of a girlfriend faded into exhaustion over the blocks, and by the time I got home I was a stumbling zombie. I locked the door behind me, dropped my jacket right there, and fell face-first onto the futon.

Wu's voice sounded in my ear. "It's late, Gabrielle. You need to start getting to bed earlier."

With a growl, I yanked the covers up and fell asleep.

Chapter Twenty

*T*hree days later. Countless cups of coffee. No cake left. No more painting done. I slumped on the stool, where I'd pretty much been perched the entire time I'd been here.

Madame La Rochelle convinced me to stay at her place so I could work every minute I wasn't at the Pour House. She was freaked out over my lack of progress.

I was freaked, too. Not just by my inability to paint, but by the thought that some creep was going to follow me home and steal the scroll. Or worse—that the creep would turn out to be Rhys, and once he had the scroll I'd never see either of them again. So I stayed.

Except I'd gotten nothing done. Aside from battling to keep *tǔ ch'i* under wraps, I had sudden pangs of anxiety over leaving the scroll alone. Totally irrational. No one knew the scroll was in my refrigerator. It was safer than if I'd kept it on me.

On top of it all, I felt this crushing sadness and I was afraid that it had to do with not having seen Rhys in days. I wanted to ask Madame if she'd heard from him, but each time the impulse came, I bit my tongue and forced myself to keep silent.

With a groan, I stood, put my things away, and washed the dishes I'd accumulated in the sink. I wished I could take a nap—struggling to keep a lid on *tŭ ch'i* was taking a toll on me—but my shift started in a couple hours and I needed to go home to change (I'd run out of clean clothes).

I didn't know where Madame was, and I wasn't about to go find her. The last thing I needed at the moment was a lecture on how my paintings weren't going to paint themselves and that I was blowing the greatest opportunity I'd ever be presented as an artist. So I jotted a quick note to let her know I'd left and sneaked out like a thief.

Wu accosted me as soon as I walked in the door to my place.

"Where have you been?" He stopped pacing to glare at me. "You haven't been home for days, and it's after five this afternoon. I've been waiting to talk to you."

I shrugged, only because I knew it'd infuriate him. "I had someplace to go."

"You. Had. Someplace. To go." He clenched his fists and hovered off the ground.

Neat trick, but he looked like he was going to pop. Could ghosts explode?

The few pieces of furniture I had began to quiver. I grabbed the only vase I owned before it crashed onto the ground. "Whoa. Calm down before you break all my stuff."

"Your stuff is the least of my concerns," he said so quietly I got worried. The last time I'd heard him speak *that* quietly was when my brother Paul totaled Mom's car. Correction: it was at Mom's funeral, when he said she'd be alive if it weren't for me. "We need to start training. The scroll—"

"I'm handling the scroll." I shook out of my jacket.

He became still. "What do you mean?"

Nothing, really—I was talking out my ass. I had no clue what to do with it. If I could only get rid of it permanently—

Get rid of it permanently.

I blinked, dropping my coat on the floor. Rule number four played in my head. *The Guardian possesses the powers as long as he possesses the scroll.*

Since *tǔ ch'i* and Wu went hand in hand with the scroll, destroying the scroll would solve everything. I could get on with my life without constantly worrying that someone was going to break into my refrigerator and end the world. I wouldn't have to worry about it falling into the wrong person's hands, but neither would I have to sacrifice my life to it. No one would be able to get it.

My duty would be done, and I'd be free.

I'd know for sure if Rhys wanted me or not.

But I'd be destroying an ancient artifact. I glanced toward the kitchen, uncertain. Maybe I needed a glass of water while I thought about it. And while I was in there, I'd just take a look to make sure the scroll was okay. One quick peek wouldn't hurt . . .

"Gabrielle?"

Wu's voice startled me. I jerked awake, frowning as I found myself gripping the refrigerator handle and about to tug open the door.

"Now isn't the time to get something to eat," Wu said crossly. "Not that you'd find anything in there other than mayonnaise."

How did I get here? I stepped back from the fridge,

mildly concerned. Okay, I was totally freaked out, because unless I was mistaken the scroll had just manipulated my thoughts.

"*Gabrielle.*"

"What?" I snapped at him.

He glared at me. "What did you mean, you're going to handle the scroll?"

"Just what I said. I've got it all under control," I lied. I didn't, but I would very soon.

All the more reason to destroy the scroll as soon as possible. "You have nothing to worry about."

"I have a bad feeling about this." His eyes narrowed. "You're planning something. I can tell."

"You can't read my mind?" I feigned surprise to piss him off. "Ghostly abilities a little limiting, are they?"

The glass in my cabinets began to shake. "I am not a ghost. I'm a spirit."

"Semantics." I raised my brow at him. "Shouldn't you be more Zen in death than you were in life?"

He visibly made an effort to calm down. Finally, he said, "Gabrielle, you have to take this seriously."

I did take it seriously. And I was seriously going to get rid of the scroll. It was the best option for everyone.

But first I had to serve drinks, which was in some people's opinions the most important job in the world. I strode through the kitchen into the living room. "I'm changing clothes. You better stay out."

I grabbed a skimpy top out of a drawer and shimmied into it. My jeans and boots were fine. Wrapping a scarf around my neck, I slipped into my coat. I was about to leave when Wu materialized in front of me.

"Gabrielle, you aren't ready to take over guarding the scroll, and—"

"Wrong." I walked around him and headed for the door. "I can still kick ass."

He frowned, "Guarding the scroll is more than fighting. It's learning how to give and take from the earth's *chi*. The power was gifted to you to help you on this journey. I realize your lack of education is my fault—"

Wu admitting he was at fault? Now I knew the world was coming to an end.

"—but we have to work together to fix this."

"Um, excuse me." Opening the door, I held up a hand. "If you recall, we tried to work together, and we didn't do very well. What makes you think you'll be more successful this time?"

"*We have no choice.*"

The desperation in his voice wasn't pretty. Even *tŭ ch'i* responded to it. The damn energy pulsed under my skin, and my birthmark tingled annoyingly. But I steeled myself and forced a shrug like I didn't have a care in the world. "I do."

I closed the door in his face and walked to work.

Something occurred to me as I was serving a cosmopolitan to a preppy girl who had no call being in the Pour House (but that was another story). If Wu was tied to the scroll, how was I going to get it away from him long enough to destroy it? And was he capable of stopping me? I imagined he could, since he could vibrate my furniture.

Dilemma.

Vivian sauntered over after I finally finished serving the preppy girl and her friends. "A man came by earlier looking for you."

My life was suddenly overly full of men. Jesse, Rhys, Paul . . . Who now? "When?"

"Earlier." She shrugged.

I recognized the shrug for what it was: something to annoy me. But I couldn't call her on it, because I was guilty of the same with Wu. I had the urge to tweak her nose, but reverse psychology worked better with her than brute force. So I turned my back on her and cleaned up some of her mess.

"Aren't you going to ask who?"

I grinned at the exasperation in her voice, only because my back was turned to her. Even though I was damn curious, I shrugged and put away an unused martini glass. "I figured you'd have told me if you knew."

She huffed, her hands on her hips. "Well, if you aren't interested . . ."

I looked at her, blinking innocently. "Oh, do you know more?"

Her eyes narrowed. "Not really. He just asked if you worked here. But he called you Gabrielle Chin."

My heart skipped and then began again, beating fast. The last time someone called me by that name I got a ball and chain in the form of a scroll slapped on my ankle. I tried not to show any emotion at hearing my real name, but I don't think I was successful, judging from the gloating expression on Vivian's face.

She went on in an unassuming way, but I could tell she was doling out information just to see what my reaction would be. And to see if she could gather anything to use against me later. "I told him there was a Gabrielle who worked here, but that your last name was Sansouci, not Chin. Though you're part Chinese, aren't you? That's why your eyes are squinty, isn't it?"

Oh, please. Vivian wasn't the immediate problem, though—the person looking for Gabrielle Chin was.

Tŭ ch'i rippled through me, echoing my unease. Only one reason someone would look for Gabrielle Chin: the scroll. Otherwise why would anyone from the past have cause to look for me? Mom was dead, Wu's ghost knew exactly where I was, and Paul would have called my cell phone if he needed me.

I knew if I showed any interest in the man, Vivian would clam up or simply tease me with scraps of info. But what choice did I have? "Did he say who he was?"

"Hmm." She tapped a finger to her mouth, pretending to be in thought while being careful not to smudge her siren red lips. "I can't remember if he did."

Did I know her or what?

"But he did say he'd come by again. Later."

Great. Something to look forward too. Let the harassment begin. Thank you, Wei Lin, for bestowing this curse upon me and my people.

Assuming the scroll was why the mystery visitor had shown up. But I couldn't think of any other reason someone would ask for me by my real name, so I stuck with the assumption.

Only something was wrong if someone else had found out I possessed it. The Guardian was supposed to walk in anonymity, or something like that. No one but the Guardian and his successor was supposed to know about the scroll. Maybe the Guardian's family, too.

I thought about my brother. Paul knew it existed and where to find me, only he'd never spill the beans to anyone. He'd always basked in the honor of our family being singled out for the Guardianship.

There was Rhys.

No. I shook my head. No doubt in my mind—Rhys would never tell anyone I had the scroll. Whether he'd kill me and take it was still up in the air, but he'd never rat me out.

Vivian brushed by me, bumping into me more than was called for. "I hope he comes back tonight, for your sake."

Thank God I wasn't pouring something like cranberry juice at that moment. "Why do you say that?"

"It's been a long time since Jesse dumped you, hasn't it?" Her smile held pure malice. "You must be hard up for a date."

"I wasn't aware you kept track of my life so closely."

She flushed. "I don't. I just happened to notice."

"Uh-huh." She probably had a serial killer notebook tucked away in her purse that catalogued everyone's habits. She had that kind of detail-oriented mind. I always wondered why she was a bartender and not a scientist, but we weren't on good enough terms that I could ask something personal like that. I hardly felt like I was entitled to know when she was working next, much less details about her life.

Not that she had any such compulsions. She rivaled a crowbar when it came to prying.

A wave of people drifted in and occupied the two of us. I got so into my zone that an hour and a half passed before I knew it. I looked around, expecting Vivian to be gone (she often left without giving me a heads-up), but she was still there, shockingly enough.

I leaned toward her to put a bottle of vodka back in the well. "Didn't your shift end half an hour ago?"

"I thought you could use more help."

Ha. Altruism wasn't exactly one of her traits. More likely she was either waiting for Jesse to come in or for the other guy to return. Or both.

I tried to get Vivian to leave, but she stuck around until closing, not going until it became apparent neither man was coming. Of course, that didn't mean she helped close, even though she was there. Mostly she just got in the way and then left the mess for me to clean.

Which was fine. Cleaning gave me time to think, and by the time I'd finished I knew exactly how I was going to get rid of the scroll.

Duh. I should have thought of it sooner. Eager, I locked up the bar and started walking down Mission Street toward the all-night convenience store on my way home.

I hadn't gone even five steps before I felt someone watching me. The feeling persisted down the block, so I casually checked behind me and then across the street. Nothing. A different guy than before? Someone who was better at shadowing?

A sleek black car with tinted windows pulled up next to me.

Rhys again. My heart began to beat double time, I wanted to believe in anger rather than expectation.

The window rolled down. He leaned onto the passenger seat as far as his seat belt allowed. "Get in."

It was on the tip of my tongue to say *no,* which he must have realized, because his jaw tightened and he growled, "Don't bloody compromise your safety because you're in a pique."

"In a pique?" My voice rose with each word. Eyes narrowed, I yanked the door open and hopped in. "I think *a pique* doesn't begin to describe the state I'm in, and justifiably so."

"Buckle up," was all he said. The lock clicked and he sped off from the curb.

I sputtered as I grabbed the seat belt. "You know, for all

I know you're the one following me. The facts fit. You're always showing up right as I'm feeling like someone's spying on me." I looked him up and down with contempt. "You're certainly shifty-looking enough. It'd totally explain the menacing feeling. Hell, you admitted you'd kill for the scroll."

"I would never harm you." He stated it as though it came from every fiber of his being.

Wrapping my arms around my middle, I sunk lower in my seat. "You already have."

His hands gripped the steering wheel hard, and he stared ahead like the road desperately needed his attention. Then he softly said, "I'll always regret that, Gabrielle, but you asked me, and I didn't want to lie to you."

Not knowing what to say, I huddled lower. I heard the apology and remorse in his voice, but he could have been faking it.

I just didn't know anymore.

Rhys broke the silence. "Where should I take you?"

"Twenty-fourth and Mission."

"You live there?" he asked as he made a sharp left to get us on track.

"Close enough."

"I'll take you to your front door." His glance dared me to fight him on this. "So I can make sure you're safe and tucked in."

Tucked in conjured up all sorts of images, and none of them involved sleeping. I shifted closer to the car door, afraid that I'd break down and let him if he touched me. I couldn't give in—I still wasn't convinced he wouldn't take the scroll at the first opportunity.

The sooner I got rid of it, the better. "I have a stop to make."

"I'll wait for you and then take you home."

"No."

The car roared to a stop in front of the convenience store. Rhys shoved the gear into park and then faced me. "Punish me however you choose, but I will *not* allow you to put yourself at risk simply because you doubt me. *I will not allow it, Gabrielle.*"

Before I had a chance to react, he grabbed my scarf, hauled me toward him, and crushed my mouth with his.

I never had a chance. *Tŭ ch'i* came to life instantly— eagerly—as if it recognized Rhys's own energy. It rushed forward to greet him, opening me to his onslaught. It accepted everything he gave in return, until I smoldered with the feel of him. Until I wanted to beg for more.

As if he knew what I was thinking, he pulled me across his lap, holding me with fierce possessiveness. One hand tangled in my hair, and the other found its way through all my layers of clothing. His palm scalded my skin, and I hissed in pleasure. No pretense, no hesitation, he skimmed up my abdomen until he cupped my breast.

It was too much and not enough at the same time. I squirmed—if anyone had asked, I wouldn't have been able to say whether I was trying to get away or get closer.

Fortunately, Rhys decided for me. Closer.

He deepened the kiss while his fingers teased my nipple to aching hardness. Under me, I felt his cock surge to the sound of my moan, insistent and hot even through all our clothing.

He nudged my head back and nibbled that sensitive spot on my neck. "Come home with me," he whispered against my skin.

My body burned for him, and I speared my hand

through his hair. It was on the tip of my tongue to scream *yes*.

And then his hand brushed my hip—over my mark.

It sparked unlike anything before, pain and pleasure combined. I gasped and jerked his hand off me.

He looked wild, like a mad crusader of old. A warrior who'd claim what he wanted even if he had to destroy whatever stood in his path. Or whoever.

And if he still wanted the scroll, that whoever was me.

"Stop." I sat up, pushing myself away from him.

To his credit, he didn't muscle me back, though God knows he would have been successful. He let me get off him, watching me silently with his all-knowing gaze.

I didn't say anything—what was there to say? I righted my clothing and slipped out of the car. The cold night air hit me, and for a moment I felt lost. But then I remembered what I had planned.

The scroll.

Instead of walking directly into the store, I went around the block. When I got back, Rhys was gone. My heart lurched with disappointment.

"Stupid," I muttered, entering the store.

The lighters were next to the register at the front counter. I picked the first one I saw and paid for it. I usually had matches at home, but I couldn't remember if I'd used them up the last time I lit candles. I didn't want to take a chance. Armed with the Bic, I strode into my hovel and headed straight to the refrigerator.

Relief flooded me when I saw the scroll. I withdrew it from the fridge. For a second, *tǔ ch'i* surged through me in excited joy. I wanted to unroll it and read some more.

Frowning, I tamped down that desire, hurried to the

bathroom, and locked the door. Not that it would stop Wu's ghost from entering, but it made me feel better.

I held the scroll over the toilet. Ignoring my birthmark's stinging, I pulled out the lighter and flicked it. A long, fat flame burst into life.

My hands shook as I brought the scroll and flame closer together.

Was this really the right thing to do? I paused, overwhelmed with the need to protect it. Sweat broke out on my forehead. I could just hide it. Or maybe I could take it and run away . . .

I shook my head to clear my thoughts. No, the scroll was dangerous, and getting rid of it meant freedom for me. No one would miss it, and this way everyone stayed safe. Because I was a walking time bomb.

"I'm a menace to society," I reminded myself, my hand inching toward the paper. And then there were the future generations of Chins I was saving from this fucked-up fate.

An image of a little girl with my mom's blue eyes, Rhys's brown hair, and a broadsword-shaped birthmark popped into my mind, and I gasped. I would *not* pass this curse on to my own daughter.

Burning it was the only answer.

Tŭ ch'i welled up in me, and I almost dropped the scroll.

"Mom died because of it." I clutched it tighter. "I'm saving someone's life by doing this."

Holding that thought in my mind, I ignored the sharp jolt of energy that shot through my body as I set the flame to the parchment.

Chapter Twenty-one

*I*t didn't burn.

Frowning, I let go of the tab attached to the flint, waited a couple seconds, and flicked the lighter again. This time, I shifted the scroll to give the flame more surface area to catch.

The parchment didn't even singe.

"Damn." Maybe it was rolled too densely?

"Gabrielle? Are you in the bathroom?"

Wu. I froze. "Yes. And don't you dare come in. I need privacy."

There was a pause. Not even a rustle, which made sense considering he was a ghost.

Keeping an eye on the door, I untied the leather string binding the scroll and unrolled it, revealing the familiar fluid strokes of calligraphy. I steeled myself, waiting for *tǔ ch'i* to erupt.

It didn't. Instead, it calmed to a gentle burbling. I sighed in relief and unfurled it all the way. I vacillated between wanting to read it and just getting rid of it.

For all I knew, if I destroyed it, a storm of locusts would rain down on the planet. The next time I had to take on something so critical to the world's safety, I'd make sure I knew a little more about it.

"Gabrielle, are you done? It's imperative that we discuss our plan of action."

I had to get moving on this before he noticed something was up. No telling what he could do, and I didn't want to be stopped. So I reignited the lighter, held it to the bottom of the scroll, and waited for it to go up in a whoosh of flames.

"I made a schedule for training. Some physical, because you're in terrible shape, but mostly mental training to increase your control over the *chi*."

Nothing.

"We'll need to discuss your work schedule so you can arrange it around the eight hours of training you need to do every day."

It wouldn't catch.

"Gabrielle?" There was an element of concern in his voice this time.

"Damn." I shook the lighter for good measure, lit it, and tried again. I stared unbelievably when the parchment remained singe-free.

"Gabrielle, I'm coming in."

"*Damn.*" I tossed the lighter in the trash but wasn't able to roll the scroll up before his head appeared through the wall.

His eyes bulged when he saw the parchment in my hand. "What's going on here? Why do you have the scroll out?"

Feigning calm, I rolled up the one in my hand. "Just checking it out."

"In the bathroom?"

I shrugged. "It's the only place I have privacy these days." I placed it back in the box and opened the door through his body. "That's just creepy."

He ignored me and focused on the scroll—of course. "You're up to something. Your eyes always shift to the right when you're up to no good."

It was infuriating that he knew me so well in some ways but not at all in the ones that were important. But I didn't want to think about this right now. I had to think of another way to get rid of the scroll since my brilliant plan didn't work.

Since he didn't seem inclined to get out of my way, I walked through him. I shuddered violently as I passed through the thick, frigid air.

"Remind me never to do that again," I mumbled as I strode to the refrigerator and tossed the package back in there. Maybe it'd get moldy. Can bacteria eat up paper?

"*Gabrielle!*"

I winced at the roar. He probably found the—

"What is this lighter doing here?"

Before I could answer, there was a rush of frigid air and he hovered over me. He glowed brighter, which I figured meant he was pissed. A safe bet, really.

"You tried to burn it, didn't you?" he asked after a long moment.

If I told him the truth, then he'd be extra vigilant the next time I tried to destroy the scroll. But if I lied, I'd be playing into the same patterns of deception I'd followed in my youth, and I didn't think I could respect myself if I did that. I was an adult. I'd claimed my life. I wasn't going to compromise myself for him. Not ever again.

So I leaned my hip on the counter and crossed my arms. "Yes, in fact. I did."

"*Gabrielle.*" His voice reverberated in my body. "*You cannot burn the scroll.*"

"No kidding. I found that out the hard way." My eye caught the faucet, and I stood up straight. If fire couldn't get rid of it, maybe water would. It had to have some sort of weakness, right? Since it was the Book of Earth and water dissolved dirt . . .

I eyed Wu. Would I be able to submerge it before he caught on?

"I don't understand you. What are you trying to prove?" He began to pace like he used to in real life, only it was more like he floated from point to point. "What were the ancestors thinking, marking you?"

Hurt mingled with my anger. But if anything, his slam made up my mind for me. I moved to the sink, plugged it, and turned the faucet on. Warm water, because it'd probably dissolve the parchment faster.

"Instead of discussing the situation with me, you gad about, doing whatever nonsense you do on a normal basis. This is serious. You're a disaster waiting to happen. You've been given a great power but have no control over it. I can feel it ready to unleash. You know what the consequences of that happening are."

All the more reason to get rid of it once and for all. I strode to the refrigerator and pulled the box out again.

Wu was so agitated he didn't notice. He continued the float-pacing. "You don't understand the ramifications. If you did, you'd obviously take this more seriously. The bartending job is a good cover. It offers a paycheck and flexibility. Besides, who would suspect a mere bartender of being a Guardian?"

Ignoring his degrading speech, I surveyed the water in the sink. Not deep enough, but there was enough to get started. I submerged the entire package—carefully so his attention wouldn't be drawn by what I was doing.

"But the rest of it," he went on, "has to stop. Painting has always taken precious time needed for your training."

"Not even in your dreams," I mumbled, watching the package dissolve. *Yes.* Finally things were looking up again.

"That's where I went wrong before. I allowed your mother to sway me and I let you paint. But no more. From now on I will not allow you to dally with your so-called art."

I snorted. Like he was going to stop me. I figured since he was tied to the scroll that as soon as it was destroyed he'd move along, too. I could not wait. I'd lived rather happily without him for long enough to know I didn't need him. At all. I turned off the faucet and poked the package with a knife that had been sitting for God knows how long in my dish drainer.

"It's time—"

It was his gasp that made me turn to glance at him over my shoulder. He looked part outraged and part supremely horrified, kind of like a startled guppy. I poked at the scroll harder. *Come on.* I pictured the faces melting in *Raiders of the Lost Ark* and tried to will *tǔ ch'i* on the parchment. Unfortunately, it lay dormant. Maybe destroying the scroll was already taking effect.

"*Stop!* You *must* stop this."

I stabbed harder.

The scroll lifted straight out of the sink and levitated through the door and into the living room.

"Damn it, I wasn't done." I followed Wu, who was wavering like a mother hen over the dripping paper. Rushing past him, I grabbed it before he could stop me.

The scroll didn't feel mushy like it should have. Frowning, I unrolled it, expecting the ink to be running and smeared.

It was as pristine as before.

I watched a drop of water roll down the parchment and fall on my boot. Was it treated with some kind of oil that would repel water? But then, shouldn't it have gone up in flames instantly?

"You cannot destroy the scroll," Wu said softly. "It's infused and protected by *tŭ ch'i*, much like you are. You have to accept your fate."

"The hell I do." I clenched it in my fist and returned it to the refrigerator.

"What are you doing?" Wu asked over my shoulder.

"Going to bed." I went back into the front room, kicked off my boots, and fell onto the futon in my clothes. I wasn't giving up on getting rid of the scroll—I just had to find a better way. Which I would after a good night's sleep.

Chapter Twenty-two

"The only thing the killer did wrong was getting caught," Jerry said with great authority.

Milo rubbed his chin thoughtfully. "So you're saying murder is okay if you don't get caught?"

"If he didn't get caught, did he really do the crime?"

I glanced up from the limes I was wedging. I was used to their philosophical debates, if you could call them that, except usually their discussions didn't extend to murder.

But their banter was a welcome distraction from my thoughts. I'd been racking my brain for the past four days, trying to come up with a safe method of disposal for the scroll. Nothing.

Which made me feel panicked. I was running out of time. I couldn't paint—at all. At this rate, I wouldn't make my deadline even if it was extended twenty years. It didn't help that Chloe, Gallery 415's director, had left a message to check on the status of the contract and paintings.

I hadn't called her back yet.

And moving to Madame's had been a mistake. I was

putting her in danger. Every time I was near her it was like I was waving a loaded gun in her face—with only a matter of time before it went off.

I would *not* let anything happen to her.

Worse than the logistical issues, I was starting to see enemies in every shadow. I felt like a conspiracy theorist with baddies lurking behind every corner. That morning while I was in the shower I thought I saw a shadow in the bathroom doorway. I'd gotten out to check and found no one. Why would I? No one except Jesse knew where I lived. But no matter how much I tried to dismiss the incident as my own paranoid delusion, my gut told me I needed to be careful—even at home.

Hell, if I didn't get rid of the scroll, I'd have to be careful the rest of my life.

For a brief moment, I considered asking Jesse for help. Given how he moonlighted, I figured he'd be good at getting rid of things without a trace. But it didn't seem right to contact him only when I wanted something from him.

Rhys would help me. I just wasn't sure what he'd help me with—getting everything under control or relieving me of the scroll.

Milo's voice cut into my thoughts. "That's a little bit like the tree falling in the forest. Did we ever come to a conclusion about that?"

Jerry shot me a sidelong look. "I may need another round to jog my memory."

Nodding, I wiped my hands on my apron. "Can I ask you guys a question?"

"Of course, sweetie." Jerry winked at me. "But I can't guarantee we'll answer."

"What brought on this topic?"

Milo downed the last of his beer and pushed the glass

toward me. "You didn't hear about that guy that was killed in the Financial District?"

"What guy?" I asked as I pulled out fresh glasses.

"Some suit." Jerry shrugged. "They found him in an alley off Sansome."

For some reason, both Rhys and Paul came to mind, and the idea of either them being hurt caused fear to spike my system. "He got a name?"

"Here's the paper. It has more details if you're interested."

I set the glasses down and grabbed the paper. When I saw the victim's name, I closed my eyes and exhaled in relief. Not Paul. Or Rhys. Pulling myself together, I drew a pint and set it in front of Milo.

Jerry snatched it and replaced it with his old glass.

"Hey." Milo glared at him. "She gave that to me."

"Possession is seven-eighths of the law." He took a greedy sip.

"Nine-tenths of the law," Milo corrected.

"That's what I said." Jerry drank another mouthful. "Anyway, we were talking about the murder because the weapon was in a Dumpster like ten feet away from the body. Stupid."

"How do you mean?" I asked, pushing Milo's fresh beer across the counter.

"Well, if you're going to kill someone, you don't leave evidence like that around," Jerry replied. "Getting rid of the weapon in a Dumpster is a good idea, but the killer went wrong by not taking it to a different, unrelated location. If I'd killed the suit, I would have thrown the gun away in a trash can across town. No one would have thought to look anywhere else—there'd be no reason to—

and the gun would have ended up in a landfill with no one the wiser."

I shook my head. "Okay, now you're scaring me, Jer."

He grinned and toasted me with his glass. "Just got a lot of time to think on shift, you know?"

"So you think about how to dispose of—" I blinked as it clicked. I might not be able to destroy the scroll, but I could get rid of it—literally. No one would know to look for it in a garbage dump. If it ended up in a landfill, all the better. It'd be lost forever, which meant it'd be safe. I'd have done my duty. According to Rhys, I wouldn't be rid of my powers, but at least I wouldn't have to worry about it falling in the wrong hands—or playing me in hopes of getting it. Maybe my powers would fade over time, if I were lucky.

"Jerry, you're brilliant." I reached across the counter, grabbed his face, and planted a big one on his cheek.

He went beet red. "Shoot, Gabe. You're compromising my tough-guy rep."

"What about me?" Milo asked plaintively.

I gave him a smacker, as well.

"Don't think that kissing us will increase your tip," Jerry said with mock severity.

"You can't blame a girl for trying." I winked at them, because we both knew they were more-than-generous tippers, and went back to cutting up limes.

With each wedge, I went over the new plan to make sure there weren't any holes. Other than the fact that Wu would be doomed to purgatory, there weren't any.

Did I care? I paused, frowning at the pang I felt in my chest. I didn't want to care. I just wanted to be free of the burden.

Tŭ ch'i surged as if it protested, but I clamped down and refused to let it sway me. I had to do this.

Damn—*Wu*. Would I even be able to do this without him finding out?

"Don't think about it," I muttered under my breath. I'd deal with that when the time came, because I doubted he'd think my plan was as ingenious as I thought it was.

Happy Hour came and went. Vivian arrived, and for the first time ever I was happy to see her, only because it meant that in a few hours I'd be able to go home—just long enough to pick up the scroll and go on a little jaunt.

Sometime around nine, Vivian sashayed over and jabbed me with her sharp elbow. "He's back."

I looked around for Rhys, although I was positive he wasn't here. I'd feel it if he walked in, no matter how distracted I was—our physical connection was that strong. I felt a rush of disappointment nonetheless. "No, he's not."

"Yeah, he is." She jerked her pointy chin at a guy sitting at her end of the bar.

As I studied him, one word resounded in my mind: *thug.*

His flat face was pockmarked, and his nose wide and crooked, like it'd been broken a couple times. His hair was slicked back with some crap that made it look shiny—not healthy but greasy and dirty.

It was the shifty way his eyes roved around the bar that made me suspicious. That and the fact that I didn't notice him earlier—like he was trying hard not to draw my attention.

Unnerving. Only was this a legitimate be-wary situation, or was I projecting again? I shook my head and tried not to show my alarm. "Am I supposed to know him?"

She looked at me like I had the intellect of a beetle.

"He's the guy who wanted Gabrielle Chin. I never forget a face." She smirked. "I think you guys would look totally cute together."

I looked at him again. He knew we were talking about him—I could tell by the way he angled himself away from us. "I don't know, Viv. He looks more like your type."

She ignored my statement. She had excellent selective hearing. "Of course, you'll have to educate him on your name. But it's not the first time a guy didn't remember your name, is it? At least you haven't slept with him. Yet," she added cattily.

Normally I would have put her in her place, but the guy chose that moment to get up and walk out. Odd, since Vivian said he'd asked about me. Of course, with Vivian you could never tell if what she said was true or not. For all I knew, she was blowing smoke out her butt.

My gut told me otherwise in this case. As if to confirm, my birthmark prickled in warning. Rubbing the spot on my hip, I stared at the front door. What if he hijacked me after work? What if he had a gun?

My heart pumped with fear. I hated guns.

Forcing myself not to imagine any scenarios involving the thug, me, and deadly weapons, I checked the time. Still half an hour to go. I walked around Vivian and started closing down my station. When it was time, I took off my apron, wadded it into a ball, and tossed it in the dirty rag bin. "I'm out of here."

Vivian batted her eyes, trying to look innocent but failing miserably. "Have fun with your little friend."

I hated the frisson of apprehension that shot through my system, but I didn't deign to reply. I strode to the office and put on my jacket and scarf. As I walked out of the bar,

I surveyed the area. Hypersensitive about safety? Yeah, but what could I do?

I was tempted to dance a jig when I went for a couple blocks without feeling like I was being followed. Sad. I didn't like living on edge like this. I was going to celebrate big-time when this was all over.

Which led me to my next task.

As I walked, I thought about the best place to dump the scroll, and I decided Noe Valley was it. For one, it was easy to get to from where I lived in the Mission even at this time of night. But the main factor was that it was yuppieville, which meant there were virtually no homeless people. The residents and homeowners wouldn't tolerate street people—it'd bring down property values.

Why did I care about the homeless? They went through trash bins looking for discarded treasures, and I didn't want some hapless street person pulling out the scroll before the garbage guys emptied the trash and took it away.

I was between the bar and home when I felt like I was being watched—again. The thug from the bar?

Without being obvious, I scanned the street. There were people around, but no one I recognized. And definitely no one that was paying more attention to me than usual.

"Maybe I'm losing it," I muttered, but I doubted it. I picked up the pace. I managed to give my shadow the slip by going to a convenience store and sneaking out the back.

Wu was waiting for me when I got home. Of course. "How dare you leave earlier? I was speaking to you."

Locking the door behind me just in case, I faced him. "Who exactly knows that I was supposed to be the next Guardian?"

He scowled. "If you think this will distract me—"

"I'm being followed."

That shut him up. His brow furrowed, three thin creases all the way across his broad forehead.

I touched my forehead. I got lines like that when I was really worried. I was torn between hating that we had that in common and anxious that Wu the Unflappable was unsettled.

After a long moment of silence, he asked, "Who is it?"

"If I knew who it was, would I be asking you?"

"What did he look like?"

I thought of describing Vivian's friend from the bar, but I wasn't entirely certain it was him. "I didn't see him."

"And yet you think you're being followed?" He said it thoughtfully, like he was processing my remark.

Which freaked me out. I'd expected him to blow me off as delusional. The fact that he didn't dismiss me outright made the pit of my stomach churn. "So who knows that I'm supposedly the next Guardian?"

"Not supposedly, you *are*," he said with a distracted air. Then he waved his hand. "The only person who knows is Paul."

And Rhys. But neither one would never tell anyone. I knew that as certainly as I knew I was meant to be an artist.

Wu nodded as if I'd commented out loud. "Paul is not an issue. He does what he's told."

Implying I didn't. I didn't know what pissed me off more: that, or the casual way he dismissed his own son. Paul didn't deserve Wu's disdain. "Why didn't you just leave the scroll to Paul?"

He frowned at me. "He wasn't born marked. When are

you going to accept the fact that you were chosen? There's no one who can take your place. Not yet, anyway."

Hovering back and forth again in a semblance of pacing, Wu muttered. "This is graver than I thought. How will I ever prepare her in time? The fate of—"

This was my cue to grab the scroll and get the hell out of there. Casually, so I didn't draw attention, I went to the kitchen and withdrew it. Resisting the urge to kiss it hello and flex the power that surged through me when I came in contact with it, I stuck it in the waistband of my jeans and pulled my top over it. Not the best cover, but better than nothing.

Shrugging, I strode into the living room. Wu was still ranting at himself, his glow intensified. Not saying a word, I picked up my jacket and went to the door.

He looked up like a startled deer when the lock clicked open. "Where are you going?"

"The store," I lied. "I'll be back soon."

"Gabri—"

I hurried out the door, slammed it shut, and jogged until I was a block away. I paused, looking over my shoulder, expecting him to be right there. I hoped I frustrated him enough that he wouldn't follow me, but I waited just to be sure.

No sign of him.

Once I did this, I'd never see Wu again. Grief hit me like I was finding out he'd died all over again. Except this time it was my fault. Maybe I should go back to tell him—

What? That I'd miss our relationship? I shook my head. He hadn't earned any father-of-the-year awards in the short time he'd been back.

"Pointless," I muttered. Huddling into my coat, I continued on my way.

A block later, the feeling returned—like someone was spying on me. Intently. With malevolence. I shuddered and drew my jacket closer. As nonchalantly as I could, I looked around for the source.

The only suspicious thing was a guy leaning against a building next to an alley up ahead, but his back was to me, so he couldn't be watching me. Probably a dealer waiting for customers. (It was easy to score in the Mission if that's what you were into.)

Still, I wasn't a dummy—I gave him a wide berth just in case. As I passed him, my unease increased. I started to turn around when he grabbed my arm, pulled me into the alley, and shoved me against a wall.

Tǔ ch'i spurred me to action, like a shot of adrenaline. I grabbed his crotch and twisted his nuts. As he yowled and doubled over, I brought my knee up to strike his nose. He cried out again, his head jerking up.

A distant streetlight lit his face. I blinked, startled but not sure why. I should have known my attacker would be the mystery guy from the bar.

In the moment I stood there gaping at him, he grabbed me in a bear hug.

"Damn it," I cursed at myself. I shouldn't have given him the opportunity to get me like this—I knew better.

"Why are you after me?" I managed to get out despite his death grip squeezing my lungs.

He replied by shaking me. "Where is it?"

The scroll. Panic surged, but I forced myself to calm down. If he was asking, he didn't know that I had it tucked in my jeans.

And he wasn't going to find out. I headbutted him,

hitting his nose again. The sharp *snap* of cartilage breaking evoked both satisfaction and revulsion in me.

He shrieked like a little girl, dropping me to hold on to his face. Blood flowed through his fingers, and I swore I could hear each drop hit the ground.

Rubbing the sore spot on my forehead, Wu's voice whispered in my memory. *Keep your opponent as close as possible, Gabrielle.*

Nodding, I stepped in front of the punk, wrapped my arms around his neck, and lodged my shoulder under his jaw to lock the choke hold. I had a few things I wanted to find out. "Who are you, and what do you want with it?"

Glaring at me from slitted eyes, he tried to break my hold.

I dug my knuckles into a pressure point at his collarbone.

He gasped, and his knees buckled.

"Why are you after me?" I put more pressure on that spot. I needed to make him talk fast—my hand was getting tired. Even as I had the thought, *tŭ ch'i* rippled through me and lent me strength.

"Bitch." He spat at me.

Caught off guard by his loogie, I let go enough for him to counter and take me off balance. Then he punched my ribs.

I gasped at the shock of pain and tightened my obliques to protect myself. His next strike didn't hurt quite as much. At least that's what I told myself.

"Bitch," he growled, punching me again. "Tell me where it is."

As much as I wanted to get rid of the scroll, I didn't want it falling into some thug's hands. So I said the logical thing. "Bite me, asshole."

He cocked his fist. I could tell he was going to hit my face this time, and my eyes scrunched shut reflexively.

Only I felt a surge of energy draw up from the ground, and before I could grab it back, it burst out of me. My eyes flew open, afraid I was going to see the thug lying dead in front of me. I wasn't sure if I was relieved or disappointed when I saw him still standing there.

He gawked at me, his fist frozen an inch away from my face. He tried to push it forward to connect, but it bounced back like it smacked an invisible rubber wall. "What the—?"

Not giving him time to recover, I stomped on his foot— a girly move, but it distracted him enough for me to pivot and elbow him in the nose. As it hit, I could feel *tǔ ch'i* gather and unleash with the blow. I winced as bone crunched but immediately kneed the inside of his thigh. He doubled over, and I brought my heel straight down on the back of his neck, feeling *tǔ ch'i* draw up with the arc of my leg and add power to the strike.

The crack of his head echoed in the chill night. I wanted to think it was from hitting the pavement. Hard to convince myself of that when it sounded before he reached the ground.

Worse: he didn't get up.

Walking to him cautiously, I prodded him with my boot. He didn't stir.

"Shit." I reached down to check his pulse. I wilted in relief when I felt its steady beat.

Instinct told me to get the hell out of Dodge before anyone else showed up. Common sense told me to find out who he was. So I leaned over and patted him down. My hand stilled at what felt like a knife.

Gulp. God, I was lucky he hadn't pulled that out. I used

to be good at knife fighting, but that was fifteen years ago. It wasn't like I could count on *tǔ ch'i* protecting me—I had no idea what I did to create that barrier.

At least it wasn't a gun.

I swallowed again, put the knife in my coat pocket, and continued searching. Finding his wallet, I slipped it in next to the knife and hurried away before someone noticed me with him. I walked fast—but not so fast that I attracted attention—all the way home.

Inside, I leaned against the front door, locked it behind me, and then started to shake. I knew it was adrenaline letdown. Okay—maybe it was a little shock, too. Being attacked was the last thing I expected tonight.

He'd wanted the scroll. How did he know I had it? And who the hell was he?

I reached for his wallet, fumbling with my pocket because my hands were trembling so badly. I dropped it. Tucking the knife under the futon mattress, I picked up the wallet as I sat and opened it.

There was no ID—no driver's license, no credit cards, nothing that gave a name. There *was* a scrap of paper with my name—my real name—written on it, as well as the address of the bar. And a wad of money. Hundred-dollar bills.

Frowning, I pulled them out and quickly thumbed through them. Thirty. Three thousand bucks in cash. To get the scroll? What else could it be?

I'd figure it out later. Right now, I needed to make sure the scroll was safe and hidden. I'd attack this plan again. In daylight. Maybe with a hired bodyguard. I stood up, touched my waistband, and froze.

It wasn't there. I felt down my pants legs, but it wasn't there, either.

Gone.

Where could it have—

Oh, *shit.* I lost it during my skirmish with the thug.

I dashed back out the door. I *really* didn't want to go back to that alley, but I had to check to see if the scroll was there.

I ran the whole way to the scene. Knowing better than to rush into the dark alley, I leaned against the brick wall and peered around the corner. Nothing. He was gone.

"Damn." After a quick survey of the area, I walked to the spot where I'd left him knocked out. There was no sign of anything. Including the scroll.

As if in punctuating the situation, *tŭ ch'i* slammed through me until I felt like I was drowning in it. The scroll wasn't in my possession anymore—logically, it shouldn't have been this strong now.

Using all my willpower, I choked it back, and the effort left me wilted. Somehow I stumbled home, slamming the door open in my haste to get inside. "Wu, come out. I need you."

No answer. Contrary bastard that he was, I knew he could be hiding. I picked up a pillow and looked under it. "Wu? I'm pouring kerosene on the scroll and I'm going to torch it again. You better come out and stop me."

I waited for several long minutes, but there wasn't any sign of him—not even a rustle of chilly wind.

He was gone. I knew it instinctively.

Dropping my head in my hands, I sank down onto the futon. What would happen to him? I'd wanted him gone, but I didn't want him in some bad guy's hands. Would he be okay?

Guilt stuck in my throat. I wanted to get rid of the

scroll, but not like this. Not to some unknown thug who would use it to rob banks. Or something worse.

Armageddon flashed in my mind.

"Oh, God." I dropped my head in my hands. "What have I done?"

Chapter Twenty-three

I *hear footsteps behind me. I look and see a man—*
shadowed and hulking.

My heart pounds. I run.

He chases, his footsteps echoing in the dark.

Go faster. And faster. But he gets closer—I can feel
him gaining on me. His breath hisses in my ear.

An alley ahead.

Go—lose him. I turn.

And I stop. He's lying in the middle of the path. I know
he's dead.

Have to check.

I inch forward, kneel next to him. Grab a shoulder
and pull. Heavy. Pull harder. The body rolls over, onto
my legs.

I look down.

Not the man—Mom.

"No." I scream, but there's no sound.

Her lips move, her eyes lifeless and unseeing.

"What?" I bend to hear her.

Her voice is a whisper. "So many deaths, all because you failed."

I bolted upright, scrambling back until my spine hit the wall. I looked down and folded in relief when I saw there wasn't a body across my legs.

"It was just a dream." Sweating, I worked to calm myself.

Tŭ ch'i slammed into me like a ton of bricks.

I gasped, grabbing the comforter as the energy attacked me. It exploded up into my body, violently invading every nook and cranny. It filled me, stretching me until I felt like it was going to tear me apart. I could feel my molecules separate with its strength. My teeth gritted against the agony, I screamed.

Everything began to rumble—not a superficial shaking, but a deep-in-the-bowels-of-the-earth quake. The candle at the side of my futon jiggled off the crate I used as a bedside table, and I heard dishes falling out of the cabinet in the kitchen.

Had to get it under control before I did some serious damage. I closed my eyes and visualized gathering all the escaping power to me.

It hurt. And felt futile. Like I was trying to cram it all into a vessel that was already overflowing. My muscles strained, and for a moment I thought I was going to explode.

"Will. Not. Fail." Yelling to gain strength, I swallowed the energy back.

The earthquake died. However, unlike the other times, *tŭ ch'i* hardly waned at all. Instead, it seethed close to the surface, potent and violent, like it waited for me to be inattentive so it could erupt again. Ten times more intense than before.

I sat there, panting and tense, afraid to relax. I crawled under the covers, knowing I wouldn't fall asleep again. I couldn't—I didn't trust myself not to cause the Big One that caused San Francisco to fall into the ocean.

My phone rang. Without moving, I flailed around until I found it on the floor next to the futon. I looked at the caller ID.

Rhys.

Not thinking, I flipped it open. "What?" I croaked.

"Where are you?" he asked brusquely.

"In bed." I paused. "That wasn't an invitation."

He ignored my comment, which gave me an indication at how serious this call was. "There was an earthquake—"

"We're in California. There are earthquakes every day."

"This was no ordinary earthquake, and you know it. Why are you being so bloody obstinate?"

"You have to ask?"

He exhaled in frustration. "Just tell me if you're all right."

My heart constricted at the caring in his voice. I wanted to lean on him, to tell him everything. To let him help me. He'd know what to do. I opened my mouth to accept his offer, but the words stuck in my throat.

"Gabrielle?"

I shook my head. "I'm just peachy." Before he could question me further, I said, "Gotta go to work. Later." And I hung up.

Queasy from the energy burbling inside me, tired from the lack of sleep, and disappointed—big-time—I rolled out of bed. I was back to square one. Behind square one. Not only had I lost the scroll, but *tŭ ch'i* felt even stronger—even wilder—than before.

What was up with that? And I couldn't ask Wu—I knew without a doubt that he was gone.

Guilt. As I gingerly shuffled to the bathroom, I tried not to think of all the things that could happen to a lost spirit. Maybe he'd be more peaceful wherever he ended up.

Yeah. Pipe dream.

The mirror wasn't my friend today. I looked like I'd been hit by a Muni bus. I hurt. Bad. Every cell in my body throbbed, and I knew it wasn't all from the punches I'd taken from the thug.

I gently touched the dark bruises on my side. At least nothing was broken. A broken rib hurt like hell. I knew—eighteen years ago, Paul and I had been sparring with staffs and he'd whacked me hard enough to crack a couple. I winced, remembering how Wu lit into him about that.

The hot water from my shower eased my soreness a little, but I knew the only thing that would really make a difference was if I started training in earnest. Not just forms and shadowboxing, but hardcore sparring. I'd gotten out of the habit of getting pummeled. It sounds bad, but you have to be able to take a few punches in order to handle fighting. "Add taking classes at a studio to the list. Because I've got so much free time."

Getting dressed in comfortable clothes (jeans and a cotton tank top with a long-sleeve scoop neck to layer), I put my hair in a ponytail (for convenience) and dabbed on a little lip gloss (a concession to looking nice). I pulled on my boots and coat and walked to the bar, taking a route that didn't lead me past the alley.

Not that I was worried that the thug would be waiting for me again—lightning didn't strike in the same place twice, right? I just didn't want to tempt fate, especially since it seemed fate was toying with me lately.

I let myself in, turned on the lights, and unlocked the front doors. Opening a bar didn't take much effort—unless Vivian closed the night before. And, true to form, she'd left things messy enough to tweak me.

Today I didn't care. In fact, I welcomed it. The more to do, the better. I attacked everything she left and tried to brainstorm—*tried* being the operative word.

Around three, two suits walked in. The moment I saw them I knew they were cops—it was in their stance and the way they scanned the bar. Since they were so dressed, they had to be detectives of some sort.

Frowning, I studied them while they checked out the one boozer in the bar. The older one was beefy—not fat, more like an aged linebacker. Laugh lines made his face look open, and his nose was sunburned. His clothes were rumpled, like he'd been sitting in a car for too long.

The younger one was sharp: his clothes, his dark hair, his dark eyes. Latino. I pegged him for his early forties, only because of the gray at the edges of his hairline and the world-weary look in his eyes. He looked relentless. Crisp. Uncompromising.

Tŭ ch'i leapt to the surface. I could feel the earth begin to stir, but, hands clenched, I capped down on it tight before anything weird happened.

Without warning, his eyes latched on to me and did a thorough visual inspection. I couldn't tell if it was business or masculine appreciation, but given how I looked, I figured it was the former.

Which in turn made me frown, because buttoned-up

men weren't my thing. Especially if they were cops. "Can I help you?"

He flipped open his badge and held it up. "I'm Inspector Rick Ramirez with the SFPD Homicide Detail. This is my partner, Inspector James Taylor."

"But not that James Taylor." The linebacker flashed his badge and a smile as he perched on a barstool. "I'm more handsome."

Not knowing how I was supposed to answer, I nodded politely and quickly returned my attention to the younger cop. He was the one to watch out for.

"We'd like to ask you a few questions," he said, taking a small notebook out of his breast pocket.

I broke out in sweat as I remembered beating up that guy and leaving him in the alley. "Regarding?"

"A murder that happened last night a few blocks from here."

"Oh." What a relief—this had nothing to do with me. For a moment I'd thought the thug was pressing assault charges. "Sure. I don't know how much help I'll be, though."

He studied me for so long it made me uncomfortable.

Even his partner noticed it. "Are you going to just gawk at the pretty girl, Ramirez, or are you actually going to get on with this sometime soon?"

He shot the linebacker a look that would have silenced most people.

The older cop just grinned. "May's making a pork roast tonight. You know how much I love her pork roasts." He turned to me. "There's a whole lot about May I love. Damn fine woman. Too bad she won't marry me."

"Why won't she marry you?" I asked.

"Says it'd interfere with her independent nature." He shook his head. "Are you married?"

"No."

"Shame, pretty girl like you." Inspector Taylor gave his partner a meaningful look before asking me, "I suppose you're an independent woman, too?"

His beleaguered tone made me grin. "Afraid so."

Ramirez rubbed his temple. "Are you two done?"

"Just waiting for you to get started, boy."

Shaking his head, Ramirez flipped open the notebook. "What's your name?"

"Gabrielle Sansouci."

"Gabrielle, huh?" Taylor's face scrunched in thought. "French?"

"My mom was French. Everyone calls me Gabe." I watched the younger one scribble the info down. Even his handwriting looked crisp.

"Were you working last night?" he asked after he finished.

"Yeah. Until ten," I preempted, knowing it'd be his next question.

"Alone?"

For a second I thought he was asking me if I went home alone. I blushed when I realized my mind was the only one in the gutter. "Alone until seven. Then Vivian came in. Vivian Redding, one of the other bartenders here. She closed last night."

"Will Ms. Redding be in later today?"

"Around seven." Or eight. Punctuality wasn't one of Vivian's strong points.

"Gabe, did you notice any unusual activity around the bar?" Taylor asked.

Pursing my lips, I shook my head. "It was pretty much

like any other night." Including that I'd been followed home, but that was a different story.

Ramirez reached into his inside breast pocket. "Can you tell me if this man came into the bar last night?"

Leaning across the counter, I looked at the picture he held out. It was an official mug shot, stark and bright, but I'd recognize the guy anywhere. It was the thug. "Is this the suspect?"

"No, he's the victim."

Swallowing a gasp, I squinted at the picture like I was studying it hard. Really, I was trying to get my equilibrium back. Finding out a guy you beat up was dead kind of rocked your world.

"What is it?" Ramirez asked, his gaze sharp.

I cleared my throat. "Nothing."

"Do you know him?"

"No," I replied quickly, conscious of the way he catalogued my every reaction and how his eyes narrowed in suspicion.

"Goes by the name Chivo," Taylor said. "He was a goon-for-hire of sorts."

I wanted to push the picture away and tell them I had no idea who the bastard was, but if the inspectors talked to Vivian they'd find out I'd lied. And I had the impression Ramirez would be like a shark in bloodied water if he caught me in a lie.

So I pulled myself together to give a coherent answer. "He looks like a guy who sat at the bar last night, but I didn't wait on him."

Ramirez held my gaze for a long, uncomfortable moment before he asked, "Approximately what time was he in here?"

"Maybe around nine. If it's the same guy, he left before I did." Because he was lying in wait for me.

Tŭ ch'i surged as if it heard the thought. I frantically clamped down on it before it could burst loose. I could do without having to explain *that* to a couple nosy cops. Shudder.

"So you had no contact with him last night?" Ramirez pressed. "If it's the same man who was in here?"

I shook my head, more to bring my focus back to the matter at hand than a denial. "No, I didn't talk to him while he was here."

"Did you notice if he was with anyone?" Inspector Taylor smiled as if to encourage my confidence.

I shrugged. "I didn't notice. I was busy with my station."

"Did he talk to anyone?"

"Not that I saw."

"But you noticed that he was here?" Ramirez asked skeptically.

"I felt his eyes on me, so I glanced up." I frowned at him. He didn't believe me. "He's a little scary-looking, don't you think?" My hackles rose as he continued to stare at me with skepticism. "Are you interrogating me?"

"Friendly questioning," Taylor broke in quickly, shooting his partner a frown. "We wouldn't call it an interrogation."

I snorted. "That's how the Inquisition started."

"A little before your time, wasn't it?" Ramirez asked seriously.

It was all I could do not to roll my eyes. "Listen, do you have more questions? Because I've got to get back to work."

He glanced at the only customer in the bar. "I can see how you're busy. Do you live in the neighborhood?"

The abrupt change of subject made me blink. "Yeah," I answered cautiously.

"And you didn't notice anything unusual when you left here last night?"

"*No.*"

He cocked his eyebrow again. "Nothing?"

"Don't you think I'd remember if I saw a murder?"

He made some sort of noncommittal sound as he scribbled some more on his pad. Then he slapped it closed, stuck his pen into his breast pocket, and pulled out a white card. "If you remember anything later, please call me."

Ignoring Taylor's smirk, I slipped it into my apron pocket, knowing I would never call.

Ramirez's nod was barely civil. "Thanks for your time, Ms. Sansouci."

I shifted uncomfortably, wishing he'd leave already. As each second went by, I had the impression he was more and more suspicious that I knew more than I was saying. Of course, it might have been my guilty conscience projecting.

His partner smiled and shook my hand. "We'll contact you if we have more questions."

"Right." I watched them stride toward the door. I was almost in the clear when I heard myself call out, "Inspector Ramirez."

He turned around. "Yes?"

"Did it seem like a mugging? So I know whether or not I have to be extra careful walking home."

"It's always a good idea to be careful, but this looked like a gang-related death. He was shot in the head after being beaten. His nose was pulp. His pockets were emptied, though, so it could have been a druggie stealing money for a fix."

My mark pricked me, and I swallowed thickly. "His pockets were emptied?"

"Yeah. We found nothing on him." His gaze sharpened. "Why?"

"No reason." Except I thought he'd had the scroll on him. I smiled weakly.

He gazed at me a moment longer and then followed his partner out.

Well, at least I knew he didn't die because of any trauma I'd caused. Not that him being shot rested easy with me. But what were the chances it was related to me or the scroll?

"Yeah." I shook my head. "Stupid question."

Chapter Twenty-four

*T*he world's going to hell in a wastebasket." Shaking his head, Jerry took a deep swig of beer.

"In a hand basket," Milo corrected.

"That's what I said."

Milo and I exchanged a look, but we didn't say anything.

And Jerry didn't notice. "It's all a sign that Armageddon is on its way. All the earthquakes, for example."

I couldn't tell them the earthquakes were me and not Armageddon. Though, come to think of it, I could very well be Armageddon, too. I ducked behind the bar to finish stocking beer bottles—and so they wouldn't read the guilt on my face.

"When have we ever had so many earthquakes?"

"Seismic activity is to be expected when you live on a fault line," Milo replied.

"But not regular, large ones like we've been having. They've been predicting that California's going to fall into the ocean. I'm telling you it's gonna happen soon."

Especially if I didn't get a grip on *tǔ ch'i,* I thought as I crammed a couple more bottles into the fridge.

"And all the recent murders," Jerry continued.

"Murder rates are always high in metropolitan areas," Milo pointed out. "That's no sign of Armageddon."

"Gabe, tell the moron that things ain't what they seem."

Wiping my hands on a rag, I stood up and looked back and forth between the two of them. "It's kind of unsettling having someone murdered so close to where you hang out, isn't it?"

Jerry smacked his palm on the countertop. "That's what I'm talking about. I knew she'd understand."

Hell, yeah, I understood. I understood too well. I scrubbed the bar more vigorously than it needed.

It's shocking to the system to find out a guy you had a scuffle with was murdered. But when you thought the guy had something that belonged to you, and now that something was missing, there was this feeling of unease that bordered on severe nausea. Because I'd been pretty sure he'd had the scroll. Where else would it be?

Tǔ ch'i shoved at me—again—as if punctuating my thought. *Shut up,* I hissed mentally, pushing back. Picking up my ginger ale, I took a sip to ease my queasiness, which had tripled over the afternoon and evening. Not that it helped, because I wasn't nauseous from my stomach but from the roiling of *tǔ ch'i.* It was comforting, though. My mom used to give me ginger ale when I was sick.

Sigh. I pushed the glass aside.

"We're outta here, Gabe," Jerry called as he stood up. "You look peaky. Maybe you should head home early tonight."

Milo whacked him in the shoulder. "You don't tell a woman that."

"What?" Jerry frowned as he dropped a couple bills on the counter. "I'm just concerned about her."

I did my best to smile at them. "Thanks, guys. Maybe I'll do that since Vivian's here tonight."

Both their noses wrinkled at the mention of her name. I smiled genuinely for the first time all day. "You need to get going. You're here late. I don't want your wives coming in accusing me of keeping you."

"More like they'd thank you." Milo patted my hand. "You take care when you go home. You should find a man, then *he* could make sure you get home safely."

As if on cue, Rhys strode in.

My back stiffened, and my face went slack. I hadn't expected to see him so soon—I don't know why—and I wasn't prepared.

Milo must have sensed my uncertainty, because he said, "Or at least take a cab, okay? It's not safe on the streets these days."

Didn't I know it?

They waved on their way out, and I waited for Rhys to come over to me.

What would he say when I told him I no longer had the scroll? Would he pack up and go back to wherever he came from? I studied his face, trying to gauge his mood. He just looked implacable.

"You hung up on me," was all he said by way of greeting.

Shrugging, I wiped the counter. "I had things to do."

His brow furrowed. "What's wrong?"

"Why? Do you sense something about my scroll?" I asked, trying not to sound worried but knowing I failed.

"No." He looked confused. "Only you are tied to your scroll."

"Then what makes you think something's wrong?"

"You're moving stiffly." His frown grew more pronounced. "Are you favoring your ribs?"

My arms wrapped around my midriff without thought.

"Lift your shirt."

I sputtered in shock before I could answer. "You can't command me to disrobe at will. Especially while I'm at work."

He looked like he wanted to argue the point. Instead he raked his hair and said, "Gabrielle, either you find a private place to show me your where you're hurt or I'll strip you bare right here."

Despite his deceptively mild tone, there was no doubt in my mind that he meant it. Glaring at him, I wadded my apron, tossed it under the counter, and called out to Vivian that I was taking a break. Without a word to Rhys, I walked toward Johnny's office. Like he wasn't going to follow.

I let him in and closed the door behind us. Leaning against it, I watched him warily.

"Your shirt, Gabrielle," he prompted, hands in his pockets. He looked calm, but his tight jawline gave him away.

The urge to push him overcame me. I lifted my chin. "I—"

Suddenly he had me pressed against the door and my shirt pushed under my armpits. For comfort, I'd decided against a bra today, and the air pebbled my bare nipples. I thought he would have noticed, but his attention was a bit lower.

"Bloody hell." He inhaled sharply. "Who did this?"

"No one."

He impaled me with a death stare.

And I caved. With a shrug, I said as carelessly as I could, "This guy attacked me last night—"

His fist slammed into the door, and I felt the impact through my body. I knew if I turned my head, I'd see an imprint in the plywood, but taking my eyes off him didn't seem wise at the moment.

Not that I thought he'd harm me. For some reason, I felt completely safe. Unbelievable, considering his recent confessions. *Tŭ ch'i* had apparently addled my brain more than I realized.

Rhys's touch as he traced the bruises was beyond gentle. The look in his eyes—not so much. "Tell me who did this," he commanded, his voice raw.

"Some thug. He's long gone." Slight exaggeration, but he didn't need to know that.

His jaw clenched and unclenched. To my surprise, he dropped to his knees in front of me, his hands spanning my waist.

Uncomfortable with him bowing like this before me, I tried to move away. "What are you doing?"

"Stay still."

I could feel his breath on my skin. Goose bumps rose all over, and my body went on alert (some parts more than others). Excitement and fear gripped my chest so my own breath came in shallow pants.

Slowly—ever so slowly—he inched forward. His lips brushed the edge of one of the bruises, so lightly I thought I imagined it. Then he pressed, and heat suffused my skin.

"Rhys." I gasped, grabbing his head. "What—"

"Shut your mouth and let me do this for you."

"I don't know what *this* is," I protested.

"This." He kissed another bruise, and another, lingering until I squirmed under his fiery mouth. He licked a trail up my rib cage, stopping just below my breasts. He sucked my skin there, and I went up in flames.

His fingers lingered under the swell of my breasts, and I held my breath wondering if he was going to grace my nipples with his kisses. God, I wanted it.

He lifted his head, his eyes searing. "How do you feel?"

Hot. Wet. Edgy.

Then it occurred to me my ribs didn't hurt as much. I twisted my torso, frowning. "Better."

"Next time you get in trouble, call me." Standing, he pulled my shirt back down.

I almost groaned in disappointment. "Next time?"

He nodded. "I have the feeling trouble follows you quite closely." He dropped a brief but electric kiss on my mouth, moved me aside, and walked out of the office.

Lifting my shirt, I looked at my midriff. The bruises weren't nearly as livid as before. How did he do that? More importantly, could *I* do that? And would he teach me if I took him up on his offer?

As I went back to my station, I wondered if I should have told him I lost the scroll.

No. The answer resounded in my head. I had no doubt that he'd find the scroll. Then he'd either return it to me or take it for himself and leave. Neither option thrilled me.

Around nine, I was debating leaving Vivian to deal with all the customers (murder—especially if it was a couple blocks away—was good for business) when Inspector Ramirez walked in again.

Shit. I whirled around to put away the vodka bottle in my hand—at least that's what I would have said. Really, I wanted to compose myself before he ferreted out anything I didn't want him to know. I was still a little dazed—and turned on—by Rhys's healing kisses.

Vivian inhaled sharply. "Wow. Talk about sexy."

My hackles rose at the thought of her even looking at Rhys. Eyes narrowed, I turned to warn her off when I saw it was just the inspector.

And he was headed this way. Damn.

Like before, he was completely buttoned up. I wondered how anyone could be so restrained all day.

Time to buck up and deal. I nodded at him. "Inspector."

"Hello, Ms. Sansouci. I was hoping you'd still be here."

Looking around him, I asked, "Where's your partner?"

He smiled faintly. "May's pork roast."

His business was so important that he came on his own? That couldn't be good. As if echoing my sentiments, *tŭ ch'i* stirred. Uncomfortable, I tried not to fidget. "Did you have more questions, Inspector?"

"I was hoping to talk to Ms. Redding first."

Vivian shoved me aside to stand in front of the inspector. "I'm Vivian."

I rolled my eyes at the way she drawled her name.

Ramirez saw—of course—and he cocked an eyebrow at me before turning to Vivian. "Miss Redding, I'm Rick Ramirez with the SFPD. I'm investigating the homicide that happened several blocks from here last night. I'd like to ask you a few questions."

She leaned across the counter in her signature move to

flash him more of her cleavage. As if her tank top didn't bare enough of her enhanced features.

Shaking my head, I went to count out my register—not because I was eager to leave, which I was, but because it gave me the best vantage point to listen to their conversation. Maybe Ramirez would say something important— like that they found an ancient scroll under the body and it was in police custody.

He flipped open his notebook and got down to business. "Ms. Redding, what time did you leave work last night?"

She pouted thoughtfully. "It was after four."

I couldn't help raising my eyebrows. That was late. Usually whoever closed was out of here by two—our crowd usually moved on by one.

Ramirez picked up on it, too. "Isn't that a little late?"

She gave him what I knew she thought was a sex kitten smile, but it looked like a piranha to me. "I was *talking* with a friend."

"Eew." I grimaced. The last time she and a friend "talked," I found a used condom in the office.

Suddenly aware they weren't talking, I looked up to find them staring at me. I blinked and held up a dollar bill. "It's sticky."

Vivian rolled her eyes like I was an imbecile before turning back to Ramirez with her predator smile. She leaned more on her elbows—the better to show off her plastic boobs. "Go on."

Unfortunately, he asked pretty much the same questions he asked me. Which meant no word on the scroll. But then he reached into his jacket pocket and pulled out the picture. "Do you recognize him?"

She gasped as she grabbed the mug shot. "This is the guy who came in looking for Gabe a couple nights ago."

Shit. I could feel Ramirez's gaze boring into me, but I kept my head down and pretended I was doing my own thing.

"He came back last night. But she was here and he acted like he never asked for her." She shrugged and handed the picture back. "I thought they'd look cute together, but then he walked out without talking to her. Weird, but Gabe likes weird, so it's a shame he's dead now."

"So Ms. Sansouci and this man never talked?"

"Not here." Vivian's eyes flashed.

I groaned. I knew that look. It was right before she eviscerated someone and left them twitching in her wake.

"But who knows what happened after she left work," she added slyly.

"Thank you, Ms. Redding. I'll be in touch if I have more questions." Ramirez slapped his notebook closed. "Ms. Sansouci, you got a minute?"

Did I have a choice? I shut the register and said to Vivian, "I'm out for the night."

She straightened indignantly. "But it's not time for you to leave—"

"It is now." I tossed my apron aside and went to get my coat from the office.

Ramirez waited for me right outside the bar. "Why didn't you mention he'd asked for you?"

I nodded at a couple regulars who said hi as they walked in. "I didn't think about it."

"You didn't think about it," he repeated slowly.

His tone sounded like Wu when he was angry—tight and controlled—and I didn't like it at all. "Like that's surprising considering you were questioning me about *a murder*."

Deep in the earth, I felt an answering rumble echoing my anger. Faint and distant, but working its way to the surface.

Breathe. I began walking briskly down the street, hoping the activity would work it off. "Besides, he barely looked at me when he was in. I thought Vivian was joking. In case you didn't notice, Vivian isn't the most credible source of information."

Though I walked fast, he didn't struggle to stay in step with me. "So are you saying Ms. Redding lied?"

"No." I huffed in exasperation. "I'm saying I didn't believe her. We aren't exactly bosom buddies. And the guy barely glanced in my direction last night. If he asked for me before, why wouldn't he have said something to me when I was there?"

"I don't know. Why wouldn't he?"

I shot him a withering look. "You don't believe me, do you?"

His mouth firmed into an astonishingly straight line. "I just found out you'd not only seen the victim but he'd asked for you before his murder, a fact you didn't choose to disclose earlier. What am I supposed to believe?"

I opened my mouth to tell him.

He cut in before I could get a word out. "Funny thing is I've had this gut feeling all along that you're hiding something. So now that I've found out you lied—"

"I never lied," I said adamantly.

"—I'm wondering whether you know more than you're letting on."

If only he knew. I kept my eyes forward and continued to march ahead.

"I'm giving you the opportunity to tell me everything you know about last night. Right now."

"I told you everything. If he was actually in the bar, I didn't wait on him. I left the bar at the end of my shift and walked home. End of story." At least that was the end of *that* story. I counted what happened after that as the beginning of a different one.

Ramirez studied me. I was amazed that he didn't walk into a pole or anything. Maybe they taught how to stare someone down while walking in detective school.

We continued in silence for several more beats. But then with casual certainty, he said, "Ms. Sansouci, I'll find out, you know."

"There's nothing to find out regarding your case," I replied in all honesty. His dark gaze was steady on me. I arched my eyebrows. "Do you have more questions? Because otherwise I'm heading home. It's been a long day."

He raked his hand through his hair. "Fine."

I nodded at him and turned to hurry home.

"But I'll be in touch," he called after me. "You can count on that, Ms. Sansouci."

A threat if I ever heard one. I waved over my shoulder and strode faster away from him.

I'd walked two blocks when Rhys pulled alongside me. This time, the passenger door just popped open.

Hands on my hips, I decided to take the path of least resistance and just get in. "Presumptuous of you," I said as I closed the door.

He raised an eyebrow. "I'm not offering you a ride."

That stopped me. "Then what are you offering?"

"This." He dragged me closer by my jacket and kissed life into me.

Or, rather, out of me. *Tŭ ch'i* leapt to meet him, and

with every lick of his tongue, every nibble of his lips, I was less and less weighed down by the force of it within my body. When he finally broke the kiss, I felt light. Like anything was possible.

Rhys nuzzled my nose with his. "You can go now."

I blinked. "What?"

"You won't let me take you home, so we're at an impasse where the only solution is for you to get out of my car and for me to go home." He sat back in his seat and stroked a finger over his scar. "Isn't that right, love?"

He used my words against me. I didn't know whether to be pissed or admire his strategy. So I shrugged and slinked out, knowing he'd backed me into a corner. "'Night."

The window rolled down. "Gabrielle."

I looked in.

"The day will come when I have you. And I won't let you go." The window rolled back up, and he took off while I stood there gaping.

I didn't realize what he'd done until I got home. He'd drained *tŭ ch'i*. At least it felt that way—the incessant power was strangely peaceful. Had he done it specifically, to help me cope?

Yes, I suspected. Did I call him to thank him? I shook my head. I was afraid I'd invite him over if I talked to him, and that wasn't a good idea.

Instead I took advantage of the clarity. I slipped on a CAL sweatshirt I'd adopted from a long-gone *amour* and a pair of socks and went to my studio. I glanced at the last painting I did with the mysterious enshrouded figure and knew what I had to paint next.

Propping a new canvas on the easel, I picked up an

old four-inch house brush, dipped it into a combination of azure and black, and attacked the canvas.

The change of night giving way to dawn brought me back to the present. I sat back and did what I never do: inspect the work I just did.

Looking out at me from the stark gloom of the canvas was a pair of blue eyes. Vivid. Omnipotent. Eyes that saw beyond my clothes, deep inside to where I hid secrets.

Rhys's eyes.

Chapter Twenty-five

*T*hose eyes haunted my dreams.

Not only his eyes but his mouth, his hands, his body. I woke up the next morning turned on beyond belief, writhing under my comforter with the feeling that he was there with me, caressing every inch of my skin.

I rolled onto my side and snuggled into the comforter. Every time I closed my eyes, Rhys's intense face filled the darkness in front of my eyelids.

Hyperconscious of the warm throbbing between my legs, I grazed a hand over my nipple and it tightened painfully. *God.* Biting my lip, I ran my hand down my abs until my fingers touched the elastic of my panties. I hesitated, torn between needing relief and not wanting to give in to him. Kind of illogical, but in my gut I felt like he'd intended to torture me this way.

No way would I let him have the upper hand. I fished my phone out of the clothes discarded on the floor, settled back into bed, and called him.

To my surprise, he picked up, but I beat him to the punch. "It won't work, you know."

"What won't work, love?"

"You won't have me unless I decide I want you to have me."

Silence. I could practically hear him thinking. When he replied, his voice swept over me like a caress. "I wouldn't want it any other way."

"Ha! You'd be thrilled if I bowed down and did whatever you wanted."

"No, I rather fancy you fighting back. It'll make your willing surrender all that much sweeter."

"I won't—"

"Oh, love, you will." His sexy whisper enflamed my already heated-up body. "One day you'll lay yourself open before me and beg me for what I can do to you."

Don't ask. I bit my lip to keep from giving in to temptation.

Rhys chuckled. "I don't have to tell you, love. You're perfectly capable of imagining it, aren't you?"

My body burning from his kisses? My legs wide and welcoming? Begging him to finally kiss me *there?* Yeah, I could see it. Quite vividly.

I frowned. "You—you . . . *wanker.*" I hung up.

That didn't go precisely how I envisioned. To add insult to injury, I was still horny.

Pressing a hand over my panties, I considered taking care of myself, but how embarrassing would it be getting caught by Wu?

Except Wu was gone, I remembered a second later. The thought should have made me relieved, but I just felt regret. And guilt.

Confused, overwhelmed, lonely, I rolled out of bed and

headed to my studio and the picture of my mom for comfort. But as I stepped in front of the easel, I got distracted by my work.

Needing to see both paintings side by side, I set them next to each other and studied them, hoping plain daylight would reveal flaws. If they had flaws, I could chalk them up to an experiment, set them aside, and continue working on the series I already had going.

But no flaws. They were just as, if not more, startling, especially side by side. They told a story of forbidden desire, hot and potent and dark. And I liked them—more than the *Enter the Light* series. A lot more.

"Damn." I rubbed my forehead, feeling a headache coming on. Maybe the original series wasn't as dull as I remembered. I resolved to go to Madame's house and reacquaint myself with it. To help get back into the groove.

So I got dressed and jogged the entire way to Madame's house. When I arrived, I was dripping sweat despite the frigid coastal wind but feeling marginally calmer than I was before.

"Thank God," I muttered as I rang Madame's bell. Usually levelheaded, I was letting this emotional upheaval get to me.

It was probably exacerbated by *tŭ ch'i*. I could feel the pulsing inside me, welling up more and more by the hour. That had to be the reason I felt torn about Wu when I should be happy he was out of my hair. Or why I felt so hot for Rhys. It wasn't really me.

My head throbbed, too. *Tŭ ch'i*'s fault, as well. Although maybe I just wasn't used to thinking so much.

Madame's voice echoed through the security intercom. *"Oui?"*

"Bonjour, Madame. C'est moi."

"Gabrielle?"

"*Oui, bien sûr.*"

There was a slight pause and then the gate buzzed open. When I let myself into the house, I found Madame waiting for me in the foyer. "*Qu'est-ce qui s'est passé?*"

I air-kissed her cheeks so I wouldn't subject her to my sweat. "Why do you think something's happened? Can't I just visit you?"

"Yes, but lately you act unusual." She frowned at me. "Do you come to paint?"

"No, I came to see you."

She stared at me like she didn't believe me.

"Really."

"You should be here to paint."

Didn't I know it? Because I knew she wouldn't give it up, I threw her a bone. "I started another painting last night."

She narrowed her eyes. "You did?"

"God, you're suspicious. Yeah, I did. It's good." No need to tell her I wasn't planning on showing it to anyone.

Studying me for another long, silent moment, she nodded and shuffled down the hall. "*Viens.*"

I followed her to the kitchen, waving her to a seat. "I'll make coffee."

She eased herself onto a chair. "You should have brought the painting. *J'aimerais le voir.*"

"Um, yeah. It's still wet. I didn't want to move it," I lied. I took my time setting the kettle on the burner and grinding the coffee beans. I fiddled with cups and saucers, even pulling out a tray. But I couldn't put it off any longer, so I glanced over my shoulder to the corner where the painting was propped on the easel.

"*Fais attention, Gabrielle.* You will burn yourself."

"Oh." Turning around, I retracted my hand from the stove. "Thanks."

Madame frowned. "You seem distracted, *mon chou*. Is there anything you need to talk about?"

Ha! "No, not at all."

The kettle hissed. I waited for the water to reach a vigorous boil and then poured it into the press pot. Bringing the pot with me, I sat down at the table.

And then I popped back up and strode over to the painting. I'd just look and get it over with. I was obsessing over nothing. It was going to be better than last night's hastily scratched-together work.

It wasn't. It was still really good, but the other paintings had a violent, ferocious passion, while this one was—well, more placid.

My shoulders slumped. "Damn."

"*Ça va, Gabrielle?*"

"*Oui, Madame*," I said, hoping she wouldn't hear differently. Massaging my temples, I pasted a reassuring smile on my face and turned around to join her at the table

"Not that I do not enjoy your company, *mon chou*," she said as she pushed the sugar toward me, "but this is not like you. You have been acting most bizarre. However, I cannot tell you how happy I am you started *la prochaine peinture*."

She wouldn't be too happy if she found out the painting was off topic. I couldn't afford to get distracted—I knew this, just like I knew she wouldn't hesitate to remind me of it.

Distracted. Right. I didn't think I could get any more scattered if I tried.

As if I didn't have enough to deal with, *tŭ ch'i* began

to stir from its long slumber. A calm churning at first, it quickly mutated until I felt like I was just this side of staying in control.

I pushed my coffee aside and, using the table as support, got to my feet. "Gotta go."

Madame frowned. "But you haven't finished your *café. Et des biscuits,* do you not want?"

"No cookies. I just have to go." I pecked her cheeks absently and picked up my jacket. As I stumbled out of the house, I got out my phone and called Rhys.

No answer. I stood on the sidewalk, wondering what to do. What could I do? Arms wrapped tight around myself, physically trying to hold it in, I trudged toward the bus stop.

Halfway there my cell phone rang. *Please let it be Rhys.* I looked at the incoming caller ID.

Jesse. Panic gripped my gut, followed by a feeling of being let down. Where was Rhys? I needed him.

Tŭ ch'i surged in sympathy to my emotions. Caught off guard by the comfort it offered, I allowed it in.

Only it took advantage of the freedom, becoming a raging torrent in a split second. Amplifying my emotions, it mingled with them until they filled me to the tips of my fingers. The ground rumbled, first deep in the earth and then more superficially under my feet. I heard the rattling that accompanies earthquakes—it rolled through me. I swelled with power.

Strong. Exhilarating and vindicating. Right now I could do anything. I felt invincible.

But then the earth pulled me, like it was trying to suck me in. Startled, I tried to pull back.

I couldn't.

Trapped. I struggled against it, suddenly not able to

breathe—as if I was being buried in dirt. I lost balance as the earth shifted under my feet and landed on my hands and knees.

Closing my eyes, I tried to reel it in. It started to retract, but just as I felt I was getting it under control it lashed back.

I cried out at the pain that lanced through me. My heart was going to burst. I shook as badly as the earth. I was going to explode—I knew it. They were going to find pieces of me splattered all over Pacific Heights. And I'd never get to see my work hanging in a gallery. All because I got tempted by the dark side.

"Not. Going. To. Happen," I said through gritted teeth. I put my palms flat on the ground and shoved with everything I had.

It resisted, burning me like I'd been caught in the path of a volcanic eruption. I screamed even as I pushed harder.

Slowly, the flow diminished until it went back to that ever-present pulsing beneath the surface of my skin. Drained and sweaty, I lay panting on the ground, thankful that I was in Pacific Heights, which didn't have much foot traffic during weekdays. If anyone had seen me, they probably would have sent me to the emergency room. Or the psychiatric ward.

Light glinted off something metallic to my right. My cell phone.

My body racked in pain, it seemed like it took forever before I reached it. I scrolled my call log and hit send when I found Rhys's number.

"Pick up," I urged.

He didn't.

Chapter Twenty-six

I slammed a vodka bottle back into the well as another wave of energy undulated from the ground through me. I swallowed it, body tense, waiting for it to surge again. It didn't—this time.

I wanted to blame someone. There were so many people to choose from—Wu, Madame, Rhys, Paul. Hell—the monk Wei Lin. What kind of bastard ruins an innocent woman's life hundreds of years before she's even born?

"Excuse me. Is that my sea breeze?"

Lifting my head, I frowned at the overly blond woman pointing at the glass in my hand. "Yeah."

She tipped her chin with attitude. "Think I can have it?"

I held on to it for a few seconds longer before I slowly pushed it across the counter.

Flipping her hair, she gave me a dirty look, dropped a couple bills in front of me, snatched her drink, and turned to join her friends. But not before she mumbled, "Bitch."

Tŭ ch'i flared, hitting me harder than before, as if it

was punishing me for losing the scroll. I wrestled with it. By the time I was certain it wasn't going to break free, I was gripping the counter, breathing like I'd run to Ocean Beach and back.

"Shit," I muttered under my breath. More of this and I was going to come apart.

After I shoved the money in the till, I pulled out my cell phone from under the counter and glared at it. Rhys had a way of making *tŭ ch'i* calm down. I could call him again. Ask him for help . . .

But I'd already called, and he hadn't answered. Or called me back.

I threw the phone back on the shelf.

"You know that kind of treatment isn't conducive to keeping your electronics working for long," Carrie said as she slipped behind the counter.

"The sucky thing about cell phones is you can't slam them down." I kicked the shelf for good measure. "They don't give you as much satisfaction."

She laughed as she tied her apron around her waist. "Good thing I don't have a life and could come in to help you out. As edgy as you are tonight, you'll probably scare away the clientele."

"I'm not sure I see a problem," I grumbled.

"Not a problem, but a real shame. Especially when they're hotties like him." She jerked her chin at the entrance. "Darn, you get all the luck. He's headed straight for you. He didn't even glance at the half-naked girls to his right."

I looked to where she motioned. Inspector Rick Ramirez. What was he doing here? "He does want me."

Carrie's eyes lit up. "Really?"

I nodded. "For murder."

Moving away from her before she could ask me anything else, I met Ramirez halfway down the bar. Just as I was about to hit him with a clever remark, *tŭ ch'i* hit me—hard.

"Damn it." I hissed. It rolled over me like a ton of rocks. I turned around and breathed through it, but that helped less and less. I felt my fingers begin to vibrate, like the energy was going to escape from their tips. I kept my hands clenched until I felt less like the Incredible Hulk and more like me again.

"Ms. Sansouci? Everything all right?"

I turned to find the inspector's too-intelligent eyes studying me, concerned. I made an effort to smile. "Just peachy. Get you something to drink?"

He didn't look like he believed me, but he played along. "Shot of Patrón, neat."

I raised my eyebrows. "Hardcore."

"I'm off duty."

No wonder he was without his coat and tie, his only concession to being casual. Oh—and the first button on his dress shirt was undone.

His gaze narrowed as he studied me. "You look pale."

"The fog makes it hard to tan." I pulled the bottle down from the shelf. I sloshed a large pour into a glass and slid it across the counter. Maybe if he got tipsy, he wouldn't ask me questions I didn't want to answer. "Do you always hang out in bars alone on your nights off?"

He lifted the glass and inhaled the scent. "Only if I think it'll lead to clues about a recent murder."

The ground rumbled below me. I held my breath. *Please—not now.* As if it heard me and wanted to show me who was boss, *tŭ ch'i* swelled and threatened to spill over for a second before it receded.

"Ms. Sansouci?"

Because I didn't want to deal with questions I couldn't answer, I redirected the conversation back to the matter at hand. "I don't know what else you think you'll find here. Unless you have a suspect here you're keeping an eye on."

"You aren't a suspect, if that's what you're asking." He toyed with the glass, his sharp gaze on me. "Should you be?"

I shrugged. I could play casual, too. "I don't seem to have a motive."

"There's that, isn't there." Picking up his glass, he stood up.

"Going away so soon?" I asked hopefully.

He eyed me suspiciously. "You're not so lucky. Just mingling."

Hoping to hear something related to the murder, or to catch something that would incriminate me? He may not have said it, but I could hear his intent loud and clear.

As I watched him walk away, another person walked into the bar. I didn't have to look to know who it was—my body went taut and tingly the second he stepped in the door.

Glaring, I waited with my hands on my hips as he approached the counter. "Thanks for returning my call," I said with not a small amount of sarcasm.

"I had to fly to Los Angeles on business this morning. I called the first chance I got this evening, but you were obviously at work. Check your phone." He studied me, a faint frown turning his lips down. Then he took my hand, flipped it over, and kissed the inside of my wrist. "That bad, is it, love?"

The sympathy in his voice nearly undid me. I jerked

my hand back and whirled around to grab the scotch off the shelf. I sloshed a hefty amount into Johnny's special crystal tumbler and slammed it in front of Rhys before I moved down the counter to help another patron.

Carrie stopped next to me, shaking a martini as she checked out Rhys. "Ask your British man if he has a brother. If his brother is even half as sexy, I'll be in heaven."

"He's not my British man," I mumbled as I pulled a beer.

"Right. I guess that's why you can't keep your hands off him whenever he comes in here."

"*His* hands are always on *me*."

She grinned. "Exactly."

My cheeks flushed. "Don't you have customers to serve?"

She laughed and skipped away to finish off the drink. I glanced at Rhys one more time before getting back to work.

But I was hyper-aware of him watching me. Even with the rush we had and all the customers crowding around the bar, I was conscious of his gaze trained on me. It annoyed me.

Actually, it turned me on, which annoyed me even more.

The only good thing was that *tǔ ch'i* submitted to his presence. Normally, that would have pissed me off, but I was just happy for the reprieve. It still seethed under the surface, but at least I didn't feel like it was going to burst free.

Once I'd helped everyone and had no other excuse, I steeled my spine and went to stand in front of Rhys. He eyed me over the rim of his scotch, casually, as if this were some sort of social call.

We both knew it wasn't.

I propped my hands on my hips. "If you're going to teach me to deal with *tǔ ch'i,* we need to establish boundaries."

"That's the problem, love." He lifted my hand and nipped the pad of my palm. "Our boundaries seem to be blurred."

"Excuse me, Ms. Sansouci. Could I get a refill?"

Ramirez. At a glance, he looked blank and polite. But I could see how carefully he calculated the scene.

"Coming right up." Withdrawing my hand from Rhys's, I poured another shot of tequila and slid it across the counter. He picked it up, eyeing me and Rhys the whole time, slowly drank it, dropped a bill in payment, and left with a chilly nod to me.

"A friend of yours?" Rhys asked.

"No."

He swirled his drink. "He wants something from you."

"Don't you all?" I retorted as I set the shot glass in the dirty bin.

"I'm asking for what will result in a mutually beneficial arrangement. He only wants to take from you."

I arched my eyebrows. "Would you care?"

"Do you want me to care?"

"All I want from you is to teach me how to control *tǔ ch'i.*"

He gaze intensified, almost as if he were trying to see inside my head. Finally he said, "Are you sure?"

The only thing I was sure of was that this was going to come back and bite me in the ass, but I nodded. "Yes."

Rhys held his hand out. His fierce expression dared me to take him on.

Why did I feel like I was making a pact with the devil? Despite myself, I shook it. I expected thunder and lightning on contact—maybe the building shaking—but only my mark tingled, a sparkle of pinpricks.

Chapter Twenty-seven

Charming," Rhys said as he stepped over the threshold and into my hovel.

Frowning, I closed the door. I hadn't wanted to invite him here—I felt like I was letting a fox in the chicken coop. But I didn't have the scroll anymore, so at least I didn't have to worry about that.

Wu came to mind, and I made a face. He wouldn't have been happy knowing I'd turned to an outsider, even if he was another Guardian.

"Interesting decor." Rhys touched the half-broken lamp by the futon.

I shrugged. "My interior decorator handles it all. She charges an arm and leg, but I think she's worth it."

"Indeed." He picked up the picture of me and Paul.

Snatching it back, I replaced it next to my bedside lamp. "Stop being nosy."

"Intrigued, love. Not nosy." Hands in his pockets, he perused the room, his gaze resting on a crimson bra lying on the floor.

Crap. I reached down, snatched it, and hid it behind my back.

"Gabrielle, you surprise me."

"Because I wear red lace, or because I don't want you to see it?"

"Do you really not want me to see it, love?"

I frowned.

His lips did that little quirk, and he strolled out of the living room into the kitchen.

"Hey. Where are you going?" I stuffed the bra under my covers and hurried to follow him. I stopped talking abruptly when I realized he wasn't in the kitchen. Not like there was anything of note in the kitchen, unless you were into moldy brown bananas. Which meant he was in my art studio.

"Shit." The painting I'd started sat on the easel, totally exposed and vulnerable. I rushed back, shivering as my feet hit the icy floor. Maybe he wouldn't notice the painting. It was dark—it could happen.

No such luck. He stood directly behind it, studying it like it was by Rembrandt.

"There's nothing back here that you'd find interesting." I swallowed thickly. Maybe he wouldn't recognize his own eyes staring back at him. It was pretty abstract.

"Quite the contrary. Did you do this?"

I tipped my chin up. "Yes."

He glanced at me before returning his attention to the canvas. "Intriguing subject."

On the inside I groaned. On the outside, I pretended to study the canvas, too. "It's from a nightmare I had. I call it *The Boogeyman Is Watching*."

"Do you have nightmares often?" He faced me.

Too close. He dominated the room, making my studio

seem even smaller than usual. I wanted to step back into the kitchen, but I wouldn't give him that satisfaction.

Instead, I steeled myself from being seduced by his heated gaze and resisted the gravitational pull of his body. "I have one recurring nightmare that won't seem to go away."

He didn't move, but I swore he got closer. "Perhaps it's not really a nightmare but a dream come true."

"That, or indigestion."

He chuckled.

I warmed at the sound, and that totally disturbed me. I needed to be on my toes, not disarmed and compliant. Frowning, I crossed my arms. "I want to discuss the terms of the deal."

"There are no terms."

"Right." I narrowed my eyes. "Don't think that just because I'm letting you show me how to use the Force that I've forgiven you. I'm still angry."

He cocked an eyebrow. "The Force?"

"I'm an artist, not a writer. I couldn't come up with anything more original." I propped my fists on my hips. "And don't think that this'll get you anything. Especially anything sexual."

This time, Rhys did move so he backed me up against the doorway. His hands framed my shoulders, and I thanked God he wasn't pressed against me. "Trust me, love, when we make love it'll be because you're begging for it and no other reason."

Hoping he didn't notice how my nipples had jumped to attention, I pretended to resist. "Dream on, stud muffin."

"You'll come to me." He nuzzled the side of my neck. "Willing and eager."

Warmth stole through me, and I closed my eyes to

savor it. *Tǔ ch'i* surged up to meet him. I tensed, waiting for the backlash, but his energy rose up to cocoon mine. Safe. Considering the circumstances, it amazed me. I relaxed even though I wasn't sure how I felt about accepting comfort from him.

His breath scorched my neck, and the heat of it echoed all the way to my toes and back. I moaned, snuggling closer. *More.*

As if he heard my silent plea, fire blazed inside me. It licked up and down my body, centering between my legs, right where I needed it. His hands gripped me closer, and his hard-on pressed into me at the same spot.

Intense. I gasped. But instead of losing myself to the pleasure, I began to drown in the sensations. He filled me—overpowering—like he sought dominion.

Not like this—not if it meant losing my will. With a kung fu yell, I shoved him back, hoping that'd be enough to bring my body back under control. It worked—our connection severed.

It took me several moments before I could speak. "Teach me how to shield."

He gazed at me in silence. I wondered what he was looking for, or what he saw, but he began to speak before I could ask. "The energies, or powers, accompanying each scroll are different, which is why they have unique names."

"They do?" I thought it was all *tǔ ch'i,* period.

"Of course." He frowned at me. "You didn't know?"

I ignored his question and asked one of my own. "What is yours called?"

Rhys hesitated. "*Huǒ ch'i.*"

"How—"

"Do you want me to teach you to shield?" he asked with a cocked eyebrow.

In other words, shut up. I nodded and motioned for him to continue.

"Even though the energy from each scroll has different properties, they all essentially work the same. The energy flows from its source, much like water. Although, unlike a river, you can redirect its course at your will."

"Deep." I couldn't help the sarcasm. He sounded like he'd read the nature bullshit from the scroll.

He shot me a quelling look. "To control the energy, you need to have complete focus. Still your mind."

"Um, this is where I've been going wrong." But in the spirit of cooperating, I closed my eyes and tried to find that calm place I painted from.

Tŭ ch'i slammed into me, harder than ever before, making me stagger. I grabbed something to keep me from falling and struggled to shove *tŭ ch'i* back where it came from.

"Stop fighting it," Rhys commanded, his voice sounding miles away.

"Can't." If I stopped fighting I'd lose myself to it, and there was no telling what would happen then.

Gritting my teeth, I wrestled with it. After a moment, I felt a cushioning warmth, and it drained from me with less effort than usual. When I finally opened my eyes again, I wasn't as physically depleted as I usually was.

I was, however, in Rhys's arms. I looked up into his eyes and blinked when I saw the stunned anger reflected there.

He gripped my arms tight. "What the hell was that?"

"You're the teacher here." I scowled. "What did you think it was?"

"Why is it so strong?"

"It's strong?"

"It shouldn't have hit you so forcefully."

"The Force runs strong in my family," I deadpanned.

"Don't play games with me, Gabrielle. You nearly overcame me." He shook me just enough to get my attention but not so he'd hurt me. "If I were anyone else, you would have killed me."

That effectively shut me up.

"Something is amiss for your energy to be so out of control."

"You think so?" I couldn't think of anything amiss. Well, except for the fact that I'd lost the scroll. *Tŭ ch'i had* gone crazy after that night. Were they tied? I frowned.

As if reading my mind, Rhys demanded, "Where's your scroll?"

"Oh, no." I shook my head. "That's not part of the bargain, either."

"You don't trust me."

"Hell, no, I don't." I'd be damned if I let him find out I'd lost it. I couldn't bear him thinking I was some ditz who couldn't keep track of one scrap of paper.

Rhys studied me, his gaze so piercing I had to fight not to fidget. Finally he said, "Picture a box."

"A box?" I frowned. "Like a shoe box or what?"

"Any box strong enough to hold the energy in it."

I instantly visualized a high-tech safe with foot-thick walls. "Got it."

"Place the energy inside and lock the door."

"That's it?"

"Until I know why it's trying to drown you, yes. You can't handle anything more at the moment."

That stung, but I tried not to pout. "Well, I could have come up with something like this."

"But you didn't, love." He raised an eyebrow. "Now concentrate."

Sparing a second to shoot him an *eat dirt* glare, I closed my eyes and pictured my safe. I began to mentally gather *tŭ ch'i* in my hands. It slipped through my fingers and stubbornly evaded my herding, so I put it in the safe little by little until I had almost all of it gathered.

Only suddenly Rhys's hands spanned my waist and snaked up my T-shirt. I gasped, mentally scrambling to keep all the energy in the safe. "What the hell are you doing?"

"Making sure your concentration is strong enough," he said a moment before I felt his teeth scrape over a sensitive spot on my neck. "Focus, Gabrielle. I can feel your energy struggling to break free again."

Gritting my teeth, I forced my mind back to the task at hand. Harder this time. Especially since he slid his hands up my abdomen to rest just under my chest. Sweat broke out on my skin—I'm sure from the strength of my effort and not his touch. But I was painstakingly winning the battle against *tŭ ch'i*.

"Gabrielle," he murmured, nibbling at the base of my neck. "You aren't wearing a bra."

"Shut up. I'm concentrating."

His palms rubbed over my nipples before they closed over my breasts.

I lost control of *tŭ ch'i,* and it slammed out of me and into Rhys.

Pain. We gasped at the same time. The ground began that deep-in-the-core rumbling that signaled an oncoming earthquake. His hands dug into me, almost burning.

And then it changed. His warm energy wrapped around me, encasing me and *tŭ ch'i* so it wasn't so intense. Then his power moved through me, flames erupting all over again.

His body pressed mine into the wall, and we both groaned with excruciating pleasure. He rolled the tips of my breasts between his fingers, lowering his head and feeding one to his mouth through my shirt. Letting my head fall back against the wall, I rubbed myself against the leg he'd worked between mine, wanting to feel that scorching heat where it counted.

It was different this time. This time, both of us spun out of control and the push-pull of the energy between us was equal. I grabbed his shoulders to hold the feeling close.

"*Gabrielle.*" He jerked one hand out of my shirt to grip my butt, grinding me against him. "Concentrate."

I didn't want to. I'd never felt so connected to anything ever. Delicious. Hot. Tempting to just stay lost in our combined power.

Tempting, but I had responsibilities. I gathered my will and focused on *tŭ ch'i*. I imagined a trap door under my feet. I mentally stepped back and opened it, visualizing *tŭ ch'i* draining through it—every last bit until there wasn't a trace left inside me. It started to shift back up, but I slammed the door shut on it. I pictured a lock on the door and flipped the key before slipping it into a mental pocket.

As suddenly as it happened, all Rhys's heat dissipated. I shivered. Not cold—bereft. And unfulfilled. Opening my eyes, my gaze collided with his.

He looked like he'd just fought a battle. His chest heaved against mine with the effort to catch his breath.

His hair stood on end like I'd raked my fingers through it, though I couldn't remember doing so, and his clothes were less pristine than I'd ever seen.

His eyes got me, though. In them, the fire still raged. And I mean *raged*. I'd never seen a blue so violent. Not a physical violence, but violently wanting.

Me.

I licked my lips, glancing at his mouth. "I'm crumpling your suit."

"I don't give a bloody damn about the suit," he all but growled.

My hands slid to the top of his shirt. I slipped a couple fingers inside his collar, teasing him before I gripped the two sides and tugged so the first two buttons tore off.

The creak of the front door opening camouflaged the *ping* of them hitting the wooden floor. I must have forgotten to lock the door. Frowning, I looked over Rhys's shoulder and gasped. "Jesse."

He said nothing as he took in the scene. His gaze fell to my chest, and his hands clenched.

Glancing down, I winced when I saw my nipple in stark relief against a large, translucent wet spot.

Then I realized I was still in Rhys's arms. Damn it. I didn't want Jesse, but I didn't have to flaunt another man in his face. I let go of Rhys and pried myself loose. "Jesse—"

"I stopped by the bar, but you were already gone. Vivian said I should try you at home."

I was going to strangle that woman.

"I didn't realize you had plans." He nodded coldly at Rhys. "I'll get out of your way."

"Wait." I rushed to catch up to him before he walked away. "Jesse, let me explain."

He faced me from the bottom of the porch steps. "Nothing to explain, babe. We're just friends, right?"

The streetlight illuminated the pain on his face, and I cringed. I walked barefoot down the steps so I stood before him. "I didn't mean to hurt you."

He trailed his knuckles softly down my cheek, his smile regretful. "I know you didn't."

"I—" I shook my head, feeling like I needed to say something but not sure what. I had the impulse to explain my relationship with Rhys—Jesse wouldn't feel so bad if he knew what happened in there was because of an invisible Force and not because of normal attraction. It was all artificial, and if I told myself that a few hundred more times, I was sure I'd believe it, too.

Sighing, he lifted my chin with a finger and lowered his mouth to mine.

Without thought, I stepped back before his lips touched mine.

Understanding twisted his lips into a bitter smile. He stepped back and stuffed his hands into his pockets. It suddenly felt like there was an enormous gulf between us, which grew when he said, "I'm going out of town soon."

"Oh." I wanted to ask him where he was going and why. But that was none of my business, so I bit my lip to keep from saying anything.

He ran a hand over my hair and rubbed my cheekbone with his thumb. "See you around, babe."

My heart skipped, and I reached up to grab his hand before he pulled away. "That sounded like a good-bye."

He flipped his hand so he held mine in his. "Do you care if it is?"

Yeah, I did. I opened my mouth to tell him, but the words wouldn't come out.

Jesse dropped my hand and turned.

"*Wait*." I gripped the back of his leather jacket, and the words tumbled out in panic. "I do care."

"Know you do, babe," he said sadly, gently disengaging my hand from his coat. "But that's not enough, is it?"

His gaze swept over me one more time, like he was taking a mental snapshot to pull out later. I wished his last look wasn't of me mussed up by another man's hands.

Guilt stabbed me as I watched him walk away. He was right—he deserved more than I could give him. I sucked.

Dazed, I walked back into my house. The first thing I saw was Rhys, standing in the middle of the room. Actually he was only thing I saw.

He stalked toward me, eyes narrowed and looking wild with his disheveled hair, tattered dress shirt, and bared, tan chest. Looking as if he was going to knock me over the head and drag me off by my ponytail.

I braced myself. "Listen—"

Spearing his hand in my hair, his forceful lips met with mine. I wondered if what I tasted could be jealousy, and why the flavor appealed so much.

Too soon, abruptly, he lifted his mouth from mine, keeping me so close his blue eyes filled my vision. He let go of me and headed for the door. "Remember the visualization."

What the hell? I whirled around, scowling. "That's it? What about training me?"

He looked over his shoulder as he stepped out. "In due time, love."

Mouth gaping, I watched the door close. What just happened?

"My world shifted on its axis, that's what happened." I

shoved my hair back, knowing I had other things to think about other than how Rhys had ignited me.

Except I could still feel his energy—part of him— inside me.

Frankly, I didn't put it past him to have taken advantage of the situation. He knew what he was doing. He'd deliberately left me this way, still throbbing and achy and branded by the feel of him, inside and out.

"Bastard." I wrapped my arms around myself and paced my shack. I paced myself right back to the studio.

His eyes stared at me from the shadows, oddly lit by ambient light from outside. It was eerie, how well I'd captured them. I shivered, and then took and replaced the painting with a blank canvas.

I hadn't planned on painting, but one glance at the white space and I knew what should fill it. Exhaustion gave away to exhilaration, and I picked up a brush.

I hesitated right before it touched the canvas. I thought of my unfinished painting at Madame's house, knowing I should start the next painting in that series. But again, I couldn't do it. I just couldn't.

Stifling the logical voice that said I couldn't afford to waste my time on something that wasn't commissioned, I attacked the canvas. Life wasn't a piece of cake. It held dark shadows and uncertain feelings. Gray mingled with the black and white. Blue eyes blazed with violent passion.

Sometime around dawn I petered out. Standing up to stretch, I studied the unfinished work. The beginning of two figures, a vortex of crimson and black surrounding each of them like forbidding auras, keeping them apart. Looking at it left me feeling both pleased and unsatisfied. One thing I knew for certain: it was damn good.

Stiff, achy, and exhausted, I moaned as I tried to work out the kinks of being hunched over the canvas for so many uninterrupted hours. After a half-assed cleaning of my brushes, I tumbled onto my bed.

My lonely bed.

Chapter Twenty-eight

$\mathcal{M}$y cell phone rang a few hours later. Jolted awake, I tried to rub the fatigue out of my eyes as I fumbled it open. "What?"

"Gabby? Did I wake you up?"

"'S okay, Paul." Yawning, I sat up and pushed my hair out of my face. "What's up?"

"I have an hour clear in my morning schedule, and I thought I could bring brunch to share at your place. What do you say? You won't even have to get out of your pajamas if you don't want to," he said with humor.

I looked around my place. I'd never cared about the squalor, but after seeing my brother's suite I wasn't sure I wanted him to come here. I just couldn't see him sitting on my secondhand futon. "No, it's better that I meet you somewhere. It won't take me long to get ready. Twenty minutes?" I asked, hauling my ass out of bed.

"I have a meeting at one, so that won't give us enough time to eat. I already had the hotel pack us a picnic brunch, and I'm not far from your home."

"What?" I frowned. I hadn't told him where I lived.

"I'm assuming you live close to the bar." He paused. "But if this isn't a good time, maybe we should try again later."

I wanted to see him, but the more I thought about it, the less I wanted him here. So I nodded. "Another time might be better. I'm not a real morning person."

"Gabby, it's almost noon."

"That early?"

He laughed. "You haven't changed at all. Remember how Dad had to practically pry you out of bed in the mornings for your workout?"

"Ugh." I scowled at the memory. "That was inhumane."

Still chuckling, he said, "Go back to sleep. I'll call you later to arrange another time."

Easier said than done. After I got off the phone, I was too awake to try to sleep again, so I got out of bed with a groan and stumbled into the kitchen to find something for breakfast.

Something turned out to be half a Milky Way bar I found in a drawer. I was propped against the sink, chewing, when I realized I didn't have a headache or feel like I was going to bring the building down around me. Cautiously, I probed inside myself.

Nothing. Rhys's visualization still worked.

I smiled wide. If he were here, I'd kiss him.

If he were here, I'd do more than just kiss him.

As if he were tuned in to my thoughts, Rhys called me right at that moment. "How are you?" he asked.

"If you're asking about the Force, it's still locked away." I hesitated and then just blurted it out. "Thanks, by the way."

"You're welcome."

"Is that all you called for?"

"No. I was thinking about you," he said, his voice going husky.

My body recognized that tone and went on alert. "What were you thinking?"

Pause. "Wicked things."

A shock of pleasure shot through my body.

"Where are you?" he asked.

"In my kitchen. Why?"

"I want to picture you. What are you wearing?"

I looked down at my ratty sweatshirt. "Lace. Black lace."

"Perhaps later you'll show me."

"Perhaps," I said noncommittally. "Is that to say I might see you later?"

"Perhaps." He chuckled. "Until then, love."

I hung up, the image of posing for him wearing nothing but scraps of lace firm in my mind. A shiver of excitement ran down my body, and I had the sudden urge to paint the feeling. I went into my studio and sat down at the easel. Picking a brush, I attacked the canvas.

An hour later, my phone's alarm went off. Work. I made a face, resenting the interruption. Biting my lip, I debated what to do. I was tempted to call in sick. Vivian wouldn't have hesitated, and for lesser reasons. At least I had a valid need.

But I couldn't leave the bar in a lurch. Torn, I decided to let it rest on the result of one phone call.

Carrie answered, sounding her usual bright self. "Hey, Gabe. What's going on?"

"I was wondering if you could do me a favor," I said quickly, uncomfortable with asking for anything.

"Name it."

"I have the early shift, but I was struck with inspiration, and—"

"You need to paint," she concluded for me. "Sure, I'll take your shift."

I blew a relieved breath. "Thanks, Carrie. Really."

"Heck, you're actually doing me the favor. I could use a little extra cash this month."

"Let me take you to dinner after you get off," I said, surprising myself with the impulsive gesture. A couple weeks ago, I would have justified it by saying I needed to eat, too, but I knew better. I genuinely liked spending time with her, and I wanted to share my excitement about the paintings.

"I'd kill for a burger," she admitted. "You don't have to treat, though."

"I want to. We'll go to It's Tops." We made arrangements for me to meet her at the bar at nine, and I hung up feeling good.

I worked clear past dusk, stopping at eight to take a shower and dress. I'd been thrilled while I'd been working, but now, thinking about it, the influence Rhys had over me frightened me. He was worming his way into my life, becoming more and more important, and I didn't have control over it.

Pensive, I bundled up and headed to the Pour House to pick up Carrie. I got there right as she emerged from the bar.

"Hey." She grinned and gave me a quick hug.

Not used to such easy affection, I patted her back awkwardly.

She didn't comment on it. Instead she looped her arm through mine and began walking. "Vivian was really put out when she saw it was me instead of you. I think she had grand plans of torturing you all night."

"What else is new?" I didn't know what to do with my hands, so I stuck them in my pockets.

"It's so high school. I wouldn't be surprised if she t-p'ed your house." She barely took a breath before she said, "How'd the painting go? Did you make headway?"

"Yeah." I made a face. "It's different than what I'm supposed to paint."

"Really different?"

I pictured the original series. "Um, you can say that. Night-and-day kind of different."

She grimaced in sympathy. "How's that going to go for you? I altered my topic on my thesis once and my advisor practically had a coronary."

I nodded. "That about describes it."

"Don't worry." She patted my arm. "If you painted something different, there was a reason for it."

Yeah—Rhys. Today I'd ended up painting a man and woman, twined so closed you couldn't tell where one stopped and the other began. I sighed, long and heartfelt.

"There's a man behind that sigh, I can tell. I bet he has a British accent," she taunted in a singsong voice. She laughed at the look I darted at her. "Why are you so glum? If he inspires you, he inspires you. Embrace it. Embrace him."

My cheeks burned as I remembered last night.

"Or maybe you already have," Carrie said with a sly grin. "Was he good?"

So good I felt myself getting moist just thinking about it. "He was adequate."

She laughed.

"What?" I asked, frowning at her.

"Gabe, even a simple Midwestern girl like me can see there's nothing *adequate* about him. He's the kind of man who'd ruin you for life."

A scary thought. And fairly accurate. "I don't want to talk about him."

"Uh-huh."

"I don't."

"Okay."

We walked in silence for a couple blocks before I broke down. "He's driving me *insane*. He shows up out of nowhere and invades every corner of my life. Then he *kisses* me, for frick's sake."

"The jerk."

I narrowed my eyes. "Are you laughing at me?"

"Not much," she said with a grin.

"You wouldn't laugh if you knew how he kissed."

"Oh, no." Looking stricken, she laid a sympathetic hand on my arm. "Don't tell me he's a slobberer. That'll shatter my image of him."

"He's not a slobberer. He's got the best technique I've ever experienced. His kisses set me on fire," I said glumly.

"Then I'm not sure what the problem is here. He's hot, he's rich, and he likes you. The bonus is that you like him back. Underneath it all," she added quickly when I began to protest.

"Maybe."

She snorted. "Definitely. If you didn't like him, you wouldn't be this worked up over him. I may be an academic, but I'm not a dummy. I saw how you were with Jesse, and you're completely different with this guy."

I frowned. "How was I with Jesse, and how am I with Rhys?"

"You held Jesse at a distance. But Rhys ignites your passion. You've been different since you met him. More open somehow. Rhys arouses you."

To put it mildly. But Rhys also wanted the scroll. He said he picked me over it, but how could I be sure? Wu loved my mom enough to marry her, but in the end the scroll was more important than she was.

The scroll was more important to him than I was, too.

Fortunately, we arrived at It's Tops, and the smell of sizzling grease was enough to distract Carrie.

Unfortunately, once we ordered our hamburgers, she began the inquisition again. "So what's really the problem with him?"

I toyed with my silverware. "This girl-talk stuff is really weird."

Sympathy softened her gaze. "You don't have many friends, do you?"

"I've been busy with work and painting."

She nodded. "Since I moved here, I haven't had a girlfriend, either. Not a real one, in any case. My mom's great, though. We're pretty close, although I can't tell her everything." She smiled ruefully. "Not that there are any juicy details in my life."

"My mom died when I was eighteen," I admitted.

"That's so terrible for you." After a moment of silence, she shook her head. "I can't even imagine what that must have been like for you. And just when a girl really needs her mom's guidance."

Something in my chest eased, knowing that she understood. "It's been a long time."

"But that's not something you just get over. I bet you still mourn her."

She didn't know the half of it.

Carrie leaned forward. "If you think you've distracted me from our discussion about Rhys, you're delusional. You're going to tell me what the deal is, you know. You're just putting off the inevitable."

The waitress arrived with our food. I waited until she left before I admitted, "I don't trust him."

"Why not?" Carrie asked as she poured ketchup all over her burger and fries.

"He wants something from me."

"No kidding." She smirked as she lifted her burger for a bite.

"Not *that*." I frowned as I poked at my fries. "Well, okay, that, too. But he had ulterior motives in the beginning."

"And now you don't know whether he wants you or still has ulterior motives." She nodded. "Tricky."

"Exactly."

"Maybe you can just give him what he wants and see what happens." She shrugged. "That way at least you'd know."

"Yeah. Except I don't have it anymore."

She mashed a few fries into the puddle of ketchup. "Does he know?"

"Not yet."

"Tell him. I'd bet a year's tuition he still pursues you."

"Maybe." I wondered how he'd react if I told him I lost the scroll. I winced as I imagined his disappointment in me.

Carrie polished off her food in record time, eating some of my untouched fries, too. I'd lost my appetite somewhere along the way, but I managed to get down a couple bites of the burger. I paid for our dinner, layered up, and followed Carrie outside.

"That was so much fun. Thanks, Gabe." She hugged me.

"I feel like I monopolized the conversation." This time I was more prepared and actually managed what I thought was a decent return hug.

"No way." She smiled. "I loved it. It's so much more interesting than what I've got going on. But I'm more than happy to discuss the rise and fall of the Ming dynasty next time."

"Tempting," I lied with a grin.

"We should do this again soon." She gave me a sidelong look. "Maybe after you give me some pointers in kung fu."

I groaned.

She laughed. "If I mention it enough, I might wear you down. Persistence is one of my most endearing qualities." She waved over her shoulder as she started walking down Market. "Good night."

I headed down Valencia, toward home. Somewhere around Sixteenth Street, that feeling of being followed crept up my spine. I picked up my pace, keeping to the busier streets. Once I thought I caught a shadow of a person in a store window, but when I turned around, there wasn't anyone behind me.

On alert, I turned the corner—

Then suddenly someone slammed me into the building on my right.

"*Oof.*" My head hit the brick wall, hard enough that I saw stars. I hadn't even caught my breath from the blow when my assailant landed a punch to my stomach.

I curled into myself, moaning. The strike knocked me for a loop, but I was lucid enough to know it wasn't that bad. I counted myself lucky that the guy didn't know enough to hit vital targets. Punching my stomach would only really result in me vomiting all over him—punching my heart could be fatal.

"Bitch. This one's for Chivo." He hit again, and I doubled over, gasping for breath.

In the small corner of my mind that wasn't overwhelmed with pain, I recognized I needed to stop the beating before he caused some real damage—like a broken rib. Figuring *tǔ ch'i* was my best bet, I pictured the trap door and knew I just needed to unlock it. So I reached into my mental pocket for the key.

It wasn't there.

What the hell? It had to be there. It wasn't like I had that many pockets in my head. But I searched and I couldn't find it, not where I thought I'd put it and not anywhere else.

"Damn." I opened my eyes as his fist plowed into me again.

Never take your eyes from your opponent, Wu said once in a past lesson. *Especially if they are winning. It's when they think they have you that you'll see an opening for a counterattack.*

Lifting my head enough to look from under my lashes, I saw him cock his arm again. I waited until I saw his fist descending and then shifted my body—just enough so his fist brushed by me and smashed straight into the wall.

He howled like a little girl, clutching his hand to his waist. "*You fucking bitch.* You fucking broke my hand!"

Another figure loomed behind him. Shit—I should have noticed he had a friend. I was screwed.

But then the man spoke—in a crisp British accent. "You're going to wish your hand is all that was broken when I'm done with you."

Rhys grabbed the creep by the collar, whirled him

around, and hit with a right hook. As his fist connected with skin, I heard the sizzle of burning flesh over my attacker's shrill scream. My stomach lurched. Of course, my queasiness may have been because of all the hits I took, too. I eased down the wall, crouching to regroup, but I still watched the fight.

He followed up with a quick succession of body shots—liver, spleen, groin—all vital areas that'd cause maximum damage.

I decided to feel awe in Rhys's fiery power rather than horror. The creep was down for the count, hunched over, his grunts of pain muffled by his jacket, and it was done for my protection and well being. Just like when he healed me.

Rhys paused, his expression ferocious. He must have decided the guy wasn't far gone enough because, torquing his body, he launched a spinning crescent kick that snapped the guy's jaw.

Absolutely beautiful.

I shifted, and Rhys's battle-sharpened gaze fell on me.

"You need a sword," I said with careful lightness.

"It didn't go with this suit." The anger that still tightened the planes of his face belied his casual tone. He lifted me into his arms.

God, that hurt. I managed to stifle most of my whimper, but a little bit escaped. I could tell by the way his jaw constricted he heard. To distract us both, I asked, "What are you doing here?"

"I was on my way to see you. It was purely chance that I saw him grab you."

"And you rushed to help? Why is that?"

He gave me a dark look. "Why do you think?"

What I thought and what I felt were at odds. And, really, I wasn't in any shape to analyze either at this moment.

His car was around the corner, and he had me home in record time. Double parking right in front of my place, he came around to my side. "Your key?"

"In my pocket."

He extracted it and then lifted me out of the seat. He carried me all the way inside and placed me on the futon.

"Aspirin in the bathroom." Wrapping my arms around my middle, I pointed him toward it.

Rhys shook his head and unzipped my jacket. "My way is better."

Remembering the way he'd kissed my aches away last time, I shivered. Yeah, I had to agree.

With tender care he eased me out of my coat, the hoodie I wore underneath, and my tank top. He left my bra on, which surprised me. Maybe he liked the look of black lace.

He scowled, running his hands along my ribs. "I should go back and beat that git all over again for laying a hand on you."

For some reason, my heart warmed and some of the pain—as well as some of my doubts about him—faded. "Can I join you?"

"Always." He lowered his mouth to my navel, flicked it with his tongue, and then began his fire-kissing thing over every inch of my battered abdomen.

I sighed. "Will you teach me how to heal, too?"

"Of course, love," he murmured against my skin.

Relaxing, I let him take my pain away. By the time he finished, I was practically writhing under him. Swollen and wet, I knew just one touch would send me over the edge.

He knew it, too. His lips trailed down my stomach to the waistband of my jeans. He nibbled my belly, his hand idly toying with the button. Then he popped it open.

What about the missing safe key?

Damn it. I'd forgotten about that. I almost wished I hadn't remembered that at *this* moment, but now that the thought had cropped up I couldn't ignore it. I didn't know whether he purposefully tricked me into locking away *tǔ ch'i* or not. Should I get physical with him despite that?

Sigh. I grabbed him by the hair and lifted his head. "I need to ask you about the Force."

"Yes, young Jedi?" he murmured, turning his head to kiss the inside of my arm.

"Stop that. This is serious."

He echoed my sigh and sat back on his haunches. "What is it?"

"Remember how you told me to put *tǔ ch'i* in a strong box and lock it?" I waited till he nodded. "Well, I couldn't unlock it again. Did you do something to keep me from it?"

The outrage on his face was answer enough, but he also said, "I would never endanger you, Gabrielle. Nor would I take away something that's a part of you like your *tǔ ch'i*."

Oddly, I believed he meant it. That meant one thing. "Then I think I lost the key to the safe place."

Rhys stared at me blankly for two seconds before his lips curved into an unholy grin.

"This is not funny." I pushed him with my foot.

"Oh, but it is, love." Chuckling, he shook his head and stood up.

"Fine. Be amused. But are you going to help me find my key?"

"It'll cost you."

Of course it would. I frowned. Was I willing to pay the price? Like I had a choice. I couldn't leave myself vulnerable—the next time Rhys might not show up. I nodded once.

Satisfaction colored his eyes. "Be ready tomorrow."

"For what?"

"You're going to work off your debt, and then I'll help you unlock your safe place." He grinned again and headed toward the front door.

"Work off my debt how?" I called after him.

"We're going to spar."

"Spar?" I frowned. "Why—"

"Lock the door behind me, love."

I grabbed my pillow and threw it. Unfortunately, it hit the closed door and slid weakly to the floor. I heard Rhys's sexy chuckle outside, followed by the purr of his car's engine.

Sparring tomorrow. I curled onto my side and stared at the closed door. I wanted to find some kind of ulterior motive for him, but not even I was that creative. It was simply thoughtful.

And confusing. Because only one motive came to mind: concern. And that was just as scary as the alternative.

Chapter Twenty-nine

I don't know why we had to start so goddamn early," I grumbled as Rhys raced through the city the next morning.

He glanced at me, a smile flirting with his lips. "It's after ten."

"God, that's more indecent than I thought." I frowned at the passing scenery. "I should be painting, you know. I only have three weeks left till my deadline."

"You can't work if you're laid up with injuries from being beaten."

I couldn't argue with that. "Why are we out here? Are we going to work out on the beach?"

"No."

When it became apparent he wasn't going to say more, I rolled my eyes. "Then where are we going? We can't be going to Sea Cliff."

"Why not?"

"Because I don't think the homeowners in Sea Cliff would appreciate us sparring on their lawns." A closet in Sea Cliff cost more than most condos anywhere else. "We'd lower the property value."

"Speak for yourself, love."

I looked him over. In a Nike sweatshirt and workout pants, he was still *GQ* chic. Even this early in the morning. I, on the other hand, looked like I'd stumbled off the streets. I sat back and closed my eyes. "We should have stopped for a mocha."

The only reply I got was a low chuckle.

The motion of his smooth driving must have lulled me to sleep, because the next thing I knew we were parked in the circular driveway of a Spanish Mission style home.

Though *palace* may have been a more accurate description. This place made Madame's house look like a shack. It dwarfed the other houses surrounding it.

Rhys brushed my face with the back of his hand. "Awake, love?"

"Yeah." I shook off the goose bumps his touch caused and hopped out of the car. I inhaled the salty air as I listened to the soothing sound of ocean waves breaking against the shore. Nice. Surveying the yard, I wondered who lived here. Someone super rich. And connected, because I was pretty sure the sculpture on the lawn was an authentic Rodin.

Joining me, Rhys took my hand and led me up the steps to the front door.

Before I could ask him who lived here, he unlocked the door and motioned me inside.

My mouth fell open. "This is *your* place?"

He nodded. "I have a workout area out back."

Gawking as he tugged me down the hall, I noted the open space, warm lighting, and rich textures from the brief glimpses of the rooms we passed. My curiosity was piqued—you could tell so much about a person from their personal space. But Rhys was obviously on a mission, so I didn't get a chance to explore. Maybe another time.

Not that I'd have occasion to come back here. It wasn't a smart idea, in any case. Rhys appeared to be my kryptonite. The more distance I had from him, the better.

I glanced down at my hand curling around his, but I couldn't bring myself to let it go.

He strode purposefully through the lower level until we ended up in a bright, modern kitchen.

"Morning, boss." A tall, beefy man looked up from the sink with a smile. The frilly apron he wore was at complete odds with his Marine looks. His gaze widened when he caught sight of me, checking me out top to bottom. He darted a quick glance at Rhys before nodding politely at me. "Miss."

"Brian, this is Ms. Sansouci." Rhys placed a hand on my back. "Gabrielle, Brian is my majordomo."

Brian eyed the way Rhys touched me and his smile warmed. He reached for something next to him and held it out. "I thought your request was strange. This mocha must be for you, Ms. Sansouci."

Taking the proffered cup, I blinked at Brian. "A mocha? How—"

"I called while you were asleep," Rhys explained.

I beamed at my new best friend Brian. "You are a god among men."

He laughed, uninhibited and from the belly.

Rhys wrapped his arm around my waist and tugged me to him. In a mild voice that belied the irritation on his face, he said, "Don't flirt with the help, love."

"I can't help it. He's so manly." Conscious of the avid

way Brian watched us, I tried to extricate myself from Rhys's arm.

But he held tight, a spark of challenge in his eyes. "Manly, is he?"

"No sissy British accent." I smiled sweetly, surreptitiously elbowing him.

Brian laughed again. "I think you've met your match, boss."

Rhys looked into my eyes and replied, seriously, "I have." Before I could react, he turned back to his employee. "We'll be working out, Brian. Perhaps you can prepare a snack for us."

"Something chocolaty, please," I added with a hopeful smile.

"I like this woman." Brian grinned. "I'll set out a buffet in the parlor."

"Thank you." With a curt nod, Rhys guided me out of the kitchen.

"You have a parlor?" I asked as we walked down the hall to the back of the house.

"Several, in fact."

"How Jane Austen of you." I frowned. "I thought you were just visiting San Francisco."

"I am."

"But you own this house." I pursed my lips at a particularly expensive-looking vase we passed. "And keep it fully furnished."

"I like my creature comforts," he replied simply. "And I prefer my own space to staying in hotels."

It was on my tongue to ask him if he owned houses in every city he visited, but I got distracted when we stepped through an archway into a large solarium.

It took me a moment to realize this was the workout

room. There was a mat on the floor and a variety of weapons mounted to the wall: swords, knives, and an assortment of different sticks—eskrima sticks to staffs and even canes. He had bamboo weapons for practicing, as well as the real deal.

One sword in particular caught my eye—a sleek broadsword, hung separately from its scabbard. Thin silver designs decorated the dark hilt—flames, of course. Gravitating to it, I stood so close I could smell its metallic tang. My fingers itched to dance along the face of the gleaming blade, to feel the blood grooves, knowing it'd be warm and alive to the touch.

But I didn't, because I knew without a doubt this sword was Rhys's—his personal favorite—and you never touched a person's special weapons without permission.

"I don't know. Seems like you could wear this sword with just about any outfit." I turned to face him, pursing my lips as I pretended to size him up. "Maybe you don't know how to handle it."

He sauntered to me. "Are you questioning my ability?"

Knowing I was playing with fire but unable to help myself, I glanced at his crotch. "Do you have good form?"

He pulled me against him, so close his personal weapon pressed into my belly, right over my birthmark. "I believe I'm fairly assured of victory."

The mark tingled to life, and I had the urge to rub it against him. "Cocky, aren't you?"

His smile was positively wicked. Without a word, he released me and pulled his sweatshirt over his head.

He wore nothing but taut muscles and tanned skin underneath. I sought out his mark, right over his heart, a mirror of my own. Then my eyes followed the thin trail of hair that disappeared mysteriously under the waist of his pants.

Don't look down. I lifted my gaze and frowned at the scars on his torso, particularly the vicious-looking one on his left side, which I hadn't noticed the night he'd first shown me his mark. I nodded at it. "Looks like someone tried to cut out your heart. Former girlfriend?"

"Former business associate." He tossed the sweatshirt aside.

"Ah." I nodded. "And the rest of the scars?"

"Remnants of various scrapes."

"To do with your Guardianship?"

"Some," he said after a brief hesitation. He went onto the mat. "Ready?"

More than ready, just not for fighting. Not with Rhys, in any case. I knew I needed practice—with a real person and not my makeshift sparring dummy—but rolling around on the mat with him, his body up against mine, his breath against my skin . . . Fighting would be the last thing on my mind. "I'd rather discuss your scars."

Stretching his shoulders, he cocked an eyebrow. "Careful, love, or I'll think you care."

"Just curious." Toeing the edge of the mat, I cleared my throat. "I don't know if this is a good idea."

"You need to be able to defend yourself. I don't want last night happening again." His jaw tightened. "I won't see you hurt again."

"Last night I was just taken by surprise. It won't happen again."

He rushed at me, grabbing me around my arms and swinging me off my feet. Caught off guard, I froze for an indecisive moment.

Just as quickly he dropped me onto my feet, stepped back, and smirked at me with an infuriating superiority.

Hands on hips, I lifted my chin. "I never said I was ready."

"Unfortunately, love, an attacker on the street isn't going to wait for you to tell him you're ready." He circled around me. He set his weight, going into predator mode, something I sensed more than I saw. "While you don't have to walk around in a state of constant heightened awareness, you do need to train your reflexes to react instantly."

No kidding. "I—"

He attacked again, getting me from behind this time. I dropped my weight, reared my head back to hit his nose, and grabbed his groin—all at the same time.

Grunting, he set me down. "Again." And he came at me, startling in speed.

My weight and breath rose before impact, and we tumbled to the ground, Rhys rolling so he landed under me. But that lasted a second before he reversed our position so he was on top, my arms trapped at my sides.

Damn it.

Don't rush, Gabrielle, I heard Wu's voice in my head. *Rushing like a bull will only make the struggle harder. Slow down and wait for the right opportunity.*

I took a calming breath, relaxed my body, and opened my senses. Rhys let up on his hold, and I saw my opening. I punched the inside of his thigh with my knuckle to make him straighten his leg and while he was off balance rolled us over so I mounted him.

Before he could counter, I raised my fist and dropped it, stopping an inch from his nose. "I win."

His eyes narrowed. "Barely."

"Sore loser?" I asked with a sweet smile.

Something in his gaze shifted, and he went into wolf mode. Holding on to my hips, he lifted his pelvis. "I wouldn't call this losing, love."

His hard-on pressed into me, impressive and hot even with the layers of clothing between us. I couldn't help rocking on it, a sharp shock of pleasure zinging through my body.

His hand slipped down to my thigh, massaging there before applying the barest pressure. I didn't realize he was using my leg-straightening move against me until I was on my back with him cradled between my legs.

"You fight dirty." Hoping he'd take my breathiness as exertion from fighting, I wrapped my legs around his waist.

Pinning my arms next to my shoulders, he lowered his mouth and nibbled down my neck. "Ah, love, I haven't even begun to get dirty yet."

I arched my back, watching him work his way down. He hovered over my breasts, barely visible through my sweatshirt except for two sharp, protruding, eager points.

He took one between his teeth, biting with just enough pressure to make me gasp. I raised my arms until he held them stretched over my head and then bucked my hips hard. He sailed off, landing next to me, and I immediately rolled over onto him.

To my surprise, he chuckled. Pulling me down over him, he kissed me, warm and soft, and then patted my butt. "Up. Let's do this again."

We spent another hour with him coming at me with different attacks—from more grabbing to coming in with punches and even charging with knives. By the end of the hour, I was out of breath, hungry, and more turned on than I'd ever been. During the fight it was all business, but the transition moments in between fights, when our bodies pressed against each other and we had to untangle, were pure torture.

Which is why I finally called a halt to the session. I dropped onto the mat. "Enough. I need chocolate now."

He walked to a small refrigerator I hadn't seen and took out two water bottles. "You weren't bad today."

"Not bad?" I snorted, catching the one he threw me. "I was pretty awesome and you know it."

"Your technique is good, but that's not your problem."

"What's my problem?"

"Your mind." He frowned as he opened his. "You're holding yourself back."

"I didn't want to hurt you," I said, trying not to sound defensive.

"You wouldn't."

I narrowed my eyes. Arrogant bastard.

"You're struggling against the inevitable. Stop fighting it. Accept the situation and do what you need to do." He sat down next to me and took a quick swig of water. "Hesitating could prove to be deadly. Even if it's a second, that's one second your opponent has the upper hand on you. A good opponent will use that second to win." He tucked back a lock of my hair that had come loose from my elastic. "I don't want that to happen."

I stared into his eyes, mesmerized by the fire banked there. "Even if you're that opponent?"

His thumb brushed my lower lip. "I'm not the threat to you, Gabrielle."

"I wouldn't bet on that," I murmured as his mouth closed on mine.

No tender lead-in, no gentle buildup. The moment

our lips touched we ignited. I didn't even try to resist—I speared my fingers into his hair and sat on his lap, facing him, to get closer.

He groaned, his hands snaking under my top. One kneaded my back, holding me firmly. The other sneaked up my side to cup my breast.

I rubbed myself into his hand and moaned. When his fingers pinched my nipple, I moaned again, letting my head loll back.

"You taste perfect," he whispered, nuzzling my neck.

"I taste like sweat."

"You taste like you." He playfully nipped the sensitive skin below my ear. "Tart."

"Hey." I yanked his hair—hard—to arch his head back.

He laughed, a husky sound I felt in my belly. His hands soothed me, but the look in his eyes was anything but.

I took advantage of his exposed neck to do a little exploring of my own. Starting at the hollow at the base, I slowly nibbled my way up to the edge of his jaw.

His cock pulsed, and I rolled my hips to tease him. But it backfired when his hand lowered to my butt and gripped it to encourage my surging motion.

Dropping my head to his shoulder, I groaned, loud and long, as the pressure hit just that right spot. My entire body felt lit and ready to explode. Needing to explode. I wrapped my legs around his body and ground in earnest.

Someone cleared his throat. Dazed, I looked up to find Brian in the doorway, watching with unconcealed interest. "Brunch is laid out in the parlor, boss."

"Out," Rhys commanded.

With a grin, Brian saluted me and retreated.

I rocked myself against him. "We shouldn't be doing this."

"Then stop." His mouth bruised mine, his kiss devouring. Demanding.

I jerked my head away, panting. "I don't trust you."

His eyes glittered with passion and something I couldn't identify. "Then why are you here?"

Excellent question. Not knowing how to answer it, I sucked his lower lip.

He returned the favor, briefly, and then asked, "Is it really me you don't trust, or yourself?"

Both, but I wasn't prepared to give him that much honesty.

He pulled me tight against him. Then, lifting me off him, he set me on the mat and leaned back on his hands. "I won't have your regrets. If you want this, you'll have to take it."

God help me, I wanted it. I wanted him. Anyone else and I could have stopped and taken care of myself later, but I knew my own touch wouldn't be enough. Rhys did more to me even with all the clothes between us than I'd ever felt before.

Just this once. We weren't naked—it wasn't like we were having sex. Not really. I could forgive myself this one lapse.

He must have read the decision on my face, because fire leapt into his eyes. He stayed where he was, letting me come to him. The only indication of his feelings was the tautness of his jaw.

I climbed back onto him, straddling his lap and rubbing myself on his cock. It felt so good I let my head relax to one side, watching him from under my lashes. Because it didn't seem like he was going to touch me, I took the initiative. Sliding a hand under my top, I squeezed my nipple, careful to leave it covered.

Teasing him excited me. I rocked myself on him faster, closing my eyes. Moaning, I felt the first tremors of an orgasm building.

"Not without me." Rhys tipped me back onto the mat, covering my body with his, thrusting his hips so the hard ridge of his erection hit me right where I needed it.

I opened my eyes to see his face above mine, intense and focused, all on me.

He lowered his head and licked my lip. "Come."

His fiery energy engulfed me and I cried out, totally consumed. With one last push against me, he groaned, head thrown back as he came, too.

He collapsed on top of me. I tried not to notice how comforting the weight of him was, or how his heartbeat complemented mine. Not to mention how much I wanted to do it all over again, minus the clothes.

Not able to take the silence, I cleared my throat and said, "When are you going to help me unlock my safe placc?"

He paused a beat before saying, "I won't help you unlock your powers until I'm certain you won't harm yourself with them."

"What the hell?" I pushed at him to create some breathing room. "That's what today was about—working off the debt toward helping me regain *tŭ ch'i.*"

"Arguing with me won't change my mind. Your power is almost abnormally strong. I'm afraid you'll hurt yourself." He tenderly brushed the side of my face. "You can't fault me for being concerned about your welfare."

Not knowing how to combat this tactic, I scowled. "I

should go. I need to paint, and you probably have meetings or whatever important people like you do."

Rhys lifted his head and searched my face. He dropped the lightest kiss on my lips before rolling off me. "You can't hide from me, Gabrielle. I'll always find you."

Scary thing was I believed him.

Chapter Thirty

*M*y episode with Rhys haunted my thoughts—and my body—all week.

Except it also inspired me. By Friday, I had some finishing touches to make to each canvas, but I had four canvases in my new series. The final one eluded me, but with my renewed surge of creativity, I knew it'd come. I just needed some rest.

But first I had to tell Madame that I'd jumped subjects. She wasn't going to be happy.

After a long shower, I got dressed and called a cab. When it arrived, I carefully arranged the canvases so the still-wet paint wouldn't smear and gave the driver the address. Ten minutes later, the cabbie pulled in front of Madame's house and helped me out with the paintings.

Propped against the flowerpot next to Madame's front door, they looked like findings in a garage sale. But Van Goghs had been unearthed in garage sales, so I took a deep breath and opened the door. "Madame?"

"J'arrive, Gabrielle. Je suis dans la cuisine."

"No," I said quickly. "I'll come to you."

I hefted a painting in each hand and propped them against the furniture in the living room. I made one more trip before I locked the door and joined Madame in the kitchen.

She looked up with a smile that turned into a concerned frown. "*Tu as l'air malade, Gabrielle.*"

"Gee, thanks." I bent to kiss her hello. "That's what every woman likes to hear when greeted, that she looks sick."

"I cannot help it. *Tu as des bleus sous les yeux.*" She brushed papery fingertips under my eyes.

Guess my attempt to camouflage the dark circles didn't work. "I was up late working."

"*Ah, oui?*" She perked up.

I grinned. "So I can look sick as long as it's for a good cause."

"*Ne blague pas, Gabrielle.* Do you have another painting? *La directrice,* she is anxious, *tu sais?*"

"Yeah, I know. And, yeah, I finished a painting. Do you want some coffee?" I took the kettle from the stove and filled it with water.

"Why do I feel as though you are not saying something to me?"

"I have no idea," I lied.

She carefully lowered herself onto a chair. "*Rhys était très impressionné.*"

"Rhys?" I whirled around. "You've talked to him? Recently?"

"*Mais oui, bien sûr.* He is a friend, *non?*"

No, I wasn't sure he was. Crossing my arms, I leaned against the counter and swore to myself that I wouldn't ask her what he said about me.

She smiled cunningly. "The water boils, Gabrielle."

"Oh. Right."

"He tells me he saw your painting."

I sloshed some hot water, barely missing my hand. "Shit."

Madame waved in the direction of a dishtowel. "He says it is very good, your painting. *Remarquable, il a dit.*"

An eager pleasure caught in my chest. Horror followed quickly behind it, that I could be so affected by his opinion. "What else does he say?" I asked suspiciously.

She shrugged expressively. "Rhys, he is a man of few words."

"No kidding," I muttered as I moved the coffee service to the table.

"When will I see the painting?"

"Soon."

"We will need to show *la directrice* also," Madame said as she took the cup I offered her. "She will be much reassured when she sees it, *n'est-ce pas?*"

I squirmed, nearly knocking over the sugar bowl.

"What is wrong, Gabrielle?" She frowned. "You are not usually so—how does one say *maladroit* in English?"

"Clumsy."

"Yes." She eyed me closely. "You are certain you are not sick? Have you eaten?"

"No, but that's not it. I have something to tell you." I looked into her wise gaze and felt more nervous than I'd ever felt in my life—even more than the first time I dared to tell Wu I was thinking of being an artist instead of a Guardian.

"You look like you face the guillotine, Gabrielle. *Dis-moi.* I will not be upset." She pursed her lips. "Will I?"

"Well—" I cleared my throat. "Maybe."

Her eyes narrowed.

"I'm reconsidering the paintings I owe the gallery."

Madame was silent for several long seconds before she said, "What does this mean, reconsider?"

"It means I haven't been working on the paintings for the rest of the series I have to complete." When she didn't explode, I quickly went on. "I started a new series."

The silence was painful.

"That's what Rhys saw, one of the new paintings." I leaned across the table. "Madame, I think the new series is the best thing I've ever painted."

She nodded slowly. "I see. But the gallery contracted the other series."

"Yeah." I pursed my lips. "Do you think they'll be upset if I turn in something different?"

She shrugged in her expressive, Gallic way. "*Je ne sais pas. C'est possible.*"

My heart sank.

"Unless we give assurances to them that the new paintings are better."

Hope flared in my chest. "Can we give them assurances?"

She shrugged again. "Anything is possible, *non?*"

I deflated with relief. "*Merci, Madame.*"

"I have done nothing yet," she said as she poured two cups of coffee.

"You didn't say I completely screwed this up, which is enough for me." I warmed my hands on the cup she pushed toward me.

"Of course, one will need to see them."

"I brought them with me."

She pushed herself out of the chair. "Then we go see them, *non?*"

"Now?" But she was already tottering out of the kitchen. Pressing a fist to my queasy stomach, I got up and followed her into the living room. Thank God I hadn't had anything to eat—I would have hated to hurl on one of her expensive rugs.

The light had changed in the half hour I'd been there. I always forgot how early the sun set in the winter. But the remaining light brought out the mystery of the paintings in a way I couldn't have staged.

Hands shoved in my pockets, I stared at Madame, who stood in front of the first painting—the one Rhys had called remarkable. Would she recognize his eyes? How could she not? Why didn't she say something? Maybe she hated it. Maybe she was wondering how she was going to salvage her reputation from this debacle.

Not able to take it any longer, I moved to the last one I'd painted. I stood in front of it and looked at it impassively.

It was frickin' spectacular.

I knew it without a doubt. It held the same element of darkness as the other paintings. The same danger, but seductive. It looked like a series of undulations in shades of black and gray and hints of deep scarlet, but if you looked closely you could make out two bodies intertwined. Sexy—definitely sexy.

Madame shifted toward me. "*Laisse-moi voir.*"

I moved over so she could stand in front of it to take a look. I forced myself to exhale. The urge to ask her if she liked it, if it was as good as I thought, if she thought the gallery would go for it, was overwhelming, so I bit my lip to keep quiet.

I thought I was going to explode when she finally nodded. *"Bon. Je les amenerai au gallerie."*

I practically wilted in relief. For Madame, that was as good as saying they were fantastic. "Do you think Chloe will like them?"

She shrugged. "We shall see."

"Okay." I nodded. I could deal with that. With Madame in my corner, I knew my chances were excellent. "Well, I'll just get out of your way now."

She waved a hand dismissively. "As your prefer, *mon chou,* but you do not need to go. It is always a pleasure to have you here."

"I need to get something to eat. I'm suddenly ravenous." I bent down and hugged her tight. *"Merci, Madame.* For everything."

She clung to me for a moment before she patted my shoulder and disengaged. "You did well, Gabrielle."

I grinned. "Didn't I?"

She snorted. "You are too modest. Now go and eat, and perhaps have some fun. You have worked hard."

"I had fun this afternoon with you," I said as I slipped into my coat.

"Bof." She waved her hand. "You must do something more than have coffee with an old woman."

I grinned. "Are you giving me permission to rage with my peeps?"

She rolled her eyes. "So full of anger, this generation. In my day we did not rage, as you say."

"What did you do?"

Her eyes twinkled wickedly, and for a moment she looked as stunning as I imagined she did when she was younger. "Use your imagination, *mon chou.* Or perhaps call Rhys and use his."

My cheeks went up in flames.

She chuckled. "Is his imagination so very good, then?"

"Gotta go." I kissed her again and hurried out. "Don't forget to lock up after me."

I hopped the 22, thinking about what she'd said. Have fun. Problem was I wasn't sure I had anyone to have fun with. At one time, the logical choice would have been Jesse. He would have come over with dessert and a pocket full of condoms for a whole night of fun.

That seemed a long time ago.

Rhys popped into my head, and I wondered what his idea of fun was. I'd bet my favorite red sable brush that it involved dark chocolaty dessert and a box of condoms.

Shiver. Best not to go there.

Carrie had suggested hanging out—that would be fun. I chewed on my lower lip. Plus . . . she was normal.

God, I needed some normalcy.

Before I could talk myself out of it, I pulled out my cell phone and called. Not that she'd answer. For all I knew she'd be at work. Or the library.

But she answered on the second ring. "Don't tell me Vivian didn't show up again."

I grinned. "I'm not at work, so I don't know. But I wouldn't be surprised."

She laughed.

"I finished the bulk of the paintings due to the gallery and wanted to get out and, um, so, I was wondering what you're up to?" I said clumsily.

"Studying." She sighed. "It's all I ever do anymore."

"Oh." I frowned, surprised at how disappointed I felt. "Well—"

"But I could use a break, and we should totally celebrate. I'd love it if you came over."

"Okay," I said before she could change her mind. "Tell me where you live."

She lived on O'Farrell close to Polk, so I got off at Mission and transferred to the 49, which would get me close enough to walk to her studio. I was shocked that she lived in the Tenderloin—it made the Mission look as safe as Noe Valley. She didn't seem tough enough to live someplace where she had to dodge crackheads and prostitutes. The rent was probably all she could afford as a student.

Carrie buzzed me into her building, and I ran up the three flights of stairs to her studio, holding my breath so I wouldn't breathe in the stale smell of urine.

She was waiting for me in her doorway, her bright smile a contrast to the dingy hallway. "Gabe, I'm so happy you called. Come in before someone propositions you."

Grinning, I slipped out of my jacket as I entered. "I could always use the extra cash."

"This is the Tenderloin. You'd be lucky if you were offered enough to cover a latte." She closed the door and triple locked it. "I don't have champagne, which is what we should really have, but I do have tea."

"Tea is great."

"Make yourself at home, such as it is," she said, waving to the small space. Her kitchenette was in the corner, and she already had a teapot on a plate warmer. "I hope you like Earl Grey. It's all I had. Congratulations on finishing your paintings! I can't wait to see them."

"I still have one more to complete."

"But you must be so relieved that you're going to make the deadline. One day I'll be able to say I knew you back when."

Smiling, I wandered around the room. Although her studio was tiny—even smaller than my place—it had a cozy feel. Clean and without clutter (except for a couple textbooks and some paper on the crate next to the futon), but warm thanks to the splashes of color she had.

"What's the verdict?" She flashed a dry smile as she pulled out two mugs. "Be honest. I can take it."

"Actually, it feels good here." I plopped onto her futon.

"Astonishing considering how many needles you had to step over on the way here, huh?"

"That thought had crossed my mind."

"Now you see why I want you to teach me self-defense." She brought out the two mugs and handed one over before sitting next to me. "So what do you say?"

I frowned. "To what?"

"To teaching me self-defense. Remember? I've only been asking you forever. Like that night you almost decked me."

"Oh." Wince. "I'm sorry about that."

She waved off my apology. "No worries. I thought it was cool how you just instinctively went for the kill. I want to do that."

Wrinkling my nose, I curled into the corner of the futon. "Trust me, it's not that cool."

"Yeah, it is." She nodded enthusiastically. "It'd be so great to know that I could take care of myself no matter what. My mom would be less freaked out all the time, too. It ain't like Iowa here, you know?"

"Is that where you're from?"

"Born and bred," she said proudly. "I came here after I got accepted to Berkeley for my master's. I liked it here so I thought I'd stay for my PhD, too. Besides, not much demand in Iowa for people with doctorates in Chinese history."

I gaped at her long enough that she asked, "Are you okay?"

Shaking my head, I said, "I didn't know you studied Chinese history."

"Yeah. East Asian history, though I specialize in China's Imperial era. Love it. I think I was a Chinese princess in another life." She winked at me. "I probably kicked some major kung fu ass, too. I think it's my destiny to learn to fight."

I nodded, but I was too weirded out to say anything. Coincidence that she was into Chinese? Hard to believe. What were the chances she knew about the scroll? Wu would have questioned her motives in befriending me.

Did she have ulterior motives? I studied her. I didn't think so. She was just too open—too trusting. And my gut didn't tell me there was anything wrong.

Fortunately, she didn't notice my internal debate. "So what do you think? Am I *grasshopper* material? I swear I'll roam the earth to avenge your death if you teach me."

I shook my head. "You don't know what you're asking."

"I do." She nodded earnestly.

"I don't know that I'm the right teacher." I pictured myself in a *gi* with my arms crossed and a scowl on my face as I told my students what to do. The image was too much like a feminine version of Wu for my comfort. Shudder.

"I think you'd rock as a teacher. How long have you been studying?"

"Too long," I said morosely.

"How long?"

"Since I could walk."

"Wow." Her eyes widened.

"But I haven't really practiced in a long time." Barring the short sessions with my duct-taped sparring partner and the one time with Rhys.

"And you still automatically wanted to kick butt." She shook her head. "You don't know how cool that is. All I know how to do is calligraphy. And I mix a mean sex on the beach. So what got you started in martial arts?"

"My dad. Do you go back to Iowa very often?"

"I think you should teach."

I rolled my eyes. "You're like a blond pit bull. Let go of the bone already."

She grinned. "I think you seriously underestimate the hero worship I've got going on here. I've always wanted to learn some sort of martial art."

Gripping the mug, I swallowed thickly. I knew she wouldn't drop it, and though I didn't want to tell her—or anyone for that matter—I couldn't let her go on thinking I was something I wasn't. "If you really knew me, you'd know I'm not worthy of any type of hero worship. And fighting isn't fun. It's hard and painful and scarring."

She shrugged. "I can take a couple scars."

"Emotionally scarring." I took a sip of tea to steady myself.

"How?" she asked relentlessly.

"There are"—I paused to find the right word—"consequences to having knowledge like this. There's responsibility."

"Life is full of responsibility," she replied philosophically.

"Not like this." Not when your actions dictated whether or not someone continued to live. "I wouldn't want to pass that curse on to anyone."

She stared at me, a frown furrowing her forehead. Then she shook her head with conviction. "From the first day I met you at the bar, I knew you had a core of steel. For you, it's not a curse. It's just who you are. And you're good at it. You need to stop seeing it as an albatross around your neck and see it as what it really is."

"What is it?"

"The thing that makes you unique and powerful. What makes you *you*."

My birthmark tingled, and a shiver ran up my spine. It was like she was talking about the Guardianship. In my head, I heard Wu's voice say, *The first step, Gabrielle, is acceptance.*

If I didn't know better, I would have suspected her of being a plant. If Wu were going to trust anyone, a strawberry blonde from the Midwest would be it. Only he didn't trust anyone, and he'd never recruit help—no matter how dire the situation.

As I stared into Carrie's big, guileless eyes, I knew she was right. I had to buck up and decide to do this. Well. Because so far I'd approached the whole thing in a half-assed manner that not only almost caused me to go insane but got me indebted to a dubious man. Oh—and did I mention that the scroll I was supposed to be safeguarding was still missing?

But decide to do something I'd spent so many years resenting? I didn't know.

Carrie gazed at me, waiting for my response. I nodded. "I see what you're saying."

"I know." She smiled at my frown. "It's not like you're stupid."

Sometimes that was debatable.

"And about teaching me some moves?" She waved her hands around in a poor imitation of *The Matrix*.

"Um, can I think about it?" I just wasn't ready to become Wu yet.

"Of course." She grinned brightly. "That's all I can ask for. I do want to tell you I'd be the ideal student. You tell me to wax off and I won't question you."

Laughing, I untangled my legs and stood up. "Good to know."

She stood and followed me to the kitchenette. "I'm so happy you thought to call and stop by. Let's do this again, okay? I enjoyed myself."

"I did, too," I said, shocked that I actually meant it. I set the mug by the shallow sink and retrieved my jacket.

Carrie gave me a quick hug by the door. "Be safe."

Zipping up my coat, I headed to the Muni stop on Van Ness to catch the 49 back to the Mission. But a hunger pang made me get off at Market Street, and I walked to It's Tops for fries and a Coke. I splurged on a piece of chocolate cake, which I got to take away.

Instead of taking Muni or a cab, I walked home. I should have been too tired—or too serene from my little trip into the normal world of having a friend—but I felt wired and jittery. Like something loomed in the foreground, waiting to pounce on me.

"I feel a disturbance in the Force," I said to myself in an effort to lighten the feeling.

I didn't feel comforted when my birthmark pricked.

Somehow, however, I made it home without incident. I was congratulating myself as I ascended my porch steps when a shadow by my front door moved. I tensed for a moment, but I instinctively knew who it was. It was in the way my body came to life.

"Hello, love," Rhys said, leaning against the door.

Wary, I stopped just out of his reach. "Why are you here?"

Without a word he pulled me to him and lifted my chin to meet his gaze. His other hand slipped under my clothes, hot and insistent on my back.

His mouth hovered a breath away from mine, and I melted in anticipation. Knowing his kiss would be explosive, I grabbed his lapels to brace myself and squirmed closer. If only there were fewer clothes between us. A lot fewer clothes.

But then he lifted his head and studied me, his thoughts inscrutable.

I asked the obvious. "Why did you stop?"

"Because I wanted to leave you wanting more." He retracted his hand from my back, a slow caress that I felt all through my body, and stepped around me.

"More? I didn't get any." I gawked in disbelief as he headed down the porch steps. "That's it? You're leaving?"

His smile was enigmatic as he walked toward his car, which I now noticed parked down the block.

Standing there, I watched him drive off. If I weren't careful, he'd slowly steal my heart, piece by piece.

Scary thing was, I was afraid he'd made pretty good headway already.

Chapter Thirty-one

*C*ursing Rhys, I let the evening air cool my overheated body. He'd succeeded in leaving me wanting more—a lot more.

"Bastard," I muttered as I went inside my shack. At least I had cake. If you couldn't have sex, chocolate was the next-best thing.

I dropped my jacket on the floor and headed to the kitchen to get a fork. I was almost through the archway when I realized something was wrong. Frowning, I turned around.

Wu sat on the futon, shaking his head. "Gabrielle, you have to get your head out of the clouds and into the present."

Actually, he was hovering more than sitting, but I found it hard to care about semantics at the moment. "Where did you come from? Are you okay?"

He ignored me and continued with his ranting. "I could have been a hired assassin waiting to kill you. You could have been dead by now."

"How did you get back?" I tried again. "I thought you went hand in hand with the scroll."

"At least you were listening to that much." He gestured next to him on the futon.

The scroll.

It looked like a tattered piece of parchment, benign and unimpressive, and I'd never felt so relieved to see anything in my life. I set the cake on my dresser and hurried to the futon, stopping abruptly as I reached for the scroll. I hadn't managed to unlock *tŭ ch'i* yet—if I touched it, would it come rushing back? I wanted to be prepared. "Tell me something. How come my powers didn't decrease while the scroll was, um, gone?"

"Losing the scroll only magnifies *tŭ ch'i* so you're more able to retrieve it."

No wonder. I'd been right. "How do you know?"

"Your inattentiveness will have to stop," he said as if I hadn't asked a question. "No one has ever lost the scroll in the history of our family. *No one.*"

And I was a disappointment—I could read between his lines. I couldn't disagree with him this time. Not only did I lose the scroll, but I didn't do anything to get it back—it returned on its own.

I frowned. Actually, since it couldn't walk, someone had to have returned it. Only one person came to mind— the same person who accosted me on my doorstep and kissed me senseless.

Rhys.

Ignoring the pain constricting my chest, I turned to Wu to verify what I suspected. "Where have you been?"

"You're too trusting." He pointed a transparent finger at me. "I knew you should have kept away from that man, but—"

"What man?" I asked hoarsely, needing to hear it.

"The one you brought home that night. The hoodlum."

The hoodlum I brought home? Rhys would never be mistaken for a hoodlum, and I hadn't brought him home until after Wu and the scroll were already gone. That meant— "Jesse?"

Wu shrugged. "Is that his name?"

"It's not possible." I shook my head, gaping. "I never told Jesse about the scroll."

"He knew." Wu's brows drew together. "I just don't understand why he brought it back."

"I don't understand any of this." Even as I said it, I remembered that night I thought I was being followed and found out it was only Jesse. Had he actually been following me? I frowned. But we'd known each other for a couple years—way before I got the scroll. And I'd never mentioned it—*that* I was certain of.

With the exception of the night I asked him what he'd do if he inherited an heirloom he didn't really want.

My heart clenched.

"No. I can't believe that." There had to be some kind of explanation, like maybe he found it, realized it was mine, and simply returned it. I scooped my jacket off the floor as I headed for the door. "I'm going to find out what's going on."

"Wait a minute."

I looked over my shoulder as I shrugged on my coat.

"You can't just leave the scroll lying here."

Rolling my eyes, I strode to the futon. I hesitated for a split second before I grabbed it. I held my breath, hoping nothing happened while also wishing that the contact would unlock my safe place. But all I felt was *tŭ ch'i* tapping on the trap door, as if it were testing it to find a way out. My mental safe held strong.

With mixed feelings, I took the scrap of paper and stuck it back in the fridge.

"Yes, that is ever so much better." Sarcasm dripped from his every word.

I didn't bother to reply. I had to find Jesse to get some answers. I fished my cell out of my pocket and tried calling him, but he didn't answer. I'd have to go to his flat. I paused halfway out the door and then turned around.

"What are you doing?" Wu asked as I came back in.

"Just in case." I stuck my hand under the futon mattress and pulled out the knife I'd taken from the thug. I slipped it into my coat, not wanting to analyze why I felt I might need it. "Try not to get yourself ghost-napped again," I said on my way out.

"Gabrielle—"

I shut the door on him and jogged down the porch steps. Too impatient to wait for a bus, I grabbed a cab and told the driver to take me South of Market to Folsom and Tenth.

During the day, SoMa was full of warehouse-based businesses. At night, it was where everyone flocked to go dancing in one of the many clubs. Jesse lived right in the middle of it all, not because he was into clubbing but because his garage was just a few blocks away.

The cabbie dropped me off right in front of the building. The interior-decorating store under Jesse's flat was closed and completely dark. No lights on in Jesse's apartment, either.

Wrapping my coat around me tighter, I went to the call box next to the gated stairs and pushed the buzzer. After waiting a minute, I tried it a couple more times, but I instinctively knew he was already gone.

"Damn." I looked up. I looked around. No one. So I grabbed the bars on the gate and hefted myself up and over. I righted my clothes and jogged up the stairs to his front door.

It was closed, and I stood before it wondering how to get in. I didn't have lock-picking skills. Frowning, I tried the doorknob. It twisted and the door swung open.

"Hmm." I stared at it for a long moment. In the movies, when a door was left unlocked it meant that either there was a dead body on the other side or a killer waiting. Maybe I needed to rethink this.

"No, I need to find Jesse." On guard, I slipped in the door, silent and stealthy. Back to the wall, I pulled the knife from my jacket and held it in front of me as I did a quick search of the apartment.

No one waited to jump me, and Jesse's corpse wasn't bleeding out on the floor. Thank God. I returned the knife to my pocket and looked around. I didn't find anything, but I did notice some of Jesse's things were missing. He'd actually left.

Frown. When he'd told me he was leaving, I (egocentrically) thought it was because he needed to be away from me. Now I wondered if it wasn't because of the scroll.

Where would he go? I strode into the kitchen, where his phone was. No notes, no pad of paper I could color with pencil lead to detect anything. I hit redial to see if that'd give me a clue, but I just got Big Nate's Barbeque.

"Hell." I dropped the phone back in the cradle, slipped back out the same way I came in, and considered my options as I walked away.

His garage wasn't far from here—it couldn't hurt to check it out. I turned around and hoofed it up Folsom.

The garage was in the center of the block, and from the corner it looked deserted, as well. Damn it. But then I noticed a faint light in one on the far windows—I think it was the office. Hope surged and I rushed forward.

Sure enough, the office light was on. The door was unlocked, too. I let myself in quietly, closing the door behind me, and tiptoed in.

Jesse stood in front of his filing cabinet, rifling through folders. The paper shredder was working furiously next to him.

I stepped into the room. "Hey."

He whirled around, a gun instantly in his hand and pointed at me.

"What the hell?" I exclaimed, recoiling. I hated guns. Guns killed. Knives could kill, too, but not without intent. Guns went off accidentally all the time.

"Shit, Gabe." He slipped the gun into his waistband and returned to his hurried shredding. "You shouldn't be here."

No kidding. I goggled at the bulge in his jeans—a different, more lethal bulge than I'd ever seen on him. Then I focused on what he was doing. "You're really leaving. For good, aren't you?"

He smiled without humor. "Does it matter?"

"Yes."

"Does it?" His eyes searched mine as he closed the file drawer. "Really?"

I knew he was remembering Rhys's hand up my shirt with me begging for it. I tipped my chin up defiantly—I would not feel guilty about that. It wasn't like I had the market cornered on betrayal. "Why did you take the scroll?"

"Because he was hired to take it," someone said from behind me.

I whirled around, weight set and ready to pounce.

Paul stepped into the office, a grim smile twisting his face and a big black gun pointed right at my chest.

Chapter Thirty-two

*P*aul?" I blinked, gaping.

He nodded. "I'm sorry, Gabby."

"Are you here to help me?"

"That's one way to look at it." He held the gun steadily trained on me.

"I don't understand." I *hated* guns. I glanced at the cold steel and then back up to his face. "Why don't you put the gun down? This is all a misunderstanding."

"There's only one misunderstanding here." He shifted the gun to point at Jesse. "We had a deal."

"What kind of deal?" I asked, directing the question to both of them. "Is Jesse servicing a car for you or something?"

Paul nodded. "Or something."

Jesse's expression hardened. "Just let her go and we'll deal."

"Deal's off." He walked into the office, his hand steady. "You were supposed to deliver the scroll this afternoon."

The scroll.

"*You* stole the scroll for *Paul?*" I gaped briefly at Jesse before focusing on my brother. In a pained whisper, I asked, "So it was all a lie? The loving-brother stuff? Wanting to help me? Wanting to protect me? You didn't mean any of it?"

"I meant all of it," he said firmly. "I was so happy to find you again. You may have been a pest growing up, but you were my *sister*. I missed you."

"Then why this?" I waved between us.

He gazed at me, almost sadly. "You wouldn't give me the scroll."

"And you want it bad enough to pull a gun on me?"

"I tried, Gabby. I tried everything I could think of to get you to hand over the scroll. You never should have been marked. You didn't even want it." He shook his head like that didn't compute. "But I wanted it. I was the oldest: the mark should have been passed on to me."

My hurt made me bitchy. "But it wasn't, was it?"

"*It should have been.*" His face darkened, and his hand with the gun shook.

Did I mention how much I hated guns?

"But the mark is inconsequential. When I hired Byrnes to tail you the past couple years—"

"The whole time?" I looked at the back of Jesse's head and stepped back, wishing I could see his eyes. My head reeled, and I had to fight to breathe. I couldn't decide which hurt more—Paul or Jesse's betrayal—but combined, they felt devastating.

Paul frowned at the two of us. Then his face twisted into a mask of anger. "Did you fuck my sister? That wasn't part of your instructions." He turned to me. "I didn't ask him to touch you. I just wanted him in place in case you got the scroll before I did."

"Jeez, that makes me feel better." Then I frowned. "Before you did? When were you ever supposed to get the scroll?"

"When Dad amended his will." His shoulders sagged, as if misery weighed him down. "Chivo couldn't do anything right. He was only supposed to rough Dad up, not kill him before I convinced him to change his will."

My stomach twisted. For a moment I thought I was going to throw up, but I got myself under control. "You killed Wu."

"*I* didn't." The gun wavered in his hand, and his eyes filled with sorrow. "It shouldn't have happened. I only wanted Dad to recognize that I was the best choice. It was always about you."

He was right. Our childhood was littered with examples of Wu ignoring Paul's accomplishments.

"Dad didn't know I existed. It's not right for the firstborn to grow up in the shadow of his sister. *It's not right.*"

It wasn't, but it didn't justify any of this. "Paul—"

"Do you remember my high school graduation?" His voice wavered with emotion. "I was valedictorian, and I'd spent a week practicing my speech, 'My Father, My Greatest Hero.' I was going to surprise Dad at the ceremony."

"But—"

"But he didn't even show up," Paul yelled. "He was too busy training his precious marked warrior. He always ignored me because I was missing what's basically a flaw."

Jesse stepped forward. "Paul—"

"*I'm not finished.*" He aimed the gun with sudden steadiness at Jesse's heart, but his attention stayed focused on me. "Remember the old *Batman* episodes we used to watch, Gabby? Every bad guy got his big info dump at the end. You can't deny me my moment."

Not sure what to say or do, I gaped at him in shock.

"I said all those things to you at Mom's funeral out of guilt and hurt, but it worked out in the end. You left. I thought for sure Dad would start noticing me. That he'd see I was the better choice to carry on the Guardianship. But no, I wasn't *enough*."

He began to pace, muttering almost like he was talking to himself. "I graduated summa cum laude. I started my own business. I have money, power, and the respect of the most successful men in the country. But my own father still wouldn't respect me." He shook his head. "And like an idiot, I tried and tried to get him to accept me. It was finally working, but I got impatient and sent Chivo to speed things up. He was only supposed to rough Dad up."

Tears flowed down Paul's cheeks. I gulped thickly, scared, horrified, and speechless

Without warning, his gaze flew to mine. The gleam in his eyes chilled my blood and gave me goose bumps. "As if that fuckup wasn't bad enough, he couldn't even retrieve the scroll from you."

Wait a minute. "He didn't take the scroll? Then who—"

"I did," Jesse said so only I heard him.

My mouth fell open.

But before I found my tongue, Paul hissed. "That was Chivo's last mistake."

He'd killed the thug, too. Oh, God. "What happened to you?" I whispered.

His face became hard. "You happened to me. Wu *knew* I'd be a better Guardian, but still he picked you."

"He didn't pick me. I was marked."

His laugh chilled me. "Even the universe picked you."

"Paul—"

"This is your fault, Gabby," he said coolly. "If you had just accepted my help, everyone would be happy. You'd be able to paint in peace, I'd have my place in our family, and we'd still be close." He held the gun steady, pointing it at my head. "But you fucked it all up."

Jesse pushed me behind him. "I still have the scroll, and I'm willing to deal."

I blinked. No, he didn't.

Paul didn't look like he believed him, either. "Where is it?"

He jerked his chin forward. "In the garage."

"Get it."

Jesse shook his head. "Let Gabe go, and then I'll give it to you."

Paul barked a laugh. "What kind of fool do you take me for?"

Nodding, I murmured, "Yeah, I almost snorted at that, too."

Jesse flashed me an exasperated look. "Whose side are you on, anyway?"

"Any side that doesn't point a gun at me." I raised my voice. "How about we all go get the scroll?"

The men paused. I could feel Jesse's disapproval at my suggestion, but frankly he had no choice. Paul wasn't going to let me go—not after confessing to one murder and being accessory to another. Our best chance of survival was to get into the garage, where there was more cover and potential for more distractions.

Paul waved the gun. "Fine. Go. And don't try anything. I won't hesitate to shoot you in the back."

"That's shocking," I muttered.

Jesse pinched my waist and then pushed me in front of him.

His protectiveness made me sad, which in turn pissed me off. "A little late for the chivalrous impulses, don't you think?"

"No."

"Shut up," Paul commanded from behind us.

"Think about this, Paul," I said loudly as Jesse guided me to the other side of a table that had all sorts of tools on it. I saw a large metal cabinet and knew instinctively that was our goal. "You don't have to do this. Let it all go, and we'll call it even. We can all go on with our lives."

"It's not that easy, Gabby." The despair in his voice pained me. "I need it. I need to prove I'm worthy."

"If this is about Wu—"

"It's about everything," he interrupted. "Wu, Mom—"

"Mom?" Something in his voice made me freeze. I turned around and stepped out from behind Jesse. The illumination from the office cast shadows across the sharp plains of Paul's face, making him look sinister. "What do you mean?"

"Didn't you ever wonder why Mom rushed out to where you and Dad were practicing that day?" He shook his head mournfully. "You were so quick to take the blame it never occurred to you that maybe you weren't the only one at fault."

My breath choked me. I felt Jesse's hand on my back,

but I shrugged away from it and took a step toward my brother. "What are you saying?"

"I told Mom you were badly hurt." All the emotion fell away from his face, and his voice became wooden. "I thought it'd distract you into making a mistake so Dad would see how unfit you were. I didn't mean for her to rush out like that. I didn't mean for her to die." His eyes pleaded with me. "I'm sorry."

"*You bastard,*" I shrieked. I leapt forward and would have attacked him if Jesse hadn't grabbed the back of my jacket and jerked me behind the metal cabinet. Out of the corner of my eye, I saw him draw the gun from his waistband as he dived after me.

I felt the bullet strike the cabinet right before I heard the loud crack of gunfire. Jesse leaned to one side and fired off a few shots at Paul.

Head in my hands, I closed my eyes and saw it all over again—Mom standing in front of me, shock widening her eyes as *tǔ ch'i* hit her. I saw her collapsing, and then I was kneeling next to her. She gasped like a fish out of water, and I lifted her head, trying to help her. She stared at me, only this time I recognized the expression in her eyes to be relief, not recrimination or accusation. Relief that I was okay.

A willing sacrifice to keep me safe.

A senseless death because of my brother's jealousy.

The bastard.

Withdrawing the knife from my pocket, I shifted to my knees and scooted to the other side. As I was about to pounce around the corner, Jesse grabbed my jacket again and yanked me backward.

"Ow." I hissed, scowling at him. "That hurt my ass."

He hissed back just as harshly. "What the fuck are you thinking? He has a *gun*."

I looked down at the knife I clenched in my hand. "I can take him."

"Idiot," he muttered. A barrage of shots hit the cabinet, and he jumped to cover my body.

I looked up into his concerned face, confused and not a little brokenhearted. "Why?"

He didn't pretend to misunderstand. "I owed him. Figured it'd be an easy way to pay my debt. I didn't count on falling in love with you. And then I couldn't do it anymore."

"But you did." I ducked as a bullet pinged on the floor next to us.

"Shit." He rolled us to the left and shot off several rounds before glancing down at me again. "That night Chivo attacked you—"

I gasped. "You knew about that?"

"I saw it," he said as he reloaded gun. "I followed you and was about to step in when you took him out. Good moves, babe."

"Thanks." There was, perhaps, a touch of sarcasm in my voice.

"I saw you drop the scroll, and I picked it up before he came to. I was going to return it to you right away."

"Right."

"I was. I hoped you'd confide in me. I was waiting for you to trust me." His gaze was filled with regret as he brushed the hair back from my face. "Wait here."

"Wait—" I reached to grab him, but he rolled off of me and jumped up shooting. The volley of returning fire made me cringe, but I shifted so I could look around the corner of the cabinet.

Jesse hid behind a car that was seriously riddled with bullet holes. I couldn't see Paul, but I thought he was hiding behind another car, based on the sound of gunfire. I sat in a crouch, surveying my options.

No arsenal at my disposal.

Wait for the police? I shook my head. Jesse's garage was located on a strip that was completely abandoned at night. The chances that someone would hear and call the cops were slim.

There was a shelf over the spot where I thought Paul was hiding—if I could create a strong enough earthquake to cause the shelf to fall, he could get knocked out.

Totally doable. If I could get *tǔ ch'i* out of my mental safe place. And if I could control it enough so it did what I wanted it to do.

Two very big ifs. I closed my eyes and focused.

A bullet ricocheted off my cover, startling me out of concentration. Too close. I needed to make something happen—fast. Trying to ignore the violent gunfire, I visualized the trap door.

There it was: thick and dusty and heavy with a gigantic lock securing the latch. I felt for any mental pockets where the key could be hiding, but I found nothing.

Damn Rhys.

A shot hit the ground to my left, and I stifled a shriek. I hated bullets.

"You aren't going to get out," Paul yelled.

"You aren't going to get the scroll," I yelled back.

"We'll see about that."

I heard gunfire and then a grunt.

"Jesse?" I couldn't see anything, so I rolled the cabinet until I saw him propped against the car he was using as a shield. He gripped his shoulder, and even in the darkness I could see the grimace on his face. "Jesse!"

"Stay there," he said through clenched teeth. "I'm good."

"You are not good." I scooted myself and the cabinet toward him.

A bullet pinged off the metal drawer, and I yelped as I ducked. Jesse yelled, "Damn it, Gabe, stay back!"

Right. Like I was going to sit here and let him get shot up by my insane brother. He might have sold me out, but I still didn't want to see him hurt.

Focus. Squeezing my eyes shut, I went back to the trap door. It was my safe place—I should be able to open it. I mentally felt around it, looking for weaknesses. I yanked on the latch, but it didn't budge.

I heard Wu say, *There is no division between you and the scroll. You are a delicate balance that creates one.* Rhys's voice chimed in with an insistent, *Stop fighting it.*

Taking a deep breath, I relaxed all my muscles, from my eyebrows to my toes. In my mind, I put my hand on the latch again. Instead of forcing anything, I simply accepted that it'd open. On an exhale, I yanked it again.

It opened.

I was patting myself on my back when *tŭ ch'i* slammed into me.

The power overwhelmed me, rushing to fill me to the brim. Pain, like my cells were going to explode, wracked every inch of my body.

"Gabe!" Jesse called out, his voice sounding faint as if he was miles away. "Are you okay?"

No, I wasn't. I whimpered, feeling the ground open,

wanting to swallow me whole, suffocating me with its pressure.

Stop fighting it.

Only I felt if I didn't fight it, it'd take me over. At the same time, I realized my way hadn't worked so far. What did I have to lose?

Opening my arms, I let go of my control and let *tǔ ch'i* take over. For a moment, it shot through me. I flattened my palms on the floor to keep myself upright and felt it burst out of my hands into the earth.

Everything began to quake, a deep, bowel-wrenching rumble. Distantly, I heard both Jesse and Paul cry out, followed by the metallic crash of tools hitting the cement floor.

Balance—giving myself up to *tǔ ch'i* wasn't balance. I tried again, reaching to pull the energy back into me. I didn't force it—I didn't wrestle it. Accepting that it had a place inside me, I let it nestle in me.

Shockingly, it did just that. I could still feel it—its pulse still echoed through me—but I didn't feel dominated.

Exhaling in relief, I tuned in to what was going on in the garage. Silence. No shots being fired. I checked around the corner of the cabinet. Nothing. Paul must be reloading.

Now was the time to strike. Gathering *tǔ ch'i*, I looked at the shelf I wanted to collapse onto Paul.

It wasn't there.

Craning my neck, I saw its contents scattered on the floor. My earthquake must have shaken it loose. Was Paul knocked out?

As if answering me, a volley of shots burst out from that side of the room.

"Gabe!" Jesse yelled.

"I'm fine," I answered, retreating behind my cover. But this had to stop.

I should have taken up Rhys on his lessons sooner. Maybe then I'd know what to do with my power. Because even while it was at my fingertips, I had no idea how to use it. Other than sparking earthquakes, I had no idea what I could do.

But I *could* go back to basics and disarm Paul with my hands. Yeah, it'd been a long time since I'd practiced disarming someone with a gun (I'd never make fun of Wu for teaching me that *ever* again), but I still remembered the essential principles. Of course, it involved getting really close to the gun, but Paul wouldn't shoot me before he got the scroll. Probably.

I calculated the distance and picked a path. I could do it. "Jesse, cover me."

"*Gabe*. Hell."

I heard him open fire as I duckwalked behind my metal shield to the outside of the garage. A moment later Paul started shooting back. I ignored the vicious cracking—God, gunfire was loud—and moved steadily toward my goal.

I got behind him.

There were a table and a couple other obstacles between us, but I could make out his form kneeling behind the car he used as cover. I debated throwing my knife at him, but it was dark and I hadn't practiced throwing knives in years—the chances that I'd miss him were too big.

Creep up on him. Nodding, I silently darted out from the cabinet to the table.

Jesse let loose a yell, followed by an empty click. I froze. Did that mean he was out of bullets?

Paul stood up, hands bracing his handgun directly in front of him, shooting indiscriminately toward the spot where Jesse hid.

I had to do something. I looked down at the knife. Here went nothing.

I rushed out from behind the table as quietly as I could. I was behind Paul before he realized. I sliced upward under his raised right arm.

He screamed, pressing his arm to his side. But as I hesitated, he swung his uninjured arm around. His flapping hand caught my cheek. Dropping the knife, I gasped and rocked back, seeing stars for a second before my vision cleared.

In time to feel him press the gun against my forehead.

Chapter Thirty-three

$\mathcal{N}$o," Jesse yelled.

Damn.

Double damn as I remembered Rhys telling me my moment of hesitation would give my opponent the advantage. I hoped I stayed alive to tell him he was right.

"Stay back or I'll shoot her." Paul's lips twisted as if he were in pain, but he shoved the gun harder into my temple. "Don't make me hurt her."

The hard metal triggered a memory of Wu holding a rubber gun to my head. *Fight your opponent—the gun is not the enemy. Pretend to cower. This will disarm your opponent, making him feel he has won. Then strike to a vital area.*

My gut spasmed with nerves. Right. I could do that. Even though I hadn't practiced it in forever. And even though it was totally different having your brother press a real loaded gun to your head.

But I wouldn't think about that.

With a shaky breath, I hunched my shoulders and

brought my hands up to my face, just like Wu had instructed. I even whimpered for good measure.

"Hurt her and I won't give you the scroll," Jesse yelled.

Something metallic slid across the paved floor, and I knew he was moving. I wanted to tell him to stay put, but I knew he wouldn't listen.

Had to act. *Now.*

Whirling into Paul, I did a right up-windmill. The moment I struck, *tǔ ch'i* rose, strengthening my block to knock his gun arm wide. Not letting the sharp crack of broken bone distract me, I stuck my thumb in his eye and held on, hoping it'd force him to drop the gun.

"Son of a bitch." Paul screamed, clawing my hand with his good one. Then he surprised me by kicking my knee.

My hands lost their grip, and he jerked his head back, his eye streaming and red but not popped. He shoved me back and pointed the gun at my face with his unhurt hand.

"Shit," I muttered.

"I'm sorry, Gabby, but you wouldn't cooperate." He pulled the trigger.

No. Picturing the shield that had protected me from Chivo, I focused *tǔ ch'i* in front of me.

The bullet hit the amorphous air and ricocheted right. Before he could react, I pushed the energy out to hit him in the chest.

He staggered, hitting the car behind him. The gun clattered to the ground, and he slid down the driver's-side panel, wheezing on his knees like the air had been knocked out of him.

The image of my mom lying dead in my arms flashed in my head, and anger forced *tǔ ch'i* to rise again. I stepped forward, knowing I could take him, knowing I could make him pay for everything he'd done.

But the sadness I remembered in Mom's eyes, even after her death, stopped me. My shoulders slumped, and the energy withdrew inside me. As angry as I was, as much as I thought Paul deserved to hurt, this wasn't the way. "This has to stop, Paul."

He lifted his head, and the dark emotion that poured from his eyes made me take a step back. "I couldn't agree more."

Lunging, he grabbed the knife off the floor and scrambled to his feet to charge me.

Tŭ ch'i spilled forward, deflecting the blade as he stabbed. Acting on instinct, I grabbed his wrist, held it up, twirled under his arm, and twisted it back toward him. We both gasped in surprise when it sank high in his abdomen.

I looked into my brother's eyes—Wu's eyes—and sank into a black hole of hatred and anger. His lips twisted, and he jerked back from me. I felt the knife slurp out of him, and I pressed my lips shut so I wouldn't give in to the urge to retch.

Paul stumbled backward and collapsed against the side of the car. His arms hugged his wound, but I could see blood seeping through his clothes around the edges

His smirk became a pain-ridden grimace. "You'd think this was the worst day of my life. But it's not. It was the day you were born."

His hatred choked me. I backed away, horrified by the flecks of frothy pink spit that gathered at the corner of his mouth as he coughed. I wouldn't think about him. I wouldn't feel guilty that my brother was dying.

Damn it—this was his fault. He'd engineered both Mom and Wu's deaths. This was how fate repaid him.

If only that bit of logic lessened the guilt I felt. I was death on people I cared for. No wonder I had no family and so few friends.

Jesse.

Tucking the knife back into my pocket, I turned around and scanned the garage.

Kicking the gun out of Paul's reach—just in case—I wove through the trashed bay toward the car where Jesse had been hiding. I skirted around some kind of rolling tool cart when I tripped on something. Looking down, I gasped when I saw Jesse lying there, eyes closed.

Covered in blood.

"Jesse." I dropped to the floor next to him.

His eyes cracked open. "Did you take care of him?"

"Yeah." Did shoulder wounds bleed a lot? I didn't think so—not unless an artery was nicked. I pushed his hands aside and froze when I saw not just the one wound but a second bullet hole directly over his chest.

His lips twisted—with humor or pain, I couldn't tell. "Got in the way of that last bullet. Ironic."

Panic surged through me. I gripped his clothes and tried to yank him up. "Come on, we've got to get you to the hospital."

"Too late, babe." He covered my hands with his. "No regrets. My fault. But you're worth it."

Tears blurred my vision. No—I couldn't break down now. I had to save him. I blinked them away and applied pressure on his wound. The blood bubbled through my fingers with each breath he took. "Don't give up, damn it."

Rhys healed me—maybe I could heal Jesse. As angry as I was for his part in all this, I didn't want him dead.

My cheeks burned remembering how Rhys did it. Knowing Rhys, he'd probably just taken advantage of the situation to kiss me. I doubted anything that intimate was required.

Pushing his clothing aside, I placed my hands directly on his wounds. Trying not to panic at the amount of blood, I pictured him healing.

Tŭ ch'i didn't stir.

Another thin gush of wetness seeped through my fingers.

"Heal, damn it." I opened my eyes and concentrated everything on healing the gaping hole.

Nothing.

I went inward and touched it in its resting place. Still there. Why wouldn't it do anything?

He lifted a bloodied hand and shakily pushed my hair behind my ear. "Love you."

I opened my mouth to tell him I loved him, too. I did love him. Maybe, I thought. In a friendly way.

But I couldn't say a word.

Regret lined his face. Then his eyelids lowered and he went limp.

"Jesse." I was about to try one more time, but I felt him leave. It wasn't violent; it wasn't more than a feeling that he'd passed on and I was alone.

I bit my lips to hold in my sadness. Maybe if I had better control of *tŭ ch'i*, this would have turned out differently. Maybe if I loved him, I could have saved him.

So many maybes.

Righting his clothing, I placed a kiss on his forehead. I still had to take care of Paul. Pulling out my cell phone,

I started to redial 911, but it occurred to me to use the garage's phone instead. I slipped mine back in my pocket and stumbled to the office. After placing the quick call, I went back out to where I left Paul in the garage.

I rounded the car he'd propped himself on and blinked. He was gone.

Chapter Thirty-four

Covered in blood, I couldn't call a cab. So I ran home, careful to take the more deserted routes through SoMa to the Mission.

Rhys was leaning against my front door when I got home. He looked immaculate, untainted, and I felt a stab of need mixed with jealousy. I didn't think I'd ever feel untainted again.

It took me a moment to catch my breath—from running but also from seeing him. Then I walked up the porch steps, keys in hand. "This is becoming a bad habit."

His gaze sharpened, and he pushed away from the house. "Gabrielle, what—"

Holding a hand out, I shook my head. "Don't touch me. Your clothes will get messed up."

"I don't bloody care about my clothes. Are you hurt?" He carefully took me in his arms, running his hands over me as if checking for injury. "You're shaking."

"It's not my blood." I tried to squirm out of his hold, but he held me, gently but without question. "Let go."

"You're the one who needs to let go, love."

As if his words flipped a switch, tears flooded my eyes and overflowed down my cheeks. I tried to hold it in, but a sob escaped. Then another. And then I was enfolded in the comfort of Rhys's arms.

Holding me close, he stroked my hair gently, soothingly. "What happened, Gabrielle?"

"Jesse died. I couldn't save him," I whispered hoarsely.

"Jesse? Your friend?" Rhys stilled. I held my breath, wondering if he was going to launch into a jealous tirade. He surprised me by simply saying, "I'm sorry."

I put my hand over the calming beat of his heart—over his mark—and burrowed closer. "I managed to unlock *tŭ ch'i* and tried so hard to heal him. Why didn't it work? I put my hands over his wound and thought healing thoughts."

"Each scroll has different properties, lending different powers," he said into my hair. "I'm not sure thinking healing thoughts are the way to approach it with yours. Only you'll know for sure how it works."

No, Wu would know, too. "But you still think you can coach me into learning?"

"I'm positive." The confidence in his voice reassured me. "The person who taught me didn't have practical knowledge of my scroll, either."

Frowning, I looked up at him. "Who taught you?"

"A monk at the monastery where the scrolls originated."

"They know about the scrolls? I thought—"

"There's one monk who's entrusted with the secrets. He keeps track of the lineages. Which is how I found you." He smiled deprecatingly. "I borrowed his record of the five families."

"But—"

"Enough for now," he interrupted. "You're shivering. You'll feel better for a bath." He pried the keys out of my death grip, unlocked my door, and guided me inside. "We need a bag to put your soiled clothing in."

"I can handle it." Shrugging out of his hold, I headed to the kitchen for a bag. And to put some space between us. I hadn't shown anyone that much emotion in—well, forever. "You can leave."

The only sign of annoyance was his taut jaw. When he replied, his voice was all cool reason. "Not until I see you cleaned up."

To see me stripped even barer? That scared me.

He must have read my thoughts, because his hand grabbed my clothes before I could step away. "I need to make sure you're okay, Gabrielle. There's no compromise in this."

Something in his voice made me look up. His eyes blazed with concern, fury, and—

I shook my head. Exhausted, I obviously wasn't seeing straight. But I was too weary to fight it, so I led him to the kitchen and fished two bags from under the sink. I placed the knife in the first one, rolled the top closed tight, and stuck it in the fridge with the scroll.

Struck by the urge to take it out and hold it, I paused. Then I looked at Rhys.

He stared into the fridge, a faint frown around his mouth.

If he were going to take the scroll, this was the time. Considering the state I was in, he had an edge over me. I waited to see what he'd do.

Turning away, he picked up the other bag. "Bathroom, love?"

The breath I didn't know I was holding whooshed out of my lungs, and hope bloomed in my chest. Nodding, I closed the door. Rhys held out his hand, and I took it and led him away.

We squeezed inside the tiny space, me facing him but looking down. "I—"

He placed the softest kiss on my lips, halting my words. "Let me," he whispered. "Please. I need to do this."

Swallowing thickly, I nodded.

He slipped my jacket off and dropped it to one side. He efficiently stripped every layer of clothing until I stood in just my panties. Then he wrapped his arms around me and held me tight.

His body thawed me, and slowly my trembling stopped. I burrowed my head in the crook of his neck and, without thought, placed my hand over his heart—over his mark.

He inhaled sharply, and his arms clasped me closer, his hands soothing my back. He murmured words into my hair—words I couldn't hear but that comforted me nevertheless.

"Gabrielle, I need—" He swallowed and, hoarse with emotion, asked, "Where is your mark?"

Without thought, I covered the spot on my hip with my hand.

He released me, taking a small step back. I was going to protest when he dropped to his knees, his hands gripping my waist. He looked up, his gaze fierce, not asking permission but wanting me to give it anyway.

I let my hand fall away.

Triumph flushed his face. Slowly, he lowered his gaze

to my right hip, just inside my pelvic bone at the elastic of my panties.

My mark.

He ran his thumb over it, and I felt it like a caress across every inch of my body. Then he leaned forward and touched his lips—one brief, electric, heart-stopping kiss—right over it.

Gasping, I arched into it. *More.*

As if he heard me, he gently bit my thigh before kissing it again, longer this time.

By the time he stopped, we were both panting. He nuzzled my panties, hooked his fingers in the elastic at the sides, and caught my eyes.

My heart pounded with excitement and, truthfully, fear. I knew what he was waiting for—I knew if I said yes there was no going back. I also knew I didn't want to consider the ramifications of what I was flirting with. I just needed to feel something besides hate and sadness. I needed to feel love, and for some reason I knew no one but Rhys could give that to me.

So I placed my hands over his and started to shimmy my underwear off.

His hands caught mine, stopping me. "Be sure, Gabrielle."

At the moment, it was the only thing I was sure of. I wanted this. I wanted him. Pushing his hands aside, I slipped out of my panties and tossed them aside.

His eyes blazed with emotions so deep I thought I could drown in their depths. Slowly he lowered his gaze, skimming over my lips, down my neck, my breasts, and abdomen, to rest at the juncture of my legs.

I widened my stance. Just in case he needed encouragement.

Rhys dipped one long finger in, grazing ever-so-lightly over the moist folds. Suddenly, he popped to his feet, tangled his hands in my hair, and brought his mouth down to ravage mine.

Every lick of his tongue was like a fire burning inside me. I ran my hands over his shoulders and down his arms to pull him closer. It turned me on to feel him dressed against my completely bare skin, but I knew it'd turn me on even more to feel him naked. I tugged his jacket and murmured into his mouth. "Off."

"Bed?" he asked without breaking our kiss.

My futon. But that was in the living room, and I was afraid if we took the time to relocate I'd come to my senses. Plus, who knew where Wu was and when he'd turn up. I shook my head. "Here."

He lifted his head and stared down at me. He frowned a little, but I didn't care, since he grabbed my butt and set me on the counter.

Wrapping my legs around his waist, I dragged him tight against me. The fly of his jeans rasped me intimately, and when I pressed closer I felt how hard he was. For me.

He shrugged out of his jacket and tore his shirt over his head. I let my legs fall open so he could take his pants off. Watching me hungrily, he pulled a condom from his pocket and undid the top button of his jeans. "Touch yourself."

"Bossy," I accused, but I slid a hand down to brush over my clit. I gasped, the feeling so much more intense than when I touched myself all alone, and I wondered if it was because Rhys had me so primed or because I wanted him so much. Much more than I'd ever wanted anyone else.

Dipping my finger lower, I moaned. Wet—so wet. I imagined Rhys doing this to me, his strong finger buried in me, his mouth making love to me. I moaned again and let my head fall back.

And I hit the mirror behind me. "Ouch."

"Next time we'll use my bathroom," he said, unzipping his jeans. "It's bigger."

I surprised myself by smiling. I hadn't thought I'd ever smile again. "It's always about size with you men."

He frowned, his eyes narrowing. He shoved his pants and underwear down and clasped me against his chest. "Don't mention other men to me," he said before he kissed me to an inch of my life.

Just when I thought I was going to pass out from the intensity, he arched me back to kiss down my neck to my breasts. He hovered there a moment before he covered a nipple with his hot mouth.

It was like flames licking at me, and, grabbing his hair, I cried out. *Tŭ ch'i* pulsed to life, echoing the pounding of my heart. Instead of repressing it, I let it flow through me and mingle with Rhys's energy.

With a low groan, he switched to my other breast, laving it with the scorching attention. Conscious of his hands resting at my hips, I didn't know whether to tell him to hurry it up or slow it down so I could hold on to this feeling forever.

I opted to hurry it up. And because actions spoke louder than words . . . I slipped my hand between our bodies to clasp his hard-on.

We both froze as I explored what I had a hold of. Thick. Silky. Hard. Really hard. I gave it a test squeeze.

Rhys growled, his hands tightening on my hips. "Don't toy with me, Gabrielle."

"I'm not." I looked into his eyes, seeing how close he was to losing it. And it thrilled me. "I want you."

Something shifted in his gaze. Tearing the condom packet open, he unrolled it over his erection and, with another growl, he tilted me back, positioned himself, and pushed himself into me.

Full. Hot. Perfect.

Gasping, I speared my fingers into his hair to bring him closer. I clenched his waist with my legs and rocked against him.

His hand snaked up to cup my breast, and the gentle abrasion of his palm felt so good I undulated against it. He placed one hand on the small of my back, tilting my hips, and thrust.

We groaned together.

Leaning in, he bit the curve of my neck, soothing it with a kiss. "You make me burn."

Panting, I shook my head. The heat of him scorched me on the inside, and the friction with his every surge only made me hotter. "You've got that backward."

"Do I?" he said, his breath choppy. Staring into my eyes, he sank in and out of me, slowing his pace as if to make sure I felt every smooth inch of his cock.

"Yeah, pretty sure you do." I moaned again as he rubbed against just the right spot.

"Yes, love," Rhys whispered, his blue eyes filling my vision as limitless and open as the sky. He began to thrust longer and deeper. "Give yourself to me."

He was just as close—I felt it in the way his hard-on throbbed and the greedy grip of his hands on my body. I clutched him with my legs to match his movements, wanting to drive him over the edge as much as I wanted my own release. Just as I felt myself start to swell with my climax, he rolled my nipple and squeezed.

I cried out as I came apart. Then I heard his answering

shout, saw the blazing passion in his gaze, and, with one last driving push, felt him come, too.

My hands still tangled in his hair, I slumped against his chest. I could feel him still firm inside me, distantly noting that he pulsed in tune to my heartbeat.

He held me to him, safe and secure.

"I could stay here forever," I murmured against his mark.

His arms tightened around me. After a moment, he pressed a kiss on my temple and slowly withdrew from me.

Frowning, I blinked at him. "What—"

A soft kiss silenced me. "You've yet to take your bath."

Oh. Right. I sat on the counter, befuddled as he turned on the faucet and adjusted the water's temperature. When the bathroom began to steam up, he lifted me into the shower.

"You aren't joining me?" I asked when he started to close the curtain.

"Next time, love." He ran a finger over my mark, and I shivered, my body instantly taut with need again. He shook his head and said, "We have all the time in the world," but I saw the desire flare in his eyes all over again.

He snapped the curtain shut, and I stood under the spray, listening to him getting dressed. Hoping. But then I heard the door open and shut, and I resigned myself to showering alone.

Overwhelmed by everything that had happened tonight, I closed my eyes and soaked under the shower. The hot water brought me back to the moment, renewing me in a way I hadn't thought possible an hour ago.

Or maybe Rhys had done that. I paused as I scrubbed myself, trying to pin the emotion churning in my chest.

When I finished, I found a clean set of sweats on the counter next to the sink and all my bloodied clothes taken away. Rhys was waiting for me in the living room when I came out.

So was Wu.

"What is this man doing here?" Wu demanded when he saw me. His arms were crossed and his mouth set in a severe scowl. "Do you know who he is?"

Not now. But at least he hadn't barged in while we were having sex. I glanced at Rhys. "I'm sorry, but you should go."

He came to me and took my hand. "I assume the ghost is friendly?"

"Spirit," Wu corrected.

Blinking, I gaped at Rhys. "You can see him?"

"I can see a vague outline. He speaks to you?"

"You can't hear him?"

"No. Who is he?"

"My scroll ghost." I frowned at the way he cocked his eyebrow in question. "Your scroll didn't come with a ghost?"

"No." Rhys reached out, hand still several inches from Wu. "Interesting."

Wu glowed brighter, showing his agitation, and waved his arms frantically. "Get away from him, Gabrielle! He's another Guardian. He's after your scroll."

"Tell me something I don't know." Shivering from the creepy cold as his arm passed through me, I waved Wu away. "Stop that."

"*Think,* Gabrielle," Wu exploded. "What other reason can he have for finding you and being here with you?"

"None." At least for finding me. For being here . . . I glanced at Rhys, remembering how reverently he touched me. Wanting him to love me like that again.

Wanting him to love me. Period.

As if he sensed my surprise, Rhys squeezed my hand. "What's happened?"

My brother had turned out to be the bad guy, and the bad guy was turning out to be my Prince Charming— that's what had happened. But I said, "Wu, my father's ghost, thinks you only want my scroll."

"I only care what you think."

"I—" Confused, I shook my head.

"Gabrielle, I came to you with less-than-sterling intentions. I've told you, I won't apologize for them. I can't be sorry I was led to you. I found a woman I never dreamed existed. A spirited, talented, passionate, beautiful woman who set me on fire in a way my powers never did." He lifted my chin, his gaze solemn and earnest. "I found home. None of the money in the world can buy the home I've found in your arms."

Tears flooded my eyes, and I tried to duck my head.

He held firm, not letting me hide. "I am sorry I hurt you, but believe that I want the best for you. I want to help you develop your powers. I want to protect you. I want to love you."

My heart clenched, elated and afraid. "Pretty words—"

"Which I mean." His eyes burned with sincerity. "Don't judge me for my original intentions. Judge me on what you've seen with your own eyes."

"Tell me you don't believe him," Wu demanded from the sidelines.

"I don't know what to believe," I said, addressing both at the same time.

Rhys brought my wrist to his lips. "Believe that I love you. I love you with the force of my being."

Wu drifted next to us, scowling fiercely. "He loves your scroll."

Overwhelmed, exhausted, completely depleted, I disengaged and stepped back. "I need time."

The silence was painful as they both stared at me.

Finally Rhys nodded. "We'll talk later. I'll take care of your blood-soaked clothes." At the door, he picked up the bag and looked over his shoulder at me. "We are *not* done, Gabrielle."

And he walked out of my house.

"Blood-soaked clothes?" Wu hovered next to me. "What blood-soaked clothes?"

Ignoring him, I headed for the kitchen. There was still one more thing to take care of before I could rest. Or fall apart. Both were viable options at the moment.

"Are you injured?" Wu demanded, following me into the kitchen. "Whose blood was it?"

"Jesse's, the guy who stole the scroll," I said tiredly as I took out the paper bag from the refrigerator. "And Paul's."

"Paul?" He stilled. "What's Paul doing here? To help you? He was always a conscientious older brother. I wouldn't expect any less from him. He understood the importance of our legacy."

Anger roused me from the dazed disbelief of the night's events. Why couldn't he have revered his son like this sooner, and to his face? I wanted to tell him how Paul was the reason Mom died—not to mention the cause for his own death—and that with a little attention from him it could all have been avoided.

But as I glared at him, my mouth opening, I just couldn't do it. Instead I asked what just occurred to me. "Why didn't you heal Mom?"

"Heal?" His glow diminished. "What do you know about that?"

"Answer the question."

His shoulders slumped, making him look more like an old man than ever before. When he spoke, it was without his usual arrogance. "I never learned how."

Gripping the counter, I nodded. At one time, I would have rejoiced to find out the incomparable Wu didn't know how to do something. Now I just felt sad.

One thing was certain: if I didn't buck up and learn what I needed to, it'd just get worse and worse. I felt that in the pit of my stomach. More earthquakes, more alienation, more deaths. I shuddered, imagining something happening to Madame. Or Carrie.

Or Rhys.

I heard Carrie's words from earlier in my mind and knew she was right. I needed to own this. I needed to make it work. All of it. The Guardianship, my career, my life—all of it. The sooner I did that, the sooner I'd have balance again.

I could do it. I had to do it.

Because my jacket was trashed, I pulled on another sweatshirt and wrapped a thick scarf around my neck.

"Where are you going?" Wu drifted beside me. "I have questions."

There was so much mingling inside me, I didn't know which emotion to focus on. Anger felt safe, so I faced him and let it rise to the top. "I *will* learn to be a proper

Guardian. On my own terms. With or without any of you, I will learn about the scroll and *tŭ ch'i*."

His mouth snapped shut on whatever he'd been about to say, and he gawked at me in stunned silence. Finally he nodded, said, "Good," and disappeared.

Picking up the bag, I headed out.

No one followed me. No one watched. It was like I was the only person in the world. Walking through the Mission this late at night was often like that, but tonight it was especially stark.

I walked all the way to Noe Valley. I dropped the knife in a trash bin. For good measure, I went to a kiosk that offered a free publication, crumpled up a few copies, and tossed them in, too. Then I slowly walked home.

By the time I got back, it was early morning. I was crawling into bed when I saw the picture of me and Paul on my nightstand.

Fury rose in my chest, suffocating me. Grabbing it, I gripped it in my hands. I'd tear it into pieces. I'd burn it and forget about Paul—he deserved no less.

But I couldn't do it.

A tear fell down my cheek and onto the picture, landing on my five-year-old face. I'd trusted Paul. I'd trusted Jesse.

Would trusting Rhys have a different outcome?

Don't think about it.

Tucking the photo under my mattress so I wouldn't have to see it, I pulled the covers over my head and hoped my nightmares would be forgiving.

Chapter Thirty-five

*I*nspector Ramirez was waiting for me—alone—outside the Pour House when I arrived to open the next day.

The second I saw him my heart started to beat triple time, but I allowed only a small frown to show. His shirt was buttoned all the way and his tie was cinched tight, so I knew he was here on business. It didn't take a genius to figure out that business had to be about Jesse and Paul. "Inspector Ramirez. What a surprise."

"Do you have a minute? I have some questions I need to ask you."

I went still at his overly somber tone. Had they found Paul? Was he dead? Tears rose to the surface—tears of anger and bitterness instead of sadness and regret. At least that's what I told myself. Because Paul didn't deserve the latter.

Tipping my head so he wouldn't see the telltale moisture, I pretended to be flirtatious. "It sounds like I have no choice."

"I know you're opening." He took my elbow like he

was afraid I was going to bolt. He escorted me in and locked the door after us. "I'll make it short."

Disengaging from him, I flipped on a couple lights and walked to the bar. "You're minus your partner today."

"He's covering other ground."

I could feel his eyes on me. I hoped he was watching my ass and not calculating how long he could throw me in jail for.

Calm down. It wasn't like he had anything on me—from last night or the night with the thug. At least I didn't think he did. "So what brings you out today? Need to harass a few honest citizens?"

"Are you honest, Ms. Sansouci?" he asked from right behind me.

I whirled around. "Jeez. Respect the personal space, will you?"

He didn't crowd me anymore—at least not physically. Mentally he was right on top of me. I backed up until my lower back hit the rim of the bar.

Ramirez studied me with his dark eyes for what stretched into forever before he spoke. "Jesse Byrnes was found shot to death last night in his garage."

But what about Paul? I wilted onto a barstool. Tears popped back into my eyes. A part of my mind was satisfied by my reaction—made me look credible.

Sometimes I hated that part of me.

He pulled out his notebook and pencil from a breast pocket. "I understand Byrnes was your boyfriend."

Not even close, especially after the news Paul dropped on me last night. I swallowed thickly, forcing the tears down. "Where did you hear that?"

"A source."

The source definitely wasn't Vivian. "Jesse and I had, um, a relationship. Of sorts."

"Of sorts?" Rick stopped jotting his notes and stared at me. The pencil creaked in his hand. "What does that mean?"

"It means we dated casually. But we'd been platonic for over a year."

"What about the rich guy from the other night?"

Rhys. I didn't know how to explain him, and I didn't want to. One thing I did know was I didn't like Ramirez's accusatory tone. "Excuse me, but I think judging me is not part of your job."

"I'm not judging you. I'm trying to establish your relationship." He studied me carefully. "How close were you and Byrnes?"

"We were friends for a couple years." A couple years where he was reporting my comings and goings to my brother. My lip quivered. I bit down on it—now wasn't the time to get distracted.

"Did you know he was leaving the city?"

I nodded. "He said he was going out of town for a bit."

"He wasn't leaving for a bit. He'd sold his shop to one of his mechanics and was leaving for good." He watched for my reaction. "Did you have a fight?"

"No. We weren't even dating anymore. I'm sure his decision to leave had nothing to do with me."

A partial truth. Jesse *had* planned to leave because of me—not me directly, but me in conjunction with the scroll. Only that was none of Ramirez's business.

"But you didn't fight?" he asked coolly.

"There was nothing to fight about," I replied sadly.

"Not even your new boyfriend?"

"I don't have a new boyfriend." Crossing my arms, I glared at him. "And if I did, Jesse wouldn't have cared."

"I bet the rich guy would, though."

"What are you saying?"

Ramirez leaned in, his eyes narrowed. "I'm saying maybe your new friend didn't like Byrnes hanging around you and decided to get him out of your life permanently."

Stunned by the scenario, I laughed incredulously. "Trust me, if Rhys wanted Jesse gone, he wouldn't have to resort to murder."

"I'll still need his contact info."

"Here." I reached for a pad of paper and a pen next to the register and scribbled Rhys's number. How pathetic was it that I knew it by heart? As I handed it over, I said, "Be careful with him. I bet he'll have a team of shark lawyers waiting to take a bite out of your ass."

He tucked the scrap into his breast pocket. "Did your brother have reason to fight with Byrnes?"

I started at the abrupt shift in questioning, conscious that he watched me like a hawk. "My brother?"

"There was another person's blood found at the scene. I'm assuming it was your brother's, since the murder weapon was registered to him."

Shit—I forgot all about the gun. "Is Paul a suspect?"

"The lead suspect."

That meant he was still alive, damn it. And if he was still out there, he'd come after me. I didn't doubt that for one second—arrest warrant or not.

"Do you know why he'd have cause to be at Byrnes's garage in the middle of the night?" Ramirez asked.

"I didn't even know they knew each other." As soon as I said it, I knew it was the wrong thing to admit.

Ramirez lifted his head like he scented something amiss. "You didn't know your boyfriend and your brother knew each other?"

"No." I crossed my arms and glared at him. "I wasn't close to my brother. I hadn't seen him in fifteen years, not until he came in here recently. Our father left me something in his will, and Paul wanted to make sure I got it."

"What did he leave you?"

"None of your business."

"It is if it's the reason Byrnes and your brother were fighting."

How ironic that it was. But I couldn't very well tell the inspector that. The scroll was supposed to be kept a secret, and too many people knew about it already. I shook my head resolutely and lied my ass off. "It was a family heirloom. I'm positive it wasn't the reason Jesse and Paul fought, if that's what happened."

He tapped the pencil against the pad. Then he said, "Is that the story you want to stick with?"

"That's the truth."

"Damn it." He slammed his notebook down on the counter. "I can tell you're lying to me."

"I'm not." I was just giving him an abbreviated version of the truth.

"Let me tell you the way I see it." He leaned in on his hand, crowding me so his anger-darkened eyes filled my vision. "I've got two corpses on my hands, both killed by bullets that came from the same gun. A gun registered to your brother. Which makes him wanted for questioning as the lead suspect for two murders. To top it all off, the first corpse was seen asking about you hours before he died, and the second was actually involved with you."

Gulp. "Put that way, it doesn't sound good."

"What it sounds like is you're the key to the whole mystery."

A key was good—I could be a key. Anything as long as I wasn't a suspect. "I wish I could help you."

"Do you?"

I nodded. "Jesse didn't deserve to die."

He frowned. "You sound upset."

"How could I not be? Despite everything, I"—I swallowed—"liked him."

Ramirez stared at me like he was peeling all my layers down to the core. Finally, he took a step back. "Don't leave town."

I hadn't planned on going anywhere, but I bristled at being told what to do. "Why? I thought Paul was the suspect, not me."

"He is, but I can't get past the feeling that you're mixed up in this somehow." He picked up his notebook. "I'll find out, you know."

Not if I could help it. "There's nothing to find out. I haven't broken any laws."

"There's an APB out for your brother." He pulled a card from his pocket and held it out to me. "I recommend that you contact me if you hear from him."

"I have your card already." But he didn't waver, so I sighed and took what he offered. "For the record, there's no love lost between me and Paul. I'm the last person in the world he'll contact."

Ramirez shook his head. "Why don't I believe that, either? See you around, Ms. Sansouci."

"Not if I can help it," I called after him. But I knew I wouldn't be free of him until Paul was captured.

I knew I wouldn't be free of Paul, either.

Chapter Thirty-six

*A*rrête, *Gabrielle*." Madame La Rochelle managed to frown at me even while she smiled at a nicely dressed couple that walked by "You make me nervous."

"*Désolée, Madame*," I said apologetically as I fidgeted some more. "I can't help it."

"Have a glass of champagne."

I shook my head. That's all I needed— to get a buzz going at my first solo art opening. "You know I don't drink."

"Perhaps this is the time to make an exception, *non?*" She lifted her fluted glass to her lips. "I do not comprehend why you worry. You are *un grand succès*. All your paintings sold."

A fluke. Or a joke. I was waiting for the moment I'd wake up to find I'd dreamed it all.

I looked up at the gallery walls where all my paintings hung—the older canvases as well as the new series I'd painted—each with a small round sticker that signified they'd been purchased.

I'd been so apprehensive about the director accepting the new series, which I'd titled *Dark Forces*. But in the end she'd been more enthusiastic about that than the previous works she'd contracted. I glanced at the room in the back where she'd showcased them. I hadn't been able to go in there yet. I couldn't handle seeing them—especially the last one, which depicted a body wrapped in darkness and a woman's form reaching out to it. In the top left corner, a pair of brown eyes glared—so like my father's, only malevolent and envious.

Yeah, my life literally splattered on canvas. Not that anyone knew but me. And Paul.

And one other person.

I searched the crowd for the millionth time. Rhys wasn't here. I didn't know if that was a disappointment or a relief.

Actually, I hadn't seen him since that night. At first, it'd been by choice. I'd needed time to think.

It didn't take long to realize his actions *did* speak louder than his original intentions. He'd helped me come into my own—with both *tǔ ch'i* and my art. I hadn't made huge progress with my powers yet—I still didn't know how to heal—but in accepting them, I found living with them more natural and less a struggle.

Most importantly, he'd never lied to me. He could have—it would have made life easier for him. I'd never have known differently. But he never did.

Honorable.

Still, something kept me from calling him. If I didn't know better, I'd think that some girly side of me wanted him to make a move. To win me.

That's when his notes started arriving.

Small, written on expensive vanilla paper in bold black

handwriting that I knew without a doubt belonged to him. They showed up everywhere—under my door at home, at Madame's, at the bar. The first one was propped on my easel in my studio.

Some sweet, some sexy, all affecting, I eagerly read each subsequent one. Devious on his part, because I started to anticipate receiving them.

I pressed my hip, feeling the last one I received tucked into the waistband of my thong, next to my mark. It said, simply, "Forever."

A week ago I'd broken down and called him. I tried to rationalize that I needed to set up training sessions again, but I couldn't lie to myself. It was Rhys I really wanted.

Except Brian told me Rhys was out of the country. And I still hadn't heard from him.

"Gabe." The director, Chloe, swept up to me in her black cocktail dress and squeezed my hand. "This is a success beyond imagination. All your paintings sold. *All* of them. It's unheard-of."

"Great." Sad that all I could think of at the moment was that I looked like a giraffe next to her. I tugged the strapless top of my shimmery peacock blue dress one more time.

Madame nudged me and hissed under her breath. "*Arrête.*"

"I could have sold the *Dark Forces* series ten times over." The dollar signs in her eyes made them shine brightly. "As it was, an anonymous buyer called early and offered to pay three times what I'd priced them."

"Peachy," I said nervously. My gut told me the anonymous patron was Rhys. Was that a good sign? He knew how personal they were—he'd recognize the emotion behind each stroke. But then why wasn't he here?

"I wonder how he heard about them. He asked for them specifically." She flagged down a waiter and snatched a glass of champagne from his tray. "So much for my grand plan of cloaking you in mystery to drum up curiosity. I was so careful not to let word leak out, too."

"Curious." I glanced at Madame, who was suddenly very intrigued by the fringe on her shawl.

"He wasn't pleased when I told him the fifth painting had already been sold," Chloe said with capitalist glee.

"Sold?" I blinked. "Someone else bought the last painting? Who?"

She shrugged. "It was another anonymous sale."

My gut lurched. *Not Paul.* That painting was intimate—part of my soul. It'd be sickening if Paul possessed it. Creepy, even. Please let it not be him.

"And as long as the check clears, I really don't care. Unless it's someone famous. Then I could use that for PR. Be sure to mingle." Chloe squeezed my hand one more time before she dropped it and went to continue schmoozing.

"I must say hello to a friend I see." Madame smiled at me. "I am proud of you, Gabrielle. I could not have been prouder if you were my own daughter."

My heart leapt into my throat, and I had to swallow a couple times before I could speak. "*Merci, Madame.*"

"You must celebrate tonight, *mon chou*. You look—how does one say?—as if your best friend is lost." She pulled me down, kissed my cheek, and glided away, leaving a scent of vanilla.

"Gabe!"

I turned around in time to catch the bundle of seafoam chiffon that threw herself at me.

Carrie's embrace squeezed the air out of my lungs. For a small woman, she had a grip.

She let go, her face suffused with wonder and excitement. "This is *so* incredible. I had no idea you were so talented. I mean, I knew you were talented, but these—" She waved at the room, her eyes wide in awe. "These transcend."

Tears filled my eyes. First Madame, now Carrie.

"Oh, no." With a horrified gasp, she grabbed my arm. "Did I say the wrong thing?"

I shook my head. "You said the perfect thing."

"Oh. Good." She grinned. "The next perfect thing I'd like to say is that you look amazing. Vivian would die if she saw you in that dress. Actually . . ." She pulled out her cell phone, flipped it open, and took a quick picture. "I'm going to pix that to her later."

Laughing, I hugged her. "I'm so glad you came."

"I wouldn't miss this for the world." She took my hand, her eyes solemn. "It means a lot to me that you wanted me to share this night with you."

"I—" I wanted to tell her that it meant a lot to have her there. That I valued her, that her friendship was treasure to me. I just didn't know how. I sucked at this emotional crap.

She smiled and squeezed my hand. "I know. Me, too."

"Are you sure you aren't a mind reader?"

"Nah. We're just on the same wavelength." She peeked over my shoulder. "I see a man over there who looks like he's dying to fetch me a glass of champagne, so I'm going to let you mingle with your adoring public."

I laughed. "Go. I'll call you tomorrow. Maybe we could have tea."

Her face lit from within. "I'd love that."

Sighing, I watched her walk away. At least I had one thing to look forward to.

I rolled my shoulders. Sore. In the past weeks since the thing with Paul (I had no idea what to call it—*incident* seemed such a pale word), I'd been working out hard. Mostly to get myself back in fighting shape. Partly because it helped take my mind off Rhys.

Sometimes.

Wu didn't think I was mentally prepared for the scroll, so he'd been reluctant to teach me anything real yet. I tried not to act bratty like Luke Skywalker in *The Empire Strikes Back,* but it was difficult. With Paul still at large, I needed all the resources I could get.

Of course, I did have a virtually constant police escort. Aside from the plainclothes detail that followed me all the time, Ramirez made a point of stopping by at least once a week. He'd sit at the bar and have a drink. Once, I asked him why they bothered to keep an eye on me if Paul had been spotted in South America. He said his gut told him Paul would show up to see me, and he'd wait patiently for that day.

I waited for my brother to show up, too. Not so patiently. We had a score to settle.

"Enough," I mumbled under my breath. I was supposed to be basking in the limelight. I pasted a smile on my face and turned to find someone to talk to. Checking out the scene, I bypassed the snooty people I should have been kissing up to, in hopes that there'd be someone more interesting.

Then my eyes fell on him. *Tŭ ch'i* leapt to life, and the tension gripping my shoulders for the past few weeks melted.

"You look bewitching," Rhys said in his sexy James Bond voice.

"You look like a penguin." Actually, he looked hot

in his tux. The only way I thought he looked hotter was naked. "Where have you been?"

"Away on business." He lifted my wrist to his lips and kissed it so lingeringly that I swore I heard two women behind me sigh. "Miss me?"

"Hardly," I lied. I wanted to rail at him for declaring that we weren't finished and then falling off the face of the world. Except for his damn notes.

He must have known, because he placed a finger on my lips. "Hush. We're declaring a truce. No arguing for this one night."

I frowned at the foreign concept. "We won't have anything to talk about."

He chuckled, stepping closer. "I think we can find something, love. Like your smashing success."

His heat enveloped me, and I leaned in, eager to feel it wash over me. "It's pretty hopping, isn't it?"

"Not surprising, however. Clothilde La Rochelle is never wrong about talent."

I couldn't help myself—I had to ask. "Why did you pay so much for those paintings? Was it so I'd feel even more indebted to you?"

"There's no debt between us. I give to you freely and without intent." He tugged me so he held my hand cupped in his between our hearts. "And those paintings were *mine*."

I blinked at the fierceness in his voice.

"You painted them for me. Deny it as much as you like, but I know they were meant for me. The way you were meant for me."

Not knowing what to say to that fierce declaration, I ignored it and said as casually as I could, "I heard someone else bought the fifth painting."

"A mistake I'll rectify soon." He tangled his free hand in my hair, which I'd worn loose tonight, and arched my neck back. "What's mine, I keep."

He seared my lips with a kiss before I could reply. He breathed fire into my mouth, and then I didn't want to say anything. I grabbed his lapel and pulled him as close as we could get in public.

Too soon, he lifted his head. For once, his eyes weren't so guarded, and I felt like I could see deep into the fiery pits of his soul. I pulled him closer, letting what I found there warm me. "You really do love me?"

"With my every breath," he said without hesitation.

My birthmark tingled, a sparkling shower of happiness. I nodded. "You told me to think about this, and I have."

He stilled, the way a predator does so he won't startle his prey. "And?"

I slipped my hand inside his coat and rested my palm over his mark. "I think it's time to discuss a new deal."

"What sort of new deal?"

"A lifelong one."

He tugged me flush against his body. "Do you feel you have enough leverage to negotiate successfully?"

Grinning, I wiggled against his growing erection. "I feel I've got quite a lot of leverage here."

He grabbed my hips and held me still. "I'm ruthless, you know. I won't compromise. It's all or nothing with me."

Looking up into his blue eyes, I nodded. "I find myself willing to agree to those terms."

"Tell me," he urged, his voice low and sexy. His thumb pressed on my mark and a corner of the note I'd tucked in my panties.

I lifted my chin and said the words clearly, straight to his heart. "I love you."

Triumph. He lowered his mouth to mine, sealing our deal with a slow, engulfing kiss. I sighed, feeling warmth spread through my body, in all the places that counted.

"Gabrielle," he whispered against my lips, "I'm going to need to look over the terms. Very thoroughly."

And very soon, if I had anything to say about it.

Would anyone miss me if I slipped out? I looked over Rhys's shoulder, across the room and right into Madame's eyes. An older woman who dripped diamonds stood speaking to her, but Madame watched Rhys and me. As if she read my query, she tilted her head and winked.

I looked back at Rhys. "What do you say we take this to my office?"

He shook his head. "No, *my* office. I'd wager I'll be better equipped."

"You're already well equipped," I said, toying with the waistband of his slacks.

His grin widened, hot and wicked. Taking my hand, he placed a slow kiss on my wrist that promised all manner of sins, and then he led me out of the gallery and into the night.

Chapter One

I can't believe I'm doing this." With a furtive glance behind her, Carrie tiptoed down the dark stone corridor. At the beginning of the monastery tour, the guide had explicitly said it was forbidden to wander from the group, and since she'd been on the tour ten times in the past ten days, she couldn't play blonde and clueless.

But she hadn't come all the way from San Francisco to China to go home empty-handed. Her best friend, Gabrielle, would have told Carrie that if she wanted something, she should go for it wholeheartedly.

She wondered if Gabrielle—Gabe—would condone breaking and entering.

Stop thinking. She had only so much time to find the room and look for what she needed before the tour group caught up to her. She hurried down the hall.

There it was to the left. The innocuous wooden door to the room that held the monastery's archives.

Heart pounding, she scurried to it and slipped inside. Carrie held her breath. She tensed, waiting, certain someone was about to bang on the door and demand what she was doing.

No one.

Just nerves. She exhaled and slumped against the door at her back. Even working as a bartender in San Francisco's Mission District didn't cause this kind of anxiety.

It wasn't her fault. She'd tried to go through proper channels. She'd contacted the monastery and asked for access to their manuscripts. They'd turned her down cold.

She was a scholar of Chinese at UC Berkeley, for God's sake—studying manuscripts was her job. And the fact that the monks had turned her down was a good indication they had something to hide.

Carrie bet that mysterious something was what she wanted. And since she'd blown her entire savings to fly six thousand miles, she was determined to get what she came for. But her return flight was tomorrow.

The room looked just like it had the other nine times she'd been in it. A long rectangle, dim but with enough light for reading. It had that musty smell she always associated with old libraries. She imagined generations of monks sitting at the table at the end of the room, carefully working on their calligraphy. The walls were lined with shelves filled with the fruits of their labor: thousands of rolled parchments and bound tomes.

One of them was Wei Lin's journal.

She hadn't been sure what to look for—there were literally thousands of rolled parchments and old bound texts on the shelves. It could be anywhere. She bit her lip, willing her nerves to calm. She was getting close. On her sixth visit, she'd noticed one shelf that looked different from the others.

Her eyes zoomed to it. The one shelf in the room suspiciously free of dust, as if someone cared for it or accessed its contents on a regular basis. The scrolls that lined it were different from the ones on the other shelves: thicker, tightly bound, and a third as wide.

Her fingertips tingled as she headed straight for the shelf. One of its scrolls had to be the one.

She'd tried to get a closer look the last three times she'd taken the tour, but it'd been impossible under the tour guide's hawklike vigilance. Which was why she'd had to take matters into her own hands today. She ran her finger along the shelf's smooth wood. Breaking away from the tour had been risky, but giving up wasn't in her makeup. And truthfully, she felt a rush at her own daring, too. She kind of felt like Indiana Jones.

Carrie slung her bag across her body and kneeled on the floor in front of the scrolls. Her blood raced in anticipation.

"Don't get ahead of yourself, girl," she muttered. She was operating on a hunch here. She didn't know for certain that the monastery had a copy of the journal—it just made sense that it would, as Wei Lin had spent his life here seven hundred years ago.

She bit her lip, helplessness combining with her nerves to create a nauseous cocktail in her stomach. She had to find it. Her future depended on it. She'd worked her butt off for a tenured position at UC Berkeley, only now her advisor, Leonora, said the board didn't believe her doctoral thesis was "sexy" enough.

Sexy enough. Squaring her shoulders, Carrie picked up one of the scrolls. She'd show them sexy.

Untying its leather thong, she started to gently unroll the fragile paper. The other scrolls on the shelf shifted, and another scroll caught her gaze. It didn't look as old or brittle as the rest.

Did monks still write on parchment? Oddly drawn to it, she ran a finger over the newer-looking scroll and felt as though her fingertip trailed in icy water. Goosebumps rose on her arms.

"Weird," she mumbled. She felt oddly compelled to unfurl it. She reached for it—

Wait—she had one in her hand already. Might as well start there. Shaking her head, she sat back on her heels and unrolled enough to read a few lines. She read the first line of the tiny but beautiful black script.

> *My name is Wei Lin, and I have appointed myself Keeper of the Scrolls of Destiny.*

"*Yes.*" Relaxing her grip so she wouldn't crush it in her excitement, she scanned it. Her heart beat faster with every word.

Five scrolls, each based on a Chinese element.

To save them from a greedy warlord, Wei Lin stole them and marked five worthy people as their Guardians.

The Guardianship passes on through each family to the next marked person.

Whoever possesses the scrolls possesses the elements' powers.

Wei Lin was Keeper of the Guardians, but he broke his own rule.

He brought together all the Guardians to help the emperor.

Bingo. All Chinese scholars knew the myth about how a monk named Wei Lin, in giving support to the emperor, brought forty years of peace to the kingdom through mystical means. *With the aid of the elements,* it was said.

But it wasn't a myth. It was real.

She'd just found her holy grail.

Instead of jumping up and doing a triumphant dance, Carrie pulled out her digital camera and began methodically photographing the journal. She glanced at the shelf. There had to be another dozen scrolls there, plus a few bound texts. Installments of Wei Lin's journal? Made sense. She checked the time. She needed to hustle.

Even as she thought it, Carrie heard the tour guide's resonant voice. It sounded like the group was just down the hall. Which meant they were headed for the archives room, because Carrie knew for certain nothing else in this wing of the monastery was shown on the tour.

Crap. She hadn't even finished photographing this one scroll, much less the rest. She took a hasty picture of the end and rolled it back up. Her hands fumbled with the little leather strip, dropping it as she tried to retie it. "Goshdarnit."

The tour guide's voice seeped through the walls. "And this is the archives room, containing the writings of centuries of monks, as well as recordings of the region's history."

Carrie retrieved the strip, haphazardly retied the scroll, and shoved it on the shelf. Unfortunately, as she retracted her hand, her sleeve must have caught on another scroll, because about six of them tumbled into her lap.

"Because of the delicacy of the documentation," the tour guide continued, "touching the texts is not allowed. But the library is impressive nonetheless."

The door creaked. Carrie watched in horror as the door slowly swung open. She grabbed the scrolls and tried to shove them back on the shelf, wincing at how brutally she was handling ancient artifacts.

But the scrolls just tumbled back down into her lap.

"*Crap,*" she mouthed, panic choking her. She looked over her shoulder to see one of the tour guide's calves as she backed into the room.

She couldn't get caught. Her mom would *kill* her if she got thrown in jail for stealing from monks, and she could kiss that tenured position good-bye.

No choice. She opened her bag, stuffed the scrolls in, and ducked under the table in the back. She could pop up and rejoin the group as they were leaving, no one the wiser. She hoped.

And she'd have the journals to study.

She grimaced. She'd just borrow them. She'd send them back as soon as she copied their information. She swore it. And she'd treat them very carefully.

Her heart thundered so loudly it was a miracle no one heard her. She couldn't even relax when the tour guide began her spiel. Holding her breath, Carrie waited. Every second stretched like hours.

A white Reebok stepped dangerously close to her hand, and she retreated farther under the desk. Gosh, she hoped no one noticed her stowed away under the desk.

The guide began shepherding the small crowd out. Finally. Carrie peeked out from under the table. They shuffled slowly out the door. Seeing her chance, she jumped up and quickly rejoined the group.

No one said anything to her, but that didn't ease her nerves. She ducked her head and slid the elastic band from her hair so her curls bounced forward and covered her face. Huddling her shoulders, she hoped she looked unremarkable and guilt-free, but that seemed a tall order.

In China, her blond hair was like a beacon. Fortunately, the tour was almost over. All she had to do was hang in there for the walk through the garden, and then she could rush back to her hotel and lock herself in her room. With her stolen booty.

Oh, gosh, what was she *doing?*

No one saw, she reassured herself as she trailed behind the group. *No one knows. Just be casual.*

They stepped out into the garden, and she breathed a sigh of relief. Almost home free. Just a few more minutes.

But as she had the thought, she felt an accusing gaze at her back—penetrating and cold. Her shoulders twitched with the need to whirl around to see who stared and why.

Silly, because no one knew what she'd done. It wasn't like the monastery was outfitted with spy cams. At least she didn't think it was.

She was *so* not cut out for a life of crime. She even hated keeping library books past their due dates—what made her think she could do *this?* From now on she was walking a straight and narrow path.

The person watching her turned up the intensity.

Maybe she should drop the scrolls and run.

No—she'd bankrupted herself for this. Her future was on the line, and she was so close. Yeah, she was breaking the law, but she was doing it with pure motives—if that counted for anything. She was going to return them. And the fact of the matter was, if someone had seen what she'd done, she would have been apprehended already.

Stop being a wimp. Whoever was staring was probably only entranced with her blond curls. The past ten days should have taught her how mesmerized the Chinese were with her hair.

Can't take this. She'd never been good at burying her head and hiding—she had to look. Wiping her clammy palms on her jeans, she turned to face her watcher.

Her heart gave a quick thud.

A man in monk's robes was at the end of the garden. A Western man with rough-hewn, carved-in-stone features and silvery blond hair that fell in shaggy layers around his severe face.

No way was he a monk.

She stared, not sure why she was so certain of that. It wasn't as if it was against the rules for a monk to be all intense. Or hot. Or to inspire wicked thoughts instead of peaceful ones.

But a monk wouldn't have such turbulent gray eyes. She met them and shivered. They had none of the gentleness and compassion she'd seen in the eyes of the other robed men. Their gray depths glinted, judging and accusing and unforgiving. His gaze seemed to penetrate, stripping aside all her layers to her soul, and found her lacking.

Her arm tightened on her bag. He couldn't know what she'd done. There had been no one in the hallway to see her enter the room, and she'd left with the group. She needed to get a grip and relax, otherwise she was going to give herself away.

She turned back around, pretending to be engrossed in the last of the tour guide's speech. She told herself not to look back—he'd go away.

Only she couldn't help herself. As nonchalantly as possible, she glanced over her shoulder.

Still there.

Why he was staring at her like she was an apple fritter and he was on Atkins? He couldn't know she had the scrolls—logically, it was impossible. Maybe he had a weakness for corn-fed Midwestern girls? And he'd come to China to work it out of his system, only here she was tempting him. She grinned at the thought, looking him over again. She wished.

"This concludes our tour," the guide said in her sing-song voice. Carrie's attention snapped back to the woman, and she exhaled in relief. "On behalf of the monks, I bid you farewell. Walk in peace."

Carrie sneaked one last glance at the supposed Western monk and hightailed it peacefully out of there. The entire way to the bus, she felt his cold gaze on her back, like a sharp knife across her skin.

Taking care to hide himself, Max watched the tour group emerge from the archives room. In his seven years at the monastery he'd grown accustomed to the daily on-slaught of tourists, but something about the blonde drew him.

She had the face of a cherub with big brown eyes, creamy skin, and rosy cheeks. Her strawberry blond hair made a stubby ponytail at the nape of her neck. He watched as she undid the ponytail to release a mass of curls that bounced onto her shoulders and into her face. The embodiment of innocence.

Except for her bowed lips. Her lips were pure sin.

But the innocence was a ruse. He stilled, feeling waves of elemental energy emanating from her. The way she clutched her bag to her side like it contained precious treasure confirmed what he already felt.

She'd taken the Book of Water.

He took a step toward her before he stopped himself. This wasn't his concern—he wouldn't get involved this time. Let someone else deal with her. Max looked around for another monk but found no one.

Anger flooded him, cold and steely. It was like fate taunted him. He knew he couldn't let her get away, but he'd be damned if he had to deal with another less-than-angelic woman with light fingers.

No way in hell.

He followed the group silently into the garden, keeping his gaze on the woman, willing another monk to show up and intervene.

Only then she turned around.

Max wasn't prepared for the shock of her doe-eyed gaze meeting his. She studied him as if she had nothing to hide and everything to offer.

It infuriated him.

And then she grinned, and her face lit artlessly.

Damn it—he'd forgotten what a turn-on innocence was. He hated himself for wondering if she'd taste as sweet as she looked. Or if she'd feel as soft. He shifted, uncomfortably aware of his groin tightening.

She gave him one more sweet smile before she followed the dispersing tour back to the bus, unaware of the havoc she'd wreaked in him.

Should he go after her? His soul answered *yes,* but he doubted it was for moral reasons. Frankly, if he got his hands on her, he didn't trust himself not to strip her bare and sink in deep. He told himself it was because he'd been without a woman for seven years—such long abstinence did something to a man.

His conscience pointed out that he'd seen other women in the seven years—the tour guide, for example—and not had this strong a reaction.

He told his conscience to shut up.

The bus's engine growled to life.

Max looked around. Still no one. He glared at the bus. No choice. Teeth grinding, he went to head it off.

He'd taken only several steps before a strong hand clutched his arm. Caught off guard, he trapped the hand and automatically arced the wrist in a leverage.

The calloused hand reversed the leverage instantly, letting it go almost as quickly. Max spun around, bringing the knife-edge of his hand up to chop. He stopped an inch from his mentor's neck.

Sun Chi's peaceful face shined up at him. Its serenity irritated the hell out of him. How could he be so still when his throat had almost been crushed?

When the Book of Water had been stolen?

Max looked over his shoulder to see the bus winding down the mountain road back to civilization.

"Damn it." Angry and frustrated, he scowled at the old monk. "The Book of Water is riding away on that bus."

Sun Chi stared after the bus. Max waited, expecting a barrage of questions, starting with why he hadn't done anything to stop the thief. But his mentor just studied him quietly before turning and shuffling away. Motioning with his hand, he said, "Come."

What the hell? Max stalked after the smaller man, wanting to interrogate but knowing he'd get no answers until the monk was ready. As a teenager, when he'd just become a Guardian and was sent to study with Sun Chi, the man's stoicism had infuriated him. As the only child of rich bluebloods, he'd always had everything handed to him when he wanted. Since then, he'd learned patience.

For the most part.

Following Sun Chi into the archives room, Max closed the door behind him and watched as the monk kneeled before a shelf in the back. He hadn't realized how much he'd wanted to be wrong about the woman stealing the scroll until he heard Sun Chi's gasp and felt the corresponding sinking in his chest.

"Gone." Sun Chi looked up at him, his gaze bright. "The Book of Water. The journals of Wei Lin. And my own."

He steeled himself for recriminations. When nothing was forthcoming, he asked, "Why would she take the journals?"

"For names of present Guardians." Sun Chi gazed at him levelly. "With one scroll, she gains ability to find the other four. You understand?"

"Yes." And that was an unmitigated disaster. No single person could handle the powers of all the scrolls. The influence of only one was corrupting enough if you weren't strong. Possessing all five . . . He shook his head. "I thought the Book of Water was sent to its next Guardian."

"Sent. And refused." Sun Chi stood and walked the room in slow, measured steps, hands behind his back.

Max frowned. "The Guardian didn't accept his duty?"

"Some Guardians are thickheaded." He tapped Max's shoulder before returning to his contemplative stroll. He suddenly stopped and lifted his head, piercing Max with his all-knowing gaze. "You must stop her."

From the moment the bus drove away, he'd known this was coming, but a part of him still didn't want to accept it. All he wanted was to go back to his cell and forget he'd ever seen the duplicitous angel. "No."

His mentor nodded as if Max hadn't spoken. "You use family's diplomatic connections."

"I gave up all that seven years ago. I'm on a different path now."

"You choose wrong path. Your path is to follow woman." The monk waved toward the door. "Find who she is and follow. Get scroll and journals."

"No," he said again, shaking his head. "Seven years ago—"

"Seven years ago, you come to monastery to heal," Sun Chi interrupted. "But you stay in monastery to hide."

"I haven't been hiding," he said, but even as the words came out of his mouth he knew they were a lie.

"You hide. From past, from present, from future." His mentor's narrowed gaze dared him to contradict that statement. "You let yesterday kill tomorrow."

"My future—"

"Your future is back in your world." Sun Chi pointed at him. "You are not monk. You are Maximillian Pierpont, Guardian of the Book of Metal. Heir to your own dynasty. Your path"—he pointed into the distance—"leads out, into world. After that woman," he said, his voice low and insistent. "You find woman."

Max knew from experience that Sun Chi's will wouldn't be denied. To fight it was wasting energy. He gritted his teeth. God help that woman when he caught up to her. "What will I be up against?"

The monk had the grace not to gloat. "Book of Water is not claimed by Guardian, so powers free. Affect person who holds it."

Remembering how unprepared he'd been for the onslaught of his own powers, he said, "That could be to our advantage."

Sun Chi shook his head. "Powers weaker than yours. Unless woman studies scroll, learns scroll's secrets. You get scrolls first. You not let anyone find other Guardians."

In other words, silence her. Max had expected that. What he hadn't expected was the pang of regret he felt at the thought of stifling her innocent light.

He shouldn't care. He didn't know the woman. She'd stolen. She was guilty, despite her innocent demeanor.

Seven years ago, he'd let Marley's appearance sway him. But she'd swayed his best friend, too. In the end he'd been betrayed by both.

He rubbed his neck, his fingers sliding over the familiar ridges of the burn scar—a constant reminder of that night.

Sun Chi placed a hand on his shoulder. "To heal, you must go. This last step exorcises ghosts of your past."

More likely this was just going to attract another ghost—one with big doe eyes and lips made for sin.

But Max didn't comment. Instead he bowed his head and strode out of the room, not happy in the least to be reentering the life he'd left behind.

THE DISH

Where authors give you the inside scoop!

♥ ♥ ♥ ♥ ♥ ♥ ♥ ♥ ♥ ♥ ♥ ♥ ♥ ♥ ♥ ♥

From the desk of Susan Crandall

Dear Reader,

Oh, how I love to write a twisted villain, preferring the play of psychological tension to physical gore. Villains are so complex, for who in this world is completely good or completely evil? Hollis Alexander in SEEING RED (on sale now) provided a wonderful opportunity to explore the depths of darkness that can lurk in the soul, the evil behind the mask of physical beauty and agreeability.

I always like to center my novels on what I call an "everyman" story, one that could happen to any of us (although we certainly hope it doesn't). I like to make it personal, to delve into the emotions of my antagonist and my protagonist. Therefore, I rarely venture into the arena of irredeemable evil. Hollis Alexander is the exception. He's bad and that's all there is to it. He's smart and uses mental manipulation to its fullest—this, to me, is the scariest kind of villain. And if I admit that I really enjoyed writing him, does that make you worry about my mental state?

Well, I did. I loved it, even though the idea of a *real* Hollis Alexander gives me chills and makes it difficult to sleep. Luckily, the idea of the *real* Nate Vances, our real-world heroes, makes me feel safe enough to turn out the lights and close my eyes.

Thanks for coming along with me on this journey. May our real-world heroes always be there when you need them.

Happy Reading!

Susan Crandall

www.susancrandall.net

♥ ♥ ♥ ♥ ♥ ♥ ♥ ♥ ♥ ♥ ♥ ♥ ♥

From the desk of Kate Perry

Dear Reader,

Have you ever wondered what it'd be like to have superpowers?

If someone gave me superpowers, I'd be stoked. Or would I? Gabe Sansouci, the sassy heroine in MARKED BY PASSION (on sale now), inherits an ancient Chinese scroll that does just that, only she finds out really quickly that having powers isn't all it's cracked up to be.

Don't get me wrong—if someone tapped me

with a magic wand and said I could fly, I'd *so* be soaring through the sky. But there are a few powers I'd turn down:

I Can't Go for That, No Can Do: Three Powers Kate Doesn't Want

1. Causing earthquakes.

I'm just being practical with this one. Like Gabe, I live in San Francisco. If I made the earth tremble every time I got upset, there'd be chaos. San Francisco is beautiful; it'd be a shame if it lay at the bottom of the Pacific Ocean.

2. Reading minds.

Shudder. The idea of reading minds is so horrifying to me that I couldn't bring myself to even torture Gabe with it. Imagine your Aunt Millie thinking about sex. I rest my case.

3. Killing by touch.

Gabe has the capacity to harm people through touch, but she also has the balancing ability to heal. Um, in theory.

Of course, Gabe's not alone in this thing. With the help of Rhys Llewellyn, man of mystery and all-around hot guy, she's sure to get a handle on her new powers. Eventually.

Hope you enjoy MARKED BY PASSION! And

keep an eye out for CHOSEN BY DESIRE, the second book in the Guardians of Destiny series.

Kate Perry

www.kateperry.com

♥ ♥ ♥ ♥ ♥ ♥ ♥ ♥ ♥ ♥ ♥ ♥ ♥ ♥ ♥ ♥

From the desk of Kelley St. John

Dear Reader,

One of the best parts of writing a novel with a multitude of passionate characters is learning that your readers want to know more of their story. That's what makes it so much fun to give you the "what happened next" portion of their lives, because, as you very well know, those characters continue to live in your heart . . . and mine. Thankfully, you can revisit several of your favorites, since they tend to find their way into my other books. For example, Lettie Campbell's sister, Amy, from GOOD GIRLS DON'T, is one of Rissi Kincaid's best friends in TO CATCH A CHEAT! And—you guessed it—if Amy's there, then that means her sexy cowboy Landon is also along for the ride. So if you didn't get enough of Amy and her sex toys or Landon and his famed massage oils in GOOD GIRLS DON'T, then you can have another delicious taste in TO CATCH A CHEAT!

And if you're one of the many readers who sent the request (okay, the demand) for sexy-and-sizzling Jeff Eubanks to get together with wild hellion Babette Robinson after meeting them in REAL WOMEN DON'T WEAR SIZE 2, I promise you that FLIRTING WITH TEMPTATION (on sale now) will give you exactly what you've been asking for—and then some!

Ever true to her impulsive nature, Babette is still changing jobs, addresses, and hair colors as often as possible. (And changing men just as frequently!) Even though she can't find a man who will stick, she's finally found a job that will: Birmingham's "Love Doctor," where she heals love that's gone wrong. Her business is—*until* Kitty Carelle hires Babette to get her back with her ex— none other than Jeff Eubanks.

Jeff believes that women—not men—are the ones who can't commit, and he has the power to completely ruin Babette's new career if he refuses to take Kitty back. So Babette is determined to make him see things her way, even if it means adhering to his ridiculous challenge of no flirting for a week. She can do it. She *can*. In fact, she could do it rather easily, if the no-flirting policy only applied to beach hunks who didn't have the last name of Eubanks. Because Jeff is looking mighty good, and Babette has been a long, long time wanting . . . everything he's tempting her with.

Have mercy, seven days never seemed so long!

Happy Reading!

Kelley St. John

Kelley@kelleysbooks.com
www.kelleystjohn.com

Want to know more about romances at Grand Central Publishing and Forever? Get the scoop online!

GRAND CENTRAL PUBLISHING'S
ROMANCE HOME PAGE

Visit us at www.hachettebookgroup.com/romance
for all the latest news, reviews, and chapter excerpts!

NEW AND UPCOMING TITLES

Each month we feature our new titles
and reader favorites.

CONTESTS AND GIVEAWAYS

We give away galleys, autographed copies,
and all kinds of fun stuff

AUTHOR INFO

You'll find bios, articles, and links to personal
Web sites for all your favorite authors—and
so much more!

THE BUZZ

Sign up for our monthly romance newsletter,
and be the first to read all about it!